A Life Worth Living

Monica McCallan

By The Author

A Life Worth Living

© 2023 By Monica McCallan. All Rights Reserved.

First Edition: February 2023

Acknowledgments

Haley, Lucy, and Erica, thank you for listening to me agonize over anything under the sun—including my long overdue return to writing. Your friendship and support means the world to me.

To Breezy and Deej. You've both become wonderful friends this past year, and I don't want to think about what my life would be like without you.

Dedication

This book is for anyone who sometimes feels overwhelmed by the world and their place in it.

Synopsis

Nora Gallagher can begrudgingly admit that she and Gray Ferris are both stellar Philadelphia real estate agents, but that's the beginning and the end of the similarities between them.

Nora's life has been in a self-imposed holding pattern for half a decade. Depending on people in her personal life only leads to disappointment, and she has no plans of making that mistake again.

Gray Ferris is extroversion personified. Bubbly. Conversational. Vibrant. She's trying to make the best of life, even if it hasn't always gone her way.

When the two women begin to learn that maybe they're not as different as they think, they may finally figure out the most important thing they have in common when it comes to finding a life worth living.

Chapter One

Nora was on her feet the second the meeting ended. Curious brown eyes caught hers as Gray Ferris loitered in the conference room but made no move toward Nora. At least the woman had some sense.

Nora's heels clicked across the hardwood floors, carrying her out of the meeting space and through the open floor plan that made up the Philly Finds real estate office.

The situation Nora found herself in was truly her own personal version of hell. Why Cynthia wanted to torture her was unclear, but it was also irrelevant. An explanation wouldn't change the fact that her boss had just announced in front of their ten-person company that Gray would also be going on the trip.

If there was ever a time for takebacks...

Storming into her boss's office, she didn't let out a breath until she felt the soft thud of the door. "Seriously, Cynthia. What was that about?"

If Cynthia Lennox, her boss, mentor, and sometimes friend, was surprised to find Nora in her office, she didn't let on. She was already seated at her desk, peering down at her computer through glasses she wore when staring at a screen. Her blonde hair had streaks of silver, the only sign that she was on the other side of fifty. The sleeveless navy wrap dress she wore hugged her frame and long, toned arms were balanced on the edge of her desk.

"What was what about? Also, I like that jacket," Cynthia said with an appraising look, brown eyes now focused on Nora.

Nora refused to fidget. Purposefully, she walked over to the window that overlooked their Philadelphia office on Frankford Avenue. She wouldn't give Cynthia the satisfaction of watching her squirm. "Don't flatter me."

"Glad you're getting some use out of it now," Cynthia said, giving her jacket another appraising stare. "You won't need it when you're 'funnin' and sunnin'.'"

"Why is Gray going on this trip?" There was no point in prolonging the inevitable. This year, partly to celebrate the company's five-year anniversary, the real estate agency had instituted an all-expenses-paid trip to Bermuda for the agent with the highest value in home sales. Nora had known since it was announced she'd be the winner, but hey, a little healthy competition never hurt.

"Because she won, too?" had to be the most half-assed answer she'd ever heard come from her boss's mouth. She hoped that Cynthia could see the clench in her jaw.

Nora ran her hands over her lapels, smoothing the navy garment before fiddling with a gold button. It was a nice jacket. At least Cynthia recognized that, even if she was intent on driving Nora insane. "Except those weren't the rules. It was supposed to be one person going on this trip, and now it's two. For some bullshit category that I didn't even know existed until you announced it at the meeting."

A quick look at Cynthia was all it took to know that she was loving every second of this. "Gray's closed more hard sells than anyone else at the company. More deals, in fact. She may not be putting up your sales profit numbers, but she's been invaluable in making connections within the city and bringing us a bigger client base."

Nora turned around and squared her shoulders, standing ramrod straight. This was bullshit, and they both knew it. Whether Cynthia was willing to admit it remained to be seen. "So she gets rewarded for low numbers and being good at putting lipstick on a pig?"

Cynthia's downturned lips told Nora she'd come close to offending her, but they quickly tipped back up into a vibrant smile. "If you want to put it crudely. And if you don't, she's made a lot of clients very happy these last few months. That's not nothing."

"So have I," Nora said, needlessly. They both knew she was inarguably the strongest agent at Philly Finds, the real estate agency Cynthia had founded five years ago. Nora had been by her side since the beginning.

"Which is exactly why I wanted to recognize you both." Cynthia's nod when she spoke made it seem like the conversation was done.

Too bad Nora wasn't finished.

She hadn't been on a vacation in years. Granted, it was her own fault, but that still didn't temper the sting of being stuck with some wide-eyed newbie on what should be a relaxing, *private* vacation.

Because the truth was, she didn't want to socialize. Hell, she didn't know if she remembered how to string a coherent sentence together with the sole purpose of getting to know someone if it wasn't work-related. And if she was listing her grievances... she didn't want to have to entertain a human being more closely aligned in personality to a golden retriever than a person. All she wanted to do was get drunk on the beach at her all-inclusive resort and maybe read some smutty romance novels.

"You could have given me a heads-up." Except that once she got the words out, she deflated.

Cynthia leaned back against her desk and crossed her arms. "And what would you have done? Withdrawn from contention or thrown your last few deals to lose?"

Her eyes narrowed. "I'd never lose on purpose."

"I know that."

"I just don't understand why you did this. Why couldn't we get separate trips if you were going to pick two winners?"

Cynthia laughed, a light but rich sound that told her exactly what she thought about Nora's irrefutable point. "It's not some conspiracy, Nora. I don't have a personal assistant. It was just easier to do everything together. Two flights. Two hotel rooms. Two people on the excursions."

Oh good, the anger was back, hot and itchy, like her skin was too tight. She was already feeling trapped, and the trip hadn't even happened yet. "Excuse me? Excursions?" she said indignantly. When she couldn't stop herself, she added, "I hope they're refundable."

Cynthia studied her. "You're acting like I'm trying to send you to a monastery for a month on a silent retreat. I booked you a damn boat for the day, that's it."

In all her years working with Cynthia, Nora had only ever seen her truly angry once. She wondered if she was about to double that record.

And god, she wished she could rein it in. No one beyond the door to Cynthia's office would likely believe what a brat she was behaving like right now. Sure, she was rigid. And maybe a little bit domineering. But petulant? Not a chance. She didn't have to 'get her way' because she paved the way. In sales. In effort. In sheer determination to be the best.

But she'd been looking forward to this vacation. Finding her best laid plans completely tipped on their side and stomped on in the most unexpected way had all her perfectly calculated thoughts swirling around chaotically.

She was on edge, and it was showing.

Nora could feel the heat creeping up her neck and splotching scarlet on her cheeks, but she wouldn't back down on this. She couldn't.

Cynthia gave her a look of genuine concern, her brows drawn together. "Are you okay? Is this really about the trip?"

She nodded her head quickly. The other parts of her life— the ones that hadn't worked out—had been shoved in a box years ago. Then she'd put a lid on it. Duct-taped it. Thrown it into the Mariana Trench.

Cynthia pulled Nora's attention back from chewing on that thought for any longer than she had to. "I know that you and Gray aren't the best of friends, but it's not like I'm sending you with Julian."

Cynthia laughed when Nora's nose scrunched up in aversion.

"As if he'd have the numbers, regardless of how you slice your wackadoodle criteria."

"Nora, you have always been a leader on this team because of your hard work and drive. You're one of the most talented, dogged agents that I know. It's one of the reasons you will have a place on this team as long as you want it."

Classy of Cynthia to ignore the wackadoodle comment and compliment her on top of it, which only served to further darken the warm splotches on Nora's cheeks.

"I appreciate you saying that."

"But with that being said..." Cynthia held Nora's stare and

clasped her hands together on her lap. She looked like a disappointed parent. It was a look Nora had seen often growing up, whether deserved or not.

She was suddenly feeling like there wasn't enough duct tape in the world to box away her problems. Still, she'd done a respectable job the last five years if she said so herself. And considering she didn't ask for anyone else's opinion, save Cynthia's from time to time, she was the judge, jury, and executioner of her own life these days.

"Just say it," Nora muttered.

"Your attitude as of late has been lacking."

"What, so you're allowed to make jokes about Julian but I'm not?" She doubted the rest of the office knew how funny she could be.

Cynthia pushed her fingers against the bridge of her nose and sighed. "That's not the point I'm making, and you know it."

Nora sulked over to the small leather sofa in the office's seating area and threw herself down on it. "It should be. He heats his fish up in the communal microwave. Who does that?" She paused for dramatic effect and crossed her legs. "He's a psychopath."

Cynthia let out another one of her vibrant laughs, and Nora could see a hint of the tension in Cynthia's shoulders rolling away. She hated when her boss was frustrated with her, but she couldn't help it. Why was everyone so oblivious to social mores? Do great work. Go home. No need to be besties with your colleagues.

She didn't want to know about Trent's fantasy football league, and she'd rather die than join it, as she'd said in much kinder words—probably—for the last three years in a row.

As if it mattered what Callie's children had said or done in some sugar-induced fit of mania the past weekend.

Kelvin couldn't understand that she wouldn't be caught

dead at a rooftop patio with him for happy hour, with kids who looked like they weren't old enough to drink. Some days she felt like she was thirty-five going on sixty, but that wasn't any of Kelvin's business either.

Grant and Tamara and Sage and Kelsey had all tried to build similar bridges with her during their time at the company, but none of them had made it through. Some got the hint easier than others. The ones that didn't got a little hurt after a while at her unwillingness to be anything other than ambivalent co-workers with them, but they got over it eventually.

The world didn't stop spinning because she refused to stay for a post-work cocktail lesson or because she took her Friday morning waffle from the waffle bar to her desk and ate in silence while looking over her daily schedule.

And then there was Gray.

She'd been with Philly Finds for about a year, the newest member of the team. She'd caught Nora on an especially bad day for their first run-in. Nora meant that literally. Coming around a corner, Nora had been surviving on about two hours of fitful sleep and late to a client appointment when their paths had crossed.

It wasn't hard to guess how it had played out.

Maybe Nora had said some words that weren't the nicest, and there'd been a moment where Gray's terrified eyes had flashed with hurt, but they'd gotten over it. Nora never brought up how she could still remember the coffee as it'd soaked into her skin, sticky and pungent. And when Gray had brought her cookies the day after to apologize for ruining Nora's favorite blouse—not that Gray could have known that—she'd even accepted them with a tepid smile.

So everything was fine. Gray had given Nora a wide berth since then, though she seemed to ham it up with the rest of the office. Nora was sure that Gray, with her bubbly enthusiasm, had already formed lifelong friendships with each and every other person on the team.

Well, this pin wasn't going to be knocked down by the bowling ball of charm that was Gray Ferris any time soon.

Nora knew that with the same surety she'd known that the trip to Bermuda was hers.

Cynthia's voice cut through Nora's mental walk through the office and all of its strange inhabitants. "Did you hear me?"

Nora blinked once. Then again. She doubted that Cynthia had been wholeheartedly agreeing with her about Julian's psychopathy. Her boss had some restraint.

"Can you repeat what you said? Unless it was to further chastise me for my behavior, in which case, that message was already received loud and clear," she said weakly.

Cynthia smiled before relaxing back against the edge of her desk. "I wasn't going to mention this until after the trip, but given your response, I figured we'd better discuss it now."

She sat up a little straighter against the soft leather, her lower back twinging. Her six a.m. yoga classes weren't improving her posture like she'd hoped. "Discuss what?"

"The company's been doing well."

"That's always good to hear."

Cynthia nodded in agreement. "So well, in fact, that I'm considering restructuring some things as we continue to grow."

That caught Nora's attention. She liked how things were. She liked her autonomy. She liked that she knew everyone and that, more importantly, they'd all been trained to leave her alone.

"What *things*?"

"I'm splitting the company into two teams. I'll lead one, and someone will become the senior agent on the other. I'm in a difficult position, though."

Nora picked at a piece of lint on her pants and ignored the

way her throat constricted. She was good at ignoring lots of things. "And why's that?" It hurt to push the words out.

"Because you're the best agent I have, but your people skills, at least as far as co-workers go, leave something to be desired. Based on your sales, you're a shoo-in if you want it, but based on soft skills..." Cynthia let her words die out with a shrug. They both knew she didn't need to say the rest out loud.

"So you're saying that I could possibly lead a team if I wanted, but you don't have a lot of confidence that they wouldn't all quit on the spot when they find out they report to me?"

"In a nutshell, yes," Cynthia said.

Nora could feel Cynthia watching her, studying Nora's expression to see how she was absorbing this information. She looked up and met Cynthia with a determined stare. "Why are you telling me this? It's your decision."

"Because I'm trying to give you agency. I know you don't want to be friends with your co-workers after... well..." Cynthia stilled and schooled her with a look before her stare softened. "Anyway, past experiences aside, I'm unsure if you actually want to lead them. Teach them. Support them."

"I'm not sure they'd like that." If that wasn't an honest statement, Nora didn't know what was. No one was ever going to vote her 'Most Outgoing' in the Philly Finds yearbook, and she'd spent years making it this way. Annoyance simmered just below the surface that she even cared, and she tempered it with an indignant huff.

"Would you like it?" Cynthia asked, as though she were reading her mind.

Nora hated that the scars of her past experiences hadn't lessened over time. Instead, they'd hardened her into something, like they'd been etched across her body so deeply they'd formed armor over her skin. "I don't know," she answered honestly.

"Well, maybe this trip can be a first step in figuring that out. Building bridges. Learning to communicate. Understanding what the newest person on the team has experienced in the last year after coming to work here. I think it could give you a new perspective on things and hopefully help you come to a decision."

"So you're turning my prize into a work trip?" Her half-decade-long default had been sardonic bitchiness, and in this moment, she couldn't have turned it off if she'd wanted to.

Cynthia rolled her eyes. "Not if you don't want it to be. And even then, these are all great skills to have regardless."

"Was this all some kind of weird setup?"

Cynthia shook her head. "No. Gray has truly earned this trip. She's breathed new life into the company over the last year —not that you've bothered to notice."

That one stung a little. Nora spent as little time in the office as she could, mostly shuttling herself between client appointments and keeping her schedule as packed as possible. It wasn't just to avoid her co-workers, but it was absolutely an added benefit.

She took a few seconds to compose herself, letting out a soft, deep exhale. It didn't have the desired effect. "When are you planning on making this decision or rolling the new structure out?"

Cynthia smiled. "I want to get things set up in the new year and have the two arms running smoothly by the time sales pick up in the spring."

Nora did some quick mental math. "That's, like, four or five months away."

"I know. I won't be announcing it to the rest of the team for a few months anyway, so it will be business as usual for everyone else."

"And for me?" She could hear the strain from her own uncertainty laced through her tone. She'd never admit it, but she wanted Cynthia to tell her what to do.

"Well, if you want the job, you know who you need to impress."

"You?" Nora asked hopefully.

Cynthia pointed through the glass panel on her door to the open-concept office. "Them."

Nora could practically smell the microwaved fish from here.

"So," Cynthia continued with finality, "take your vacation. Have a wonderful time. Maybe learn to be a team player. And when you come back, you can decide if you want to invest time in becoming a more ingrained member of this team with the eventual goal to lead part of it."

Nora sat there, helpless to come up with another argument that would put her life back to the way it had been fifteen minutes ago. "Just that simple?"

"Life is nothing more than what we make of it," Cynthia said, walking over and opening her office door.

Dismissed—and feeling more than a little dressed down—Nora stood up and ran her hands down her blazer.

The unhelpful lesson she took away from her conversation with Cynthia was that she should be more careful about what she wished for. Because when she walked out of Cynthia's office, being stuck on a tropical island with Gray Ferris for a week was suddenly the least of her worries.

Chapter Two

"Nora did not look happy earlier this morning when you were announced as a winner," Kelsey said quietly—at least for her—as they fixed their early afternoon coffees.

Gray had two showings later in the afternoon, both close by. Fishtown was a hotbed of activity lately, and her office being located where she lived was just an added bonus. She didn't even mind that it was a few miles outside the hustle of Center City. She loved the mostly residential area, with its own main drag that had started to swell with a number of bars, restaurants, and stores over the last few years.

"Hmmm..." she said absently, focused on stirring in her oat milk until the coffee was the perfect soft chocolate color she loved. She knew exactly what Kelsey was implying, and she was mostly surprised her co-worker had managed to keep that to herself all morning.

Not that Gray had been around to be on the receiving end of Kelsey's Spanish Inquisition. After their all-hands meeting, she'd schlepped down to South Philly, over to Brewerytown, and then to West Philly to show new clients a few prospective houses at each location.

But truthfully, she'd only been back for about ten minutes, so maybe Kelsey didn't deserve as much credit as she was giving her.

"I mean, I thought she was going to have a meltdown. Did you see how she snuck into Cynthia's office? They were in there for a while."

Gray shrugged, the ends of her hair grazing the tips of her shoulders. "Honestly, I didn't. I had to run out right after the meeting to get to my appointments."

Gray tried not to gossip.

She would chat. Shoot the breeze. Ham it up.

Sure.

But she always made sure to focus her questions on the person she was talking to instead of them both talking about someone else. Especially when it came to Kelsey.

"Well, all I have to say is good luck on your likely not-so-relaxing vacation."

Gray picked up her coffee to blow on it before placating Kelsey. "I'm sure it'll be fine."

Long, blonde hair almost dipped into Gray's coffee cup as Kelsey shot a furtive look past the kitchen area and into the open office beyond. "She's intolerable."

"She's a good agent. There's a reason she won the trip too."

Kelsey leaned in conspiratorially, eyes narrowed. Gray braced for whatever mean jab was coming. "Good enough to act like a complete bitch to everyone?"

"It's not like any of us really know her," Gray said, not exactly sure why she was coming to Nora's defense, with the exception of common decency. It's not like Nora had made Gray's life any easier than the rest of the team, but still, she didn't think it was fair to bad-mouth someone if they weren't there to defend themselves. She knew what it was like to have people talk around you instead of to you; how quickly the office gossip grapevine took on a life of its own.

She didn't wish it on anyone.

"Because she acts like we all have a communicable disease," Kelsey retorted. "I can't believe she closes so many deals. Does she morph into a completely different person with clients?"

"I don't know. You should ask her," Gray deadpanned before taking a long sip of her coffee and then staring at Kelsey over the rim of the cup.

The conversation about Nora Gallagher always came up eventually when Gray was out for a night with her co-workers. She never participated, but Nora was almost mythical at this point in her refusal to engage with the rest of the team. In an office made up of fewer than a dozen agents, with Nora being the most senior based on both tenure and performance, it was honestly impressive.

"She doesn't bother you?" Kelsey's voice was almost exasperated, like she was throwing chum into a shark tank and couldn't believe the lackluster results.

"It seems like she just wants to do her work and go home." Maybe Gray did sometimes wonder what Nora was like outside of work, but she wasn't going to admit that to Kelsey, the office gossip, of all people.

The indignant huff Kelsey let out made it hard for Gray to keep a straight face, but she managed. Barely.

"Fine, you don't want to do this. I get it. Will you at least tell me if she's batshit crazy on the trip? I don't think any of us have ever spent time outside of work with her, except Cynthia."

It was the first time Gray had really considered the reality of her situation. She'd be spending almost a week with Nora, and it wouldn't be about work. She'd see more of her austere colleague than she, or probably anyone else in the company, ever would. A quick pang of guilt sluiced through her that she was even going. It seemed like Nora liked her privacy, and Gray's mere presence had thrown a colossal wrench into that aspect of her vacation.

No wonder she'd followed Cynthia into her office. The trip was never billed as a group vacation, and Gray had been just as surprised as Nora when it was announced she'd also won.

Of course, she didn't feel badly enough to give up the trip. That would be idiotic. She'd go and give Nora all the space a twenty-square-mile island could provide. Maybe they'd have a few nice conversations; maybe they wouldn't.

At worst, she'd get a fantastic end-of-summer tan to pull her through winter and knock a novel or two off her ever-growing to-be-read pile of books. At best, she'd finally know more about Nora the person instead of Nora the kick-ass real estate agent.

It was easy to be intimidated by her, and maybe Nora liked that. Top dog in the office. Unapproachable. Focused and dedicated. Peeling back the layers would prove what Gray already knew, even if Nora didn't want her to see it: that she was just a person, with regular problems and frustrations and hangups like anyone else.

If, for some reason, it was important for Nora to keep up that facade for some semblance of self-protection and control, Gray would be fine with it.

And really, it wasn't like they'd be trapped together.

In the logistical sense, traveling with Nora was exactly like Gray had expected it would be. She'd shown up at the gate an hour before boarding was set to begin, and Nora was already there.

What she hadn't expected was that Nora would be wearing

a soft-looking pair of black joggers and an even softer-looking white, V-neck T-shirt. It was a far cry from the business attire she wore in the office—though, sure, Gray liked those too. The woman had a knack for picking out blazers that must have been bespoke for her frame. Today, like all days, her hair was immaculate, its tousled, blonde waves bouncing just above her chin.

Gray noticed her before Nora realized she was there, so she stole a few moments to take it all in. How one of Nora's sneaker-clad feet was resting on top of her suitcase. The way her usually stoic expression was much softer, her lips eased into a gentle smile from something she was reading on her Kindle. Her fingers absently curled around a tendril of hair as she played with it. She almost looked... cute, if Gray didn't know what an absolute menace she was at work.

Maybe she wouldn't ever make the menace comment to Kelsey, but having thoughts wasn't illegal. Gray tried to temper them as best she could, but ever since the first time they'd met, she'd felt like she could do no right where Nora stood.

And coming on this trip? Well, it would either jumpstart their relationship or blow it to oblivion. Gray had already accepted that in the darkness of night a few hours ago as she'd tossed and turned in her bed.

She'd wondered in the week leading up to the trip if Nora would try to soften the potential awkwardness of them traveling together. A few more hellos. Maybe an exchange of pleasantries in the office.

None of that had happened.

If anything, Nora was even more absent from the workplace, to the point that Gray wondered if she was actively avoiding it.

Sure, she could chalk it up to Nora doing as much as possible since she'd be out for the week, but Gray's clients had all been prepped that she'd be unavailable and given an interim agent to support them, and she'd assumed Nora had done the same.

After about thirty seconds of indulgent staring, like she was watching a creature she'd never seen before, Gray made her way over to the gate and cleared her throat. "Morning."

When Nora looked up at her, the soft, easy features on her face were already gone. "Morning."

"Do you mind if I sit next to you?" She pointed at the chair two seats down, as Nora's smaller bag was already resting on the one to her left.

Nora shrugged. "I assume we're sitting together on the plane anyway."

"Makes sense." Gray shuffled her roller bag next to her and placed her backpack between her feet.

And then they sat, silence enveloping them as it clung to the recycled air circulating through the building. It was cloying in a way that made it hard to focus on browsing on her phone. Nora went back to reading her book, and even if Gray wanted to ask what she was reading, she knew she never would. The best thing, as far as she could assess, would be to let Nora take the lead. Maybe she'd have to chime in if things became desperate, but her grand plan was to try and act like a completely normal human and hope it all worked out.

Gray made it about five minutes before all her best laid plans crumbled. "Can I ask you something?"

Nora's sharp, blue eyes stared at her for long seconds before she answered. "Yes?"

"I know you weren't expecting me to be on this trip. I wasn't expecting to be on this trip, so I don't want you to feel like I'm intruding or anything. I'm just hoping we can both have a nice vacation, regardless of how much or little interaction we have."

For the briefest moment, she thought Nora's lips turned

upward in a slight smile when she said, "I don't remember hearing a question."

Gray waved her hand, flustered. Heat crept up her neck, and she shifted in the uncomfortable chair. "Fine, call it a comment on the reality of the situation. I just don't want you to think I expect anything of you."

It mesmerized Gray how Nora's brow lifted up on one side, her features open and almost amused for the first time in Gray's memory. "Expect things of me?"

"Like hanging out. Or going to dinners. Or acting like we're friends or something." Gray fumbled through her words. They were surprisingly hard to get out with Nora's focus entirely on her.

Because... god, was Nora Gallagher attractive. And that shouldn't have mattered, but dressed so casually, her blue eyes leveled in Gray's direction for maybe the longest period ever, it was making it a little hard for Gray to think on her feet.

"I'm sure you'll bake me cookies to make up for it if you cross any lines," Nora said, full lips now definitely smirking.

"To be fair, that was an accident."

"Because you weren't paying attention." Nora's voice was matter-of-fact, and it stirred something combative in Gray that tempered the swell of attraction she'd felt only moments ago. It was strange how quickly one emotion could push another to the side, as the memory welled up in her.

Gray had thought of that day many times. It had been her first day at a new job after she'd left her last agency. She'd already been nervous, only to find herself squarely on the shit list of the company's top agent. She'd spent weeks thinking Nora's subsequent behavior toward her was because of what happened and not because that was how Nora acted toward everyone.

It wasn't until she'd settled in, growing comfortable in the

A Life Worth Living

homey embrace of Philly Finds—despite Nora's less-than-warm welcome—that she'd realized Nora treated everyone, with the exception of Cynthia, with an almost cool derision. She wasn't openly hostile, but anyone with a modicum of social awareness could tell that Nora didn't want to engage in anything more than business-related conversations. And given they all had their own book of clients, that didn't need to happen often.

"I could say the same for you," Gray batted back without thinking, too lost in the moment and how she'd felt at the time. Philly Finds was her fresh start, and she regretted for even a moment that she'd let Nora make her feel anything less than cautious optimism about it.

The eyebrow raise leveled at her deepened in a way Gray chose not to appreciate. "Is that so?"

"Feels like Bermuda's neutral territory," Gray said with a shrug, trying to find her way back to balance. "You're not the top agent there, and I'm not the newbie."

"We're not in Bermuda yet."

Gray pulled out her phone. "Do you want me to take notes and follow up there?"

"I'd rather you didn't," Nora said, but there was no malice in her voice. Her stare tracked across Gray's face, curiously. Leaning closer, Nora rested her elbow on the armrest of the chair between them.

"So..."

Nora's stare dropped down to Gray's lips with the elongated word before she dragged her focus back up and those icy blues narrowed to about half their normal size. "So what?"

It took a lot for Gray to hold back an exasperated puff of frustration. "So, how do you want to play this? Do you want me to leave you alone on the trip?"

Nora shrugged. "I don't know if that's going to be possible."

"That's a non-answer. I didn't ask what was possible. I

asked what you wanted." This woman may honestly be the death of her. Nora must have been actively trying to be obtuse.

"What I want is to shut down my brain, sit on a beach, and not be asked questions like this," she said with finality before she continued reading.

Gray briefly fixated on the idea of Nora on the beach, all long legs and fair skin. She enjoyed the little surge of warmth that shot through her, and even smiled when she thought about how Nora would probably shoot daggers at her own feet for capturing sand between her toes.

But it extinguished quickly when she considered Nora's words. Nora didn't have any interest in being friends with Gray. Hell, she was implying she could barely tolerate polite conversation with her.

The warmth lingered, but now it was from the uncomfortable heat of realizing that she'd been dismissed.

But they were stuck together. In this airport. On the plane. In Bermuda.

Still, she didn't need to make it any harder on herself than it needed to be. She'd extended an olive branch, which Nora was intent on swatting away like a feral cat. At least she could say she'd tried, but giving Nora even a second more of her time was just a waste.

"Good to know," she said, popping in her earbuds. She turned up the volume to block out any possible response Nora may or may not have given and focused on a plane taking off in the distance.

Chapter Three

Nora rolled her carry-on about a foot and waited in the customs line in the Bermuda airport, Gray behind her but not making any attempts at further conversation.

So maybe she was being a little bit of a bitch. She hadn't meant to be so cold, especially with Gray looking at her so earnestly in the airport, but it was hard to flip that switch into a more neutral mode on command.

But people, save her clients, never looked at her with any sort of expectation. Gray, with her big, brown eyes and perfect, pursed lips, had been acting like they could change the tides. That this trip could be whatever they made it.

As if life were that easy.

Some days, Nora felt like a ball of yarn, wound up so tightly for her own protection. Because it wasn't just a question that Gray was asking—it was a string she was pulling. And all the strings needed to be kept in place or Nora's carefully crafted existence would unravel.

It was a system she'd worked out over the last five years, and it kept her moving through the days with limited fallout. Reject everything. Change nothing. Exist in stasis as the world spun around her.

She knew how it sounded, even in her own head, but it was ingrained at this point.

On the plane, she'd briefly considered apologizing, but there hadn't felt like a right time. And what would she say?

Whether an apology should have happened, Gray, true to Nora's request, hadn't asked her any more questions. She hadn't even taken her earbuds out again.

Not having active clients to focus on was giving her far too much time to think. Cynthia, even though she'd been out of the sales side of things for a few years now, was the only person on the team Nora had trusted to leave her active portfolio with, and she was almost sure her boss wouldn't respond to any of her text messages requesting status updates.

Actually, she knew that. She'd already reached out twice and had been sent back nothing more than a thumbs-down emoji each time. Smart of Cynthia. Silence could be interpreted as not having received the messages and would have allowed Nora to give herself the green light to keep reaching out.

But work was her *thing*, a way to direct her focus to keep from spinning out. For as much as she'd been telling herself that a week on a tropical beach was exactly what she wanted, she could feel the fear and uncertainty hanging over her like a specter. Without anything to occupy her time, how would she spend it? Unwinding? She hardly knew what that looked like. Her phone was always tethered to her. She lived for an unexpected evening call from a client who was frantic that something was going wrong. It felt good to be needed, and where these business relationships were concerned, she had to give nothing of herself in the process.

So she'd been nervous about this trip, but she'd thought that if she was going to fall apart, it would happen privately. That maybe it would be awkward and frustrating at times, but there would be no one else around to see it.

Gray Ferris was making sure that wasn't going to happen, and it felt perfectly reasonable that Nora would resent her for it, whether being here was Gray's fault or not. When she'd shown up at the airport this morning, all bright-eyed and bushy-tailed, in a pair of tapered jeans and a sleeveless tank top —looking at home and relaxed in a way Nora had possibly never felt—frustration had welled up inside of her.

And the questions. God. The questions that Nora didn't have an answer to, even if they were so stupidly simple. She didn't want Gray to know that, and she sure as hell wasn't going to admit just how utterly out of her depth she felt about this trip.

"You're up." It was Gray's even voice from behind her, breaking through above the din of the crowd queueing for customs.

She groaned and stepped up to the customs agent, fumbling with her passport. This was going to be a long week.

Sooner than she expected, though, Nora found herself alone. She and Gray had hotel rooms next to one another, though thankfully they weren't adjoining. Not that it really mattered, but she wanted all the separation she could get—physically and metaphorically.

There was something about Gray she couldn't quite put her finger on, and she much preferred focusing on that over accepting that maybe she was the problem.

Was it possible for someone to honestly be that open and

approachable? It had to be some kind of act. Cynthia's words from a few weeks ago flitted through her mind, about how Gray had been improving things at the office, like she assumed Nora hadn't noticed.

Except that she had.

She'd seen Gray float around the office whenever Nora was forced to be there, casually leaning on a co-worker's desk with a mug of coffee and chatting idly. Always the same mug—a giant, purple monstrosity with what appeared to be dinosaurs painted on the side of it.

Nora could admit that Gray was good at her job, but the rest of it? The bubbly, extroverted, "attractive in a way that said she didn't really care if you took it or left it" package? Pass.

If Gray was sunshine, Nora was midnight rain. Beyond both of them being great at their jobs—which she could begrudgingly admit—she doubted they had more in common. Even if they did, it wasn't high on Nora's priorities list to find out.

"Ugh," she said to no one as she picked her toiletry bag out of her suitcase and placed it on a shelf in the bathroom.

She needed to stop spending so much time thinking about Gray. The whole point of her self-imposed isolation was to prevent this exact scenario.

Instead, she looked around at the room she'd call home for the next five days and tried to appreciate the moment.

The hotel room itself was nice, if not slightly modest. It was hard not to survey it through the eyes of a real estate agent, scrutinizing every design choice and mentally critiquing or complimenting the layout of the resort and its buildings. But the view off her balcony was what dreams were made of, all still, clear water and gently billowing palm trees. If she was writing the listing, that'd be the front and center hook for the property.

The resort was a tropical hodgepodge of multiple seemingly well-made structures settled on different outcroppings. The main house was set atop a hill, and boasted a few restaurants and bars. At least that's what the brochure she'd been given at check-in said. There were maybe ten other buildings scattered around the main one at slightly lower elevations. They housed the hotel rooms, which all had doors opening directly onto the exterior walkways and paths meandering through the property.

Somewhere close by was rumored to be a pool and an outdoor bar, situated right off the private beach access that opened onto a sea so cerulean it looked fake. She couldn't remember the last time her entire body had felt sunlight on it, and she instinctively reached into her bag for the small bottle of SPF 50 that she'd been able to bring in her carry-on. It wasn't going to last long.

As she organized items on her vanity and settled in, she decided to give Cynthia a call, just to check in.

Ring. No answer.

She plugged her phone charger into the wall.

Ring. No answer.

The extra bottle of water she'd purchased at the airport was placed securely in the mini fridge.

Ring. No answer.

Her passport went in the safe in the closet next.

When the phone skipped over to voicemail, she disconnected the call. As if Cynthia refusing to answer would deter her from the questions itching in the back of her mind since she'd left Philadelphia this morning.

Nora – 2:42 p.m.

I was just saying hi

25

Cynthia Castellano – 2:42 p.m.

> I doubt that very much

Nora frowned at her phone. There was no point in lying to Cynthia.

Nora – 2:42 p.m.

> Okay, so maybe I also wanted to know if the Jetsons liked the open house on 14th St.

The house had come on the market Thursday, and Nora had known they'd love it. It was a feeling rooted in the amalgamation of thousands of houses shown to prospective buyers over the last ten years, not in any sentimentality at the thought of the life they could lead there. In every practical sense, it checked all their boxes. She'd sold them on the vision of family and life and happiness, but that, too, was a carefully constructed narrative.

She knew exactly what people wanted, because once upon a time, she'd wanted those things too.

Cynthia Castellano – 2:43 p.m.

> … That's not your concern this week

Nora – 2:43 p.m.

> I don't think I'll be able to enjoy myself unless I know

Cynthia Castellano – 2:43 p.m.

> Really cutting off your nose to spite your face there. You're in literal tropical paradise. Why are you thinking about work?

Nora – 2:43 p.m.

Can't teach an old dog new tricks?

Cynthia Castellano – 2:44 p.m.

You're 35, Nora. You need to give that schtick up.

Nora – 2:44 p.m.

I'm an old soul.

Cynthia Castellano – 2:44 p.m.

They loved it. We put in an offer at the open house. Now will you go have fun?

Satisfaction slid through her. She smiled into the empty room and squeezed her phone like she was shaking someone's hand. Regardless of what anyone else thought, she didn't begrudge others' happiness. She just didn't need to be a part of it—or her own—in any meaningful way.

Nora – 2:44 p.m.

The sun will feel a little warmer knowing they liked it.

The three dots appeared in their text thread and then disappeared for a few seconds before the next message came through.

Cynthia Castellano – 2:45 p.m.

Are you playing nice with Gray?

Ugh. Why did Cynthia have to bring her up? It wasn't

Gray, specifically, that had Nora out of sorts. It was the possibility of change. On the plane ride over, she'd knocked around the idea of what actually working toward this promotion would mean.

If her first interactions this morning were any indication, it would be an uphill slog that wouldn't end well for her and may leave a lot of collateral damage in her wake.

Nora – 2:46 p.m.

> She's fine.

Cynthia Castellano – 2:46 p.m.

> Gagged in a closet somewhere?

Nora – 2:47 p.m.

> Only if she asks nicely.

Cynthia Castellano – 2:47 p.m.

> She's dealt with you for the least amount of time, and she's your best chance to get the team on your side.

Nora didn't want to admit it, but it meant something to her that Cynthia still believed she wasn't beyond redemption. She'd lost faith in herself that her life would be anything more than a grind from one deal to the next. It wasn't that she was bored—quite the contrary—but she'd meant what she'd texted her boss. It was hard to teach an old dog new tricks. People didn't suddenly wake up one day and decide to be different. To make better choices for themselves.

She felt the cement of the new reality she'd solidified hardening around her every day. At first, ignoring people had been difficult, but back then, the wounds had been so fresh that doing anything without crying or screaming had been difficult. Retreating inward on herself had been safe—comforting even. And once she'd done it for long enough, it had become second nature.

She no longer thought frequently of her ex, Andrea, and the life she'd expected them to have together. Andrea had made sure there'd be no good will left at the end.

The loss of her parents, which had happened only a few months before the implosion of her three year relationship, still stung at the oddest of times. There'd been so much left unsaid between them, and that door was closed forever.

In boxing up the bad, she'd shuffled any good into the box too. Her trust in people. A want for genuine connection. An excitement for life and the possibility of what came next.

An armor like that didn't come off easily. And when she remembered back to how broken she'd been, how abandoned she'd felt in the face of her world crashing down around her, she wasn't sure that she wanted to take it off.

Nora – 2:48 p.m.

I'll take that under advisement.

And she would, even if she didn't think it was actually going to happen. Some days, she barely noticed the armor she'd constructed around herself. Other days, it felt so heavy it was difficult to breathe. She wore it because the alternative was inconceivable. To let herself be vulnerable and exposed? Not a chance.

What Cynthia was asking of her was no small feat, and

maybe it wasn't even possible. Maybe some people were just too broken to ever find their way back. Maybe she was one of them.

People acted like feelings were something that happened to you, not something you made space for, so she'd stopped making space. She couldn't be hurt if she couldn't be touched.

But she hated the idea of getting passed over for this promotion. Even if she didn't really want it. Even if it would be an uphill battle to get it.

Thirty minutes later, she was dressed for the beach in a simple black bikini that also hadn't felt sunlight on it in far too long, slathered with sunscreen in all the places she could reach. An oversize shirt and a pair of loose shorts completed the outfit, having been dug out of some recess of her closet at home.

She could do this. Get the promotion. Play nice with Gray. Prove to herself that she could still have whatever she allowed herself to.

Overthinking their run-ins and planning every possible scenario wasn't going to get her anywhere. For the first time in a long time, Nora realized that all she could do was go with the flow of the next few days and adapt as the situation unfolded. That was the rub of other people, wasn't it? That she couldn't control them, couldn't control the outcome.

She gave herself a long, scrutinizing look in the mirror before she said, "You are the only thing standing in the way of whatever you want."

* * *

It felt impossible that Gray had beaten her to the beach. Not only that, but she was already—drink in hand—wandering around the shallow water and talking to a small group of people.

The annoyance that flared up in her was almost enough to quell the awareness of the light blush snaking up her neck and fanning over her cheeks. Gray Ferris, lounging in the shallow end of the water in a purple bathing suit, was... a lot, even if Nora wished the other woman weren't here.

Every time she saw her, it was a reminder of just how many variables were out of Nora's control.

Chestnut hair billowed lazily against Gray's shoulders, like she couldn't be bothered to put it up in her rush to get to the beach. Was this some kind of power play? To get there first? Nora checked herself. That level of paranoia was a lot, even for her.

She tamped down the feeling and threw her bag on the sand next to a free beach chair, one of only a few left. Even though the official end of summer was on the horizon, the resort was still bustling with people.

It wasn't a large stretch of sand, but it was private, and there were at least fifty chairs that people had moved into varying configurations to fit their groups. She wanted to see the beach in the morning, before the rest of the guests descended and added their own chaotic touch of humanity to an otherwise perfect experience.

"First time in Bermuda?" a woman in the chair next to her asked as Nora sat down, working to minimize the sand she brought with her.

What was it about vacations that made people so chatty? She'd forgotten that, given it had been so long since she'd been on one.

"It is." She pulled out her Kindle and hoped the woman would leave it at that.

No such luck. "It's lovely here. I've been about a dozen times. Such a quick flight from the United States to find your-self in paradise."

31

Monica McCallan

Their chairs were only about a foot away from one another. Outright ignoring the woman didn't feel like an option. "I just got in today."

"Ah," the woman said knowingly, like that explained anything. The bracelets on her wrist jingled when she lifted her frozen drink to take a long, luxurious sip that only people in commercials seemed to do. "You're going to love it. I can just tell."

Nora lifted a skeptical eyebrow.

"It's a great place to relax, is all I mean." She waved her hand out toward the water. "And who doesn't need a little more relaxation in their life?"

"You've got me there." Nora eased against the back of the chair, which was so hot she sat up quickly.

"You didn't get a towel from the pool cabana?" Wow, Nora was sitting next to a regular Sherlock Holmes.

"I—"

The woman pointed behind them, toward stone steps cut into the beach. "The pool is right past there, and the bar's right next to it. If you're a drinker, I've got you pegged for loving the Miami Vice."

What the fuck was a Miami Vice, and what about Nora at all screamed that she would like it?

But she couldn't deny that lounging at the beach was best done with a towel, and she did want a drink.

Plus, it allowed her to leave this conversation. She was sold.

She stood quickly. "Thanks for the tips. Is my stuff okay here?"

"Oh sure, don't you even worry about it. I'll be here for at least the next hour, and I'll keep an eye on it. The name's Lisa," she said, extending her jangling arm.

"Nora."

"Lovely to meet you, Nora. I can tell you're going to have a

32

fabulous time." Lisa was a melty puddle of relaxation, in the way that came from being a little sun drunk after a long day of lounging.

Nora began her walk toward the pool instead of disagreeing with the woman, even if she still had her doubts.

Chapter Four

It was beginning to seem like Nora had no problem being conversational on this vacation; it was just that she didn't want to talk to Gray. At least, that's what Gray clocked from her vantage point in the water.

She'd watched Nora meander down the stone steps and onto the bustling beach. Noticing Nora was easy. She was tall. Graceful. A little oblivious. Nora had moved across the beach like she was the only person on it, somehow finding a direct path to one of the few beach chairs left unoccupied in the mid-afternoon sun.

Gray shook her head and lowered her body down, her knees bending so the water ebbed just above her shoulders, one hand above the water to keep her drink safe. She let out an indulgent sigh and fantasized about lifting her feet and floating on her back. Still, she stayed rooted to the soft sand beneath her toes, like if she finally let herself go, she would drift out to sea and never come back.

The water felt good. That's what Gray wanted to focus on. How it was almost still, with schools of tiny fish darting past her during the brief periods when she was unmoving. In the shallow end where the sea and beach met, with the sun's soft heat working its magic all day, the water had warmed to the perfect temperature.

She slid one of her hands through the sea and enjoyed the gentle resistance against her muscles. Caught up in proving herself at Philly Finds this past year, she couldn't remember the last time she'd enjoyed a day without thinking about work or making sure that her life was staying on track.

She wasn't going to let Nora take this moment from her.

She'd already made a few friends. Two men had swum over first. They'd asked all the greatest hits, like, *Have you been here before?*, *Where are you from?*, and her personal least favorite, *Are you here alone?* That was usually how it went. When three more women followed suit, she breathed a small sigh of relief. This trip wasn't going to be some magical romance, regardless of what the romance novels would have a person believe, and she liked the safety of groups.

Within a few minutes of Nora's arrival, Gray watched her lithe frame ascend back up the steps she'd come from, sans her bag.

"Do you know her?" Darcy, the woman next to her, whose name she'd learned about five minutes ago, asked between sips of an almost melted daiquiri.

Gray pulled her focus back to the cute brunette and her slightly sunburnt nose. "Sort of?"

"Gonna have to explain that one to me."

While she'd been watching Nora, she hadn't noticed the other four in the group floating away to throw a football a few feet farther into the water.

"We work together. We both won this trip, so I know who she is, obviously." Gray scrunched up her nose, trying to find the right words to explain the dynamic. "And we sat together on the plane, but that's about the extent of it."

"So... not friends, then?"

"Honestly, no. We're just two people who know one another in the real world, who ended up at the same vacation resort. Are those your friends?" Gray wanted to change the subject. She didn't want to explain Nora. Especially not how acutely and frustratingly aware of her presence Gray had been for the last few hours.

"I'm here with the two women, Rachel and Robin. We met the guys a few days ago. There's some kind of sales conference happening that seems like nothing more than a glorified party, so it's been busier than I expected."

Gray took in the information. Nora would hate a raucous atmosphere. The idea made her sort of giddy. "Have you been to Bermuda before?"

"I used to come with my parents growing up. They were big cruise enthusiasts, and this is a popular stop. In adulthood, I realized I hated cruise ships, but I still love this tiny island."

"Makes sense. Very Buddhist of you," Gray mused before adding, "You know, taking what you want and leaving the rest."

Darcy bobbed her head, her chin dipping into the water. "Exactly."

Gray held up her plastic cup and straightened her legs to stand. "I'm gonna get a refill on this, but it was great meeting you. Maybe I'll come throw the football around later if you're all still out here."

With a quick wave, she walked the twenty feet back to the shore, already missing the soft, buoying support that the ocean provided.

* * *

It became clear that Gray and Nora were going to keep running into one another. The resort wasn't that big, and the poolside bar seemed to be the central daytime hub for guests who weren't on excursions around the island.

Gray gave Nora a quick once-over, like she'd done earlier this morning at the airport, and eased into the spot next to her at the bar.

"Fancy meeting you here." It had to be the effects of her first drink, which had been a surprisingly generous pour for being all-inclusive, coupled with the heat of the sun, that had her already going back on her self-imposed rule to give Nora a wide berth on this trip.

And it was definitely the effects of her first drink that had her leaning her forearm on the bar and turning toward Nora, Gray's fingers absently plucking at a coaster that had been left behind.

Gray had always been a sucker for a pretty woman. The way Nora so decidedly fell into that category made Gray want to scream, so that obviously wasn't helping her either. Nora's oversize button-down had slipped to the side, revealing her collarbone and accentuating the long column of her neck.

Fleetingly, Gray wondered what it would feel like to cup Nora's jaw, where the skin looked soft and was probably warm from the heat of the sun.

It was easier in Philadelphia, when Nora was only around the office at sporadic intervals, always moving with purpose and never sitting still long enough to come into focus. She was only an idea of a person to Gray there, and the gaps she'd had to fill in with the bits of knowledge she did have made it easy to keep her distance over the last year.

But in another world, if they didn't know one another and Gray saw Nora standing alone at a bar on a tropical island paradise, she'd have thought maybe it was a fantasy that had come to life. Or that she had to be dreaming.

But chemistry and compatibility weren't the same thing, not that she was looking for either one with Nora—or anyone else. Still... a little thrill shot through Gray when Nora turned toward her, fingers pushing back against her temple to hold her blonde hair away from the side of her face.

It was impossible to see Nora's eyes through her oversize sunglasses, and her impassive face gave nothing else away. "A coincidence for the ages."

"Another of the same, miss?" the bartender asked when his focus landed on Gray. She saw him out of her peripheral vision, frustrated at how difficult it was for her to pull her focus away from Nora.

She was at a bar waiting for a drink. Not waiting for Nora to bestow a crumb of attention on her like she was a beggar who hadn't eaten in days.

She pushed her cup toward him. "Yes, thanks."

The extra, precious seconds of distraction helped bring Gray back to reality. In the real world, Nora Gallagher wasn't mysterious or aloof; she was rude.

Because Gray could make inane small talk with the best of them. It was one of the things she prided herself on. But Nora's absolute resistance to normalcy was starting to grate on her, in spite of the pleasant buzz of alcohol and attraction that made her feel like she was still floating in Bermuda's warm waters.

It was the wisps of wanting to lean into those indulgent feelings, however ill advised, that propelled her now. She couldn't help herself, like someone who needed to touch a surface with a sign that said, 'Hot. Do not touch.'

Or maybe she just wanted to poke the hornet's nest to see what came out—though this was so not her style that she should have taken a few extra seconds to consider what she was doing.

That didn't happen.

The idea that struck her felt irrefutable, given the few shots' worth of alcohol coursing through her sun-soaked body.

Extending her hand, she leveled her most charismatic smile at Nora. "I'm Gray. It's nice to meet you. First time in Bermuda?"

Nora looked down at her hand for prolonged seconds before she tipped her focus back to Gray's face. Eyebrows a few shades darker than Nora's blonde hair now raised above her sunglasses, she watched Gray, seemingly mulling over the offer like it was the most serious decision she'd made in a long time.

It was hard to place exactly what happened on Nora's side, but something changed. Gray couldn't see her eyes, but Nora's head cocked to the side as she drew her shoulders back.

Still, a small puff of air escaped her lips when Nora's soft hand slid into her own, her stomach swooping low. "Nora. It's nice to meet you. This is my first time in Bermuda."

Gray smiled in a way she couldn't help, like she'd finally unlocked a door with a key she hadn't known she'd had. She ignored her own surge of curiosity at what had changed things so quickly for Nora. "You look like a cruise enthusiast. What's got you on this side of the island?"

It was a little addictive, the way Nora's lips edged upward, even if it was only into the idea of a smile. "A cruise enthusiast, hm?"

There was a silky, low quality to Nora's voice that slid through her then with its impact. Gray liked it. A lot.

"Okay, so... not a cruise enthusiast." Gray pretended to really consider her options before snapping her fingers. "Then you're here with the sales conference?"

Nora took a long sip of what looked like two frozen drinks mixed together. "I wasn't aware there was a sales conference."

Gray feigned dejectedness at another wrong answer

instead of focusing on Nora's now slightly wet lips. "I really thought I had it that time."

She wanted to keep Nora talking; she felt like she was existing in a moment suspended from reality. This couldn't last, though; she knew that.

"Process of elimination is never a bad approach."

"What are you drinking?" The words were out before Gray realized they sounded like a come-on. Again, she braced for the impact when their carefully constructed facade shattered around them.

But it didn't.

"A woman on the beach told me I looked like a Miami Vice kind of person." The hint of a smile had grown fuller, like Nora herself was surprised at both the assessment and her own admission.

Gray took a chance. "I'd have pegged you more as a 'Dark and Stormy' type." She held her breath and waited for the smile to drop from Nora's face, her own blooming brighter when it didn't.

"A little presumptuous for someone you just met?" Nora parried, easing her sunglasses up onto her head. Clear blue eyes met Gray's with curiosity, like Nora was waiting to see what she'd do next.

Like maybe she was enjoying this too.

She raised her hands, palms facing up. "It's one of the classic drinks here, that's all. Considering it's your first time, I thought maybe you were soaking in the full experience."

"Seems like you're a bit of an expert then? Not your first time, I take it?"

It was stupid how heat slid through her at the soft lilt in Nora's voice. In how she was so willing to be wrong for the sake of this game they were playing. She'd never seen Nora be wrong about anything.

"Ah, the process of elimination was also not a bad approach, but you went the wrong way. This is actually my first time here." The words, *I guess we're both a bunch of virgins,* were hanging on the tip of Gray's tongue, but she didn't go there.

"So you're just a nerd for vacation-planning research?"

A laugh escaped then, low and genuine with Gray's surprise. "While that's not the worst moniker a stranger could give me, this is a very chatty resort. Rampant with conversation if you stand still for longer than thirty seconds."

"So that's my problem then? I'm not moving fast enough?" Nora had eased her elbow down on the bar so they were closer to each other's eye level now.

Gray's mouth dropped open. That definitely sounded like a come-on. But no, there was no world in which Nora Gallagher was hitting on her, game or not. "If you want to avoid conversations, then yes, that's exactly what it means."

"I'll take that under advisement."

She could feel it, the natural ending of the conversation ebbing like a low tide easing water away from the shore.

"Well, it was nice meeting you," she said with a quick second of eye contact before dropping her stare down to her forgotten, half-melted drink.

"You, too, Gray." And then Nora turned back toward the bar, making Gray feel like the entire conversation had been a hallucination.

The world felt a little tilted on its axis as she meandered back down to the beach, melty drink in hand. Apparently, Nora Gallagher actually had a personality. And more than that, when the other woman was willing to let her guard down, it was one that Gray rather liked.

* * *

Gray didn't see Nora at dinner, and she didn't seek her out. After the beach, punctuated by a few more drinks, she'd taken a decadent nap in the late afternoon. By the time she'd made it up to one of the restaurants, the families were mostly tucked away for the evening, and a much more boisterous crowd was seated for dinner.

It was a welcomed surprise when Darcy waved her over to their table. "Howdy, stranger. I was wondering if we'd run into one another again."

She was seated with the two men and women from earlier that day, and Gray was quickly ushered into an empty chair across from Darcy.

"How was the rest of your day?" Darcy asked. A few others around the table focused their attention on Gray, waiting for her answer.

Weird? Unexpected? Exhilarating in a way that still sent little spikes of adrenaline coursing through her when she thought about it?

"Relaxing." It wasn't a complete lie, but she wasn't even going to begin unpacking her interaction with Nora to these people. It would take way too much explanation, on top of making her sound certifiably insane.

"Awesome." Darcy's smile was broad and genuine, and Gray noticed her gaze linger for a few extra seconds on her lips. Which was not an unwelcome experience, but it was absolutely not where her head was at that moment.

"They're thinking about trying to get everyone out on an earlier flight," the guy seated next to her said after checking his phone.

Gray's brows drew upward. "Is the conference not going well?"

He shook his head. "The hurricane is switching directions."

"Hurricane?" She shoved down the flash of anxiety that

jolted through her. She'd known that this was the start of hurricane season, but it had seemed like a far-off concept. Bermuda was closer to the Carolinas than the Caribbean, where the storms were usually most impactful.

"It would be the first one to hit Bermuda this season," Darcy added. "You probably didn't see the bulletin board when you walked into the main building. They put up a notice today, but the hotel doesn't seem very concerned."

"They seemed concerned enough to put up a notice," said the guy... Cody... whose name Gray had finally plucked from her memories of earlier this afternoon.

"To be fair, they post weather notices every day," Robin said from the seat next to Darcy. "We're supposed to leave Friday, which is not long after the storm would hit."

"We're set to leave then too," Gray confirmed needlessly.

"At least it'll be easier to get a drink at the bar if the sales conference leaves early," Cody said with a laugh that Gray found annoying. Of course, the good old boys' club would take care of their own.

She assumed that Nora already had this information, given her overly regimented personality, but she still made a mental note to tell her next time she saw her.

Until then, she told herself with as much conviction as she could muster, there was really nothing she could do.

Chapter Five

Nora knew she'd been avoiding Gray after... whatever it was that had happened between them yesterday.

She'd begrudgingly accepted, in the quiet of her room, as she'd replayed the conversation back last night, that something had to give. A part of her that acknowledged that, for as much as Nora would like to think she was different, she was no more impervious to falling under Gray's spell than her co-workers or the friends Gray seemed to pick up like strays.

When Gray had looked at her in the shade of the poolside bar, all soft eyes and a mischievous smile, Nora couldn't help but play along with her. She'd felt her armor loosening where Gray was concerned, like she hadn't spent years learning to insulate herself.

And that was the rub. She'd been drawn in, and there was no reasonable explanation for why that had happened.

It had been itching at Nora like a bug bite since yesterday. There was something about Gray Ferris. Nora couldn't quite articulate it yet, but that woman was a chameleon. Friendly with everyone. Exactly who she needed to be at any given moment.

It was a gift, but to someone who approached everyone with suspicion these days, it could also be viewed as performative. And Nora knew—through personal experience—that it was easier to become trapped in someone's web when they showed you exactly the version of themselves that you'd personally like best.

She'd thought about it during dinner last night. And she'd mused over it during breakfast earlier. At yoga this morning. Still, it nagged at her persistently, so much so that she wondered if she was imagining seeing Gray in front of her now.

Near the entrance to the resort's main building, Gray was with a group of people. It looked like they were coming back from an excursion to somewhere else on the island. They were all chatting animatedly, heads tipped back in laughter while they clambered out of the taxi van.

How quickly the shift had happened for Nora, from completely ignoring Gray to acute awareness of her every move.

Because now, she had *questions*. About what made Gray Ferris tick. Whether she was really as open and friendly as she acted.

The itch was back.

But maybe... it wasn't just about Gray.

Sure, Gray was the catalyst, but the last few days had also been a sign that she needed to stop secluding herself so much, possible promotion or not. Her mind had felt so scattered since coming to Bermuda, and she could only imagine how that was translating into her behavior.

Still, though, there was a part of this that was definitely about Gray, specifically. If Nora actually wanted to lead a team, Gray would be a valuable ally. She had the office wrapped around her ring-clad fingers through sheer charm, regardless of its authenticity.

So if she ever wanted to get back there, even just professionally, it was possible there was something important that Nora could learn from Gray. And this trip was the perfect opportunity.

Nora caught up with the group as they wandered down a winding path that headed toward the poolside bar and the beach beyond.

"Hey," she said, her longer legs falling into step next to Gray, who looked the picture of island relaxation in a pair of shorts and a blue, sleeveless top that matched the color of the ocean water perfectly.

Something flashed across Gray's face, but it was a blink-and-miss-it look, replaced by that ineffable smile. "Hey, yourself. How's your day going?"

Treating this like an investigation, fueled by a nagging suspicion that something about Gray wasn't what it seemed, made things easier for Nora. She didn't have to chastise herself for noticing that Gray already looked more tan. Or that she seemed relaxed while she walked, like the sun had soaked into her muscles. It made her move a little more slowly, giving Nora a chance to notice the light reflecting off the rings adorning Gray's fingers. Arms bobbing at her sides, Nora's focus was drawn down to the hand only a few inches away from her own thigh. If Gray relaxed a little more, melted into a puddle of serenity, her fingers would ghost across the hem of Nora's shorts.

It was a thought that almost made Nora lose her footing.

She righted herself and took a deep breath. "I did a morning yoga class on the beach," she said before adding—because she needed to get them back to their conversational status quo—"Then I called Cynthia repeatedly until she finally picked up and gave me an update on my clients."

The loud laugh, almost bordering on a snort, that Gray let out sent a wild rooster scurrying across the lawn. "Sorry, buddy." Gray gave the rooster a mournful stare, like she really was worried she'd ruined his morning. When her moment of contrition was over, and they were off the steps and on a flatter path leading to the pool area, she finally made eye contact with Nora. "And how was yoga? Relaxing?"

Nora nodded, struck by the genuine sincerity in the other woman's voice, like she really cared. She made a note to eventually ease into her own communication style. And sure, it felt a little wrong to be studying Gray like this, but it was easier than the alternative.

"I... um..." Gray stilled, even as the rest of the group continued on and disappeared around the corner. "I assume you already know, but I wanted to just check in and make sure you'd heard about the storm."

"Storm?" Nora asked, working to keep her voice even.

"It's probably nothing, given that it's already changed once, but they said it could hit Thursday night."

Nora's face scrunched up in confusion. Not at the idea of a storm, but that she'd somehow missed it. In her goal to be totally checked out of real life, with the exception of work, she hadn't turned on her television or looked at the news. When they'd headed here, the weather had shown nothing but clear skies and an enviable amount of sunshine.

Why hadn't she considered that could change? It wasn't like her to miss something like this, and that thought nagged annoyingly, somewhere deep in her mind, even though she had bigger problems to worry about right now.

She pulled out her phone and opened the weather app and began to scroll. The aforementioned clear skies would be present until Thursday afternoon, when a torrential downpour was set to roll in somewhere during the late evening, tapering off on Friday morning.

"I mean, we'll probably be asleep, right?" Gray said breezily, but her impossibly big, brown eyes betrayed her.

And that's when Nora saw it, nested in the paragraph-long explanation at the bottom of the weekly weather report. "Oh, it's a hurricane."

"It *could* be a hurricane," Gray stressed. "It doesn't mean it will be, and even so, these buildings are practically fortresses."

Of course her first vacation in years would see a hurricane barreling toward them. Nora tried not to choke on the frustration laced into her words. "So we just... what? Spend the next few days waiting to see how bad it's going to be?"

"Or how not bad, hopefully." Nora didn't put a lot of trust in other people, and even though she found herself wanting to believe Gray, the way she was fiddling with her rings spoke volumes about her lack of confidence.

"Sure."

"Do you wanna grab lunch with us?" Gray gestured toward the poolside bar, hidden behind the lush foliage surrounding it.

"Eh..." Her instinct was to say no. It was reflexive at this point.

"No pressure if not." A shrug of her shoulders confirmed Gray's words, that it really was a take-it-or leave-it situation.

For whatever reason, that solidified something inside her. If not now, on an island where she knew almost no one, save one soul, this was the perfect place to practice being more sociable. Besides, in spite of her ongoing confusion about Gray's own motives, she didn't have the impression that Gray would use this information against her.

It was a surprising revelation, to think of Gray as trustworthy, especially when Nora had spent the last day—hell, the last minutes—analyzing her motives. The conclusion had happened in her bones, not her brain, settling through her body with startling assuredness. It was her intuition, she finally realized, grasping for the name of something she hadn't felt in far too long.

Instead of fighting it like she usually would, she smiled at Gray, anticipation whirring through her body at what felt like the first intentional step she'd taken forward in a long time.

* * *

Lunch hadn't gone as terribly as Nora had expected. Sure, Cody and Victor were annoying in the way only sales bros could be, but the other three women—Rachel, Robin, and Darcy—were all functional people who kept the conversation flowing easily. It helped that Gray had some sort of magical ability to tether two people together in discussion, almost like a sixth sense.

Frankly, it was mesmerizing to watch how she effortlessly got people talking about themselves and sharing tidbits that she'd tie into what someone else had said, almost like Nora was watching a bridge of connection be built in front of her very eyes.

Gray had teased out, in a wildly circuitous way that involved childhood talent shows, left-handedness, and ancient Chinese warriors and their juggling prowess, that Victor and Robin both knew how to juggle. This knowledge had led to a lively, if not dangerous, demonstration where they each downed a couple of shots and then tossed the empty plastic glasses until a rooster brushed against Robin's leg and caused hers to clatter on the ground.

Hours later, they walked back toward their rooms, quietly

wandering along the path, except for when Gray would occasionally coo at a passing rooster.

"Did you have a rooster as a pet or something growing up?" Nora finally asked when their building came into view.

"Just a lover of animals in all their forms. My sister, Willa, is the one known for bringing home strays."

"You're not the do-gooder type?" Nora teased, her tongue loose from the alcohol at lunch.

Gray shot her a sharp glance once they hit the outdoor staircase leading up to their second-floor rooms. "You don't know anything about me."

"I know that," Nora pushed out quickly, holding her hands up in resignation.

At the top of the steps, Gray made space for Nora to join her on the landing but stopped and turned, so they were almost standing chest to chest. "I'm a little surprised you notice anything about anyone, unless it's met with derision."

It was a punch-in-the-gut statement that knocked the wind out of Nora's sails. She racked her brain, trying to figure out what could have happened, but she came up empty. "Was I... is this about something that happened at lunch?"

And then she felt the bubble of embarrassment balloon up in her. She absolutely didn't have to take this, regardless of the better footing they'd found themselves on. She stood up to her full height, inches taller than Gray.

It didn't matter.

Gray exuded a quiet confidence that bloomed brighter when she finally answered. "I guess I'm just wondering why it took an island and eight hundred miles of distance for you to start engaging with humanity. And honestly, I don't know that I want to get used to it if you're going to go right back to being cold when we get home."

She didn't like this line of questioning one bit, even if it was warranted. Had she expected they could just continue forward and pretend like the last year hadn't happened? It was Nora who was playing hot and cold, avoidant and then engaged, like a palm tree snapping back and forth during a storm.

Nora was already tired, even after a few days of assuming ulterior motives and second-guessing Gray's intentions. It had been easy to mentally check out of life for so long, she realized, because she'd assumed the effort of this type of existence would exhaust her.

She'd been right.

They'd moved closer to one another, somehow. Gray's hands were clenched around the metal railing where Nora's arm was resting, their bodies almost touching. They seemed to do that now, whenever they both stood still long enough. It was unnerving. The situation vibrated at a frequency Nora hadn't felt in so long that she didn't even know what to call it. Frustration? Tension?

She let out a soft exhale that caught Gray's attention. Her stare shifted up to meet Gray's, whose focus was in turn trained solely on Nora. The resort was buzzing with activity, but the staircase was quiet, with only a hint of music audible from the pool at least thirty yards away.

"I'm..." Nora stumbled over her words, heat working its way up her neck. She forced the words lodged in her throat out into the space between them. "I'm sorry for how I treated you. I'd like a fresh start."

"You'd like a fresh start?" Gray parroted back, confusion etched across her features.

"I am... trying here. And I know you don't owe me anything, but I really would like to move forward with you." Nora's voice was strained with sincerity and embarrassment, but she couldn't muster the will to care.

She waited, watching Gray's soft features move through

varying expressions before her lips eased into a smile. "Okay then."

"Okay?"

Gray nodded. "I'm sorry too."

She stared at Gray dumbly. "For what?"

"For snapping at you. I don't like people assuming they know me. Call it a character flaw," Gray said with a grin that made Nora a little lightheaded. "I just don't really know what to expect with you."

Gray's eyes were piercing, and her attention made Nora forget she should answer.

Fleetingly, she wondered what would happen if she leaned in closer.

Nora shut the thought down with the intensity of a slamming door.

Cynthia's future offer pinged around somewhere in the recesses of Nora's brain, but it wasn't, surprisingly, what spurred her on. "Do you want to have dinner tonight?"

For an entirely new reason, something that felt a lot like curiosity—not suspicion—pulling her forward, she wanted to know what else she'd missed about Gray.

Chapter Six

Dinner at the resort restaurant would have to wait, but Gray was pleasantly surprised that she was going to have a *friend* on her private taxi tour of the island.

As she got ready to leave her hotel room, she rolled around the day's events in her mind. She still didn't know what had gotten into her earlier. Nora's comments about her shouldn't have cut to the quick the way they had, and Gray had let her momentary flash of anger get the better of her.

She'd felt unmoored by Nora's unintentionally cutting words, a familiar and unwanted companion from its presence in Gray's adolescence. Back then, she didn't have the language or the power to articulate her needs or wants.

Still, why had she done that? Maybe it was because, for the last twenty-four hours, it felt like she was on a vacation with someone completely different from the Nora Gallagher she'd known for the last year. And generally, people didn't change that quickly, regardless of how gorgeous the weather was. It had picked at her during lunch, like a mystery that needed to be solved.

Nora had sat across from her, long legs crossed at her ankles. She wore very little makeup, as far as Gray could tell, and the only jewelry visible was a necklace with an infinity symbol, held together by a thin, silver chain. Gray had noticed it before in the office, given that Nora wore it most days.

Nora's tousled hair had been down, and shorter than Gray's, it just brushed her jawline. It would have been a more severe haircut if not for the way Nora's blonde hair hung in soft waves to frame her face.

As Gray had gotten ready that morning, dressing in a pair of jean shorts and her favorite turquoise tank top, she considered whether there was some angle she was missing.

God, she had to stop overanalyzing this. They'd hashed things out, though briefly, and it sounded like they were both on the same page, at least as far as Bermuda was concerned.

Gray needed to let the rest of it go, which was exactly what she'd resolved to do by the time they emerged from their hotel rooms at the same time to head out on their tour.

"Winston comes highly recommended," she said as she and Nora made their way through the main building of the resort toward the pick-up point out front.

Nora raised an eyebrow while she held the door open for Gray to step out into the balmy, late afternoon air. "By whom?"

Nora was dressed in another casual look, a pair of dark skinny jeans that hugged her lithe frame and an oversize linen shirt that had a few buttons undone at the top, exposing her clavicle. She looked surprisingly relaxed. Her skin was already sun-kissed, with freckles that Gray had never noticed before prominent on the bridge of her nose.

Nora seemed to just... glow, for lack of a better word. Her nose was slightly pink. Her cheeks too. And maybe it was the subtropical sunlight playing tricks on her, but the other

---

woman's eyes seemed almost bluer here, like they were reflecting the clear water that surrounded them.

Relaxed looked good on Nora Gallagher, at least from Gray's vantage point. It was another reason she didn't want to continue to rock the tentative solidness they'd found themselves on.

"A guy I met on the beach gave me the tour guide's number," Gray responded as a minivan pulled up in front of them, with 'Island Tours' emblazoned on its side.

"Oh, so we could be living out a scene from *Hostel* right now? Getting into a van recommended to you by a guy on the beach?" Nora was making her wariness known, but there was no edge in her voice.

Gray rolled her eyes and smiled as the van door opened. "I was paraphrasing. The guy on the beach, Tom, is a frequent tourist in Bermuda. His wife, Sandy, was also there, though her tips were centered on the capital city, Hamilton."

"But we aren't going to Hamilton?" Nora asked as she climbed into the van behind Gray.

"We're going to Saint George's. It's the oldest English settlement on the island."

"That it is," the man who formally introduced himself as Winston said from the driver's seat.

Gray had only been out of the country once before this, to Canada a few years ago. That had felt criminal, given how much she loved history and architecture. Most days, she tried to focus on all the good things in her life instead of the things she'd felt like she missed out on.

But she had this trip, and she was going to make the most of it.

* * *

In the minivan, Nora sat quietly in the co-pilot-style seat next to Gray. The fifteen-minute drive up to Saint George's began to stretch on, even with Winston peppering in little facts along the way.

"That's the former Astor estate," he said, pointing to his left.

Gray moved closer to Nora's window, trying to keep as much distance between them while still getting the full view of the estate's multitude of all-white buildings sprawling along the water's edge. "But Vincent, right?"

She could feel Nora's gaze, though she didn't say anything.

Winston nodded animatedly. "Yes. John Jacob's son oversaw the construction of this estate."

Gray had gone through a hyperfixation on the *Titanic* after watching the movie as a kid, years after it had come out. It had sent her on a crash course, learning everything she could about the ship and its passengers, which had led her to John Jacob Astor's oldest son, Vincent, who'd inherited his father's hundreds of millions after his death aboard the fated oceanic liner.

"The train tracks are gone, aren't they?" Gray had always been fascinated by the way the uber-wealthy had built what amounted to small, self-sufficient cities within their estates.

"Train tracks?" Nora asked, a catch in her voice that Gray took as surprise at her own knowledge.

She decided not to pick that apart when they still had the majority of the tour to go. "If memory serves, Vincent Astor built a stretch of private train tracks that cut through the property for ease of movement, ultimately connecting it with the Bermuda railway in the 1930s."

"If memory serves?"

Gray shrugged. "I like history."

"The history of Bermudian estates?" Nora sounded almost suspicious at this point.

"It started with an obsession with the *Titanic*. Then it morphed into the people who died. Morbid for a ten-year-old, I know," she said with a self-deprecating laugh before adding, "Then I was in way too deep and started wondering about what happened to their children and their wealth. That led me to Vincent Astor at one point. Did you know he eventually sold the land that became the Empire State Building?"

Nora was looking at her like she'd just sprouted wings. "Why did you care?"

Gray shrugged again. She'd long gotten over being embarrassed about her passions. "I got curious."

Maybe there was slightly more to it than that, but being friendly didn't mean having to word-vomit her entire life story to a woman who had only decided yesterday she could moderately tolerate Gray's existence.

Nora leaned back in her seat, her long body relaxing against the black interior fabric. Now it was her turn to shrug. "Okay."

Gray knew that surprise had flashed across her face when Nora smirked and then looked back out the window. Apparently, she was holding true to her attempt to be more congenial. The other woman's exponential learning curve scared Gray a little, if she was being honest.

When they reached the town of Saint George's, Winston started talking and did not stop for the next thirty minutes.

It was fascinating to hear about the small town in his own words, partly because he was a lifelong resident and partly because Gray had no idea how intricate and unique Bermuda's setup was.

"There's no fresh water?" Nora sat up straighter again, leaning closer to Winston in the driver's seat.

"No, ma'am, not except for the rain. No fresh lakes, springs, or rivers. Bermudians are required to collect rainwater and house it in tanks on their property."

"That seems..." Nora's voice trailed off, and she never finished her thought.

Winston pushed on with his tour. "All the homes are made of stone. The roofs too. They're built in a cascading style so the water catches and drains easily into the collection tanks."

Gray was transfixed by the homes they passed. They were all built in relatively the same style—low, square buildings with white roofs and pastel-painted walls. Most of the homes had a staircase, wider at the bottom than the top, leading up to the front porch around the front door.

Gray craned her neck toward Nora's window again, where the houses dotted a street that ran parallel with the coast. "It really makes you think..."

She heard Nora's voice as she continued to memorize every detail of the homes they passed. "Think about what?"

"The functionality of architecture. How much of it is rooted in need, accessibility, the style of the period in which it was built. Everything here is so different from Philadelphia because it needs to be. It's fascinating." The wistful sigh she let out was drowned out by the hum of the minivan.

When she turned, Nora was looking at her, their faces only a few inches apart. Her pulse picked up when their stares met.

Gray was so close that she could see the lighter flecks in Nora's eyes, like they were catching the reflection of fireflies in the twilight. There were soft little crinkles at the edges of her eyes, and Gray was sure she'd never seen a look quite like it on Nora's face. It opened Nora up somehow, and made her look like an entirely different person.

Not that Gray didn't also appreciate the strong, clean line of Nora's jaw or the sharpness of her cheekbones. But those were the things she'd grown used to, and she associated them with a person who wanted to keep herself closed off, who wore those features like armor. What she was staring at now felt like someone had taken a brightly lit room and turned down the intensity tenfold before lighting a candle and putting a soft record on in the background.

It was the type of look that a person like Gray wanted to lean into, to bask in and do anything she could to see it on Nora's face everyday.

She briefly registered Winston's voice from the front seat when he said, "The houses are all made of stone to withstand hundred-mile-per-hour winds during hurricane season."

Nora tensed next to her. They hadn't discussed the possible hurricane again since she'd mentioned it this morning. Gray hadn't looked at the weather since last night, promising herself not to agonize over something she couldn't control. If the storm came, they'd ride it out. And it wasn't a certainty that it would continue its current path to the left of the island.

"So you're saying it's safe here?" Nora asked quietly from beside her. It was a wonder Winston was able to hear her at all.

"One of the safest places you can be with winds so strong they can pull a tree out by its roots."

Gray did not need that visual.

She turned and bumped her knee against Nora's. "That's good news."

Nora bit her lip before she let out a long, low sigh. It was a sound of resignation, maybe acceptance at best. "I guess it could be worse, but that's not the barometer I usually shoot for."

It wasn't what Nora said but rather how she said it that made Gray look at her then. There was a vulnerability in Nora's voice, her tone betraying the flippancy of her words. It wasn't hard to get lost in wondering what types of things kept

Nora Gallagher up at night, given how much of an enigma practically everything about her was. Even at work, Gray didn't know her. She knew that Nora didn't like to engage with others, and that she was quick to be annoyed, but she hadn't, even professionally, seen moments where she was unguarded like this.

But what did Gray know? Maybe she was making it all up in her mind. It was entirely possible that Nora just didn't want to discuss the impending storm. It wasn't like talking about it would change anything.

She stopped herself from asking what type of barometer Nora usually tried to shoot for. Probably perfection, doing things expertly on the first try and never looking back. Gray didn't have that ability, but she was usually determined to get where she wanted to go. There was no such thing as failing too many times and giving up. When she really thought back, she could only remember twice in the past few years where she'd simply cut her losses and moved on. The first was at her old job. The second, more recent time was when she'd accepted that Nora wasn't going to budge from her island of isolation at the office.

Instead of asking, she leveled a soft smile in Nora's direction and leaned back against her seat. Looking out the window, it seemed almost impossible that there was a hurricane barrelling toward them. The sky was a bright blue, and puffy, white clouds that looked painted onto the landscape hung above the horizon.

Winston—oblivious to the accidental grenade he'd lobbed into a fragile ecosystem—continued to chat animatedly about the natural beauty of the island, along with its economy and some of the more notable events that had happened in its history.

When the minivan pulled back up at the hotel, it felt like

Nora had retreated inward again. She hadn't said much the rest of the ride, save small acknowledgments of what Winston had continued to tell them.

Gray tried not to take it personally.

"Did you still want to grab dinner?" Gray asked as she watched the minivan pull away. Nora was already turning to walk into the main resort house.

Nora fidgeted awkwardly, bouncing from one foot to the other. "I didn't realize how tired I would be after today. Rain check?"

All Gray could do was nod because Nora still had that look on her face, one Gray couldn't decipher. Her blue eyes had grown darker, like they were taking on the impending storm. The relaxed look from earlier was gone, replaced with a ramrod-straight posture that looked out of place against the tropical backdrop of palm trees and roosters.

Gray waved her off. "Totally fine. I'll see you tomorrow?"

Nora nodded slowly. "Tomorrow," she echoed, like she was trying the word out for the first time to see how it sounded.

When they stood before the reception area's double doors, Gray stopped just before they would separate to head to their respective rooms.

Before she could overthink it, she ghosted her fingers across Nora's forearm. "You'll let me know if you need anything?"

And there it was again, when the flashes of different looks settled, that look that she couldn't quite figure out. A little wanting, as Nora wrapped her arms around her body and leaned forward on her toes before rocking backward.

Gray's mouth dropped open in surprise when one of Nora's hands gently squeezed her own, little sparks of awareness flickering across her skin with the touch.

"I will. Thank you."

And just like that, Nora disappeared through the glass double doors that led down the path to their hotel rooms.

After she watched Nora go, Gray turned to the right and walked toward the restaurant where she'd eaten dinner last night. She welcomed the idea of sitting on her own and rolling this strange day around in her mind.

If she was smart, she'd be a little more focused on the impending hurricane. Instead, all she could think about was the storm behind Nora's eyes.

Chapter Seven

There was no way in hell that Nora was hopping on a boat and heading out to sea today. She didn't care that they'd still be able to see land. Or that the storm wasn't set to arrive until tomorrow night.

All she cared about was being within eyesight of a building made of stone that could withstand hurricane-force winds. That was her singular focus, and she planned to stick to it.

When she'd left Gray last night, who'd been surprisingly sweet about her complete about-face when Nora had turned tail and run back to her room, she'd let herself start to fall apart.

She hated storms. Snowstorms. Rainstorms. Hailstorms. Whatever that thing was that made people like the chaotic beauty of nature, she didn't have it. She also wouldn't call it "beauty," but it was how she'd heard people describe their love of angry, unexpected bolts of lightning flashing across the sky or thick, harsh drops of unrelenting rain that coated everything in their path.

But this wasn't a storm. It was a *hurricane*. People died in those. All the time. And now, thanks to almost an entire night spent researching every hurricane for the last twenty years, she had more information than was probably safe for a person teetering on the verge of a mental breakdown.

She thought it would help calm her, knowing the statistics. Confirming that Bermuda was, in fact, as safe as Winston had mentioned on their tour.

It didn't.

Peeking out her window, all she saw were blue skies and calm waters. There was nothing about the quiet confidence of the serene ocean that gave any indication a storm was set to come within seventy miles of the small island.

The bright, seafoam-green catamaran on the small dock next to the water sports building was barely bobbing. At the water's edge, no waves lapped against the shore. There was only stillness. She could walk out to where her feet no longer touched and still see close to the bottom. Everything was calm.

She'd had moments, like the one this morning, when things had seemed fine before they weren't. A lack of indication that something was amiss was no reason to let her guard down. She'd done that before. More times than she wanted to admit. More times than she was willing to do again.

For as much—or as little—as she trusted people, she trusted nature even less. At least a person had the possibility to be reasoned with. Nature didn't care if she lived or died. It moved. It existed. It progressed across the earth, especially its storms, in paths forged miles above the ground.

She couldn't do anything except watch it happen.

Gray Ferris – 9:55 a.m.

> Were you planning to come snorkeling this morning?

Nora resisted scoffing when she looked down at her phone,

even as tension flooded her body. Just the mention of their planned excursion had her limbs buzzy and her chest tight.

Nora – 9:56 a.m.

> I think I'm going to hang around the hotel, but have fun!

She couldn't remember the last time she'd used an exclamation point in a text unless it was work-related. Even now, it was meant to hide her utter dismay. Staying in her hotel room and falling apart privately was the best-case scenario for everyone involved.

It was easy to feel like a caged animal as she paced back and forth across her room. The space was perfectly functional for sleeping and getting ready, but the point of the resort was to be out and about. On the water. On the island. In the few small cities and towns.

She watched the water from her balcony, scrutinizing it like a suspect in an interrogation. Her eyes scanned the shore, watching for any signs the current was changing. Incorrectly, she felt like a bit of an expert, given all the research she'd done in the last twelve hours related to storms and how they ebbed and flowed, swelled and abated.

She had tuned the television to a channel that was now playing almost constant weather coverage. She'd already seen the same bit replay three times in the last half hour.

That realization snapped something in her. "Goddammit," she said into the room, which was empty save her miserable form she was dragging back and forth across the well-worn carpet.

Knock. Knock.

At the same time irritation flared up in her, a small sense of relief to be pulled out of her spiral made its presence known.

She'd become so used to dealing with her inability to deal

65

on her own that it was a surprisingly welcome shock to remember that other people existed.

Opening the door, she said, "I don't need—" at the same time Gray took a small step back and yelped at the force of Nora's appearance.

"Hey," Gray said when she landed solidly on two feet again, her cheeks flushed. Her hair was pulled back in a short ponytail, wisps breaking free and framing her round face. She looked exuberant to experience the day. Nora could only imagine what she herself must look like in juxtaposition.

"I'm not going on the boat."

Gray nodded and beamed another smile in Nora's direction. "I know."

When Nora wasn't really in control of herself, there was a very small window for her to get to emotional safety. That usually involved secluding herself from everyone.

She tried to remember that she was *trying*, though, and she took a deep, steadying breath. "What brings you by, then?"

It took about all the willpower she had to cut the edge from her voice. None of this was Gray's fault. Coming on the trip. The storm. That she was a bright ray of sunshine that moved through the world, casting light instead of shadows.

Some people noticed everything when they were stressed. Sounds. Smells. They had an acute awareness of their surroundings.

Nora wasn't one of those people.

She went into survival mode, just trying to breathe and get through it. 'White-knuckling' was probably the term, if she was willing to give it a name.

Finally, she pulled her focus from Gray's megawatt smile to see how her arm was lifted at an odd angle, her elbow bent out at almost ninety degrees. She followed the path of that arm to see two face masks and two snorkels dangling between her long fingers, knocking lazily against one another.

"Um..." *Don't bite her head off*, Nora silently cautioned herself. "Did you not get my text? I was planning on skipping the boat today."

Gray nodded as her smile grew, which Nora hadn't thought possible. "These aren't for the boat. The water sports shop gives them out to guests. I was figuring we could paddle around the hotel's beach later if you're up for it."

Nora's eyes narrowed, mostly because she was trying to figure out what was going on. "You don't want to go on the boat?"

It was then that Nora noticed a light blush on Gray's cheeks as she shifted her weight back and forth, from one foot to the other. "Actually, I get seasick," Gray admitted. "It probably wouldn't be an issue, but I don't really wanna take the chance and have a dozen other people see me blowing chunks over the side of a boat while they're trying to frolic in the same water."

Nora didn't try to hide her laugh. "That's, um... wow. That's quite the visual."

"I know," Gray said, her own self-deprecating laugh bubbling up. "Since the weather has everyone's schedules thrown off, they were more than willing to let me cancel. A lot of people are trying to leave early tomorrow, so those people were happy to take our spots today."

And there it was again. The reminder that the storm was coming, regardless of how prepared for it or oblivious to it Nora was.

"Well... that's good, I guess," Nora answered lamely. What else was she supposed to say? *Oh good, glad the impending hurricane is creating some opportunities for idiots?*

"Yeah. So..." For the first time since Nora had opened the

door, Gray looked unsure, her brown eyes scanning Nora's face like she was looking for a sign about how to proceed. Gray looked a little bit like a confused puppy, and Nora, regardless of what others thought of her, didn't relish thinking she was the person who had caused that uncertainty.

"So?" Nora finally asked, trying to put them both out of their misery.

"Well... I think sticking close to the hotel today makes sense, but it's going to be nice through tomorrow morning. And with people changing their flights and everything moving around, I was able to snag a couple of massage reservations for the cave."

Nora's eyebrow lifted. "A cave massage?"

"It seemed like it could be relaxing. And then, if you're up for it, we can snorkel at the hotel. There's a reef about fifty yards out, or we can swim around to the inlet on the far side of the beach."

Nora leaned heavily against the doorframe to buy a few extra seconds. "I don't..."

"It's up to you," Gray said quickly. When she shrugged, her lifted shoulders raised the snorkeling gear and caused it to clack together. "I'm doing it either way, and I just know that sometimes having something to do takes my mind off things."

Was she really that transparent? Nora thought she had done a pretty good job of covering up her anxiety and fear with frustration. It bothered her that Gray had possibly seen through that. What was the point of having a wall up if it was made with plexiglass?

"Plus," Gray said, leaning a little closer, almost conspiratorially, before her cheeks flushed pink again. "I've never had a massage before. And in a cave of all places? How cool is that?"

Her tone made her seem younger, gave her a childlike excitement that made Nora feel something she couldn't quite place. From what she knew about Gray, the other woman had never come off as naive or sheltered. Annoyingly bubbly and positive, sure. But in this moment, she was realizing how little she actually knew about Gray Ferris.

Nora's head cocked to the side without her being consciously aware it was happening. "You've never had a massage?"

"Nope," Gray said with another shrug. She was doing that a lot today. Shrugging, like her words or Nora's answers didn't matter all that much.

Something stirred in Nora then. Another new emotion in a sea of firsts over the past few days. It took her a few uncomfortable seconds before she realized that she didn't want to disappoint Gray, who'd obviously gone through effort and trouble to coordinate a day at the hotel that would be relaxed but also distracting.

And she'd done it for both of them.

It was more solid and real than anything that had happened between them yet. Maybe Gray really was just this type of person.

Her stomach fluttered, fear mingled with excitement. It was the first time since yesterday she'd gone more than five minutes without thinking about the hurricane. And, thinking about it now, she felt relatively calm, like everything would be okay. The world was moving around them. The island wasn't shutting down yet. The rest of the guests, presumably, were in good spirits.

"Okay."

A tentative smile bloomed across Gray's face. "Okay?"

Nora nodded. "Okay. What time's the massage?"

"Eleven," Gray said, and Nora could feel the palpable excitement starting to radiate off of her.

Nora looked down at her smartwatch to confirm how

quickly she needed to move. It had warned her at least a handful of times last night that her heart rate had been skyrocketing. Stupid technology.

"Give me ten minutes?"

Gray bit her lip and nodded, scanning Nora's face. "Meet me outside the entrance to the cave. It's just over there," she said, extending her free hand to point about a hundred feet away. Then she bounded down the hallway, Nora watching her disappear down the staircase until the vibrant white of her smile was out of sight.

Nora got ready on autopilot, knowing she'd be shedding her clothing in a few minutes anyway. Humans were hardwired for connection. She knew that. As she threw things in her beach bag, she decided that the small, unfamiliar feeling bubbling up inside of her wasn't something she needed to deal with right now. There were more important things. Like a massage. Then a hurricane. Then whatever happened with the Philly Finds team when she returned home, if she was intent on getting the promotion.

Ruminating on how elated Gray had seemed when she'd practically skipped away was not making it onto the list.

Chapter Eight

A woman in an all-white uniform was waiting when Gray reached the entrance of the cave. A door behind her that led inside was drawn open. The woman's hair was pulled back in a low ponytail, and she had an easy smile on her face. Her relaxation comforted Gray, given the storm barreling toward them. Its impending arrival felt both excruciatingly slow and breathtakingly quick.

"Good morning," she said in an accent Gray couldn't place. Maybe British?

"Morning. The other person is on her way." She wasn't going to quite call Nora a friend yet, but she doubted the woman cared about the semantics of their relationship.

"I'm Tala. Celeste is waiting inside, so if you want to head down, I'll wait here for the other guest."

"Sure, thank you." Gray nodded and walked through the doorway, darkness overtaking her.

She was on a path cut through the rock, or possibly naturally existing within it, that led deeper into the cave. It took

71

time for her eyes to adjust, and her walk was lit by small Edison bulbs hanging on each side. She could faintly make out the jagged lines of rock forming the walls, and wooden planks below her feet guided her forward.

After about thirty feet of walking, the cave opened up. Gray stopped breathing, taking in the expansive oasis that unfolded before her. From her vantage point at the top of a set of stone steps, she could see at least six floating canopy tents draped in gauzy, white linens. It looked like they were built out into the water, which was impossibly clear and bathed in the soft lights hanging throughout the cave.

She'd never experienced anything like this, and it was taking all her willpower not to squeal in delight. With the soft, low music playing through hidden speakers and the absolute silence otherwise, it didn't seem like that would be appreciated.

Once she reached the bottom of the steps, another woman, whose features were harder to make out in the ambient light, gestured to her. "Hello, miss. My name is Celeste. If you'll follow me, please."

Gray nodded and wondered if the smile threatening to overtake her whole face made her look as happy as she felt.

Another planked walkway, suspended across the water, led her into the surprisingly spacious tent on the floating platform. The far side was open, looking out at that impossibly blue water in the cave. She wanted to stay here forever.

"You can get changed. There is another guest coming, yes?" The soft voice pulled her out of her quiet reverie.

Her eyes had mostly adjusted to the darkness, and she noticed for the first time the two massage beds positioned next to one another, with about a foot of space between them.

"Oh," she said softly. The word felt like an explosion in the otherwise quiet cave. She couldn't see the other suspended platforms from inside this one, but she took a chance asking, her voice barely above a whisper, "Is the other person going to be in this one?"

Celeste nodded and pointed to a small area with cubbies. "When it's booked with two people they are usually in the same area. I'd offer to move one of you, but the other beds are currently in use."

This would be fine. Right?

How Nora would feel about this activity that possibly bordered on an HR violation was another matter entirely.

She walked over to the cubby area and deposited her water bottle in it. "Okay, thank you."

"I can pull the privacy curtain between the beds closed while you get ready, if you'd prefer." Celeste's words helped the lump in Gray's throat to dislodge.

Gray walked back over to the far massage bed, nestled closest to the open water. "Yes, thank you."

Celeste pulled the white curtain between the beds across the platform. Her movement caused the suspended area to rock gently in sync with the water that buoyed it. It would have felt decadent and relaxing, except that Gray was trying to disrobe as quickly as possible to crawl under the cover on her massage bed. Within minutes, she and Nora would be naked next to one another, having what Gray was now realizing was an incredibly romantic couple's massage.

Instead of using the cubby, which was now blocked by the curtain, she let her clothing drop to the floor before pushing it under the bed enough that it wouldn't be in the masseuse's way.

As soon as she slid under the cover, warm against her naked skin, soft voices floated through the air.

"You can get undressed and myself and Celeste will be back in a few minutes. Do you need anything?"

"No, thank you." It was Nora's voice, quiet and calm, cutting through the music drifting through the still air.

In all likelihood, Nora was barely making any noise. But being naked, so close to her, had Gray's ears oriented to every noise. What sounded like clothing dropping to the floor came first, then the soft padding of feet, followed by what could only be the sheet as it was pulled back from the bed for Nora to crawl under, just as Gray had done moments ago.

And then, it was the softest, most relaxed exhale Gray had maybe ever heard, and she wondered how such an indulgent sound was possible from someone wound as tightly as Nora.

Lying naked in the quiet of the cave, Gray willed her body to relax. She had never been embarrassed by her body, except in her younger years when people had tried to make her feel that way. It housed her soul, her brain, her heart. Today, she liked to adorn it in jewelry and bright colors and makeup some-times, but she didn't think of it all that often as anything more than a vessel. She knew she was lucky in that respect.

Since she'd been a teenager, more attention had been paid to her because of her body. A chest that drew unwanted stares. Hips that men seemed insistent to put their hands on without permission. She'd rebelled during her adolescence, dressing in oversize pants and button-downs, refusing to make herself any more of a mark than she needed to be.

Eventually, she'd realized that people wanted to control her body regardless of what she wore. It had taken a long time, but she'd started dressing for herself. So that she liked the person she saw when she looked in a mirror, not to deter any type of 'unwanted' attention that was out of her control anyway.

So it wasn't the idea of being naked that was making her feel exposed right now. It was because she was naked next to Nora, who, in spite of their brief but ongoing truce, was still an enigma to her.

Her breathing stilled as one of the masseuses drew back the partition between them, and she chastised herself for not asking if it could be kept shut the entire time.

Too late now.

Gray's head was facing toward the water, and she focused on her breathing as an almost imperceptible movement rippled across the otherwise smooth surface. She watched that same movement reflect in the light that cut through the shadows of the cave.

When the masseuse's hands kneaded into her upper back, she stifled a sound of satisfaction. It felt so damn good. Better than any possible awkwardness.

Lulled by the soft music and light playing across the cave walls, she almost forgot about everything else until a groan of... something escaped from Nora.

It was low and throaty and decadent, and it reverberated through her own body, quickly dissipating in her limbs that didn't quite feel like they were attached to her anymore.

"This is heaven," she responded in what could be construed as a trancelike state.

"Mmhmm." Nora's voice was muffled, like her mouth was pressed against the massage table. That was not a visual Gray had been prepared to imagine, not that she could appreciate it, given how her thoughts felt hazy at the edges, like she was in a dream.

Hearing Nora's pure, unadulterated enjoyment was all it took for the already loosening wall of tension in Gray to crumble. She didn't want to miss how good this felt for a second.

* * *

When Gray woke up the next morning, it was still hard to believe the last twenty-four hours had happened. Post-massage had morphed into lounging on the beach in chairs next to one another, taking turns heading up to the pool bar to grab another round of drinks. Nora had mostly read, but Gray had convinced her a few times to wade into the shallow water and paddle around.

They'd separated to return to their hotel rooms and then met at the main house for dinner. Conversation had remained limited to fairly superficial topics like work and the resort, but that didn't matter. Gray was elated with how far they'd come in such a short amount of time.

She'd fallen into bed and slept soundly. She'd known this trip was a chance to rest and unwind, but she hadn't realized just how tightly she'd also been wound—trying to find her footing at a new job, avoiding the storm cloud that was Nora Gallagher (formerly, maybe), and healing from the last year.

It was a strange feeling, like something had slotted into place. Stranger because she usually didn't care if the pieces didn't fit.

The late morning light filtered in intermittently, obstructed by the clouds from the hurricane that had rolled in overnight. The storm was still predicted to be hours away, but she could see a solid gray cover where yesterday nothing but blue skies had painted the picture of tropical perfection.

After she pulled herself out of bed, she wandered over to the window and stretched her arms above her head, letting out a satisfied groan. The wind had picked up enough that the palm trees, usually billowing gently in the breeze, started to flail back and forth. A few small branches and debris littered the ground, and a maintenance crew was already scurrying below to clear the remnants.

She could see signs that the storm was on its way, but stepping into the outdoor hallway finally made her understand with startling clarity how overwhelming and powerful nature could be. The air around her seemed like it was holding all the Earth's water, heavy and thick, like she was swimming as she walked.

It was a slog up to the main house. Sweat trickled down her back in spite of the day's cooler temperature. The doors into the building were opaque from the condensation, beads of water rolling down and creating patterns along the glass, like the moisture wanted to exist on every available surface, the air unable to hold it back any longer.

She headed inside, glad she and Nora had decided to meet here for breakfast instead of walking up together. It gave her a few seconds to acclimate to the air conditioning and wipe the sweat from her brow. Thank god she'd given up on makeup the last few days or she'd probably look like a drowned raccoon.

It was only when she was giving herself a quick glance in the hallway mirror leading toward the breakfast buffet that she noticed the activity happening in the reflection. Not for the first time, she'd thought that the restaurant was what The Rainforest Cafe wanted to be. Big, beautiful palm trees grew up from the floor, and plantation fans circled twenty feet above them. The walls were all windows, floor-to-ceiling glass that, until this moment, had only seemed charming instead of terrifying.

Sadly, she hadn't heard a single rooster this morning, noting they'd probably started taking cover somewhere. Animals were like that—perceptive survivalists in a way humans had just never gotten a knack for.

Because, after all, there was a hurricane on the way.

It was all she could think about when she realized just how many people were there. She watched the scene through the reflection before turning around, like she was looking at a painting in a museum. All the tables were filled. More guests leaned against the available wall space. It looked like the entirety of the hotel was congregated, their eyes, and now Gray's, drawn to a man dressed in a blazer with shorts and bermuda socks on.

When she finally turned around, she caught Nora's eye. Nora was standing at the edge of the crowd, about twenty feet away. It was human nature to be curious about why a group was congregating together. It set off some sort of primitive part of her brain, the desire to move closer.

Quietly, as the man stood talking from atop the few steps that descended into a lower area of the restaurant, Gray wandered over and stood next to Nora, who had what could only be described as a strained look on her face.

Usually, Gray was good at rolling with things. Growing up, she had had to be. Her parents weren't what she'd call *responsible* by conventional standards. Forgotten lunches or lunch money was the norm. Unsigned field trip permission slips were almost guaranteed until she'd learned to forge her mom's signature. Missed soccer games—as in, she missed them completely —because her parents had forgotten to drop her off.

She'd learned early on that if she wanted or needed something, she had to come by it herself—or she had to align herself with people who could help her get it. Life was more predictable when it was structured, but she didn't feel like she'd ever truly suffered as a result of unpredictability. Resourcefulness and adaptability were now the cornerstones of her adult life.

Well... maybe there had been some consequences over the years. Her parents had forgotten to fill out her financial aid forms for university, which was how she'd ended up starting a semester late and ultimately heading to a community college. At least there she hadn't had to worry about taking on debt or relying on her parents anymore.

She told herself she didn't begrudge them for it. The power had been shut off multiple times during her childhood due to unpaid bills. Her parents had rented an assortment of houses over the years, always moving to try and outrun late payments. For as much as Gray tried to be unaffected by that one, it had always bothered her more than the other parts of her life that she'd always assumed were normal until she'd learned better. It was probably what had drawn her so intensely to becoming a real estate agent once she'd finished school.

So while all Gray wanted for her life was stability, she tried to be as adaptable as possible. What happened over the next twenty-four hours was going to put that to the test.

Lost in her thoughts, Gray realized she'd missed the first part of the announcements. She only slipped back into the present when she noticed the tension radiating from Nora. She was keeping her composure, but her posture was rigid, her face drawn tight. Her back was to the wall, but Gray would bet anything that she wasn't touching it. There was no point when the strain of Nora's body was holding her upright like a marionette on a string.

So much for yesterday's massage.

Gray focused her attention back on the speaker when he held up a flashlight. "Each room will be given one. We're connected to a grid that runs underground, and we don't anticipate a power outage, but we want to be prepared."

A soft groan escaped Nora's lips, but Gray continued to face forward.

"If you have electronics, you'll want to fully power them up today. In the event of a power outage, you'll also want to empty your trash bin and fill it with water to ensure you can flush your toilet."

Now it was Gray's turn to groan. Maybe she should have been a bit more attentive during these announcements, but she knew that Nora was retaining every word. Besides, Gray thought, worrying herself about the hurricane in the days leading up to it wouldn't have changed where they found themselves now.

The man held up his hands to make sure everyone was looking at him. "And lastly, I want to ask if there are any doctors or nurses here. No need to raise your hands, but please let a member of our staff know when you come to collect your flashlights. Emergency services won't be able to reach us for the duration of the hurricane, and though we don't expect to need your assistance, we'd like to be as prepared as possible."

That sent a jolt of apprehension down Gray's back. Sure, the storm may be intense, but she hadn't expected there to be an actual fear of bodily harm.

She chanced another glance at Nora, whose face had gone pallid.

"We're going to be fine," she said, knocking her shoulder into Nora's. The contact their bodies made was akin to throwing a gummy bear at a rock. There was real, true fear on Nora's usually composed face, and Gray, never liking to see suffering, wanted to do anything she could to help alleviate it. "We'll be fine, I promise."

It was then that Nora finally turned toward her, as the storm announcements ended and people began milling toward the table where flashlights were being dispensed. "You don't know that."

"Bermuda is one of the single safest places to ride out a hurricane."

"I'd rather not have to ride out anything."

Gray didn't let herself smile at the petulant sound in Nora's voice, even if she did find it surprisingly endearing. "Fair. But as it stands, this is happening. We're going to get our flashlights and fill our trash bins and we're definitely," she emphasized, "going to see how much food they'll let us pilfer away in our rooms."

"Food is the absolute last thing on my mind right now," Nora finally responded with an exasperated sigh.

"Be that as it may, I feel like you'll thank me later."

Nora rolled her eyes before her voice grew uncharacteristically quiet. She finally leaned back against the wall and ran her fingers over the smooth metal of her necklace, seemingly lost in thought when she said, "I hate storms. I always have."

It was the honesty in her voice that struck Gray the most. She didn't know if Nora had ever been as forthright in an admission with her before, except maybe when she'd told Gray yesterday, in no uncertain terms, that she strongly believed eating lunch in the office should be illegal. Gray had snort-laughed and earned a scowl from Nora for that.

"I promise you." She turned toward Nora, effectively bracketing her between Gray's body and the wall. She was surprised by the insistence in her own voice as she said, "We're going to be okay. This is one of the safest places we could be. The storm's going to be a hundred miles off the coast. The worst of it will pass by the time we wake up tomorrow."

Nora's eyes were cloudy like a stormy sea, similar to the water that had begun to break in choppy waves against the beach that morning. "You can't—"

"I can." Gray put her hand on Nora's forearm, which was bare, with the sleeves of her button-down rolled up to her elbows. "If I'm the worst type of wrong, neither of us will have to worry much about who was right because it won't matter. And if I'm only a little wrong, you can lord it over me forever."

Finally, the smallest hint of a smile appeared at the edges of Nora's mouth, even if her body was still taut like a bowstring.

Gray slid her hand down and grabbed Nora's, just enough to pull her toward the table where the line had dwindled.

"If you play your cards right, I may even be willing to make some flashlight puppets later." The normalcy of Nora's eye roll, which happened like clockwork as her punchline landed, was strangely comforting.

Chapter Nine

Nora had been doing fine—in the way that "fine" meant she was actively avoiding accepting reality.

It wasn't until a rapid knock on her door that it felt like everything well and truly imploded.

"These are for you," the woman in a housekeeping uniform said, attempting to hand her a thick stack of towels that she stared at dumbly.

Gray, to her credit, had been the far more composed of the two of them during the earlier announcement about storm best practices. When she'd gotten back to her room, Nora had read the printed piece of paper again with all the information the man had gone over, and then she'd promptly put as much physical space between it and herself as she could.

It didn't matter. It was already inked across her mind like a Rolodex she could flip through, highlighting individual points whenever something in her room reminded her of them.

She stood in the doorway, looking at the woman and then down at the towels she was trying to hand her.

Please ensure your front door is properly closed. Do not open it during the storm.

Did this count as the hurricane yet? It must not, since housekeeping was still delivering storm prep items to rooms.

The churning in Nora's stomach was back, shifting from a slow roll that she'd kept at bay to an aggressive boil threatening to pour out of her. "What?" she asked, even though she'd heard the woman perfectly—and could recount the exact phrasing on the information sheet—in spite of the blood rushing around her ears.

She pointed beyond Nora to the glass balcony doors, then down between their feet, where they stood on opposite sides of the room's entrance. "To stop any draft or water that may come through."

A pool towel will be delivered to your room in case of water seeping through the front door. Place a towel inside of the entrance door and be careful in case the floor gets slippery.

They really thought the rooms were going to flood? She wasn't even on the ground floor.

"I'm not even on the ground floor," she said aloud.

The woman peered around Nora and into the room, which wasn't hard given that her shoulders had rounded into her body and she was instinctively trying to make her tall frame smaller. Less of a target.

"Don't forget to bring the chairs and table in from your balcony."

Patio/balcony furniture needs to be moved inside your room to prevent it from blowing into sliding glass doors. Please do not leave furniture outside.

For having committed the list to memory, she hadn't been able to complete a number of the tasks, frozen in some sort of delusion that this wasn't really happening.

"Could they break the glass?" she squeaked out.

"Just a precaution," the woman said with a cheery smile,

extending the towels once more and giving Nora no other option but to take them and accept her fate. "You'll be fine, love."

Fine. Fine. Fine. She repeated the word like a mantra in her head, a buoy to cling to as the current of her thoughts threatened to drag her down. Over the last five years, it had become her guiding principle in making it through each day. Fine wasn't aspirational, but it was practical. It was where she'd crash-landed after a life of relative optimism that, in retrospect, she'd taken for granted.

Fine got her up each day and allowed her to be great at her job. But after factoring in the other ways in which she'd completely pulled back from engaging with anyone who'd required more than a superficial relationship, fine was where things averaged out. Fine was always being impeccably dressed in the office but knowing there was an indecently high pile of clothes on a lounge chair in her bedroom, collateral damage still —after all these years—from being unable to settle on an outfit every morning.

And fine was, most days, just surviving. It was what she'd taken away from the year of therapy, after everything had happened. She hadn't stuck with it, but there had been so many layers weighing heavily on top of one another that she'd had to find a way to chip away at a few of them. Once she'd gotten to a place where she felt like she could breathe again, she'd stopped going.

They hadn't even scratched the surface on her weather-related anxiety, which she was now regretting with a force that made it hard to breathe.

She'd had panic attacks before, but she'd gotten better at managing them over the years. Mostly once she'd decided with a sort of nihilist finality that nothing mattered enough for her to allow herself to fall apart over. It wasn't the healthiest coping strategy, but it was one that had allowed her to function day-to-day again.

Because Jesus... a hurricane? She'd considered it in the abstract, sure. A storm was coming, and she wasn't (completely) delusional. But as she stood alone in her doorway, the woman moving on and knocking on Gray's door, the full extent of what was happening around her—to her—smacked against her like a brick to the head.

She was trapped. On a tiny island in the Atlantic Ocean. There was no fresh water except the metric fucktons the hurricane was threatening to dump on them, courtesy of hundred-mile-an-hour gusts of wind. For hours. In the darkness that was inching closer as the sun moved lower into the late afternoon sky.

Was it better that she wouldn't be able to see the full tumult of the water outside her window? The shoreline, which she'd looked at days ago with a wistful sigh, so still it had seemed like it was frozen in time, was now an encroaching prison, creeping farther up the beach. It moved inch by inch across the white sand with a frightening, methodical precision.

The wind.

The rain.

The sheer *force* of it all.

Her arm recoiled when she felt something warm against it, shocking her system and sending little sparks of anxiety zagging across her skin. Dragging her eyes up, she met Gray's pensive brown ones. They were big as always, but with a hint of fear behind them that made Nora suddenly feel like she was going to cry. If the resident ray of sunshine in Nora's life was going to look at her like that, what hope did she have of keeping herself together through this?

Gray's words, said like it wasn't the first time she'd had to repeat them, finally cut through the noise inside her head, which a moment ago had felt like it was going to drown her before the storm could.

"Nora," Gray said firmly, now definitely not for the first time. "Are you okay?"

She became aware of Gray's warm fingers as they slid down to her wrist, enveloping it and squeezing, like she was trying to get Nora's attention.

Nora looked down, the towels laying between their feet where she'd dropped them. She dragged her focus back up to Gray's face after long moments spent looking at the ground. The towels had fallen almost perfectly, one on top of the other, only slightly askew, like they'd been placed there intentionally.

"Nora," Gray said again, her voice insistent as her fingers pressed into Nora's skin.

"I don't like storms."

"You mentioned that." And just like that, everything about Gray softened. Her eyes, which had been so dark and focused, relaxed. The expression eased across her entire face, opening it back up into the Gray that Nora had come to recognize over the last year. Seconds ago, her normally smooth skin had been drawn so tightly that it looked like a mask to Nora, so un-Gray-like with the worry lines running across her forehead, her lips drawn over her teeth like she was experiencing physical pain.

Before she could fully process the situation, to come back down to earth and settle into the world around her, surprisingly strong arms enveloped her. Gray surrounded her and became the focus of her grounding techniques, a safe harbor in the physical—and metaphorical—storm that was picking up around them.

It was Gray's warmth she noticed first, radiating from her whole body as she pulled Nora into a hug that was both yielding and firm. Chestnut-colored hair, visible from her peripheral, brushed so softly against her cheek that it almost tickled. It would have, had her nerves not felt live and exposed, raw in a way she only felt at the height of true panic. A soothing arm was running up and down her back, which, in any other circumstance, she would have recoiled at. But in this moment, the only time that—she was surprised to realize—she'd felt safe within the last day, it was a comfort she couldn't even begin to describe.

She was cocooned in Gray's presence, which was grounded and strong in a way she'd never expected Gray to be. It pulled her away from the oppressive weight of the air around them, from the smell of salt that had clung to her nostrils all morning, now replaced with the light, clean scent of whatever perfume Gray was wearing.

Gray held her like that, not speaking, just running her hand methodically down Nora's back. On the way up, she would follow the ridge along Nora's spine, tracing the indentations with deft fingers. On the way down, she'd flatten her palm, like she was smoothing the tension away.

Purposefully, Nora realized dimly, Gray's fingers began to slow when they reached the bottom of her spine for what could have been the dozenth—or hundredth—time. She pulled back then, looking at Nora with eyes that were so focused and reassuring that it felt like everything really would be okay.

Gray's voice was calm and clear, matter-of-fact when she said, "Give me five minutes to get my stuff. We're riding this thing out together."

* * *

Once the anxiety faded, the embarrassment set in. That was all Nora could think about, like a loop replaying over and over.

Gray, to her credit, didn't seem to notice from the bed she now lounged on, the one closer to the floor-to-ceiling window looking out at the ocean. If she'd noticed, she was choosing not to comment. Now that Nora was calm, she wanted to tell Gray that she could go back to her own room, that they could ride out the storm in solitude and reconvene for the aftermath in the morning.

But it was too late for that. The wind whipped against the building, darkness settling across the horizon as angry raindrops beat down around them.

An hour ago, Gray had sat Nora down on one of the beds and turned on the television. She'd felt like she was a four-year-old who needed to be distracted from a meltdown.

Which... wasn't that far off actually.

"Watch this," Gray had said, turning on *Wheel of Fortune* and putting the remote on the bedside table.

"Hoping the spinny wheel will distract me?" It had been all the humor Nora could manage in the moment, as her heart still beat erratically. She'd still felt a little like she may throw up, which wasn't likely, given she hadn't eaten all day.

"Only if you want it to," Gray had said, disappearing out the door.

And then, she'd come back, pulling her suitcase and carrying a bag that looked like it might burst at the seams.

Without fanfare, she placed the bag next to the unoccupied bed and walked back toward the door. Nora felt the sound of the lock clicking into place more than she heard it, both safety and imprisonment rolled up in one confusing sound.

Gray, she realized, didn't make a big deal out of things. She hadn't asked Nora again if she was okay. Sitting on her own bed, she'd kicked off her flip-flops and leaned back against one pillow, pulling the other one across her stomach and cuddling it like a stuffed animal.

It was exactly what Nora needed. Space, but also the calming presence of another human being.

Besides a few lights outside, ones that guided guests along the pathways winding through the resort, it was pitch-black. The sun had set, and the moon was visibly absent as the clouds rolled in, bringing the rain with them.

Nora finally felt functional enough to respond to Cynthia's multiple texts sent over the last few hours. "I'm letting Cynthia know we're okay," she said, focusing on her phone.

Gray's voice pulled her attention.

"Thank you for doing that. She checked in with me about an hour ago." Gray flicked her focus to the guide channel. "I can offer you *The Office* reruns or *Grey's Anatomy*. Pick your poison."

"Isn't *Grey's Anatomy* a little on the nose?" Nora had meant the statement as a quiet musing, but it pulled Gray's attention toward her anyway.

And then, Gray shot upright, like she'd been struck by a lightning bolt. Nora flinched instinctively, wondering what Gray saw from her vantage point closer—by a whole four feet—to the storm.

"What's wrong?" she asked, looking at Gray expectantly, trying to keep her voice calm. She hadn't come back down to planet Earth over the last hour only to ratchet up her anxiety again. She'd never survive at this rate if that was the case.

Gray, pulling herself up to her knees and cradling her pillow between her arms, had the most delightfully shocked look on her face. "*Grey's Anatomy*. Like Gray." She was beside herself, like this was the most interesting information she'd ever realized.

"I didn't really think my comment would be that much of a showstopper." But secretly, Nora was just relieved Gray hadn't seen something in the darkness outside.

"*Grey's*," she emphasized, pointing to herself and stabbing her chest with her pointer finger. "Like me."

Nora, finally feeling like she was inhabiting her own body again, quirked an eyebrow. "This is new information to you?"

"God," Gray said, slapping her hand to her forehead. "That's why in high school, Matt Jenkins kept asking me if I wanted to watch *Grey's Anatomy* with him."

It seemed like Gray was talking to herself, genuinely working out the answer to a puzzle that had been quietly simmering in her mind for years. "Because then he'd, like... wiggle his eyebrows suggestively. I never understood why."

Gray did an eyebrow wiggle of her own that was outlandishly obvious, but thinking on it, Nora could see a teenage boy doing exactly what Gray was doing now, like the joke needed explaining.

And apparently, Nora mused, it had.

"So much death on that show. Lots of blood. Medical emergencies abound. Like, yeah... there's definitely romance, but still..."

Nora brought the hand not resting on her stomach up to her face, using it to gracefully cover her smile and faking a cough to hide the surprised laugh that husked out.

It was... nice. To spend time with someone who seemed to enjoy life. Who stopped to appreciate the little things.

And again, it chipped away a little more at that nagging suspicion Nora was slowly letting go of—this idea she'd harbored that Gray wasn't who she claimed to be. Or that she was only presenting some version herself that was most appealing to whomever she was with.

The night before, Gray had made them stand outside for long minutes, listening to a sound they'd both finally agreed on was a bird. There had come a point when Nora realized they wouldn't make it inside unless she acquiesced. But it wasn't hard to do, in that moment, when Gray had been looking at her so expectantly.

"It sounds just like a text tone," Gray had said in a voice that wasn't so much trying to convince Nora as it was just stating something like it was an obvious fact. There was genuine wonder in her voice when she furrowed her brows together and added, "Imagine that."

Nora had nodded as seriously as she could manage given the subject matter. She'd never have noticed the sound if Gray hadn't pointed it out.

And then, once Gray had appreciated the experience in a way Nora was already coming to realize defied the conventions of time, she had held the door open for Nora and gestured inside. "Let's get dinner. I'm starving."

Drawing herself back to the present, Nora couldn't help but smile, too, at the delighted look on Gray's face. "I'm sure Matt Jenkins thought he'd struck gold with that one."

"Clearly," Gray said, throwing herself back against the pillow. "He asked me about a dozen times over a year. Just running at the wall as hard as he could, expecting something to change."

Comfortable silence settled around them.

When she looked up again, Gray was studying her.

So quickly, with only a handful of real interactions between them, Nora was realizing just how many looks Gray had. She'd never noticed because she was too busy ignoring everyone. Gray, with her vibrant personality, had been more difficult to disregard on an ongoing basis, but Nora was well practiced by the time she'd waltzed into her world.

"What?" Nora finally asked when Gray didn't look away. She sat up straighter on the bed, realizing for the first time—with an acceptance that was both grim and enlivened—that they were indefinitely trapped in a hotel room together.

At least there were two beds.

It was the last thought that ran through Nora's finally calmed mind before the room was bathed in darkness.

She screamed.

Immediately, she could hear—and feel—Gray moving around the hotel room. "I'm going to light the emergency candles and find the flashlights."

Her heart felt like it was in her throat in those seconds that she waited for... something. For her eyes to adjust, which wasn't possible with the complete darkness enveloping her. For the flicker of light from somewhere in the room, which Gray had promised her only seconds ago, but which felt like it took a lifetime to appear.

Fingertips dug into the soft comforter underneath her as she tried to take deep, calming breaths.

"I brought mine, too," Gray said from somewhere across the room. The crinkle of a bag she was probably rooting through sounded as loud as a jet engine in what felt like a void of time and space.

Nora didn't know if she'd ever experienced darkness like this. No lights outside, just a solid, almost sideways wall of rain that lapped against the exterior concrete in a chaotic, inevitable tempo.

She was listening to herself breathe when she heard the scrape of a match, followed by the faint scent of smoke.

"Success," Gray said needlessly as the candle flickered to life about eight feet away, another one following moments later. "You'll probably want to conserve your phone battery, but the screen should still work."

Of course. In her panic, Nora hadn't even thought of that.

"I wasn't kidding about the shadow puppets," Gray mused as she walked back toward Nora, a silhouette more than anything.

After fumbling around, Nora finally clasped her phone in

her hand and pressed her finger against the screen. Even after less than a minute of darkness, the artificial light was jarring, but with it, she noticed that Gray was carrying what looked like a laptop.

The bed dipped next to her, something she felt more than she saw. "What are you doing?"

"If you must know," Gray said, a slight edge in her voice that hadn't been there before, "my thing is that I don't love the dark."

That's when Nora realized that the edge she heard in Gray's voice was fear. She didn't like hearing it, but she was glad that she knew it. Not because she wanted Gray to be fallible and human. No, it was because she could finally be helpful instead of sucking up all the emotional energy in the room.

She scooted a little closer, moving her pillow so it just touched the one behind Gray. "So I hate storms and you're afraid of the dark. What a pair we make."

There was something about the darkness in that moment, when it felt safer to act than to think. When she didn't worry about the implications of what was happening between them.

She felt Gray's legs extend down the bed, finally able to see their bodies when Gray opened the laptop resting on her thighs. "I hope you don't mention to Cynthia that she basically sent the two of us on our own personal versions of *Fear Factor*."

"Are we going to group-journal about our feelings together?" Nora said, looking at how their bodies stretched down the bed, awareness prickling through her. "I'm sorry," she followed immediately after.

"You're stressed, I get it. But I'm not the enemy here. The power will come back on eventually, and we'll be fine. I just figured you might want to watch something while we wait. Take our minds off everything."

Which was actually a really good idea. And now Nora felt both guilty for being rude, but also stupid for not planning ahead. While she'd completely shut down today, pretending the storm wasn't happening, Gray had obviously been taking a different route, ensuring that she'd be able to ride out the situation as comfortably as possible. And, more than that, she was willing to let Nora take advantage of her planning too.

"You're absolutely right," Nora acquiesced, trying to hide her embarrassment. "What've you got?"

She forced herself to settle back against the warm cocoon of the pillow she'd called home for the last hour.

The harsh glow of the computer screen was enough to illuminate Gray's face, the white of her teeth visible as she gave Nora another one of those *looks*. Soft but also curious, like she was trying to figure something out.

Even though Nora wondered what she was seeing—because who wouldn't be curious to know what the first person to see her in this way in years was taking away from it—she didn't ask.

Maybe she didn't actually want to know.

And Gray didn't offer any assessment.

Instead, Gray leaned back against the pillow behind her, putting an arm behind her head and shifting the computer over so it balanced on both their thighs.

Nora leaned closer to Gray, enjoying the warmth where their legs almost touched. There was a part of her that was grateful for her own awkwardness, for how hard she had to work and focus to keep that tiny sliver of space between them. Even when—she could admit to herself—what she really wanted to do was press the length of their thighs together and enjoy the softness, the comfort that came from leaning on someone else.

It was something she hadn't entertained letting herself

want in a very long time. Not that she'd give into it now, but at least it gave her something else to focus on instead of the intermittent gusts of wind pushing against the building.

* * *

She didn't know when she'd fallen asleep.

Or how, in spite of not sharing a bed with someone for years, she found herself nestled into Gray's side like a puppy looking for warmth.

If anyone from the office saw this, they wouldn't believe it, she thought blearily, given that she herself hadn't accepted it was real yet.

She wasn't actually awake, which was the only reason that thought alone didn't startle her upright. It was that liminal space, hovering between wanting to give in to the comfort of sleep so badly it felt like something was physically pulling her against the bed and knowing the real world was soon going to come calling.

It was still raining, but the wind had moved through, she noticed dimly. Natural light streamed through the condensation-soaked glass. She could see it through the eye she'd managed to open; the other one was pressed into Gray's torso.

So soft. How had she never noticed how soft Gray was before?

Her hand was splayed out against Gray's hip, skin against skin where she'd found the sliver of exposed waist where Gray's tank top had ridden up.

The laptop had fallen to the side of Gray, away from both of them. They were on top of the covers, and Gray was half sitting in a position that only seemed possible to fall asleep in if you were under thirty. The arm that, at Nora's last recollection, had been balanced between Gray's head and the wall, had fallen at some point, draping itself around Nora.

Gray shifted but didn't wake, her fingers curling against Nora's back before she relaxed her palm against Nora's spine, just like she'd done yesterday when Nora had been upset.

Individually, none of her thoughts had set off enough alarm bells to warrant removing herself from the comfort and warmth of Gray's body.

There was a moment when she wanted to fall back asleep and prolong this comfort for as long as possible. But as soon as her mind started to wake up, the comfortable, sleepy sensation began to fall away, thought by thought.

Enough of them together finally punched through the haze.

The last domino to fall was the soft, contented sigh from Gray's lips. Because when Nora lifted her head enough to look up at the rising and falling of Gray's chest, everything became real.

She froze then, her loose, sleep-soaked limbs going rigid. Her mind knew—in some hazy recess she wanted to exist in forever—that something was off, but her body wasn't taking orders from her brain.

This wasn't a dream.

Gray was holding her, softly but with a quiet confidence that made Nora feel the safest she'd felt in years.

More than that, and the much bigger problem than a single awkward moment, was that Nora liked it. A lot.

That realization in itself was enough to get the blood pumping through her veins and spur her into quiet action.

She picked up Gray's arm, lifting it back across her body so she could slide off the edge of the bed. In a perfect world, Gray would never know how they'd fallen asleep, and they'd never need to discuss this.

* * *

They made it off the island later that day. Thank god they hadn't had to reschedule their flight on top of everything else. Nora felt like she couldn't take a full breath until their plane, which had taxied for an agonizing amount of time, propelled them into the air and safely away from the remnants of the storm littered around the runway.

Gray was seated next to her, giving Nora emotional space— even if, physically, they were almost on top of one another in the small aircraft.

Nora could smell the light scent of Gray's freshly washed hair, and instinctively, she wanted to move closer. She shook the remnants of last night from her mind. People trauma-bonded through all sorts of things. Their situation was no different. It was a moment in time, and that moment was over.

Last night had presented a need, and Gray had stepped in and helped when Nora hadn't been in a position to decline. But this? The pull toward Gray, the desire to recapture the comfort and safety she'd felt this morning?

Her stomach swooped low when Gray caught her eye and gave her a soft smile. *Want.*

For having gone so long without significant emotional responses to anything, Nora was surprised that she could so easily name her feelings. She liked to think of them all as packaged separately and existing independently from one another.

Because the thing was, if she added them all up and looked at the sum of their parts, they became something she wasn't willing to consider.

Her armor may have been lessening, but she had no plans to take it off and leave herself exposed.

Chapter Ten

Kelsey had Gray cornered at the coffee machine on Monday morning like she'd been staking it out. "Tell me everything."

They'd started at Philly Finds within a few months of one another. The similarity in their ages, along with, well... whatever else Kelsey had deemed important, meant that she'd decided they were friends.

Gray knew this conversation was inevitable, and she'd already resolved to stick to the facts and not the feelings, especially with someone like Kelsey. "Bermuda was beautiful. Very relaxing overall. There was a hurricane, which I would appreciate not having to go through again any time soon."

The loud "ugh" that Kelsey let out echoed through the kitchen area and out into the office. "I heard about that. Totally sucks." The look she gave Gray passed for thoughtful before she leaned against the counter and angled their bodies toward one another. "Now that we have that out of the way, tell me the good stuff."

"Good stuff?" Gray had thirty seconds left for her coffee to brew and then another thirty seconds to fix it if she stirred aggressively. One minute. She just had to stave Kelsey off for a single minute. She bought extra time by walking over to the fridge and grabbing the oat milk.

"Oh, come on, Gray. You know what I mean."

She placed the oat milk on the counter and pulled the sugar jar closer to her. "I don't, actually."

Gray hadn't been able to work out on her own how she felt about the past week, and she sure as hell wasn't going to process it with Kelsey.

Once her coffee was brewed, she pulled the mug from the Keurig machine. She poured in the oat milk so hastily that it almost splashed over the rim. And then she decided, in spite of her love of the perfect cup of coffee, that extracting herself from this conversation was paramount to the right ratio of sugar and milk. She pushed the sugar back against the wall and, with her spoon still in her mug, picked it up and took a sip.

"All right. I have a million things to catch up on." It wasn't a complete lie. She needed to get updates on her clients from Callie, who had stepped in for her last week.

With a quick wave, already moving away, she headed over to her desk, ignoring the dumbfounded look on Kelsey's face.

But when she sat down, it wasn't the catch-up she needed to do that was occupying all of her mental bandwidth.

No. That energy was being completely taken up by a tall blonde who still hadn't shown her face in the office this morning. Just another thing for a usually composed Gray to fret about. It was easy to wonder if the fragile truce—possibly even friendship—they'd found themselves in over the past week would hold up after returning to their normal lives.

Because, truly, she'd thought of little else this past weekend. Every time she thought of them—her and Nora in Bermuda—she felt more confused than before.

When she'd noticed Nora in the hallway before the

storm, not going to her had felt impossible. Instinct had driven her when she'd seen the lost, detached look in Nora's eyes.

Gray had taken the reins, sure, but Nora had let her. Let into her room. Onto her bed. She wondered how many people got to see Nora like that, real and vulnerable and just... existing in a way she didn't often let other people see.

She'd wanted to be closer to Nora. At least she could admit that to herself.

Because when the layer of frosty protection was stripped away, Nora was a lot like the type of woman Gray would be attracted to.

Intelligent. Focused. A little bit emotionally messy.

It had been easier to ignore her attraction when Nora was being her usual safeguarded self. But it wasn't like she hadn't noticed her over the last year. The blue of her eyes. The sharp angles of her jaw. The way she walked through the office with purpose, always on the move.

Now, for better or worse, she knew other things too. Like how one of Nora's brows drew upward in what looked like suspicion, but it was actually Nora deciding how she felt about something. Or how, surprisingly, she was a cuddler. That she was deathly afraid of storms. And that she experienced what looked like panic attacks, even if she was the last person on earth that Gray would expect to suffer from them.

And she'd never forget how it felt waking up on Friday morning, the warmth of Nora's body enveloping her like a hug she hadn't known she'd needed.

There were excruciatingly sweet seconds where she'd felt Nora snuggle closer into her stomach, like she was going to fall back asleep.

She'd felt Nora stiffen then, and deep down, Gray had known there was no other way this would end. She'd kept her eyes closed and stilled her fingers that wanted to run along the ridge of Nora's spine.

People always left, and Nora would be no different.

Maybe that was part of why she felt safe getting closer to Nora. There were no surprises as to how this would end.

She'd waited for Nora to slip out of bed and into the bathroom, and seconds later, Gray had popped up and collected the few items of hers that had ended up strewn about the room. A zip-up hoodie on the other bed. The emergency candle, which she assumed she had to return to her own room.

She'd agonized over whether she should leave without saying anything, but a lifetime of ambivalent parents had committed her to never wanting to leave another person confused if she could help it.

Making it as easy as possible for both of them, she'd been ready to leave, bags in her hands, when Nora had come out of the bathroom.

"Heading back?" Nora had asked, running a hand through her unruly hair. That was another new thing Gray had learned, that Nora suffered from a ridiculously cute case of bedhead in the morning.

"I'm not sure if flights will leave today, but I figured I'd give you a little space."

Nora had nodded then, her face soft. It wasn't embarrassment, necessarily, but the way she was looking at Gray had definitely changed since the night before, like she wasn't trying to hide herself anymore. "That makes sense."

And then Nora had stood, a little awkwardly, in the doorway leading out of the room, like she was gearing herself up for something.

Gray had decided to make this easier for both of them. She'd always been good at reading the room. "Well, I'll get out of your ha—"

Nora's words had tumbled out, cutting Gray off. "Thank you. I don't think I said that before, but thank you. For being here. It was a very kind gesture, and I hope you know that I appreciated it."

Gray had nodded because... what else could she do? She'd never heard Nora thank anyone. Finally, she'd found her voice. "Sure. What are friends for?"

The subtle smile on Nora's face had still felt like it could light up the entire room. "I guess this officially does make us friends."

Gray had grinned. "Sleepovers and all."

It was then that Nora had moved back into the room, making space for Gray to leave. "Probably won't be a need back in Philadelphia, but the company was nice."

Heat snaking up her neck and fanning across her cheeks, Gray's hand had enveloped the cool metal of the door. "For friends or for sleepovers?"

And... yeah. She'd spent all weekend thinking about those words, internally kicking herself whenever they rolled through her mind. Whether that was how Nora had taken it or not, she'd basically asked if they'd still be having sleepovers in Philadelphia. Which was just so problematic on a million different levels.

Unfounded rumors had ruined her last job, and she couldn't imagine what would have happened if there had been truth to them.

So that was the pin holding the grenade, just waiting to be pulled so the whole thing could blow. She and Nora were co-workers. Which was only the first, though not unimportant, obstacle to whatever was brewing. Add in a dash of the fact that Nora was obviously a private person. Layer on the understanding that there was definitely a *story* behind Nora's facade.

And... yeah. This couldn't go anywhere. Maybe to friendship, which Gray would like to see come to fruition now that they were home. Because she was a masochist like that.

But anything else?

It couldn't happen.

Leaning back in her chair, she blew out an exasperated breath that captured the attention of Trent, who sat at the desk closest to her.

"Welcome back," he said, shifting his focus away from his laptop to give her a broad smile. "How was your trip?"

* * *

Gray had settled back into a rhythm at work. There were no explicit rules regarding the time they had to spend in the office, but unless it was wildly inconvenient, she liked starting her morning there.

She hadn't seen Nora all week, except for when she'd been in twice for closings with clients. That wasn't uncommon, especially given that both of them were playing catch-up after their time away.

With multiple showings every day and a closing of her own, Gray was already exhausted by Friday morning. A TikTok she'd posted had gone viral earlier in the week, and she had dozens of new leads to sort through from the form she'd added to her profile.

Honestly, she was living for it.

Helping people find their perfect home. Closing deals that seemed impossible. Proving herself.

It was all she'd ever wanted.

She was finally feeling like she was in control of her own life, of the future she'd been working hard to build.

A shadow fell across her laptop, and she braced herself for yet another attempt from Kelsey to extract information from her about her week in Bermuda. It felt like a game of cat and mouse at this point, but with her own limited time in the office, she'd been staying one step ahead of her work friend.

Sadly, she had to stop at some point, situated at her desk like a sitting duck.

"I'm really—" she began, ready to rebuff Kelsey's protests.

"Busy?" A voice she'd be lying if she said she hadn't missed this last week pulled at her attention.

Gray took a deep breath and leaned back in her chair before looking up at Nora, who, as usual, had on an impeccably tailored blazer that made Gray swoon. Just a little bit. "Hey."

Nora, looking only a little uncomfortable, leaned against Gray's desk. Her skin still had a soft glow from their trip. It made Gray feel warm, like she was remembering the heat from the sun. Multiple people stopped what they were doing and stared. If Nora wanted to make a statement of some sort, this was the time to do it.

Friday mornings were the only time of week when everyone was guaranteed to be in the office together, since they had a weekly team meeting to touch base.

She could practically feel Kelsey salivating from the desk on the other side of Trent.

Nora ran her long finger along the outline of a dinosaur on Gray's favorite mug. "How's your week been?"

A grin split across her face that she didn't even try to hide. "Nonstop. How about yours?"

"About the same. But everything seems a little easier after surviving a hurricane." Nora looked down at her then, blue eyes searching for... something.

Gray wasn't sure what as the moment extended between them.

It was usually easy for Gray to fill a silence, to keep a

conversation going. And it wasn't that she didn't appreciate Nora being willing to talk about their trip, because she was.

What she realized, staring up at Nora, was that she wanted to say *more*. They'd literally slept wrapped up in one another, and going back to pretending like she didn't know what Nora looked like when she melted into relaxation was a hard pill to swallow.

She stifled the urge.

"Have you been in the office much?" Gray asked, sneaking a glance around the room to see whether everyone was still watching them.

They were.

Nora shook her head. "Only twice for closings," she said before she remembered something, snapping her fingers. "And Tuesday morning."

Reaching forward, Gray picked up her coffee cup. She watched as Nora's hand, which had been tracing the pattern of the dinosaur, pulled away before she rested it against the edge of the desk.

Her fingernails were painted a gorgeous plum color, new since they'd been back. She wondered if she'd notice things like that more and more, now that she was allowed to look.

It took Nora making a soft sound for Gray to come back to the present conversation. "What happened Tuesday morning?" she asked, picking up where they'd left off.

Gray was transfixed by the conspiratorial smile that Nora leveled at her as she leaned a little closer. "I came to catch up with Cynthia, but honestly, I think she wanted to make sure that you'd made it off the island safely."

Ah... that made sense. Cynthia, besides being incredibly apologetic about the hurricane—which was a freak natural occurrence and not her fault in any way—had also asked Gray about the trip. She'd assumed that it was a temperature check on whether it had gone well overall.

Gray put her coffee cup down and peered back up at Nora, tracking her expressions when she asked, "And, um... what did you tell her?"

Nora laughed then, in a way that made her whole face light up.

There was that feeling again, like Gray was becoming a little addicted to seeing and learning all the different facets of Nora's personality.

"Honestly, for a second, I got really worried," Nora said, lips narrowing like she was remembering how she'd felt. "I hadn't been in the office on Monday, and I didn't even think about whether you'd come to work. There was a flash of panic when I thought something may have happened to you this weekend, and then it got even worse when I assumed you were safe but that you'd decided to quit."

"Does Cynthia really have that little faith in her employees?"

Nora shook her head emphatically. "That was all me, not you. I promise. Cynthia's been very good to me over the years, and I'll be eternally grateful for that."

"Seems like it's a symbiotic relationship," Gray said, tilting her head to the large whiteboard that took up almost an entire wall, highlighting the currently ongoing deals and sales totals. It was no surprise that Nora was at the top.

"Even so," Nora acknowledged, a smile on her face as she looked toward Cynthia's office door, "I know I don't make it easy."

Gray put her elbow on her desk and rested her head on her palm, leaning forward. "You don't say."

Nora stood up to her full height, running her hands down

her blazer. "And just for that, I'm not going to save you a seat at the meeting."

She'd felt comfortable with Nora before, in brief moments during their trip. During dinner, when they'd discussed their more difficult clients. The afternoon spent together on the beach, when they'd sat in companionable silence and watched the bright blue sea. And while they'd slept, cocooned against one another like the world outside didn't exist.

But strangely, all of that paled in comparison to this.

Because right now, what was happening, was real. It wasn't some alcohol-induced, sun-soaked break from reality, where they could pretend that the world outside tropical paradise didn't exist.

And she couldn't help but bask in the little thrill that shot through her as Nora's attention remained entirely focused on her, bright blue eyes playful and vibrant in a way Gray had never expected to see in this office.

She definitely hadn't been expecting to be the one to cause it.

It was just about nine a.m., when their meeting would start, and not that it mattered, given the whole office was focused on them, but she didn't want to be late. And she definitely didn't want to get stuck sitting next to Julian.

She rose from her chair and shot Nora a smile. "Race you there."

Chapter Eleven

On the first day of October, Nora found herself with an unexpected gap in her schedule.

One of her very first clients at Philly Finds, the Romanos, were selling the home that Nora had helped them purchase almost five years ago. At that time, they'd been pregnant with their first child and looking to move out of their Center City apartment. Five years later, and with another kid to show for it, they were doing what many city dwellers did—heading out to the suburbs.

So they'd called Nora. Which she'd appreciated.

Their closing, which was scheduled for one p.m., an hour from now, needed to be pushed back. So she'd vacated the conference room and headed to her desk, where she now sat idly, surprised that she didn't immediately jump to fill the time and distract herself.

People could say what they wanted about her personal life, but when it came to relationship building in her professional one, she could go toe to toe with almost any other Realtor and still likely come out on top.

It hadn't taken long for her to find a house in the suburbs that the Romanos loved, in a public school district that was well regarded, a neighborhood that was close to the Main Line but a bit less expensive. She'd checked all the boxes easily.

That's what she did, and she was good at it.

The thing about a job like hers was that it was very easy to know if you were good at it or not. Life was much more ambiguous, but being a Realtor had obvious metrics for volume of home sales and deal values that gave her a clear path to success. Sure, marketing and working leads and any number of day-to-day things required a little creativity, but the path was laid out for her.

She knew that her job was a unique experience in that she watched people live out their lives. She was part of some of their biggest moments but still on the periphery. There was a lot of emotion in purchasing or selling a home, sometimes a lifetime of memories that a person was giving up to make a move.

The divorces, she'd always thought privately, were the hardest. Talk about cutting the baby in half. Either one partner couldn't afford to buy the other out, or they'd both wanted to leave the house and be done with those memories.

She knew a little something about what it felt like to want to burn it all to the ground.

Luckily, in those cases, the two people who'd come to hate one another didn't have to be in the same room. Nora had made the mistake once of having a recently divorced couple on the same text thread, which had exploded within minutes into some of the most toxic language she'd ever heard. She hadn't really been shocked that they couldn't make it as a couple, especially after reading what they were willing to say to one another in front of her, and she'd learned moving forward to always ask for a little more context on the reason for the sale.

But what did she know?

With three failed relationships, she hadn't come close, at least in the practical sense, to knowing what a divorce would entail, to understanding the emotional toll it could take on a person. Sure, her breakup with Andrea, her last partner, had gutted her. More than that, it had sent her careening down the path she'd never expected. She'd become someone she didn't entirely recognize these days—but at least there hadn't been paperwork involved.

She leaned back in her desk chair—in her coveted area in the corner of the office, where she could see people approaching from all directions—and, perplexed, touched her fingers to her lips. She was smiling. It was possibly the first time it had happened in years while she was thinking back on her past relationship.

None of the other Philly Finds agents knew Andrea, and Cynthia never brought her up, at least not by name.

Nora hadn't forgiven her. She didn't think she'd ever forgive her. But she also hadn't moved past what had happened, for as much as she tried to tell herself she had.

If things had ended on a better note, like they'd grown apart or wanted different things, maybe Andrea could have remained the reason for Nora's moratorium on workplace romances.

But their relationship hadn't ended amicably.

And instead of looking at what had happened as a specific situation that was better to know about now than later, Nora had let its toxic tendrils weave their way into every facet of her life.

It had felt like her only option was to take a blowtorch to any and all emotional vulnerability, whether it was at work or in her personal life.

Which was why she was having a hard time understanding why she was smiling.

Absentmindedly, she picked up the sticky note on her desk that she'd read when she'd sat down.

Gray, at some point later yesterday or earlier this morning, had left it. It wasn't the first one she'd received from the younger agent, but she hadn't caught Gray leaving one in the act. Yet.

This one was longer than the others, so Gray's impossibly scribbled writing was small, almost hard to read. Even if she hadn't known Gray's handwriting, which she did, there was no one else who would have dared to touch her desk, even to sit something on top of it.

The oldest-known living land animal is a tortoise named Jonathan, who is 189 (maybe 190) years old.

And then Nora had flipped it over, because Gray always had to leave some sort of commentary about the fact.

Really puts our time here in perspective, doesn't it?

Nora didn't know about that, but she had come to accept the little thrill she felt whenever she saw the bright turquoise note somewhere on her desk. To be fair, it didn't take much to throw some excitement into her otherwise aggressively regimented life these days.

This was just Gray, she was discovering. Bright turquoise Post-It notes. Inconsequential facts. Sneaking around and leaving messages just for the fun of it.

In the past few days, the last remnants of Nora's suspicion had been snuffed out like embers of a fire. She'd wanted to dislike Gray, and it had definitely made things easier when her life was more compartmentalized.

But she just couldn't.

After a few weeks back in the office, continuing to rationalize that narrative in her mind seemed stupid. Maybe there was a past version of herself that was naive, who'd loved and trusted a little too freely, but she'd never been dumb.

So the only thing she could do was accept Gray at face value, sticky notes and all.

And while she was thinking about Gray, she realized there was something she needed to do.

Cynthia's door was open, and with Nora's work area the closest to her office, she was standing in front of Cynthia's desk within thirty seconds of her original thought.

"I cannot tell Julian he can't heat up his lunch in the office," Cynthia said without looking up from her laptop.

Nora stopped herself from speaking and took a deep inhale. *Ugh. Fish. Again.*

"Surprisingly, that's not why I'm here." Even though Julian really should have been placed in a special glass box, where his obnoxious office etiquette only impacted himself.

That got Cynthia's attention, who peered at Nora over her glasses, an interested look on her face. "I guess hell really did freeze over. I've been expecting you to march in here for the last ten minutes."

"It's annoying, sure. Do you want me to lodge a formal complaint?" Nora asked seriously, though she failed to hide her smile. Which was a pretty new experience for her. She wasn't exactly prone to fits of positivity in the office.

Cynthia laughed and let her glasses, attached to a thin, gold chain, drop around her neck. She leaned back in her chair and studied Nora. "So, if not the fishpocalypse, what can I help you with?"

Nora sat down in one of the plush chairs in front of Cynthia's desk and tried to articulate the idea that had been rolling around in her brain for the past few days. "If I'm..." She took a beat, clearing her throat, watching how Cynthia stared at her with curiosity. "If I'm going to leverage Gray to help me, I'd like to be honest with her."

She'd come to that conclusion this past weekend, when

she'd popped into the office to grab a folder with paperwork that she'd forgotten. Realizing she'd forgotten something, in and of itself, had been a jarring realization, but it had quickly slipped from her mind when she'd seen a Post-It note stuck on top of the folder she'd come to retrieve.

Psycho *was the first movie to show a toilet flushing.*

And it was just such a stupid thing to see written on a tiny piece of paper that she'd laughed. Then she'd laughed even harder, imagining Gray laughing while she'd written it. Probably at her own desk, since she wouldn't have let herself get caught.

In quick seconds, the guilt had set in. She didn't like to use people. Soliciting help from someone was one thing, but actively pilfering information from Gray had suddenly felt... smarmy.

Because Gray, she had to well and truly accept, was just a really nice person. And Nora, in spite—and definitely also because—of what she'd gone through, didn't want to take advantage of the trust of others.

So telling her had just started to make sense in a way that felt obvious. If she was being begrudgingly pulled back into the world of the living, she was going to do it right.

She couldn't read the look on Cynthia's face as the seconds passed by.

"I know that you wanted to keep things under wraps for a while—"

Cynthia cut her off. "I think you telling her is a great idea."

"Yeah?" Nora asked, surprised at how much the pride in Cynthia's voice meant to her.

"Definitely." Cynthia paused then, looking at Nora with a soft smile. "I'm glad this is where you landed. And I won't make a thing of it, but I'm glad to see you're opening up a little."

Nora rolled her eyes. "I wouldn't go that far. It's just the right thing to do."

"You're right about that, but this is a conversation I couldn't have imagined us having even a few weeks ago."

"No, probably not," Nora said with a shrug. It wasn't that she felt different, but she would be stupid to ignore that things were *changing*.

"Just ask Gray to keep it to herself for a little while. Regardless of how things land, I'd rather have more time to get everything in place."

"Sure. I can do that." Nora stood up and moved to the door.

"And Nora?"

"Yeah?"

"It's good to see you smiling again."

Nora didn't answer, but she gave Cynthia a quick nod before fleeing back to her desk.

Now she just had to figure out a way to explain this to Gray without seeming like a complete asshole.

* * *

The opportunity to talk with Gray presented itself earlier than Nora had expected.

When she walked out of Cynthia's office, Gray was leaning against her desk. Which was an interesting development for their... friendship, as it had been Nora who'd come to her during their past few interactions.

This, at the very least, Nora thought she owed Gray. After all, it hadn't been Gray who'd been sullen and closed off for the last year.

Still, Nora wasn't going to try and dwell on the past, a shocking thought in and of itself, and she appreciated that Gray was making space for them to move forward from it.

Now, she just had to pepper in a little honesty.

Nora stood in front of Gray, who was still leaning on the desk, Nora's back to the rest of the office. At midday, it was sparsely populated, with only a few other agents either grabbing a quick lunch in the communal kitchen or working quietly at their desks.

"Already losing your touch for subterfuge?" Nora asked, smiling involuntarily at whatever note she might receive next.

"I have no idea what you're referring to." Gray pushed off the desk and stood up to her full height, leveling a look of pure innocence in Nora's direction. "And *if* I was here for another reason, you'd never have seen me."

Nora lifted a brow. "Is that so?"

"You doubt me?"

It was a question with layers. Nora wasn't going to pick them apart right now.

The busy push of summer, when people were more likely to move, had come to an end, which meant this was one of the first weeks that she had more time to spend in the office. Prospecting. Planning. Organizing.

It wasn't her favorite part of the job, since it required periods of self-inflicted focus, but she could do it mostly on autopilot these days.

Gray, she'd noted earlier this week, had started to dress in a wardrobe that solidified fall was coming. The light sweater she wore clung to her curves, so thin it could pass for a long-sleeved shirt.

When she realized that she was staring at Gray, she took a small step back, clearing her throat. "I don't doubt you."

A dizzyingly genuine smile worked its way across Gray's lips that made Nora feel like she'd done something important. "I'm happy to hear that."

Nora realized there was probably a purpose to Gray loitering around her desk then. "So... what brings you by?"

Gray laughed and picked up her phone from the edge of the desk. "To your little slice of heaven in the corner? I was heading out to grab a coffee. Did you want to come?"

She looked down at her watch. With her closing postponed, she had plenty of time. "Sure."

They walked out of the office, Gray ahead of her, and she could see Kelsey, from her desk closest to the door, trying to make eye contact with Gray. Generally, Kelsey didn't register on Nora's radar. She wasn't a strong agent, and whenever Nora did take note, Kelsey always seemed to be looking around furtively while in conversation, like she was afraid someone was trying to eavesdrop.

Nora stifled a laugh. Like whatever Kelsey had to say was that important.

When they stepped out into the bright afternoon sun, Gray took a long, decadent inhale. "God, I think I'm going to need to burn these clothes. I don't know if the smell of fish will ever come out."

"It would be a shame," Nora said distractedly while she made sure her phone was in her blazer pocket. Gray's complexion looked great in the soft purple color.

Gray caught her eye and smiled. "You're right. Probably the only thing worse than microwaved fish is if you burn it too."

"It may surprise you, but I've made my thoughts on the subject of lunch-safe foods very well known," Nora said with a subdued grin as they headed down Frankford Ave.

"I'm sure Cynthia appreciates your desire to improve the workplace." She could see the edges of Gray's lips tipped upward, like she was trying not to laugh.

"You know me. I'm a regular cornerstone of workplace culture."

Gray did laugh then. It had a genuine, melodic cadence that rose above the sounds of construction that were inescapable on almost every block. Fishtown's growth was fantastic for being a real estate agent, but it was a nightmare to walk more than a few hundred feet without needing to navigate around closed sidewalks and piles of rubble or dirt.

It felt good, Nora realized, as she placed her hand on the small of Gray's back to guide her across the street, the sidewalk closed twenty feet ahead. She appreciated, in some small way, being able to acknowledge that this... openness was something new for her. She didn't know why she felt so comfortable doing it with Gray. She didn't want to pick it apart either, but it helped make the whole situation feel a little less intense. Like it was okay that she was changing her behavior. That she didn't have to pretend the last year hadn't happened, but that Gray wasn't going to hold it against her.

It was...

It was space. There was a feeling that, for the first time in a long time, she had room to grow. And that, if she did, all the threads of mistrust and insecurity and anger that were still very much a part of her core personality wouldn't unravel while she did it.

Nora didn't hear the vibration of Gray's phone until she eased it out of her pocket. With a quick look at the screen, she flashed Nora an apologetic smile. "I've gotta take this."

"Sure." Nora stopped on the street where Gray did, busying herself with checking email. It wasn't uncommon to hear another agent on a work call, so she thought nothing of sticking close by instead of heading the half block to the coffee shop alone.

Gray turned away from Nora and cushioned the phone between her ear and shoulder so that her hands were still free. "What's up?"

She watched as Gray quickly shifted again, placing the phone back in her hand and listening to whoever was talking.

"I can't—" The way Gray pinched her fingers against the bridge of her nose and took a deep breath made Nora think this wasn't a welcomed conversation.

More silence on Gray's side, like she was letting the other person run out of steam.

Nora moved to walk away and give Gray some breathing room for what was quickly beginning to seem like a private conversation, but Gray held up her finger, stopping Nora. "One sec," she mouthed.

A very un-Gray-like eye roll made Nora bite down on her own lip.

Finally, Gray sighed and ran her fingers through her hair before she leaned against the brick wall of the building they stood next to. "Willa, that's not going to work. You know I don't have a set schedule." Gray shut her eyes for long seconds before speaking again. "Why don't you come over tonight and we can discuss this in person?"

Nora, giving herself more credit than she probably deserved, was trying to focus on anything else, but the strained note in Gray's voice was hard to ignore.

When Gray slid her phone back in her pocket, she looked more worn down than Nora had ever seen her. The impulse to want to help propelled Nora to take a step forward. "You okay?"

Gray blew out a long breath, and so quickly that Nora wondered if she'd imagined it, the agitation on her face was gone, replaced with a light, breezy smile. "Just my sister, Willa. All good."

With the conversation apparently closed, given that Gray had started walking toward the coffee shop, Nora quickly fell into step beside her.

Now no longer felt like the best time to be asking for a favor. Instead, Nora held open the door to the coffee shop and gestured for Gray to head inside. For the first time in their tentative friendship, it felt like Gray was the one who could use a little understanding.

Nora, surprising herself as they stood in line, their shoulders brushing, realized that she was happy to be able to give it to her.

Chapter Twelve

Gray usually felt pretty adept at rolling with the punches of life. Today was not one of those days.

A client she'd been working with had been shown dozens of homes at this point, and still, they found a flaw in every one of them. Unfortunately, said client didn't have "perfect house" money, and their expectations could never live up to their price range.

Still, she would keep trying. All she needed to do was find a way to make it click. But they'd visited another four houses today that had just come on the market, and with the supply starting to stagnate as the colder months rolled in, their options were getting limited.

But, surprisingly, given that for the last few years, something related to work was always at the top of her priorities list, that was not her current biggest concern.

She hadn't allowed herself to think too seriously about the Post-It notes that she'd been leaving at odd hours on Nora's desk, whenever a thought struck her. They held inconsequential little snippets of information that she'd picked up over the years, most of them being some fact that made no sense in the broader context of a conversation.

This thing between them was growing, and now, Gray looked forward to creatively leaving the notes on Nora's desk without being seen, whenever one flitted through her mind. Today, she'd left a note informing Nora that there was one vending machine in Japan for every forty people. She'd missed lunch, and as she'd sat at her desk in the early afternoon, she was struck by a swift pang of hunger. It was a facet of her adolescence that she'd been lucky enough to stave off in her adult years. Another reminder of how much better her life was now.

So she'd written it down. And then when Nora had slipped on her light fall jacket, likely on her way to a showing, Gray had discreetly stuck the note on the back of Nora's computer monitor, so that just an inch of turquoise stuck out below.

But no, even a work crisis or her mounting attraction to her very off-limits co-worker was not what currently occupied Gray's attention.

That honor went to the tricolored ball of fur in her bed, which had made its home in a blanket, growing more comfortable in the last week.

"Aunt Becks is coming over, and we're going to be on our best behavior, yes?" she asked the small dog seriously.

The dog picked its head up and tilted an ear like she was listening, but there was very little else to distinguish agreement.

When the front door opened—because Becks, her best friend, always just walked in, and Gray had forgotten to mention the flight risk in the form of an eight-pound (possibly) Chihuahua mix that was now living with her—she was half a second behind the eager dog.

She bellowed, "Shut the door," from the top of the landing, but the dog was already halfway down the steps.

Maybe she should sign her up for agility training?

No. This was not a permanent situation, even if the dog's time in her home was growing more open-ended by the day.

Becks, to her credit, dropped down and immediately scooped the dog up. "Who's this little cutie?"

"That's S'mores," she said in a voice laced with exhaustion, even if looking at the little gremlin made her smile.

Three pairs of destroyed flip-flops. More puppy pads than she could count. A refusal to eat dinner unless Gray sat with her. To top it all off, she was like Velcro, and if Gray was in her home, they were within a foot of one another, ideally touching if S'mores had her way.

She appreciated the genuine look of confusion on Becks's face. "When did you get a dog?"

Gray looked at S'mores. She needed to hear this. "I didn't get a dog."

"Okay, but... I am holding a dog right now. That is in your house. That you are chasing around." Becks peered around the large living room in Gray's Philadelphia row home. The space, where a dining area blended into a living room, the kitchen through a doorway behind it, took up the majority of the first floor.

It wasn't like Becks didn't know about her sister, Willa. They'd been in one another's lives long enough for Becks to see Willa's personality play out in real time. Still, it always felt like Gray was being too judgmental, even if she was only giving the facts of the situation.

"I'll give you three guesses, and I bet you don't need the first two."

"Ah," Becks said with a knowing smile as she watched varying emotions flash across Gray's face. "Whimsical Willa strikes again."

"You know it." Gray took the bottle of wine in Becks's other hand and started walking toward the kitchen. "Thank you for being willing to hang out here. I've been gone all day, and I felt too guilty leaving her."

Becks followed, S'mores still happily cocooned in her arm. "I've been living out of a hotel and eating at restaurants every night, so this is actually perfect."

As a set designer, Becks split her time between Philadelphia (cheaper) and New York City (cooler), though she could also end up anywhere in the world depending on the job she booked. It was a lifestyle that was a little too unpredictable for Gray's own taste, but it worked for her best friend.

Most recently, Becks had been in Vancouver for a few weeks, and Gray was happy to finally have some face time to catch up.

Gray uncorked the bottle of wine and poured them both a glass. "How was the shoot?"

"It was... interesting."

It wasn't what Gray was expecting to hear, given Becks's initial reticence at doing the set design for a holiday movie. That was when Gray noticed the slight tinge on her friend's cheeks as she avoided eye contact.

"Rebecca Marie Anderson, what are you not telling me?"

Becks cuddled S'mores closer into her chest. "It's not a big deal."

"If you're being all shady about it, then it's absolutely a big deal."

Becks was one of those ineffably cool people. It was just a fact, like how the sky was blue or water was wet. Becks didn't blush. Ever.

Even when they'd dated, closer to a decade ago, Becks had seemed... unflappable. Beautiful. Confident. Driven.

They'd met working in a coffee shop while Gray was going to community college and Becks was in design school. It had been Gray's first—and only—relationship. When Becks had graduated a year before her and started traveling more for shoots, both their age and the instability of building something had taken its toll. Luckily, an amicable breakup left room for their friendship to grow.

Still, she wasn't going to let this go. She hadn't seen Becks this out of sorts in a very long time. "What's her name?"

"Tatum," Becks said with surprisingly little protest.

The name didn't ring any bells for Gray, but Becks was almost always working with different casts and crews on shoots.

"You can put S'mores down, you know. She does have legs." Almost invisible, under her long, soft fur, but given the speed at which she moved, they were definitely there.

Becks cuddled the dog closer to her chest. "I like her here."

"Sure," Gray agreed while she grabbed a charcuterie board from a cabinet before opening the fridge and pulling out a variety of cheeses, spreads, and fruit. "I was thinking I could just do something simple for dinner. We could hang out on the sofa and talk."

"Sounds perfect."

Gray pointed a knife at her friend. "Now tell me more."

Becks laughed and slid into one of the chairs on the island, across from where Gray worked. "Held up at knifepoint for information. God, I've missed this city."

Unlike Becks, Gray was elated that her friend was working on a cheesy holiday movie. Sure, it wasn't prestigious or necessarily cool in the eyes of a lot of people, but Gray loved them. She was unrepentant in her excitement about what brought her joy.

And that was formulaic romance plots set amidst a wintery, wondery backdrop.

Three weeks ago, Gray had been on a beach in Bermuda, and now, she was thinking about snow and Christmas trees and the holidays. Life was starting to feel a little more "blink and you miss it" with each passing year.

So, as far as Gray was concerned, this was absolutely information worth fighting for. And the way Becks was squirming in her chair, looking around like she hadn't been to Gray's house dozens of times...

Yeah, that warranted a few targeted questions.

* * *

An hour later, with the bottle of wine long gone and a sleepy S'mores cuddled between them, Becks pushed herself up into a seated position.

How she could sit up straight in pants that tight was beyond Gray's understanding, but maybe it wasn't for her to know.

"Now you need to tell me everything going on in your life," Becks said, grabbing an errant cracker from the charcuterie board and popping it in her mouth. She chewed thoughtfully, giving Gray a chance to speak.

"I'm still processing your torrid two-week romance with the literal freaking lead of the movie."

She liked how Becks blushed a little in spite of trying to look like she didn't care. "You make it sound so cloak-and-dagger. She's just not out. I was being... discreet."

"Sure," Gray said with a sympathetic nod. "I'm sure being the face of wholesome holiday television does not put traipsing around with a gay lover at the top of her list."

But still, it made Gray's lips tip downward. Becks deserved someone who would scream about their love from the rooftops. Who would proudly walk into a room with her and make her feel like the only woman there.

Becks would absolutely hate it if she said any of those things out loud, though.

"Will you see her again?" Gray asked, plucking a grape from the board and popping it in her mouth.

She forced herself to sit cross-legged, leaning her back against the plush sofa cushions that she'd spent months agonizing over. Luckily, she loved them. Which was a good thing, considering all the pressure she'd put on them, both emotionally and physically, this last year.

"I think maybe it was a moment in time, you know? My job's not changing any time soon, and neither is hers. And she's not out, so that makes things more difficult."

She and Becks had always been two peas in a pod because neither of them forced things. Life either worked or it didn't, so what Becks was saying made complete sense.

But, for some reason, it wasn't sitting well with Gray.

She was rolling Becks's words around, trying to work out exactly why when Becks's voice cut through the din. "So what about you? Don't think I'm not aware that you're keeping all of the attention on me."

Usually, Gray spoke freely—at least to Becks—about the good, the bad, and everything in between. But she was finding it hard to come up with the words to explain the last few weeks of her life.

"Well, I'm taking care of a dog, as you know," she said, giving S'mores a belly rub.

"Yeah, what's going on with Willa? Why'd she dump a dog at your house?" Becks turned her attention toward S'mores and cooed, "Because you're a perfect baby and I can't imagine anyone giving you up."

It was easy to gesture broadly around the room when she said, "That's just Willa. Never looking before she leaps."

Even if she felt protective of her younger sister, Gray was

perennially annoyed that Willa never could seem to get her shit together. She knew exactly who that reminded her of, but she rarely let herself go there.

"While I am all for you getting a dog, if that's what you want, I'm not sure why you're left holding the bag on this one." Becks shot her a sympathetic smile. "Holding all the bags, usually, but this one specifically."

Gray had asked herself that same question too.

"She and Keith took some kind of end-of-summer trip. I'm not really sure about the details."

Keith made Willa look like the world's most focused and responsible individual. Together, they were rash and impulsive, floating through life like there were zero consequences.

"So they decided to adopt a dog on this trip? To live with them in their fourth-floor walk-up that I know for a fact doesn't allow pets?"

Willa had moved in with Keith three months ago, after they'd been dating for less than that at the time. Gray had assumed it was a horrible idea, but still, she'd helped her sister move in. Becks had been between shoots at the time, and tagged along to help.

The giant *NO PETS* signs in the lobby and on each floor they passed had really solidified the fact that their landlord wasn't going to be the type to make exceptions on this front.

Gray groaned. The whole situation was so Willa.

"Willa says they found her along the highway."

It had been like this since they were kids. Willa always brought home strays, and it became Gray's problem to deal with them.

Becks studied her carefully. "So... what's the play here?"

Gray instinctively put her hand on S'mores's stomach. "Well, it's not like I can drive back to Tennessee and try to find her owner, if she was in fact just lost and not abandoned."

If that was even the correct state, given Willa's story had changed a few times during her various retellings. Life with Willa contained a lot of half-truths, which had made Gray an expert at reading between the lines.

"That makes sense. But, you know"—Becks's voice was soft, in that way she used when Gray knew she was trying to be gentle—"it's not your job to clean up after her."

"But it's not S'mores's fault that my sister is irresponsible."

There, she'd said it. Willa was irresponsible, and there was no way around it. Dropping S'mores off last week with no plan as to what would come next was just another thing in a long line of seemingly disconnected decisions—if Gray could call them that—that made up how Willa lived her life.

So Gray had been running herself ragged to get back home every few hours between showings and work, making sure that S'mores was doing okay. It wasn't a good forever plan, but she'd never been good at thinking about things in absolute terms.

S'mores was here now, and they were figuring things out.

Becks nodded and then squeezed Gray's hand before leaning back against the sofa. She knew enough not to continue pushing the Willa conversation.

"How are things going with your bitchy co-worker?" They'd managed a FaceTime call during the few hours after Gray had returned and Becks had been set to leave for Vancouver, but nothing more meaningful since then.

Gray hadn't gotten into the night of the storm with Becks, considering she hadn't quite decided how she'd felt about discussing it the same day she'd woken up in Nora's bed. Unfortunately, time hadn't solidified her feelings on that front.

As she was finding out pretty quickly, Nora Gallagher was not at all like she'd expected.

"She's decidedly less bitchy since returning," Gray said after she'd spent a few seconds mulling over her answer.

Gray didn't want to pick apart why she was acting so guarded about the whole thing.

Apparently, her refusal to be introspective was a common theme tonight.

They had discussed Nora at length over the last year, at random times when she'd come up. Gray never gossiped with her co-workers, but Becks was a safe place to dump all the emotional turmoil that she needed to process before it leaked out in unhealthy ways.

So why, as she looked at her closest friend, who was staring back at her with a curious look, didn't she want to open the valve and take some pressure off?

Becks didn't seem to share her reticence at diving in. "Did you get The Story?"

'The Story,' as they referred to it, was whatever had happened to make Nora Gallagher more of a cardboard cutout wrapped in barbed wire than an actual person. It had been fun to speculate on, once upon a time, but Gray no longer felt the flutter of excitement that Becks was bringing it up.

Gray shook her head. "I did not. We did hang out together a couple of times, though."

Becks squinted. "Why are you being so cagey?"

"I'm not being cagey. I literally just told you that we hung out," Gray defended.

Becks blew out a breath and ran her hand through her long, dark hair while she collected her thoughts. The look of curiosity was back when she leveled her hazel eyes in Gray's direction. "You spent five days and a natural disaster with quite possibly the most buttoned-up person either of us have ever met. And you're going to, with a straight face, hit me with a 'we hung out.'"

S'mores's unexpected presence in Gray's life had taken some of her focus off of Nora, but Becks was pulling her back into it, where, Gray had to accept, it had been lingering below the surface, just waiting to bubble up.

When she didn't respond, Becks pushed again. "You're really not going to tell me? I've been waiting to hear about this for literal weeks."

"If you've been wondering this for weeks, then why did you wait to ask me?" A flare of frustration slipped out, but Becks was completely unaffected by it.

She bounced up on her knees before leaning back on her heels, looking at Gray expectantly. "Because you can't lie to me in person."

Gray rolled her eyes, knowing how true the statement was. She was already wilting like a flower in the hot sun. "I'm not trying to lie to you. I just... don't know exactly how I feel."

"Well, isn't it great that you have a person here who wants to work out all those messy, complicated feelings with you? Imagine that."

"It's just weird," Gray admitted, the valve on her feelings finally starting to loosen.

"I mean... it's not like you guys had sex or something." Gray looked at Becks, who stared back, hazel eyes growing wide like saucers. "Holy shit. Did you two sleep together?"

The cap on the valve finally blew from the pressure.

"In the actual definition of the term, yes. We did sleep in the same bed together." It felt good to say it, to acknowledge what had happened. The second the words pushed out like steam escaping, she realized how much she'd needed to say them.

Becks dropped her hand down to S'mores' chest, like she was getting ready to give her CPR. "How? Why? Tell me everything."

"It just sort of happened. The storm was coming, and Nora didn't seem to be handling it well. I'd never seen her look like that before, like a gust of wind would blow her over."

"Weird example to use when hurricane-force winds are in play, but sure," Becks teased, which was her way of urging Gray to continue.

"Shut up," she said lovingly. "So, I ended up in her room. It was all going fine, and then the power went out."

"And you probably did not like that."

Gray nodded, thankful for all the things that Becks just knew about her, without the need for an extra explanation. "Exactly."

"So what happened?"

"I lit the emergency candles and grabbed my laptop. I had some shows downloaded, which I figured we could watch. So... I got on her bed and..." Her words tapered off while she tried to figure out how to explain it. She went for simplicity. "And we fell asleep. It was all very PG, but, like... I was not expecting it."

Logically, it all made sense, the way that things had played out.

And Gray had slept in bed, platonically or otherwise, with many people before. It didn't have to *mean* anything, especially given the circumstances that had led them there.

Which was why it was so frustrating that she couldn't shake how good it had felt, and how often she had forced herself not to think about how good it would feel if it happened again.

"And..."

"And what?" Gray asked, her body deflating now that the pressure had escaped.

"Did you guys talk about it?"

"Not really? I mean, she thanked me the next morning for being so nice about the whole situation."

"That's already exceeding my expectations of her," Becks

said seriously. "So, what's the problem? Is she being standoffish again now that you're back?"

Gray shook her head. "She's being surprisingly..."

"What?"

"Great?" Gray admitted, letting the word roll around between them. "It seems like she's really trying."

Becks leaned back on her heels again, putting some extra space between them so she could look at Gray. "Permission to speak freely?"

They'd done this bit since working at the coffee shop together, when they'd become manager and assistant manager.

Gray saluted her, enjoying the bit of normalcy amidst the chaos she'd felt the last few weeks. "Permission granted."

"Sometimes, your standard for 'great' can be different from the average person's. Between your parents and Willa, the bar is set pretty low. So it's awesome that Nora's turning over a new leaf, but I wouldn't be blinded by her finally acting like a functional human."

It was the soft, sympathetic look that Becks gave her that made Gray feel like she was going to cry, the truth of her friend's statement weighing her down like an invisible anchor.

"I know. It's just..."

"I love that you are open to giving her a second chance. Quite frankly, I'm more than a little surprised, but I don't want you to move through the world not trusting anyone. I just think that if she is serious, let her keep showing up, and take what she does at face value. Don't let the fact that you have a crush on her complicate the situation."

"I don't have a crush on her," she said in a voice so unconvincing she almost laughed. There was no point in denying it, especially to Becks of all people. "Okay, so maybe I have a little crush on her."

"We can't help who we're attracted to, but...."

"You know I'd never act on it. Not at work."

Becks nodded sympathetically, though Gray didn't miss the flare of anger in her eyes. "I get why you feel that way. And while I'm obviously not against workplace romances," she said with a self-deprecating smile, "I understand why you may not want to go down that path."

"To put it mildly."

Becks's eyes narrowed into almost slits, her voice dropping to a venomous growl that Gray so appreciated when it was in her defense. "All that shit with Paul was not your fault. He was a horrible person who was jealous of your success, and he tried to cut you down to his level instead of rising up to meet you."

Intellectually, she knew that, but it still didn't calm the wave of anxiety that rolled through her. It was why she'd left her last job, when the gossip had become too much for her to handle.

She'd been at her last agency for six months when Paul had asked her out. He'd flirted, been helpful at first, had played the part perfectly of someone who'd just wanted to get to know her. Still, dating someone she'd be working with every day had felt messy. She didn't like complicated, so she'd tried to take things slowly. Get to know him but still ensure that, if things didn't work out, there wouldn't be any fallout.

It was easy to see in retrospect—and with a clarity that never came when she was in the eye of the storm—that she and Paul were not destined for anything. But he'd shown her the best version of himself, even if it was fake, and the second she didn't fit his expectations of her, their relationship had devolved.

At the time, she'd wanted to trust him. She was finally getting to a stable place in her life, where she felt like she had enough control over her environment to trust a little more freely, to open herself up to the possibility of something more with someone.

Their few fledgling dates had come during the time when Gray's star, professionally, was on the rise. She'd found her footing, and even at a large agency like Brenneman Brothers, she was making progress.

He hadn't liked that.

And when she'd told him she felt like they should just be friends, he hadn't liked that either.

Maybe if she'd been more honest, things would have played out differently. If she'd told him that she'd started to feel uncomfortable around him, that the little jabs he made about her appearance or anything unrelated to her dedication and drive as the reason she was closing deals were wearing thin.

But, at the time, she hadn't understood why she'd felt the way she had. She couldn't articulate—couldn't pinpoint—that his resentment, simmering below the surface and starting to spill over, was morphing her initial interest in him into contempt.

All she'd known was that she was doing well, and for some reason, she felt badly about it.

The whispers had started a few weeks after. It was all ambiguous at first. A few people stared at her a little longer than normal as she made her coffee in the kitchen area. A scoff in an agent-wide meeting when her numbers were released had caused a scuttle of snickers in the otherwise quiet room.

Finally, another woman who worked at Brenneman Brothers, Priya, had caught her as she was heading to her car one day, about a block away from the office.

"I just wanted you to know," Priya said, after she'd explained that there was a rumor circulating that she was sleeping with Jonathan Brenneman, one of the founders of the agency. Thirty-five years her senior. Her boss. Married with three adult children almost the same age as Gray.

She'd been struck dumb by the idea, but she'd thanked Priya profusely and then gone home and cried on her sofa for hours, all the looks and sneers and stilled conversation when she walked into a room now making sense.

They'd all thought she was sleeping her way to the top. At worst, that he was padding her numbers in some sort of sexual favor quid pro quo. At best, maybe that Jonathan was passing her off easy wins instead of divvying out the new leads in a round-robin format when new clients came in without a specific agent in mind.

Either way, her confidence had popped like a balloon.

It had been so easy, she'd realized, for people to want to believe the worst. For them to accept this narrative about her. That they wanted to like themselves better for it and dislike her more because of it.

No one had even asked if it was true. Which, a week later, she'd discovered—thanks to Priya again—was because Paul had been circulating a very casual though convincing story around the office.

Two days after that, she'd been called into Jonathan's office, where he'd said off-handedly, like he was discussing the weather, that they may as well commit the crime if they were going to be punished for it. She'd wanted to punch out his too-white teeth.

It was just another example of the people in her life who were supposed to protect her letting her down. That had been a difficult lesson to learn, that there truly was no one except herself that she could depend on.

"Why am I such a bad judge of character?" she lamented, mostly to herself.

"Hey, no." She felt Becks's hands, one braced on each of

her shoulders. "You are sweet and kind and funny. I love those things about you. And when you show them to other people, they do too. Some people are just shitty human beings. That has nothing to do with you."

Gray nodded but didn't say anything.

"And I'm glad that you and Nora are finding some common ground. Just... be careful. Yeah?" There was a tenderness in Becks's voice that had never been a given for Gray growing up.

Launching herself forward, she wrapped her arms around Becks and squeezed. "You're an amazing friend. Thank you."

Later that night, as she stared up at her ceiling, with S'mores snuggled between her legs like they'd always slept this way, she tried to absorb Becks's words. To sit with them and internalize their meaning.

Nothing had really changed, if she thought about it, except that she and Nora had found a more solid footing. Her attraction for the other woman had always been there, and she'd dealt with it well so far. And Nora was more open than she'd been in the past, but Gray had just barely scratched the surface on knowing her.

So... yeah. She just needed to slow down. Focus on work. Figure out what to do with S'mores. Take things one day at a time.

Because, the truth was, she'd been here before. To a place where she'd felt stable enough to open herself up after a lifetime of hodgepodge-ing together the pieces of the person she'd wanted to become. The second she had, it seemed like life wanted to kick her right back toward the person she'd been.

Chapter Thirteen

Today was going to be difficult, but still, Nora found that, for the first time in years, she didn't want to hide from it.

A day, she was finding, could be a lot of things to a lot of different people. For her, October 21 had been marred by sadness—and more than a little anger—for the last five years.

It was also Gray's anniversary date for starting at Philly Finds.

So Nora was committed to doing today differently.

Acknowledging Gray's work anniversary didn't have to be a big deal, and it was the least she could do to rectify her behavior from last year. And maybe it gave her a nice distraction from thinking about what this day usually meant to her.

So, instead of wallowing, she'd gone to an early morning yoga class and then taken a long walk around her neighborhood.

By the time she reached the office, she was buzzing with the optimism that only came from an endorphin rush—and maybe the red eye she'd downed at the coffee shop.

Nora placed a cup, the same order Gray had gotten a few weeks ago, on her desk. "Congrats."

Gray's hand reached out for the coffee cup with an appreciative smile at the same time that she asked, "What are you congratulating me on?"

"Is today not your one-year work anniversary?" Nora asked, knowing she wasn't wrong. She'd never get this date wrong.

"Oh, right," Gray said, leaning back in her chair and wrapping her fingers around the paper cup. She sat, lost in what looked like thought for a few seconds.

Nora leaned on the edge of Gray's desk and caught her eye. "Are you doing okay?"

They'd done this—quick chats at Gray's desk—at sporadic intervals since coming back from Bermuda. Usually it was Nora who initiated them, but it wasn't until today that she felt like she may actually be intruding.

When Nora lifted her brow in concern, Gray waved her off and took a long sip of her coffee.

It was only seconds, but Nora had a chance to watch Gray's expression morph across her face.

There was something off about her. There had been for the last week or so. They hadn't discussed it, but her usually bubbly personality was muted.

Finally, Gray seemed to answer the question she'd just remembered being asked. "I'm just tired. My sister got a dog, which she can't keep, so now I have a dog."

"That sounds... unexpected." Nora generally hated surprises, which was probably not a surprise to anyone who'd ever met her.

A puff of air pushed out of Gray's pursed lips. "It was, but that's just Willa. It's what she was calling me about last week, actually. The day we grabbed coffee."

"Got it. How are you doing with the unexpected addition to your life?"

"This helps." Gray tipped her coffee cup toward Nora before taking a long, indulgent sip. "Thank you, by the way. I should have led with that."

She caught Gray's brown eyes again, noting the faint circles under them. "I figured we can't change the past, but I'd like to change the tone of our interactions on this day."

And then she saw, in real time, as Gray's eyes sparked to life. There was that glint in them that Nora so appreciated, like she was taking everything in all at once.

Nora liked being the one who caused it, even as Gray teased her, "Because on this day last year, you berated me for our run-in."

"I think 'berated' is a slightly strong word," Nora defended herself before she quickly acquiesced, "But yes, I was not as welcoming as I could have been that day. I'm genuinely sorry for that."

"What a difference a year makes," Gray mused, leaning forward in her chair.

"And as for last year..."

Nora had thought about having this conversation multiple times in the last week. She wasn't quite ready for it, but she was finding that she didn't want to continue keeping everything bottled up.

That route worked—until it didn't.

She'd spent so long insulating herself that she hadn't realized how much her life had stagnated for the sake of self-protection.

It wasn't like she was looking to launch herself off an emotional cliff, but her first tastes of real human interaction in a long time were more than a little enticing.

Gray made it all feel easy, like it was as simple as putting one foot in front of another instead of running a marathon.

Gray's coffee cup was poised just below her full lips, her brows drawn close together while she studied Nora. "What about last year?"

"This is the anniversary of the date I lost my parents."

Emotion flickered across Gray's face before she encircled Nora's hand in her own. "Oh, Nora. I'm so sorry."

The touch was warm. It sparked across Nora's skin and up her wrist, holding her in place.

It wasn't that she talked about it often, but she could do it without the full weight of emotion in her voice. "I appreciate that. My relationship with my parents was complicated, but it was still an unexpected loss."

Gray nodded and squeezed at Nora's hand. "I appreciate you trusting me enough to tell me."

And that was the strangest thing about all of this. She did trust Gray, even though she had no objective reason to feel that way. In Bermuda, when Gray had been there for her, it had planted a seed that had started to sprout, pushing through a solid wall and creating cracks in Nora's foundation.

Pretending it hadn't was starting to feel like she was trying to merge two competing philosophies in a way that they'd never fit.

She had to pick one.

"I just..." She fumbled over her words, looking up to catch Gray's eyes, which were intently focused on her in a way that made the rest of the office melt away. It pushed her to continue. "I just didn't want you to think that last year had anything to do with you. About me not wanting you here."

The vulnerability in her voice would have embarrassed her a few months ago, like she was begging someone to take advantage of her admission. To use it against her and cut her down when she was at her most exposed.

Today, it felt a little bit like the loosening of another chain that was keeping her tethered to the past.

Gray's phone alarm buzzed, breaking the moment as reality washed over Nora.

Instead of looking away, Gray held her gaze and squeezed her hand again. "Thank you for telling me."

"Morning meeting calls," Nora said, letting the last wisps of the weight of the moment drop away, returning her to the chatter in the office.

And even though the office wasn't her favorite place, it somehow felt softer when she became aware of it again. The lights didn't feel as bright and glaring, like she was constantly on display. The precise layout felt less like a maze to wander through without attracting attention and more like a focused path. Even the noises from her co-workers, who were all making their way to the conference room, didn't grate on her like they usually did. It was a pleasant buzz of activity humming around her, more like white noise instead of nails dragging down a chalkboard.

It felt, at least a little bit, like she was finally waking up.

Lately, Nora's brain kept sticking on feeling like she'd missed so much time. It was hard to remember the last time she'd actually enjoyed fall. Not since the death of her parents, sure, but even before that.

What had she been doing?

She couldn't remember doing anything festive with Andrea in the four years they'd been together. Not a pumpkin patch or a stroll to look at the leaves or a Christmas market.

The way people decorated their lives with memories, she'd decorated hers with...

Nothing significant came to mind.

When she looked back, the entire relationship felt a lot like a blank space, and she was trying to figure out if that was because she'd blocked everything out or if it really didn't have the rose-colored tint of perfection she'd let herself believe in at the time.

Gray, in spite of trying to figure out how to take care of an unexpected puppy and working more concurrent deals than Nora had thought was possible, didn't seem to have that same issue.

Which was how, a week after the anniversary of her parents' death, Nora found herself walking to the coffee shop with Gray, something that had become a somewhat regular ritual between them.

"What are you going to dress up for on Halloween?" Gray asked, her breath visible in the unseasonably cold air.

Nora lifted an eyebrow. "Nothing?" She could honestly say the thought hadn't even crossed her mind.

She wasn't a monster, though. The big bag of candy she'd be putting out was already sitting on her kitchen table.

Gray surveyed her, though she continued to walk quickly. "I'm going to say you go for more of the classic costumes than something topical."

"I honestly don't think I've worn a Halloween costume since college." And even then, it had been a couple's costume that her first real girlfriend, Chelsea, had insisted on.

Gray stopped and spun around before she stepped in front of Nora.

It all happened so fast that Nora had to brace herself to stop the imminent collision, one of her hands falling against Gray's shoulder.

"Since college?" The sincere incredulity in her voice was almost cute.

Nora shrugged. "I didn't think that was strange. I don't have kids, and I don't go to Halloween parties. Why would I dress up?"

Gray's voice was a mix of exasperation and confusion. "Because it's fun?"

"It's fun if you enjoy dressing up," Nora pointed out.

"And you don't?" Big, brown eyes had grown impossibly wider, like Gray genuinely couldn't understand what she was hearing.

"I don't think I give it that much thought."

"You dress up for work." Gray's stare scanned down Nora's body, her outfit invisible under her peacoat. When Gray's eyes moved back up to meet Nora's, there was a faint blush from the cold tinging her cheeks.

"That's different."

Gray cocked her head to the side. "Is it, though? Really? You put on a costume every day to showcase something you want the world to see."

"I don't—"

Gray's arm looped through hers, pulling Nora forward. "We need to walk. I cannot keep standing here when it's so cold."

"Seems like you didn't do the best job with your *costume* planning today," Nora teased as Gray led her down the sidewalk.

They were only a block from heat and caffeine, and truly, stopping to have that asinine conversation had not been either of their smartest moves.

"S'mores chewed the arm on my winter coat," Gray said as they reached the entrance to the coffee shop. Nora only realized their arms were still linked when Gray separated them to open the door, and she missed the warmth of body contact. "So," Gray said, ushering Nora inside, "that's my defense. I threw it on the sofa when I came home last night, and when I woke up this morning, she'd mangled one of the arms like it was her favorite chew toy."

"Sounds like a handful," Nora said, trying to hide her smile.

"That's one way to say it. 'Free to a good home' is more along the lines of what I was thinking." Gray grinned as she made the comment, probably because they both knew that would never happen. There was a soft, sweet look that Gray got on her face whenever she talked about S'mores, even if it was to tell Nora that she'd chewed something up.

They got in a line six people deep—apparently everyone had had the same idea today—and waited their turn. It was nice, Nora realized, to do something as mundane as grab a coffee during the workday and catch up with someone.

They took a step forward. "You should bring S'mores into the office."

Gray tilted her face, eyes narrowing. "I'm not sure it's a pet-friendly workplace."

"It's worth asking. Sometimes dogs chew things because they're bored. S'mores probably wants your attention, or she needs more stimulation."

"I really don't get the vibe that Cynthia will go for it. And what about showings? Or if someone coming in for a closing is allergic to dogs? Or if someone on the team is allergic?" It was surprising, the amount of rebuttals Gray was rattling off, like she'd already considered this possibility but had talked herself out of it. "Plus, I don't have any space near my desk."

"I think you just don't want to subject her to the smell of microwaved fish."

Gray laughed then, the line between her brow relaxing. "Honestly, she'd probably love it."

"You can put a little pen up next to my desk if you want. It's farthest away from everyone on the team and from the conference room."

Nora didn't know what to make of the quick little inhale of sound that came from Gray before she said, "Oh."

It wasn't a big deal. S'mores needed a place to hang out, and she was in and out of the office anyway. That settled things in her mind. "Plus, I've been looking for a security system."

Gray cocked her head to the side, a puzzled expression on her face. "Security system?"

"Someone keeps leaving notes on my desk. I'm hoping the perpetrator will be scared off by a ferocious guard dog."

Her own lips tipped into a smile as she let the words settle between them, and she watched as Gray's confusion morphed into a devious smirk that made her look like a gleeful kid who was proud of what they'd gotten away with.

"I mean, it would be fair for her to earn her keep," Gray said as they moved up another place in line.

Nora affixed her eyes to the menu board that she already had memorized. "Definitely."

Gray looked toward the menu and clasped her hands together. Nora could feel her shifting her weight onto her tiptoes. "But, it seems like whoever's doing that is probably pretty cunning."

"It's a regular *Thomas Crown Affair*," Nora said with a smile that she couldn't hold back, which wasn't a common occurrence in her life, even if it had been happening more frequently.

"I think S'mores would look great as a bank robber."

These games, or whatever they did, entertained Nora. Like when they'd pretended to be strangers in Bermuda. Or now, when Gray refused to confess to being the Post-It Bandit. She wondered if, come Christmas, they'd be having a very serious conversation about Santa Claus and the route he'd be taking around the world.

The thought stopped her cold. She didn't really plan for the future, especially where other people were concerned. She'd just started to assume—without realizing it until this moment—that Gray would continue to be around. That they'd grow closer. Share more jokes. Build a stronger rapport.

The realization was disconcerting at first pass, and as they took another step forward, she let the idea simmer.

Would it be so bad? To assume that she and Gray would continue their friendship?

Whether it was bad or not, she realized that she wanted it. The stability of whatever this was had become important to her. She assumed it was because she'd gone so long without real human connection that it was a little overwhelming, but accepting it didn't strike fear into her or make her freeze up the way it would have a few months ago.

And whatever it was, she didn't need to pick it all apart or analyze every angle in search of immediate understanding.

Nora watched as the last person in front of them placed their order before she pulled herself out of her own head and smiled at Gray. "And, pray tell, what is the guard dog in question going to be for Halloween? Dressing up seems like a very important tradition in your family."

The brightness in Gray's eyes was arresting, all of it focused on Nora when she said, "You'll just have to come over Thursday for trick-or-treating to find out."

Chapter Fourteen

Gray – 5:15 p.m.

> Do you remember when we discussed me not simping over my co-worker?

Becks Anderson – 5:15 p.m.

> Sure do.

Becks Anderson – 5:15 p.m.

> Why?

Gray – 5:15 p.m.

> Because I am... um... not doing a great job at that. I just needed to admit it to someone.

S'mores, aware that the vibe was off, was following her around the house while Gray eyed her home from the perspective of an outsider.

Why had she invited Nora over?

Well, she knew the answer to that question.

Because Nora was, with each passing day, becoming more of a fixture in Gray's life—and her thoughts.

And then she'd had to go ahead and offer to let S'mores hang out at her desk?

Gray had been a goner.

Becks Anderson – 5:16 p.m.

What have you done?

Gray – 5:16 p.m.

I invited her over tonight to hand out Halloween candy.

Becks Anderson – 5:16 p.m.

That seems fine?

Well, yes, when she'd asked, it had seemed fine. That was, until she'd had a sex dream about Nora last night. She didn't really know how she was supposed to come back from something like that.

It had been so vivid, had felt so real that Gray could barely make eye contact with Nora at the office today. The last time she'd seen those eyes, it had been in her dreams, and they'd been staring intently into Gray's own, fire melting through the icy blue.

When Nora had asked whether Cynthia had given the go-ahead on bringing S'mores in, Gray's face had flamed just from hearing the pitch of her voice, remembering how it had sounded last night in her imagination, as Nora came in her mouth, thighs pressed around Gray's head.

This morning, she'd expected to have scratches down her back from where she'd dreamt Nora's nails had scraped across her shoulders, her body writhing under Gray's tongue.

It had been so long since she'd kissed someone. In her dreams, there'd been a lot of that too. Soft kisses. Sensual kisses. Heated kisses that made Gray's head spin.

Nora had the best lips, and Gray couldn't stop her mind from thinking back to how she'd imagined them mapping a path across her body in the darkness, both of them sweat-slicked and panting as her hands had wrapped through Nora's hair and she'd begged for mercy.

Even now, heat still pooled in her stomach, low and instinctive.

So... yeah.

When the actual, real-life Nora she was becoming friends with had asked if they were still on for tonight, her focus had flickered across the blooms of color Gray knew were snaking around her chest and neck.

Gray could only nod, give a quick thumbs-up, and flee from the office.

That had been an hour ago, and she still couldn't shake the feeling that Nora, when the protective façade—and clothing—were stripped away, was going to spell all kinds of trouble for her.

But that wasn't going to happen.

Nora was more present than Gray had ever seen, but there was still a wall. And, Nora's issues aside, Gray was working through a whole slew of her own.

She knew that what had happened at Brenneman Brothers hadn't been her fault. Still, she blamed herself for setting off a series of events that she never should have set in motion.

What was it that they always say? It's good until it isn't.

Becks Anderson – 5:19 p.m.

Gray?

Gray – 5:19 p.m.

I'm fine. Nothing to worry about.

Becks Anderson – 5:19 p.m.

I'm on the West Coast, so I'll be on set until late your time, but I can talk later if you need? Or tomorrow?

She smiled down at her phone. Even just knowing that she could be honest with someone, and that it was okay not to have it all figured out, helped quell the balloon inflating in her stomach.

Gray – 5:19 p.m.

It's okay. I just had a moment of panic. Can't wait to hear all about the shoot when you get back!

This was going to be fine. She was going to be completely fine.

* * *

It wasn't fine.

Nora arrived at 5:45 p.m. on the dot, just like they'd discussed.

But when Gray opened the door, all her best laid plans fell apart. Maybe she'd dreamt about the softness of Nora's lips against her own, but she'd gotten the visual spot-on, right down to a full lower lip that was begging for Gray to suck between her teeth.

"Hi," Nora said when the door opened, looking soft and sweet and like all kinds of trouble for Gray. She'd dressed down since work, in a dark blue sweater and a pair of light-washed jeans that accentuated her long legs and, naturally, pulled Gray's focus to them.

Which... didn't seem to be quite the giveaway she'd expected, since Nora was doing the same thing, her eyes scanning down Gray's body while Gray's tracked upward.

Her throat went dry when she saw how Nora was taking her in, from the wide legs of her pants up to the coverall's zipper that began low on her stomach.

She waited, still for seconds, until Nora's eyes lifted all the way up past the costume and settled on the aviators balanced on Gray's head. Sunglasses at dusk hadn't been her best idea, and even if she'd wanted to have them on for the full effect, getting to see Nora's appraising stare was worth it.

"I didn't peg you as a *Top Gun* fan," Nora finally said, her lips tipped into a smile. Her hands were full, a bag of candy in one and what looked like a bottle of sparkling rosé in the other.

Gray brushed her hands down the olive-green suit before she stepped to the side to let Nora in. The cold front had broken the day before, and it would be the perfect night to sit on the stoop and hand out candy. "I used to have a babysitter who loved the movie. We'd watch it all the time." Maybe 'babysitter' wasn't the right word, but it was the easiest one to share without more explanation.

Nora looked at her curiously but followed Gray into the house.

"Would you like a glass?" Gray said, holding up the bottle and heading toward the kitchen.

"Sure." Nora followed until she stopped to look at the photos on Gray's living room wall.

"You can take a look around if you'd like." Gray needed

space, a few seconds to compose herself, given how her body wanted to betray her whenever Nora walked into a room.

Especially when it seemed that Nora had been staring at her almost unabashedly seconds ago, her brows drawn down in focus—exactly how Gray had imagined them last night.

As she uncorked the bottle, she realized that in all of her dream-related anxiety, she'd barely given Ms. Gibson, the inspiration for her Halloween costume, a single thought. Not that she was on Gray's mind a lot, but she'd been popping up more and more in her memory over the last month.

She'd loved her afternoons with Ms. Gibson, a stable parental figure who'd been a fixture in her life for the few years they'd lived in the apartment in Old City, before the neighborhood had become a hotbed of arts and entertainment and her parents had picked them up and moved.

They'd gone to West Philadelphia after that, a distance that might as well have been across the country for a twelve-year-old with a bad sense of direction.

She didn't see Ms. Gibson again, but she still remembered the smell of her apartment. Cinnamon mingled with tobacco, a scent that still made her nostalgic twenty years later.

It was Ms. Gibson who'd started taking her to the library after Gray had read all the books in her neighbor's apartment.

Sometimes, they'd watch VHS tapes after school, when Gray would wander over unannounced and simply let herself in. While most kids loved after-school cartoons, Gray was obsessed with anything from the eighties. She was a captive audience, sitting on Ms. Gibson's floor with a bowl of Cheez-Its and focusing with rapt attention on the screen.

She didn't know who she would have become if not for those four years spent in an apartment that was identical to her own and yet so different. Her own home felt like it was filled with her parents' things, and she'd always felt like a bit of an outsider.

Not that her parents spent a lot of time at home anyway. She was a latchkey kid before she knew what that was, with a key she wore around her neck to unlock the door when she came home from school. Willa, five years younger, wasn't often at Ms. Gibson's house until the last year in Old City. She wondered if her sister even remembered their neighbor.

When they'd moved across the city, everything had changed. Willa was seven, and with no social network in the neighborhood, Gray had become the babysitter—the parental figure in her younger sister's life.

And at twelve, that wasn't a mantle she'd been looking to take on quite yet.

That was the first time that Gray had understood the world was going to try and tell her who it wanted her to be.

The first year after they moved, she'd been the weird, quiet kid in class who'd read a lot. Then she'd hit puberty. And that was the second time she discovered that the world wanted to tell her who she was. As her chest had come in, it was like people had assumed it had taken the place of her brain.

When people had started talking to her more, it wasn't to ask what book she was reading.

So she'd learned to play along.

Becks was the first person to break down that wall, as they'd worked side by side and developed what Gray had felt was her first real friendship. It gave her a sense of belonging she hadn't felt since those days sitting on Ms. Gibson's floor, a pile of books spread out around her.

As she poured the second glass of rosé, Nora's quiet footsteps echoed in the kitchen.

"Given your self-professed love for Halloween, I was a little surprised you didn't wear your costume to work." Nora smiled wryly, setting off a whole new wave of stomach flutters for Gray.

That had been the plan. Except waking up with Nora's name on her lips and a pleasant but excruciating tightness in her center hadn't boded well for doing anything except existing on autopilot.

Gray handed her a glass. "I don't know if my clients would have appreciated that."

Nora made a small sound, like she was imagining how that would have played out before she looked around the kitchen. "Where's S'mores?"

S'mores, now solidly a member of the Ferris family, hadn't been bothered to get up and assess the guest in their midst. Gray wondered what that felt like, since every ounce of her focus was trained on Nora.

Her gaze flicked upward to the ceiling. "Sleeping upstairs on my bed I'd assume."

"She's really settled in here."

"We're working on it," Gray admitted, smiling in spite of the unexpected intrusion. She liked S'mores, tiny snores and all.

Nora placed her wineglass on the counter and ran her finger along the stem. "So she's staying?"

Gray hadn't admitted it yet, but they both knew it was the truth. "Yes."

They stood mirroring one another, except that Gray held her wineglass up to her lips and took an indulgent sip.

Nora took a long look around the kitchen, which Gray had redone herself when she'd moved in. "I love your place, by the way."

Home meant different things to different people, and for Gray, it had been having a place to call her own, where she wouldn't be uprooted at someone else's whim. By her parents.

From landlords raising rent. It was part of why she loved being a Realtor so much—having the ability to give that type of security to someone else.

She put her glass down when she realized she was almost halfway through it. "Thank you."

"You own?"

Gray nodded. "I bought it four years ago."

Nora made another sound. "Impressive."

"I mean... I figured I should actually experience what my clients go through."

"Many people work in professions they don't take part in, whether by choice or by lack of having the luxury."

It felt like Gray was starting to edge closer to a point of friction, but she wasn't sure where the boundary was. "Do you own?"

"I rent," Nora said before she took a sip of her wine, looking anywhere but at Gray. "I considered buying for a while, but my plans sort of changed."

"Feels like there's a story there," Gray pushed. It was hard to temper her curiosity where Nora was concerned.

Clearing her throat, Nora stood up a little straighter. "I was in a relationship, and I thought we were going to buy a house together. It didn't work out, obviously."

"Their loss," Gray said seriously.

Nora's gaze flicked down to her lips before she drew her focus upward and met Gray's stare. "You don't know that."

She wondered if Nora felt it too. How the room was warmer than it had been moments ago. The way it felt like they were connected by an invisible string, drawing them closer together. Gray could still remember how Nora's lips had tasted in her dream, sweet like cinnamon.

Her stomach exploded with butterflies. She couldn't look

away as the moment shifted into something she wasn't expecting to actually happen.

The knock on her front door sounded like a bomb going off.

Nora shifted backward fluidly, her hand braced against the counter's edge. Her face was flushed, with splotches of color disappearing into the V-neck of her sweater, and all Gray could think about was feeling that heat with her lips.

"We should get that," Gray breathed into the space between them, which felt like organic matter, growing and shrinking as the seconds rolled on.

"We should." Nora didn't move.

Gray blinked once, then twice, shaking herself back to reality.

"They'll probably egg the house if I don't go out there." Gray managed a smile, finally taking a step back to truly put space between them.

"Probably," Nora said, her voice laced with a low rasp that was not helping Gray's control.

She grabbed the bowl of candy on the counter to give to the trick-or-treaters. When she reached the hallway that connected the kitchen to the living room, she stopped and turned around. "You coming?"

Nora nodded wordlessly and followed her through the house.

Yeah. This was going to be a long night.

Chapter Fifteen

The chill of the early evening air was like a balm on Nora's scorched skin. Moments ago, she had absolutely been ready to kiss Gray.

How had things gotten so out of hand?

It wasn't because Gray looked unfairly good in her olive-green jumpsuit that was unzipped down to just above her cleavage, the idea of what was underneath possibly more transfixing than it would have been if she'd been exposed. She was showing less skin than Nora had ever seen her show in one of her work outfits.

There was something about Gray that Nora had come to find comforting—which was a strange juxtaposition to her body's awareness of the soft, silhouetted curves of Gray's body. It was like she was a consistent, grounding force in her life that Nora was becoming a little addicted to.

And that was exactly what she didn't need to be feeling right now. Because when Nora let her walls down, this was what happened.

She stopped looking at things practically. She missed red

flags the size of Texas. Her own wants and needs became tied up in someone else's, so enmeshed that she struggled to figure out where the lines had even blurred because it was all one big, emotional mishmash.

After Andrea, she'd stopped cold turkey. She didn't trust herself, especially after she looked at their relationship in retrospect.

It had been something she'd thought a lot about over the last few weeks, her brain starting to wander into the new spaces that her openness was creating.

She'd ignored the reality of their relationship for the sake of staying together. Andrea was charming and driven, and Nora had been happy enough to go along for the ride. To have her value measured by someone else who'd said she was good enough, instead of her having to feel like she actually was.

And, for a while, Andrea had made Nora feel like enough. But what Nora was finally coming to accept was that their relationship had always been conditional. She hadn't wanted to lose it, so she'd continued pushing as the goalposts kept moving, meeting each of those conditions. Not overtaking Andrea professionally. Allowing Andrea to set the pace of their relationship. Settling for apologetic moments when Andrea treated their relationship like an afterthought instead of giving it the focus it deserved.

They'd made it four years on the fumes of a romance that had sputtered out long before.

And then everything changed.

When Nora's parents died, the ability to uphold their fragile balance withered away. It didn't happen immediately. At first, she'd told herself that nothing had changed. Her relationship with her parents had always been strained. The lack of her dad's acceptance that she was a lesbian and her mother's

159

inability to stand up to him about that—or anything else—were common sources of friction in her house growing up.

But every morning, it got a little harder to get up. It felt like each day, a rock was being added to a basket she was carrying.

She'd retreated inward to keep the pieces of herself and everything she couldn't deal with glued together. There was, for the first time in her relationship, no energy left over to work herself into the shape she needed to be in order to keep their puzzle pieces together.

And then one day, the basket was too heavy to carry. She didn't want to be anything to anyone, including herself.

Andrea had cheated on her within three months.

The worst part of it all was that it hadn't even been Nora who'd left after that.

She hadn't cared enough to keep things together, so why would she finally start caring when they actually fell apart?

The following months were brutal. She hated being alone. With her thoughts. With her fears. With all the pieces of the smashed mirror that was her life. She was walking around a room, trying not to get cut on the shards of glass that reflected back just how far she'd fallen.

Some days she wondered, had it not been for Cynthia starting her own agency and taking Nora with her, if she would still be working at the same office as Andrea.

There was, however, a certain freedom that finally came with not caring. She'd started outpacing Andrea at work before she'd left, quickly becoming the top agent in the office. She'd slept with more women than she could individually count until the novelty had worn off, always sneaking away during the night to save herself from any morning conversations.

She wasn't proud of the person she'd been when she was with Andrea, but she also wasn't proud of the person she'd been afterward either.

It had taken her a long time to realize that she was numbing the numbness.

At that point, she had known she needed to change but had no idea how to go about doing that.

She hadn't known how to heal, and turning inward was born out of not hurting anyone else as much as it was for her own self-preservation.

Even if she wasn't there yet, to a place where she felt like she was on solid ground, she knew that she didn't want to hurt Gray.

Gray, who was sitting next to her on the stoop, doling out candy to kids in costumes and chatting with each and every one of them.

She was the woman who left cute sticky notes on Nora's desk. She was a tether to a life of normalcy that Nora could finally see on the horizon.

And Nora didn't want to fuck that up.

So she focused on enjoying the night. This was the first time in years she'd given out candy instead of placing a bowl outside her front door.

The steady stream of trick-or-treaters went on for hours, wineglasses refilled in tandem with the exposed bottom of the candy bowl.

When Nora walked back into the living room with a full glass for each of them, Gray was closing the door behind her, the empty bowl balanced on her hip.

"The shop had to close up for the night. We've run out of inventory." Gray put the bowl down on a table next to the entryway. When she crossed the room, Nora was suddenly aware of how alone they were—S'mores's snores on the sofa notwithstanding.

Nora watched as Gray moved closer, tracking her across the room. Nora had accepted it before this moment, that she was wildly attracted to Gray. Because, in the obvious sense, who wouldn't be?

Her hair was down, wavy and a little wild, like she was perpetually on the move from one thing to the next. She had a lingering tan from Bermuda, her complexion shades darker than Nora's own fair skin, and her lips were glossy from the lollipop she'd stolen out of the bowl and had been sucking on for the past fifteen minutes.

That had been about the time Nora decided she needed to go inside and take a breather. It helped that she'd gotten a text from a client when the few extra minutes they'd bought her allowed her thrumming heart to slow down to a manageable tempo.

It was hard to imagine that five minutes ago, she'd been thinking about broken hearts and betrayals. How for so long her chest had felt like a black hole.

Now, all she felt was the heat from Gray's penetrating stare as she stood in front of her, brown eyes sliding across Nora's face like she was searching for something.

Nora wondered if she had found it when Gray asked, "Is that for me?," her gaze drifting to one of the wineglasses.

She tried to shake herself out of the heat that was enveloping her senses and handed Gray the glass. "We polished off the bottle. Not bad for a night's work."

Gray took the glass in her hand but didn't drink it. Her eyes landed on Nora again, deep and focused. Nora wanted to know what Gray saw when she looked at her.

"We can hang out on the sofa if you don't mind the ambient snoring."

The joke loosened the tension in Nora's chest, and she nodded. "Sorry I took so long. I got a text from a client."

Gray didn't respond until she was situated in the middle of

the sofa, S'mores sleeping underneath a blanket on the far side. "All good?"

Nora took the empty seat and placed her drink on an end table. "I sent over a contract earlier tonight, and they wanted to set up a call tomorrow to discuss it."

This, Nora noted, was familiar territory. She could talk about her clients—talk shop—for hours. It was easy and impersonal for her. Which made it even more jarring to realize that wasn't what she wanted.

She did, however, need to have a long overdue conversation with Gray. "I've been meaning to ask you something."

Gray sat up a little straighter and extended her arm across the back of the sofa. "What's up?"

Their bodies facing inward, it wouldn't have taken more than a few inches before Nora was pressed against her leg. Their familiarity had only grown since they'd come back from Bermuda, and, she wondered, if it had felt that good then, how would it feel now?

Even better, she guessed.

It was the wondering—that she could admit, at least to herself—that had made her avoid this conversation every time an opportunity to have it had come up in the last few weeks.

Which was exactly why she needed to have it. The part of her brain that had been making decisions lately was not her friend. It was holding out—holding off—like it was waiting for something to happen.

And in spite of the growing attraction that Nora felt, mixing business and pleasure was not going to help her in what she needed to do.

"Well, it's a little embarrassing," Nora said, hoping her self-deprecating tone lessened how aware she was of Gray's soft gaze as she patiently waited for Nora to continue.

Gray's brows furrowed. "Oh, sure," she said, a decided uncertainty in her voice.

Nora filled the silence quickly. "It's about work. I, uh... I was hoping to get your help with something."

"Work," Gray repeated, like she was hearing the word for the first time.

She bit the bullet. "Cynthia is giving me a shot at a promotion, but she says my—uh... my people skills in the office leave something to be desired."

Gray blinked. Once. Then again. The haze in her eyes grew focused. "What's wrong with your people skills?"

She didn't mean to, but Nora laughed then. Because whether Gray was saying it out of kindness or legitimate confusion, it was still a ridiculous thing to say. "I appreciate the vote of confidence, but I think we both know I'm not the social butterfly of the office."

She couldn't read Gray's face. Her lips were pursed together and her brow drew downward, like she didn't like what she was hearing. And there was something else there, settled just below the surface, something that Nora couldn't even begin to pick apart when Gray said, "Why do you need to be the social butterfly? We're real estate agents. You're great with your clients, I'm sure. You wouldn't be the best agent in the office if you weren't."

Nora only let herself take a quick pause to bask in the compliment, and she smiled earnestly in thanks. "I appreciate you saying that, but I am not known as the most approachable person." She let the words settle between them. "And I'd like to change that."

"Change it? How are you going to change that?" Now Gray seemed genuinely confused, like she couldn't understand where the conversation was going.

"With your help, hopefully."

Gray ran a hand through her untamed hair and blew out a long breath. "Nora, you're going to need to spell this out for me. I still have no idea what you want."

What a loaded statement. Nora was realizing she wanted all kinds of things lately.

"I mean... if I want to get better, I need to, like... be more of a team player?" Her words trailed up at the end in question. "And I was hoping you'd help me with that."

She watched Gray's hand shift from where it was tangled in her hair and she pointed toward her own chest, just like she'd done in Bermuda. It was cute, Nora realized, and she liked that she was starting to learn Gray's quirks. Even if they were more distracting than she'd like. "Me?"

"Well, I'm pretty sure only one of us is usually on our co-workers' Christmas card list."

Gray squinted at her. They were not on the same page about this at all.

Nora pushed on. Apparently, Gray was going to force her to spell this out in the most concrete terms, putting her own idiocy on display. "Cynthia says that I have a 'people problem' at the office. I am in talks with her about a promotion, but we are both fully aware that getting half the team to willingly take me on as their team lead is a tough sell."

"Does Cynthia know we're having this conversation?"

It was not exactly what Nora would have asked first, but to each their own. She nodded and tried to decipher the look on Gray's face, which was shifting into something she recognized, though still with an edge of suspicion. "I asked her if I could tell you."

Gray looked visibly relieved, her shoulders rounding out as she let out a loud exhale. "Okay, good," she said before she started chewing at her bottom lip. Seconds passed before she spoke again. "So you want me to... what exactly?"

What she really wanted was for Gray to lean forward and kiss her with the same lip she'd been biting. It was pulling Nora's focus more insistently with each moment they did this confusing back-and-forth, seemingly unable to find a common understanding in the conversation.

She needed to stop thinking like that.

"I'm sorry. This was a stupid idea," she said, lust mingled with embarrassment tinging her cheeks in what she knew was a deep crimson.

Nora moved to stand up, but Gray's arm encircled her wrist. It was soft but insistent as she guided her back down to the sofa.

"Hey, I'm sorry. I'm just surprised." Gray's voice was full and apologetic in a way that settled around Nora like the comfort of a weighted blanket. "You're the best agent in the office. So what if you don't care what other people think? I know you're fantastic with clients or you wouldn't close so many deals. You're obviously intuitive. I guess I just don't really understand how I can help."

The more Nora had to explain it, the weirder it was starting to sound. Because, really, what was she asking of Gray? For her to do all the legwork and get the rest of the team on board with Nora when Nora herself would reap the rewards?

"I feel like I should have given this conversation more thought before bringing it up," Nora admitted.

Because, sure, she'd thought about it the last few weeks. Spending more time with Gray. Proving to the rest of the team that she could engage. She'd even ask Julian what kind of fish he microwaved if she thought it would help.

But still... things had already changed. Their relationship wasn't transactional or tentative anymore, and asking about this like it was a business arrangement was what was making it weird. At least, that was why Nora felt weird.

She had no idea what was going on in Gray's head. Her features shifted from impassive to confused to skeptical from one word to the next. It was dizzying to watch.

"Let me try this again." She turned the hand over that was still encircled by Gray's fingers and rubbed her fingertips along Gray's palm.

Gray took in a sharp breath and her hand froze, long moments passing before it softened, and she rested the weight of her hand on top of Nora's.

Nora ghosted her fingertips along warm skin again, quickly getting lost in the sensation. She drew herself back to the point of the conversation, not without a significant amount of effort. "I shouldn't have asked for your help like this was some business arrangement. As my friend, I was hoping that you could support me with this. I know that's a very vague way to say it, but I'm going to be trying more at the office, and it would... well, it would mean a lot to know that you have my back."

She watched Gray's eyes soften, a smile easing across her lips that made heat settle through Nora's body. "Sure, I can do that."

Chapter Sixteen

Days after Halloween, Gray was still thinking about her conversation with Nora. To say she was surprised by Nora's request was an understatement.

'Did Nora want to lead a team?' was the only question she let herself consider.

Gray had no doubt that Nora could do anything she set her mind to. Hell, she'd iced out the office for literal years. At least according to Callie, who'd been at Philly Finds for the second longest after Nora.

She'd been drawn to Callie's energy immediately, a genuine friend who never pried but always seemed to be looking out for Gray. Callie was probably a decade older than Gray's almost thirty years, with a heart-shaped face and a bright smile that made her seem trustworthy. But Gray knew that there was also a keen intellect behind her green eyes.

Callie, unlike Kelsey, hadn't told Gray that in a furtive tone by the coffee station. No, she'd mentioned it to Gray a few weeks after she'd started, when it was clear that Nora's antipathy toward her was making Gray unsure about her place at Philly Finds.

Callie had walked some paperwork that Gray had left on the printer over to her desk. Her auburn hair had been tied up in a french twist, something Gray had always remembered because of how good it had looked. She'd complimented Callie on it frequently over the last year.

"It's not you, just so you know."

And Gray, scrambling to pull her gaze away from where Nora sat at her corner desk, had looked up at Callie with wide, surprised eyes. "What's that now?"

All she'd gotten in response was a soft smile that made her feel like, if even for a moment, everything would be okay. "I've been here the longest besides Nora and Cynthia. She doesn't talk to anyone."

Gray couldn't help it when she stole another glance. She could still remember what Nora had been wearing that day—a soft-looking navy blazer that was rolled up onto her forearms. Head down, she'd been filling out paperwork at her desk like Gray had now seen her do hundreds of times. Her hair was a little longer then, its tousled edges falling against her shoulders. She'd sighed, and Gray had watched the movement, the heaviness of it all.

She'd started staring initially because Nora, who was usually devoid of almost any normalcy, was chewing on a pen while reading over the document.

And it had just made her look so... human.

It wasn't until she'd kept staring that the weight in Nora's posture became evident. It was a brief moment where she'd seen past the wall into what she thought was the *real* Nora, only to be struck dumb by what she hadn't been seeing since they'd met.

Complete detachment, like she was suspended in a bubble as the world moved around her.

Gray had been transfixed, like she was looking at an optical illusion, Nora shifting back and forth between two different people, two temperaments. And layered on top was the emotional—and physical—distance, so that no one would get close enough to see either of those parts of herself.

They were two sides of the same coin. Gray had learned long ago that leveraging other people and building relationships was her ticket to success in this world. Nora had seemingly gone to the other side of the spectrum, completely ignoring that other people existed in favor of self-imposed solitude.

So it had become something Gray thought about, infrequently but enough that it would come up in conversation between her and Becks.

How was a life like that possible?

Because, really, she just couldn't understand it.

And the more she got to know Nora, the less she understood how she'd managed it for so long. Because Nora was surprisingly warm and engaged. She'd surveyed the trick-or-treaters' Halloween costumes and very seriously discussed the inspirations behind them. She'd offered to let Gray keep S'mores at her desk, even though it meant that she may become a hotbed for dog-induced foot traffic.

What a difference a year could make.

At least, it had been a year for Gray. For Nora, it had been longer than that, and Gray wondered what that must feel like.

Nora had decided that things were going to be different, and just like that, they were changing.

All the changes in Gray's life had been forced upon her. Moving so much when she was younger. The collateral damage of Willa's instability. Leaving her last job.

She was good at playing the game but made sure she never

let herself get too close. Other people brought volatility to her carefully constructed world. Toeing a line was a skill of hers at this point, but the line was blurring.

Because Nora was changing, and it was like the force of that change was creating a magnetic field that was pulling Gray in.

Which she noted with staggering clarity as she sat on the floor next to Nora's desk, setting up a collapsible playpen for S'mores to hang out in for the next few hours.

She unzipped the pen from its travel bag and started unfolding the panels. Going through the steps to construct the playpen was therapeutic. It gave her hands something to do even if she couldn't shut her brain off fully.

At the root of it all, she was frustrated. With herself, mostly, but also at the world that seemed to never stop spinning around her.

All she'd expected during Bermuda was maybe a softening of Nora's exterior, a little perfunctory effort to help get them through their trip. She'd never planned for a world in which Nora Gallagher could be the thing that spun Gray right off her axis.

Which was how they'd gotten to where they were now.

In all her confusion about Nora—in who Gray thought she was and who she was becoming right in front of her—she'd so misread the signs a few nights ago. And that bothered her. She'd obviously projected her own attraction for Nora, which had led to her looking and acting like a complete idiot when Nora had asked if she'd help her integrate with the team.

Had she not thought they were going to kiss, she would have understood what Nora was asking far sooner instead of looking like a lovestruck teenager.

Nora opening herself back up had nothing to do with Gray. Still, she was more proud of Nora than worried about herself, and she hadn't spent years cultivating stability to not build the foundation of it solidly. The axis may have shifted, but the world kept spinning.

As for her unrequited crush, she should be thankful that Nora was oblivious to her more than anything else.

* * *

Gray hadn't gone to an office happy hour since she'd been back from Bermuda.

Drinks after work were usually a hodgepodge crew of whoever didn't have evening showings or could make plans with little to no notice. Callie was usually out, since she had to get home to her kids. Tamara was hit-or-miss given that she taught an evening yoga class in Center City a few nights a week. Sometimes, there were events scheduled further in advance, but for the purposes of ingratiating Nora to the group —which still, as a whole, felt like a ridiculous thing to even consider—Gray had decided to keep it casual.

It wasn't hard to get people in a high-stress, customer-oriented job to agree to drinks after work.

Which was how, a little after six, she found herself opening the door into the warmth of Mulherin's Sons. She loved everything about the beautiful bar and restaurant located a fifteen-minute walk from the office, but she especially loved the dark mahogany interior that made the large space feel much homier. The sun was already setting, and the low lighting and candles created an intimate atmosphere.

Pulling off her coat when they walked in, she strode past the barroom situated at the entrance and peeked her head around the corner into the main dining area.

"Yes!" she said triumphantly, looking back. "Fireplace is free."

Besides Nora, Trent, Kelvin, Sage, and Kelsey had all decided to come along. She was confident that Kelsey would have chewed off her own arm to make sure she was free once she'd found out Nora was coming.

Gray often went to happy hour with Trent and Kelvin, both in their late twenties. Sage, however, was a bit of a surprise. She'd only thrown out the offer because it had seemed rude not to, but she couldn't remember a single event outside of work that Sage had joined in the last year.

Maybe Nora was a bigger draw than Gray had given her credit for.

No, that wasn't true. She knew that the rest of the office would be wildly curious. It was that her own curiosity had dimmed in the obvious ways since coming back from Bermuda, even if it was replaced with a different sense of awareness about Nora.

But Nora had asked for her help, and she wanted to do what she could.

At least in this way being co-workers was always relevant, drawn like a physical line between them and setting a clear boundary.

The fireplace lounge was nestled against one of the walls in the dining room. It was still early in the night for dinner, and they had most of the room to themselves.

Gray hid her surprise when, instead of sitting in one of the two wingback chairs flanking the coffee table, Nora sat down on the far side of the sofa. Gray followed suit and sat down in the middle. Even if her mind had made a decision about her crush, her body hadn't decided to acknowledge the memo.

Kelsey marched right past both of them and sat in the chair closest to Nora. Bold of her, but not unexpected.

Gray would never outright say that Kelsey was a bad person. She just had a very different personality than Gray.

She chose to focus on the negative things in her life, always wanting to dissect them until she felt vindicated in her own choices.

So, she could be a little frustrating in one-on-one situations, but she was usually fine in a group atmosphere.

Generally, the group would already be in animated conversation when they walked in somewhere. The conversation would start in the office, and by the time they'd get to the bar, stories about difficult clients or misrepresented homes would have been told, followed by someone else who had to one-up them with an even more ridiculous story.

Tonight, it was almost silent. The quiet conversation of the few other people in Mulherin's floated through the background, and she could hear the crackle of the fireplace.

Gray wondered if Nora realized the power in being able to cut off a well-oiled conversational machine at the head. It probably shouldn't be aspirational, sure, but it was still impressive.

The warmth of the fire had nothing on Nora's thigh. It was pressed against Gray's own, like they'd now sat many times before. And, as always, Gray got a little thrill from it. Maybe this was all she'd have with Nora, which was all the more reason to want to enjoy it.

Nora leaned forward and caught Gray's eye before whispering in her ear, "Thank you. I promise I'll be on my best behavior."

She could hear, more than see, the smile in Nora's voice, and it set off a wave of butterflies in her stomach.

"Now where would be the fun in that?" Gray asked, tilting her head to catch Nora's stare again.

She barely registered Kelsey's voice from next to them. "So, Nora. Surprised to see you here tonight."

Nora stiffened, and Gray could see how her smile faltered

before she put it back into place and turned to face Kelsey. "And why's that?"

Gray felt protective over Nora, even if there was no reason she should. Nora was an adult. She wanted to be in this situation. She knew that there would probably be some general confusion about why she was here. Maybe Gray had hoped that everyone would be polite enough not to mention it, but she'd known the alternative was a possibility.

When she'd found out Kelsey was coming, that possibility had been upgraded to a probability.

Kelsey shrugged, like she was simply making polite conversation. "Just not your usual scene."

Gray watched as Nora lifted a sculpted eyebrow and leaned a little closer to Kelsey. "And what's my usual scene?"

"Well, I wouldn't know, now would I?" Kelsey's voice was saccharine sweet, and it set off alarm bells in Gray's head. "Just interesting that you're starting to come out with us for happy hour now."

Nora leaned back on the sofa, her long arm extended along the edge of it, legs crossed like she was having a casual conversation with a friend. "I don't follow."

It was riveting to watch, the way Nora sat like a queen surveying a subject. Her face was friendly if not a little impassive, and she could already see Kelsey buckling under the weight of Nora's presence.

Mesmerized, Gray barely remembered what she ordered when the waiter stopped by to ask about drinks. Nora's blouse was unbuttoned enough that her collarbone was exposed, her long neck lengthened even further as she continued to look at Kelsey like she could respond if she wanted but that it wouldn't bother Nora if she didn't.

Kelsey sat up straighter. "You know what I'm saying, Nora."

Everyone was watching them now, waiting to see what happened.

Gray was honestly a little surprised that Kelsey was being so overt in displaying her dislike for Nora. Sure, she'd always made private comments about their co-worker, which Gray tried to quash whenever possible, but this was... something different.

It was the uncertainty about how far Kelsey would take this that made the hair on her arms stand up.

And then, Nora did something that surprised her.

She looked at Kelsey and said the two words that knocked the wind right out of Kelsey's sails. "I'm sorry."

"You're what?" Kelsey sputtered. Her drink almost to her lips was forgotten.

"I'm sorry. I haven't been very present with the team, and I haven't created the nicest environment for all of you, I'm sure. I know it's not great to feel like you're walking on eggshells all the time. So, really, I'm sorry." Nora looked around the chairs and sofa, her lips pursed and her eyes conveying genuine remorse.

"Oh, um..." Kelsey said, stalling for time like she was deciding between accepting the apology and going in for another round.

"Maybe I'll even join your fantasy league next year," Nora said, her attention turning to Trent, who looked like he'd never been directly addressed by her before.

His boyish face turned bright red, even in the dim lighting, before he recovered. "That would be awesome. I mean, player stats are basically just comps. I think you'd really kick ass," he finished before blushing again.

Apparently Nora had that effect on more people than Gray had noticed before.

And when Nora looked away from Trent, she met Gray's

stare, only a few inches of space between their faces. Gray didn't know when she'd leaned closer. It was that magnetism again, pulling Gray in whenever Nora was in the process of changing.

It was dizzying. It felt so secure but also like she was walking on a tightrope.

Everything was changing, but for the first time, as Gray let the feeling of pride settle inside of her, that Nora had done something that was obviously difficult for her, it didn't feel like such a bad thing.

* * *

Nora insisted on giving Gray a ride home when they got back to the office.

"I only live a mile away," Gray protested.

Nora opened up her car's passenger-side door at the sidewalk before walking around to the driver's side. "Yes. I know where you live."

A warm car and more time with Nora wasn't a hard sell, and she found herself sliding into the seat without protesting again. "Well, thank you then. I appreciate it."

Once Nora eased the car onto the road, she glanced at Gray. "I feel like that went decently well."

Gray nodded. Because really... it had. After Kelsey calmed down, the conversation had started to flow. Gray wouldn't have thought this possible a year ago, but happy hour was actually more fun with Nora there.

A lot of things were seeming like more fun with Nora around for them these days.

She pushed that thought away.

But the thought she couldn't push away was how Nora had

done a complete one-eighty. "I wasn't expecting you to apologize to everyone tonight."

Nora shot her a smile before focusing on the road again. "You showed me in Bermuda that I couldn't just move forward and pretend like the past hadn't happened. I was trying to bring that spirit into my relationships with everyone else."

Right. Everyone else. Because, at the end of the day, Gray's relationship with Nora wasn't special. She was just another member of the team, and even if they'd become friendly first, it was a matter of circumstance, not desire, on Nora's part.

She decided to change the subject to quell the sting of disappointment churning in her stomach. "You said something about walking on eggshells. What was that all about?"

The soft smile on Nora's face faltered. At a red light, she turned to face Gray, blue eyes sharp as they focused on her face. "Halloween got me thinking about a lot of things."

Gray exhaled softly, waiting for Nora to continue. She didn't know whether she would, but she was decidedly curious. She was sure that Nora had a lot of thoughts running around in her head all the time, mostly things she never vocalized.

Even in the darkness, Nora's bright blue eyes were piercing. Gray watched as she drew her bottom lip into her teeth, mulling over whether to continue. When the light turned green, they started moving, Nora's eyes trained on the road again.

It wasn't until they were about a block from Gray's house that Nora finally spoke again. "My dad wasn't an easy person to get along with. Neither was my ex, if I really think about it."

The air was heavy around them, and Gray was almost afraid to breathe, worried that it would disrupt whatever story Nora was on the cusp of telling.

Nora put the car in park in front of Gray's house, the engine whining softly in the cold air. Everything seemed so loud while she waited. It was hard to explain it, but sometimes things felt important to Gray before they happened. Generally, those things scared her because they meant whatever was happening had the weight to change something.

But this... she needed to know.

"On Halloween, you said that I don't care what people feel."

Gray shook her head almost before Nora was done talking. She remembered the conversation vividly, given how many times she'd thought about it over the past week. How she'd picked apart every word and movement and nuance, wondering what it had all meant. "No. I said you don't care what other people *think*. I never said you don't care about people's feelings."

"Isn't it kind of the same thing? People think things because of how we make them feel?"

It was an interesting point, a distinction that Gray would never have made. "Regardless of semantics, I didn't mean it as a bad thing."

Nora looked at her then, blue eyes cloudy with what seemed like a lifetime of memories floating through them. She knew so much more about Nora than she had before, but it was still so little in the grand scheme of things.

When Nora's stare finally softened, she let out an equally soft sigh, like she was releasing whatever was weighing on her. "For the last few years, I thought that I could insulate myself from other people and that there wouldn't be collateral damage. That it was a choice I was making that didn't impact anyone else."

Gray reached across the space between them and grabbed Nora's hand, giving it a quick squeeze before continuing to hold it loosely. It was comforting a friend. Nothing more.

Maybe if she told herself that enough times, she'd start to believe it.

They sat in silence, Gray willing to give Nora as much time as she needed to figure out how she wanted to say whatever she was gearing up to share.

"So I just... I don't know. I checked out. I'd lost my parents. And then I lost my relationship soon after. Not that either of those things were healthy parts of my life..."

Gray knew both things had happened from their brief conversations about Nora's life, but she didn't know one had come so quickly after the other. She still wasn't quite sure how the pieces fit together.

"I guess I didn't really feel like I mattered, so I didn't know how much my behavior would matter to other people." Nora let out a sound of frustration, but she didn't move away from Gray.

Knowing that Nora didn't feel like she mattered cut like a knife through Gray. It was a special kind of loneliness that she knew all too well and wouldn't wish on anyone.

"I tried for so long to play by the rules that other people made. With my dad. With Andrea, my ex. And then one day, I just couldn't anymore. I was too tired. I'd spent so long thinking that other people were the point of it all—not trusting myself and wanting to earn their acceptance."

Gray's whole body felt like a live wire, electrified by the emotion pushing from Nora. She leaned forward and wiped away a single tear that had fallen on Nora's cheek, her eyes glassy with the promise of more if she kept going.

She wasn't going to make this about her, but she knew a lot about feeling like she was living life for other people.

"And even if I didn't trust other people anymore, I still didn't trust myself." Nora's voice didn't waver when she added, "I still don't trust myself."

Nora wiped her coat sleeve across her face. It was then that

Gray realized her hand was still on Nora's cheek, cupping it gently. Nora pulled Gray's hand down with her own, fingers intertwined across the center console between them.

Gray's heart cracked open a little when Nora let out a wet laugh and said, "You've got to say something now. I feel like I've been talking for so long that I'm about to pass out."

"I think you're braver than you give yourself credit for, Nora."

Nora shook her head in obvious disagreement. "I've been hiding for years."

Gray shrugged. "Some people hide their whole lives. A few months ago, you decided that things would be different, and already, they're different."

"Feels like the bar is set pretty low." She hated the embarrassment in Nora's voice, but she was still proud of her for being honest and not bottling it up inside to stew over privately. Asking for help, especially with her mistrust of other people, was no small feat.

She squeezed Nora's fingers again, liking how well they fit together. How warm and connected Nora's touch made her feel. "If you only have fifty percent to give and you give five percent, then you've given a hundred percent of your effort."

"I'm still terrified about all of this, about engaging again, but I can't keep letting life pass me by. I can't pretend like I'm this little self-sustaining island."

"Even Bermuda needs to get things imported, even though they're pretty independent," Gray said, a wry grin easing across her lips.

The weight of the moment was lessening until Nora looked at her with eyes so arresting that Gray forgot how to breathe. "When I had my panic attack in Bermuda, you being there made all the difference. No one's ever made me feel safe in that way. So, thank you. I don't know if I really acknowledged how much it meant to me."

Gray nodded dumbly and hoped her heart wasn't going to beat out of her chest. "I'm just glad I could be there. And really, it was fun to ride out the storm together. Definitely better than spending it alone."

She still couldn't vocalize what it had meant for her, to fall asleep with Nora in her arms and feel like, even for just a night, things made sense in a way they hadn't in a long time.

And with the way their friendship was going, she probably never would.

A tiny flare of desire lit her up from the inside when Nora leaned closer. So close that it would only take a few inches of movement for Gray to close the space between them. A few inches and she'd know whether Nora's lips were as soft as they looked.

She wanted it, even though she knew it was a bad idea. Even though she knew that it would change everything. That consideration alone should have stopped her dead in her tracks. Instead, all it did was make heat sluice through her veins.

"Nora," she said a little breathlessly, giving herself over to whatever was going on in the moment.

A flash of movement caught her attention. Who would be opening the door to her house, where she lived alone?

A silhouette, similar to her own, stood outlined in the light from inside the house.

Willa.

She shook the fog of lust from her mind and pulled herself back to reality. "My sister, Willa, has apparently made an unscheduled visit."

Nora blinked, still close enough that Gray could see the flecks of amber in her blue eyes. She wanted to pretend Willa wasn't standing in her doorway, to ignore the rest of the world and lean back into this decidedly irresponsible moment.

Finally, like Nora was a little lost in the moment, too—though Gray really had no idea the main cause of it, given the emotional tumult of the last few minutes—she leaned back, the space opening between them like a chasm.

"She seems..." Nora didn't finish, instead chancing a glance at the doorway where Willa stood, peering out at them like a parent counting down to curfew. Which was laughable, given that Willa had never adhered to a set curfew a day in her life.

"I go with 'unpredictable' on my good days," Gray said, letting reality settle back around her.

It kept happening, where Nora was concerned: getting lost in moments like Gray didn't care what would change.

The two of them kissing after Nora's raw honesty would have definitely changed things.

And even if she wanted it—more than she'd wanted anything in a very long time—some balances were too delicate to upset.

Chapter Seventeen

"A little birdy told me that you joined an office happy hour last night." Cynthia stood at the coffee machine on Friday morning, waiting for her double shot of espresso to brew.

It was early, and besides Callie, who often came in right after dropping her kids off at school, the rest of the office was empty.

Nora leveled a stare in her boss's direction. "Glad to know the office gossip grapevine is alive and well."

Cynthia waved her off. "I saw a few of you come back into the office afterward to grab your things. I promise, your good name is still intact."

"We both know my name holds less water than a leaky bucket around here."

"Is that"—Cynthia leaned in, studying Nora—"self-deprecating humor?"

Nora rolled her eyes but couldn't stop the small smile that worked its way across her lips. "Even I have my moments."

"A lot more of them lately, to be sure."

A pleasant warmth spread through Nora that Cynthia had

noticed. It wasn't like she was doing all this for a response from her boss, but if there was anyone that should benefit from the fruits of Nora getting her shit together, it was Cynthia.

Nora leaned her hip against the counter while she waited for her coffee to brew. Meanwhile, Cynthia started pulling things out to set up the Friday morning waffle bar.

"I wanted to thank you, by the way," Nora said while Cynthia was rummaging around in the fridge.

Cynthia poked her head out. "Thank me for what?"

"For not giving up on me. And also for letting Gray bring S'mores into the office. That was really sweet of you."

"I didn't know you were such an animal lover," Cynthia said, her brows drawing upward. She dumped the containers of blueberries and strawberries into a colander and began rinsing them in the sink.

"Gray's been very nice to me. I'm just glad you were able to help her out on this." It was obvious Cynthia was fishing for something that Nora wasn't going to give her. Still, she admired her boss's persistence.

"Along with S'mores, I see Gray at your desk an awful lot too."

Nora started pouring the waffle mix into a large bowl. It had been a long time since she'd helped Cynthia with this Friday morning ritual. Sure, she thought as she sifted the flour, maybe Gray was at Nora's desk a little more often. And an extra chair had magically found its way to her corner, where Gray would sometimes sit while S'mores played in the puppy pen situated between them.

And maybe it had made spending time in the office a little more enjoyable, so she'd been finding her way in more often instead of lurking around in coffee shops between showings.

She waved a plastic spatula in Cynthia's direction. "Well, it is her dog. Would be a little weird if she just abandoned her with me."

Cynthia nodded seriously, though she failed to hide her smile. "Absolutely. Very responsible of her."

"It's not..." Nora stopped stirring the batter and leveled a stare in her boss's direction. "It's not like what you're implying. We're becoming friends. And given you know how long it's been since I've had a new one of those, I assumed you'd be thrilled."

Sure, she'd felt it—the crackle of electricity that sometimes sparked between them—but she chalked that up to going so long without real human interaction.

Cynthia poured the now dry berries into a serving bowl and centered it on the table. When she was finished with that, she opened the cabinet doors behind her and pulled out two waffle makers.

After she plugged them both into the wall behind the counter, she turned back toward Nora, eyes serious behind her glasses. "I think you've always had a misconception that a work-place romance was your problem with Andrea."

It was surprising how little hearing Andrea's name impacted her. It used to make her whole body seize up, like if she didn't blink, didn't move, maybe she'd be able to survive.

Now, she felt a flicker of annoyance, but nothing enough to even make her stop mixing the batter. "I acknowledge that there were many problems with my relationship with Andrea, though being co-workers definitely didn't help."

She watched Cynthia shake her head and put her palms down on the table. "Nora, there was no rule against you two being in a relationship. And technically, to your point, being an asshole isn't illegal either, though it should be," Cynthia added with a teasing smile.

"I'm worried you mean me and not her."

"You've had your moments the last few years, but I definitely mean her. You know I never liked Andrea. She acted like her success only counted if she cut other people down while she achieved it."

"I don't know if that's how I remember it..." Still, though, there was a lot in the months after her parents died that she didn't remember well.

When Nora'd met Andrea, she'd been charmed by her confidence, her tenacity, the interest she'd shown in her. By the time the cracks had shown themselves, it was already too late. At least, that's how she'd felt. Nora had craved her approval by then, had oriented her whole life around Andrea. She liked being associated with her, someone who walked into any room and commanded attention. By having someone like that choose her, she was telling Nora that she was good enough too.

Even if being chosen had started to come at the cost of her own happiness.

"I never understood why you thought the sun shone out of her ass. You are twice the agent she ever was, and you did it without climbing on the backs of others. And the one time," Cynthia said, holding up her finger, "that you needed Andrea to actually be there for you, to show up in the way a partner should, she decided that her needs weren't being met and cheated."

That one still stung a little to hear.

Finished mixing, Nora walked the bowl over to the counter and placed it between the two waffle makers. In the drawer below, she found two measuring cups to pour the batter.

With the prep done, she washed her hands again and leaned back against the counter, her full attention on her boss and mentor. Cynthia had given her a gift all those years ago, a lifeline when she'd desperately needed one. It felt like something she could never repay.

What she could do was finally start living for herself again, and that started with honesty. "When I met Andrea, I was young and insecure and wanted someone else to tell me that I was enough. She did that... for a while."

"I'll never understand why you felt that way," Cynthia said, her voice sincere.

Nora leveled a lopsided smile in Cynthia's direction. "For the sake of simplicity, let's chalk it up to a lot of unresolved childhood trauma."

Cynthia's glasses had scooted down the bridge of her nose, and she looked like a caricature of a therapist when she asked, "And now?"

Cynthia went by the book when needed and made exceptions when it counted. She was one of those indomitable personalities that Nora had always found inspiring. If she'd ever wanted someone's approval, it should have been a person like Cynthia, whose acceptance wasn't conditional.

But what she was finally realizing was that it wasn't anyone else's approval she needed—it was her own.

People were always going to pull her in different directions. They were going to for the sake of their own convenience or because they thought they knew best, because they wanted her to fit into boxes that best served their own needs—whether they did it intentionally or not.

At least, that had been Nora's experience with people like her dad and Andrea. Cynthia had never made her feel that way. It was why she trusted her, and why she'd jumped at the chance to go with Cynthia when she left their last realty agency.

"I'm working on it. At thirty-five, I'm finally trying to figure out who I am—outside of anyone else's approval."

Cynthia smiled and squeezed Nora's shoulder. "I think I'm probably really going to like that person."

Nora mirrored her smile and pushed herself away from the counter just as she noticed Gray enter the office, S'mores bundled up in her arms.

Gray caught her eye, like she knew exactly where Nora would be standing, offering a mittened wave before she pointed to the playpen at Nora's desk.

Nora nodded and watched Gray place S'mores down on the carpet. The dog zigzagged around the desks before running through the unzipped playpen's door and into a bed of blankets waiting for her.

Cynthia was already almost to her office, so Nora finally answered to herself when she said, "I think I am too."

Nora took a seat at the morning meeting, an open chair next to Gray in the conference room. The check-ins were over quickly, though sometimes Cynthia would review some type of best practice to keep everyone up to speed. It could be a continuing education class she encouraged the agents to take or a discussion of up-and-coming neighborhood trends in the city.

Usually, Nora zoned out, given that she was the one who helped Cynthia prepare the material ahead of time.

Cynthia stood at the head of the conference table, a large television screen mounted to the wall behind her. "We're officially heading into the holiday season, folks."

A stock photo of people shaking hands appeared on the screen. Nora had begged Cynthia to use something else, but she'd been promptly shot down.

Nora leaned toward Gray and whispered, "Nothing says networking like an early 2000s photo of two guys shaking hands."

She hadn't expected Gray to respond with more than

possibly a smirk mirroring Nora's own, but instead, she stared at a faraway look on Gray's face as she gazed absently out the window.

Seconds later, Gray's phone buzzed, and she flipped it over in her lap before firing off a text and then sliding it into the pocket of her jacket.

Cynthia's voice drew Nora briefly back to the meeting. "This year, we're not reinventing the wheel. As we get deeper into the winter months and sales inevitably slow, this is a great opportunity to network with local businesses and build out your referral list come springtime."

Nora nodded along, forcing herself to keep looking forward instead of glancing back toward Gray, who hadn't pulled herself out of whatever distraction had her focus.

Gray had stayed at her desk before the team meeting, which, while not the strangest thing, was a little atypical for the relationship they'd developed lately. Nora tried not to over-think it, even if her mind drifted back to the night before.

Maybe Gray was overwhelmed by how much emotion Nora had shown. Sure, they'd become friends, but it wasn't like crying had been on her list of things to accomplish last night either.

Still, it had felt good to be honest.

Whatever this thing was between them—a connection at the very least—she hoped it wouldn't disrupt the solid place they'd reached.

Was that what Gray was upset about today? Or had some-thing happened with her sister when she'd gone into the house?

"I'll send an email out later today with the upcoming networking opportunities," Cynthia was saying. "I'd encourage everyone in the office, regardless of seniority," she said, looking pointedly at Nora, "to try and attend at least a few of them. Local business leaders will be there, along with other agents."

When the meeting ended, Nora was struck by the strangest sense of déjà vu—except that a few months ago, she'd been running away from Gray and toward Cynthia's office, and now she was moving to Gray's desk, where her friend had headed without a word.

She made a pit stop on the way, scooping up S'mores in her arms and cuddling her warm body.

"S'mores isn't thrilled to be pulled from her cuddle cave, but you looked like you could use a pick-me-up." Nora leaned against the edge of Gray's desk.

"Hey, S'mores," Gray said, a soft smile on her lips. She looked tired, now that Nora had more time to take her in.

Nora handed the dog to Gray, who cuddled her against the soft fabric of her sweater.

She dropped her stare down so she could catch Gray's eyes. "Are you doing okay? You seem... unfocused."

Gray leaned back in her chair and let out a long, strangled sigh. She ran the hand not holding S'mores through her hair. "It's Willa."

"I assume her being at your house last night wasn't planned?"

"She and her boyfriend, Keith, have decided to 'consciously uncouple.'" Gray let out another strangled sound. "They were together for six months. What do they have to uncouple except the apartment, which Willa stupidly moved into with him after dating for three months?"

"That sounds stressful for everyone involved, but especially you."

Gray shot her a smile. "I love my sister, but it's always like this. She does things before she thinks. She's so..." Nora waited, knowing no good could come from her supplying any type of superlative to describe Gray's sister, even if a few choice words came to mind. "Reckless. I came down this morning, and my kitchen was a disaster because Willa 'had a craving' at midnight and decided to make breakfast for dinner. It wasn't even dinnertime!"

She'd never seen Gray like this before—out of sorts and unable to control it. There was clearly history between the two sisters that would take more than a morning check-in to talk through.

It made her next words come quickly, given the easy pretext. "Do you want to hang out on Sunday? I mean, if you want to get out of the house for a little?"

She liked how Gray's face softened, her shoulders visibly relaxing at the offer. She liked being the one who had caused that.

"That might be nice. I hate conceding my space to Willa, but she can outlast me without blinking an eye."

"There's an art fest in your neighborhood that day if you're interested. You can get some space but still hang close in case she sets the house on fire." Nora had been planning to check it out on her own regardless, and she realized that company—especially if it was Gray's—would actually be really nice.

Gray shot her a distraught look that was quickly tempered. "God, you have no idea. I can't believe I ever even gave her a key to my house."

Nora lifted a brow. "Would you really have kept her outside if she came to you, asking for help?" That didn't strike her as Gray's style, given how helpful she always seemed, but she knew from her own experience that family was an entirely different beast.

"No," Gray said, resignation in her voice. "I wouldn't. Our parents don't show up for her, so I feel like it falls to me, whether I like it or not."

Nora knew what it was like to have to take care of herself, at least emotionally, but she couldn't imagine having to support someone else, especially a person who floated through life with Willa's temperament.

"Well, whatever you do, it will be the right decision. You're a good person, Gray, and it's really kind of you to help your sister."

Gray nodded, like she was absorbing Nora's words, her hands running through S'mores's long fur in a repetitive motion. Nora wondered if it was Gray or S'mores who was in need of comfort right now.

When Gray didn't say anything else, Nora stood up from where she was leaning on her desk. "Three o'clock on Sunday? Do you have any showings?"

Talking about work brought Gray back into the conversation, her head shaking back and forth. "Not in the afternoon."

"Okay, perfect. I'll stop by your house and then we can walk over? It's just a few blocks."

Gray looked up at her then, a half-hearted smile on her face that made Nora's heart skip a few beats.

Nora squeezed Gray's forearm gently before running a hand over S'mores's back. "Do you want me to take her back to my desk?"

She watched as Gray cuddled the dog closer. "No. I'll keep her for now."

Nodding, Nora scratched behind S'mores's ears. "You two make a cute pair," she said without thinking the words through.

Gray, given her own distracted focus, didn't seem to notice.

Fifteen minutes later, Nora chanced a glance over at Gray. She was still petting S'mores gently, in the exact same spot that Nora had left her.

Chapter Eighteen

"Willa!" Gray yelled up the steps. "Seriously. What the hell?"

Gray was running late, hopping awkwardly around her living room with a single shoe on. The other, inconveniently, was on the sofa with S'mores, a hole where her big toe should go.

She'd discovered weeks ago that S'mores had an affinity for chewing shoes. Chewing anything really. They'd compromised, which meant that S'mores got all the chew toys she could handle and Gray had started keeping all of her shoes in the hall closet to avoid any situations like this.

"Willa," she bellowed again. It was after nine a.m., and she didn't care that Willa had dragged herself in at god knows what hour the night before.

After long seconds, Willa appeared at the top of the steps. "What? It's so early."

Gray grabbed the shoe from S'mores's protective paws and replaced it with a chew toy. She walked back to the bottom of the steps and thrust the shoe up toward her sister. "I asked you to keep the hall closet door closed."

In all the physical ways, she and her sister were very much alike. Dark hair. Dark eyes. Same height. They had a similar smile that Willa used to get out of trouble, something Gray had done in her younger years too. Now that they were adults, they were mistaken for twins more often than not when they went out. Gray, five years older, wanted to take that as a compliment, but even being compared to her sister physically made annoyance prickle through her veins.

Willa wiped her tired eyes, only opening one of them to peer down at Gray. "Aww, sorry, sis. I threw my jacket in there when I came home last night and must have forgotten."

Just like Willa forgot to put condiments back in the fridge. Or how she forgot to lock the door whenever she came back. The same 'forgetfulness' had caused her to use the last of Gray's coffee and not replace it. That had been an especially fun morning yesterday.

Gray shook her head and took a long breath that should have calmed her down. Instead, because it gave her time to think of another three things Willa had done in the last few days, it only ratcheted up her frustration.

How in the world had she only been here for less than two days? Living with Willa was more of an adjustment than living with a pet that depended entirely on her for survival.

No, she corrected herself, they were not 'living together.' S'mores may have snuck in through the side door and become a permanent fixture, but this was where she drew the line. Willa was going through one of her *phases*, and Gray was giving her a place to sleep until she figured out her next move. As usual.

"Sometimes I don't understand how we're related," Gray muttered under her breath, though she knew her sister could hear and likely didn't care. They'd gone through this same conversation enough times in infinite permutations that, if Willa had cared, they wouldn't still be having it.

"I'll replace them," Willa said sleepily, though Gray knew that wasn't happening and also likely assumed her sister wouldn't even remember this conversation in a few hours. "I also got more coffee."

Willa was Teflon when it came to deflecting responsibility for her mistakes. Sure, she may have said the right things in the moment, but the follow-through never matched any promises she'd make.

"I just need it not to happen again." Gray hated how she sounded like a parent scolding a misbehaving child, but she didn't know the alternative.

Over the years, she'd tried everything. Icing Willa out. Setting firmer boundaries. Trying to have serious conversations with her.

Nothing seemed to work.

"Today would be a great day to go apartment hunting," Gray called behind her as she headed to the closet to find a non-mangled pair of shoes to wear.

Willa's voice floated from the hallway, a telltale sign she was already on her way back to the guest room. "Why would I do that when it's so welcoming and lovely here?" she said in a singsong voice that made Gray want to scream. There was no one who could set her on edge faster than her sister.

Gray dropped down to the floor in front of the closet and scanned the small shoe rack she'd placed in there. If she changed her pants quickly, she could wear a pair of warmer boots instead of the flats she'd planned on.

After she grabbed the shoes, she shut the closet door and headed upstairs. The door to the guest room—she refused to call it 'Willa's room'—was already shut.

"Typical," she muttered as she headed into her own bedroom.

She switched out a pair of charcoal slacks for her dark

skinny jeans instead. With a quick look in the mirror, she applied a soft lipstick and ran a hand through her hair.

She was downstairs in less than five minutes and out the door in seven.

As she drove to the first of three homes she was showing her new clients today, she tried to push her frustration down.

Willa's surprise appearance in her life was nothing new. Neither was Willa's behavior.

Why, then, was it throwing her more out of sorts than usual?

Maybe it was because, for the first time in a long time, she felt like her life was on the right path. She owned her own home. She had a best friend she could count on emotionally. She was doing a great job at work and had finally settled into Philly Finds.

And she'd done it on her own. At least, that was how it felt most days. Willa, even with the help Gray wanted to give her, continually fell short of the mark.

Gray didn't remember it being this bad growing up. Then again, there was no such thing as breaking curfew when your parents didn't care when you came home. There was no meltdown over subpar report cards when they didn't even know what classes you were taking.

Even knowing that Willa's childhood involved very few grounding forces—since Gray had had the same experience— she begrudged her sister. Growing up the way they had wasn't Willa's fault, but the person she was today was her responsibility.

She was thankful when she showed up at the first house so that she could shut her brain off. A young couple stood outside, bundled up in the mid-November cold. This was their first home, and they were looking for a small rowhouse to start their journey of home ownership.

Unlike a lot of other things in Gray's life right now, she felt like she was qualified to handle this.

"Morning," she said when she exited the vehicle. "Looks like there's parking available, at least on the weekends." She'd never try to put someone in a house they didn't love, but she also knew it was her job to point out things they may not notice in their buying decision.

Jenna, one of the prospective buyers, rubbed her hands together. "Makes all the difference on a day like today. Lance, I love the little gate outside," she said to her husband.

Lance surveyed the small, white picket fence that ran between the sidewalk and the front of the property.

Gray opened the gate and headed toward the lockbox hanging on the front door. "This is a deep lot in the neighborhood, so along with this front paved area behind the gate, there's also a small yard in the back."

Gray opened the front door to the main living area, which was very similar to her own. A staircase ran along the right wall, and the family room opened into an area with a dining table, leaving the kitchen open to the rest of the room, where it was nestled against the back of the house.

She made a note to get the contact information for whoever had staged the house. She especially loved the light fixtures they'd chosen, a semi-flush sputnik mount that made the ceiling look taller.

Growing up, she'd lived in enough houses that she'd started developing opinions on them from a young age. But, given that none of the homes were really hers, she'd kept little cutouts of design ideas in a notebook she'd taken with her whenever they moved.

Now, she had Pinterest boards to catalog different ideas, though she always deferred to the professionals and had a few staging companies she worked with when customers wanted to use them.

Gray spent the next few minutes going over the highlights of the house, making it a point to note any information that wasn't available on the small leaflet that the sellers had left on the table at the entryway.

"The house is turnkey-ready. The previous sellers replaced the roof three years ago, and they installed a new privacy fence in the back last year."

Usually, Gray's job was much harder than this. Over the past few months, her client base had grown. Whereas she used to have to inspire people to see themselves in a space that fit within their budget, the influx of young professionals from other cities was giving them more flexibility in price, meaning that updated, modern homes were well within their range. Sometimes, it cut down her time to close from months to days.

Still, she liked helping people see the possibility of their new house.

At the top of the landing, she pointed to each door when she said, "Master bedroom in the front, two bedrooms or a bedroom and a home office or nursery, and a newly refinished full bath. I'll give you two some time to look around, but I'm happy to answer questions."

They spent about fifteen minutes upstairs before coming back down and checking out the kitchen and backyard.

When she locked the house back up, she turned to Jenna and Lance. "Okay, one down, two to go. If you had to rate this one on a scale of one to ten, how are you feeling about it?"

She found that asking people to score a property when they left was helpful in anchoring their overall opinion. Looking at sometimes a dozen homes could make them all blend together.

"I'd give it a nine," Jenna said, gazing up at the brick exterior.

Gray nodded. It was a great start, and it helped her figure out what they needed in a dream home if they didn't want to put an offer on one of the three today. "What kept it from getting a perfect ten from you?"

She liked that Jenna considered the question for a few seconds before answering. "Ideally we'd love a finished basement, but it's not a must-have."

Gray nodded again and turned to Lance. "And what about you? Love it? Hate it?"

Lance had commented less during the tour, so he was more of an enigma.

"I'm going with a nine as well. I love that it's set back from the street, since I think that'll make it a little quieter." He wasn't wrong. It was no apartment living, but you had to be okay with neighbors and street noises to make it in Philadelphia.

"And what's keeping it from being a perfect ten for you? Last question, I promise," Gray said with a rueful smile. "I'd have asked you in the house, but I find it's better to have you talk about the property when you aren't inside it anymore."

"The half-bath downstairs is a little small. We also have an older dog, and I worry the staircase is a little steep for him."

Jenna gave her husband a look of pure adoration. "That's a great point about Finn."

Now they were onto something. Gray wrapped her jacket tighter and started walking, Jenna and Lance falling into step beside her. "This is all great information. Let's discuss Finn's needs at the next house, since I don't know the legality of you agreeing to buy a house if you're partially hypothermic."

That earned a laugh as they walked through the front gate. Gray headed to her car, parked directly behind theirs. "Next house is on Cumberland Street."

Lance gave her a thumbs-up before they disappeared into their vehicle.

Gray sat for a few seconds before pulling out into the street, inventorying everything that Jenna and Lance had expressed over the first tour. She felt like they'd love the third house, though she had a few more questions she wanted to ask them at the next one.

Throwing herself into this morning had been a welcome distraction from her sister. And honestly, it had also been helpful in avoiding her mounting thoughts regarding a certain formerly tempestuous blonde who'd suddenly decided that she was going to be the perfect blend of supportive and helpful.

Gray didn't know what she was going to do about Nora, but their friendship—or whatever it was—had started to take on a life of its own.

She'd been down this path before. She'd tried to open herself up, only to be disappointed in ways she hadn't even seen coming. At the end of the day, she'd been most disappointed in herself. For trusting. For expecting that someone wouldn't prove her right.

Paul had so spectacularly failed across the board that it was a slap in the face of the tenuous efforts she'd made to trust other people.

She'd learned a tough lesson about keeping her circle small and her trust low.

Meanwhile, Nora, in the last few months, had gone from an idea to an active part of Gray's life. She was chaos personified for Gray's carefully crafted existence.

And still, Gray couldn't seem to stay away from her.

* * *

201

She had severely underestimated how cold it was going to be today. Dashing between houses for the showings had not prepared her for any extended period of time spent outdoors. Even with a bulky winter jacket, cold seeped under her skin, her fingers going numb by the time they'd made it through the outdoor vendors set up at Calloway Brewing for the Winter Arts Fest.

They'd lasted thirty minutes outside, and Gray was pretty sure that had been about twenty-nine minutes too long.

"I give up." Her words, even as they crossed the threshold into her house, made a visible puff of air into her living room.

Nora was right behind her, scarf bundled around her neck. Her face was hidden except for her eyes and the red tips of her ears.

She looked downright adorable, a thought that Gray had pushed out of her head more times today than she cared to count.

"Do I get to meet the famed Willa?" Nora asked as she unwound her scarf and looked toward the staircase.

"I think you mean 'infamous,' since she's rarely discussed in a positive light." Gray felt a momentary pang of guilt until she remembered the state Willa had left the kitchen in when she'd come back from her showings earlier today. "And no, she's a bartender at a dive bar in South Philly, so she's at work."

"At least you get some alone time on the weekends." Nora pulled off her jacket to reveal a chunky gray sweater underneath. "Things not much improved?"

Gray sighed and eased out of her boots. At least it hadn't been wet out, so it could have been worse. "I think her preferred place to live would be a frat house. I will concede that she's a surprisingly good cook, though she leaves the kitchen incredibly messy."

"Oof," Nora said. Gray appreciated the commiseration, even though she knew that Nora only heard her side of things.

Finally down to an appropriate amount of clothing for being indoors, Gray wriggled her toes in her sock-clad feet and tried to absorb the warmth around her. "Do you want a cup of tea or something?"

"Tea would be great." Nora's face was still flushed from the cold, and Gray could now see that her cheeks were just as red as the tips of her ears.

"Just a heads-up: S'mores is probably under a blanket on the sofa." She cocked her head toward an almost imperceptible lump. "I'll be right back."

Gray puttered around the kitchen, taking the few extra minutes alone to compose herself. She felt like that was a lot of what she did around Nora these days.

When the kettle whistled, she poured the water into two mugs. She didn't often use it, but she had a little serving tray with room for milk, sugar, and an assortment of tea bags. It was impractical given her day-to-day life, but she appreciated having it now as she walked cautiously back into the living room.

She placed the tray down on the coffee table. "Tea is served."

S'mores, who'd grown so lazy in her new home that she sometimes felt like a piece of furniture instead of a living creature, had crawled on Nora's lap and was sleeping soundly.

"I'm afraid to move her," Nora said apologetically.

"Because she'll never be comfortable again," Gray said sarcastically as she gave S'mores a loving pat. She leaned forward and surveyed the sachets of tea. "I have peppermint, chamomile, or ginger tea. Pick your poison."

"Peppermint, please."

Gray opened the tea bag and dropped it in one of the mugs. "Do you want milk or sugar?"

"A splash of milk would be perfect."

"Good?" Gray asked as she tipped the tiny pitcher.

"That's great, thank you."

Gray handed her the cup, their fingers brushing as she transferred the handle to Nora. Little sparks zigged across her slowly thawing skin. She shivered as the sensation worked through her body.

Nora reached for Gray's hand and enveloped her fingertips. "Are you still cold?"

The skin-on-skin contact felt so unbelievably good, except that it set off all kinds of warning bells in Gray's head. Not that her body seemed at all concerned. It just wanted to lean into the touch, into the moment, into the vibration in the air around them.

The last time they'd been on this sofa together, she thought she'd misread the signs. That she was projecting her own desire onto Nora. Now, after the last few days, she wasn't so sure anymore.

When Nora's bright blue eyes scanned her face, their fingers still intertwined, all the reasons that this was a bad idea floated into the background, barely registering in Gray's consciousness.

So what if Paul had been an asshole? And people who worked together hooked up all the time. Trusting someone, laying her emotions bare, was very different than wanting to sleep with them. Knowing what Nora sounded like when she came apart instead of what Gray imagined it to be like didn't have to change anything.

Her mind was working out a puzzle, trying to fit the pieces together in a way that made sense, when Nora's stare dropped down to her lips and then dragged upward to find Gray's likely blown pupils.

She'd been trying so hard to keep it together. To keep it professional. To keep herself separated from any type of emotional entanglement.

But right now, all she wanted was to keep Nora looking at her the way she was, like Gray was something precious that Nora wanted to keep safe.

"This isn't just me, right?" Nora's voice was low, just barely above a whisper as it floated through the few inches of space between them.

Nora's admission sent a pang of want straight to her center. Because god, she felt it. She'd been feeling it for months, even when she hadn't liked Nora all that much.

And now? Well, she didn't feel like she had enough energy left to keep fighting it.

"It's not just you." Gray gulped. "I feel it too."

Nora's stare didn't leave hers, like she was memorizing this moment, eyes tracking everything when she said, "And this is probably a terrible idea."

Gray set her mug of tea on the coffee table without looking, hoping it wasn't close to the edge. She leaned her side against the cushion and took a deep breath. At least she and Nora were on the same page. "Definitely not my best idea."

She loved the little lopsided smile that Nora gave her, even if it made her heart beat erratically. The staccato thump threatened to burst out of her chest when Nora asked, "Do you know what you want to do about it?"

They were so close now that Gray could see the light smattering of freckles across the bridge of Nora's nose. She felt it acutely then, the magnetism that whirred through her whenever they stayed still for long enough.

The edges of her lips tipped upward into a smile. "Probably nothing good."

"I'm worried this could change things between us." Nora's voice was impossibly soft.

It had been a fear Gray had, too, among so many others. "Only if we let it," she answered, plucking the mug from Nora's hands.

"Who knows?" Nora said as Gray placed the cup on the coffee table. "Maybe it won't be any good."

Gray nodded and licked her lips, anticipation vibrating through her. "Probably not."

She sighed when Nora's hand, still warm from her tea, cupped Gray's face gently. Her eyes fluttered closed when she felt soft, tentative lips ghost across her own. Butterflies exploded in her stomach as their lips slotted together, and she captured the sigh that escaped Nora.

Nora's thumb traced along her cheekbone, excruciatingly slowly. Gray hadn't expected her to be so tender, to savor this moment and imbue it with a deeper meaning than lust.

The small bit of resistance she had left in her evaporated when Nora's tongue slid across her bottom lip, asking for entry. She leaned forward and pressed her free hand into the cushion below her. What she really wanted was to wrap her fingers into Nora's sweater and pull her closer, to meld their bodies together and give herself over fully to what was happening.

"Nora," she husked out before sucking on her bottom lip and finishing with a gentle bite, loving the low, quiet growl that Nora let out.

Who knew when she'd get a chance to do this again?

Nora smiled against her lips. "Definitely no good."

Gray kissed at the edge of her mouth before answering. "The absolute worst."

The front door of her house blew open just then, like a

freight train was barreling through. Gray pulled back and looked toward the door while S'mores bounded off of Nora to investigate whatever the hell was happening.

Willa stood in the entry, staring at the two of them on the couch. "Whoops."

Gray briefly noticed the anger etched across her sister's face before it disappeared. A slightly embarrassed smile took its place, and Gray thought that maybe she'd been projecting her own feelings onto a face very similar to her own.

Confusion, then annoyance, then frustration rattled through Gray as she tried to make sense of why her sister was standing in the doorway. "What are you doing here? Why aren't you at work?"

All she wanted to do was erase the last five seconds from her life and lean back into Nora.

Willa, oblivious as usual, pulled off her boots at the door. She shrugged, and her shoulders hung heavily for a moment before she tipped her chin toward Gray, like whatever she was about to say didn't matter all that much. "That's not really gonna work out."

The frustration exploded like fire in her veins, her hands already balled into fists when she stood up. "Are you kidding me? Did you really get fired today?"

"I can pick up another bartending job. It's not a big deal," Willa said as she headed toward the kitchen.

Gray felt like she was about ten seconds away from having a complete meltdown, and that absolutely wasn't something she wanted Nora to see.

"Nora, I am so sorry, but I think you should go. I need to talk to my sister." She gave Nora an apologetic stare, proud of herself that her gaze only dropped once to Nora's still wet lips.

"Yeah. I get it." Nora took a step closer and ran her hand

down Gray's arm, blue eyes offering comfort and understanding. "Are you okay?"

She nodded, but refused to lean into the support that Nora seemingly wanted to provide. "I'm fine. We can talk about this later, yeah?"

There was a moment where it looked like hurt flashed across Nora's face, but she tempered it quickly. "Yeah. Just text me."

Seconds later, fueled by the wisps of a moment interrupted far too soon, Gray was headed into the kitchen with what felt like enough rage to sustain her for a lifetime.

Chapter Nineteen

Nora decided to stop in the office before heading home since she was in the neighborhood. Still, she knew it was fueled by a pathetic part of her that thought maybe Gray would resolve things with her sister quickly and want to hang out again.

This was why she needed to keep herself more compartmentalized.

Her nature was to wrap herself up in other people, to wrap herself around them whenever she felt a connection.

It was why sequestering herself from the world had been such a good idea. She didn't know how to do casual.

Everything about whatever was happening between her and Gray was a recipe for disaster. She knew this on an instinctual level as she unlocked the office door and hurried inside. She let out a frustrated sigh and rubbed her hands across her face.

"You okay?" Callie sat at her desk, drinking a cup of coffee and watching something on her laptop.

"Sorry," Nora squeaked, a sound she'd probably never made inside the walls of this office. If anyone had to hear it, she was glad that it was Callie, who seemed far less invested in what was going on with her than anyone else in the office. "What are you doing here?"

"My fifteen-year-old is on a date. I figured rather than head back home to the suburbs, I'd just hang out here until he's done." Callie sighed into her coffee cup, though she didn't seem especially upset by the information she'd just shared.

Nora tried to pull her kid's name from the ether of her memory. The last time Nora had talked about Callie's children, the fifteen-year-old would have been closer to ten.

"Jake," she said, the name coming to her before she'd processed it. She'd seen the kids in the office a few times over the years, for the holiday party that Cynthia forced her to attend as her once-a-year mandatory (for Nora) event. "He plays baseball?" she asked more than said.

Callie nodded. "Since he could walk. Though this year..." She stopped and gave Nora a strange look, like she'd just remembered Nora very likely didn't care. Or, at the very least, she'd never acted like she cared before.

And that was fair.

Nora didn't do well with shades of gray... no pun intended.

When she'd shut down, she'd shut down everything. Engaging about anything would have been a slippery slope for her.

She'd realized in the last few months that for all the time she spent thinking that her reticence and reclusiveness were no one's problem but her own, it wasn't true. Any time someone had tried to build a bridge with her, she'd run to her safe side and hacked the ropes with a machete.

Nora eased her jacket off and threw it on the back of an empty chair. She walked over to the kitchen and started making a coffee. "What's different about this year?"

Callie leveled a pointed but surprisingly soft stare in her

direction. "You socializing, for one, but I assume that's not what you were asking."

She liked the no-nonsense lilt in Callie's voice—god knows she probably needed it with two kids at home. "Not going to let me skate by on that one, are you?"

"A week after I started here, I came in one morning, and you'd moved your desk to the very corner where it resides now." Those were the early days, when Cynthia still sat out in the main area instead of in her office.

Nora did have the good sense to blush when she remembered that, yes, she'd done that. "It wasn't personal, I promise. I was just... going through some things."

Callie nodded and paused whatever was playing on her laptop before turning her attention more fully to Nora. "I figured you just didn't want any competition."

"Competition was fine, but I wasn't in the market for friends," Nora answered honestly.

"I was disappointed. I'd been really looking forward to doing things differently this time."

Nora met Callie's stare again as the shame washed over her. Callie had met her at possibly the lowest point in her life, but she had no idea what had been going on in Callie's life at the time either.

She walked across the room and sat in the empty chair next to Callie's desk, where she'd thrown her coat. "I'm sorry." She was saying that a lot these days, and she meant it every single time.

"I appreciate that," Callie said sincerely. "I was coming from Brenneman Brothers, and I'd really hoped this would be a fresh start."

They'd all heard of Brenneman Brothers & Associates. It was an old boys' club that was as successful as it was toxic, at least according to the rumors. With a foothold in the local real estate market for the past thirty-five years, their networking was invaluable—but it came at a cost. Unrelenting competition. Casual misogyny. A culture that seemed impervious to the #MeToo movement.

"How long did you work there?"

"A little over ten years."

"Wow." Nora let out a low whistle.

Callie laughed. "Yeah, I know."

"How did you survive there that long? I mean," she added, 'if the rumors are true?"

"I started in 2007, right before the bubble burst. It was all-hands-on-deck then, with everyone and their uncle getting a mortgage."

Nora had heard the stories of the rise and the fall. She'd gotten into real estate about ten years ago, once the market had finally rebounded. Andrea had always talked about surviving that period as if she'd been to war and back.

"Seems like that would make it even harder to stay there during that period? With the pie getting smaller and the other agents just as hungry as ever?"

"Things were fine for that first year. I'd just had Jake, so I was dipping my toes into the real estate world for the first time. I could set my own hours, and there were so many people to work with who probably would have been blocked out. I was new, so I didn't know the rumors about the company. I just knew that they were taking on new agents."

"And then?"

Callie shrugged, though her face betrayed her. "Things got uglier. Most brokerages had a moratorium on taking on new agents, so I was sort of stuck."

"That makes sense, but I am sorry you went through that."

"I had Reese two years later. And I was just so excited," she said wistfully before her face dropped. "It was about three years after that that I found out my then husband, Allen, was cheating."

"That's terrible." And truly, Nora meant it with every breath in her lungs. "I know what that feels like," she added quietly.

Months ago, the sympathetic stare Callie was giving her would have made her want to throw something. Now, all it did was make her feel that tenuous bridge that she usually tried so hard to fight.

"But you stayed at Brenneman Brothers for"—Nora did quick mental math—"five more years? Why?"

"I'd just become a single parent. My confidence was at an all-time low. I was trying to navigate raising two kids under ten while still providing a good life for them."

"I couldn't imagine."

Callie laughed and leaned back in her chair. She was always such a perfect balance of positive and no-nonsense that Nora would never have guessed what she'd been through.

"It's easy not to want to let people see us struggle," Callie said knowingly. "But once the kids were both in school and I felt like I'd sort of gotten the hang of single parenting, I decided to make the move."

"To Philly Finds," Nora said, her cheeks heating up. "Where you were met with me."

"I'd survived much worse environments, but like I said earlier, I was disappointed. I'd been excited to help build something from the ground up. To work on a team of strong women."

"I know it's probably not much of a consolation, but I do wish I could go back and do things differently. And I'm very sorry if I ever made you feel unwelcome before."

Callie nodded. "I appreciate that. And not to be obtuse, but are you in some kind of program where you're making amends or something? Seems like you've done a complete one-eighty since coming back from Bermuda."

Nora wasn't supposed to mention the possible company restructure, but as she looked at Callie, so willing to give her another chance, she realized that, though the promotion had been the catalyst for her change, it had become about so much more than that.

Gray's face flitted through her mind, but it was so much more than that too. "I was given another chance, and it seemed like a stupid thing to waste."

Callie picked up her own coffee cup and surveyed its contents before lifting her stare back up to Nora. She leaned into the walkway between the desks and held her mug toward Nora. "Well then, cheers to finally figuring it out."

They tapped their mugs together, and in the nearly empty office, save the first two employees of Philly Finds, Nora felt like she was finally on the right track.

It had been five days since she and Gray had kissed. Not that she was counting.

And still... they hadn't talked about it.

There was no reason to rush things, but there had been a definite unsteadiness between them since it had happened.

On Tuesday morning in the office, Gray had quietly asked if they could table the conversation for the time being. "Friends for now? Until I can figure some things out?" she'd asked, her voice uncharacteristically unsure.

The old Nora would have agonized about it. She'd have run through a million different scenarios and permutations and fears.

Not that this current version of herself was perfect, but she was trying. She'd gotten coffee with Callie twice since their run-in at the office, and she'd even sat at the table in the kitchen one day while Trent and Sage were eating lunch.

Progress was measured in inches, not miles.

The space, she told herself, was a good thing. She needed clarity about what she wanted—especially where Gray was concerned. In past relationships, Nora had been happy to let the other person take the lead, even if it was to her own detriment. It had always been, she'd accepted, the cost of making things go smoothly.

She now realized that just meant she had been holding on to the wrong partners because she was more afraid of being alone than being unhappy.

Unhappiness hadn't gotten her anywhere, and neither had closing herself off from the world.

So, she was trying something different.

Wrapping her scarf around her neck, she walked over to Callie's desk. "You about ready?"

On their coffee run yesterday, they'd decided to go to the upcoming Realtor and local business happy hour together. It would be the second-to-last one before the holidays, and Nora was hoping to get a few new contacts as they headed into the dead of winter.

It also didn't hurt to have a friend tag along, given that there was a very real possibility Andrea would be there. She'd managed to go years without seeing her, mostly because she avoided anything related to the broader realty world to make sure they didn't run into one another.

In their ongoing conversations, Nora had pushed herself to open up to Callie. Some parts of their lives were very different, but they both understood the desire to make it on their own, as well as the crushing sense of desolation that came with betrayal.

Still, their conversations were surprisingly positive. Spending time with Callie had already started to feel like catching up with an old friend.

"Well, I am letting Jake watch Reese tonight, so beyond the ever-present fear that they're going to burn the house down, I'm good."

Nora laughed and amended her recent thought to: mostly positive. "I'm sure they're going to have a much more fun night than we will."

Callie rolled her eyes and buttoned up her jacket. "I just have this feeling that so many Brenneman Brothers people will be there."

"Well, if they are... fuck 'em."

That earned a laugh as Callie bumped their shoulders together. "What about you? How are you feeling?"

"Like I'm sick of hiding. From myself... and definitely from Andrea."

"That's the spirit," Callie said loudly before Julian, who was on the phone, shot her a glare. She dropped her head and laughed while they walked toward the door. "Is Gray coming tonight?"

"I don't know." Which was the truth. Nora had only seen her in the office a handful of times, usually when she was there to print out paperwork.

S'mores, too, had been mostly absent.

But in spite of her own uncertainty because of the kiss—or whatever else was going on in Gray's life—she hadn't faltered.

And that was something to be proud of.

"I'm sure she doesn't want to see them either."

Nora's brow lifted as she slid into the passenger's seat of Callie's SUV. "What do you mean?"

She watched Callie realize in real time that she'd possibly

said something she shouldn't have. "Oh, I assumed you knew. She used to work there."

"Is that supposed to be a secret?" Nora asked, waiting for Callie to pull out onto the street.

Part of Nora's complete withdrawal from society was that unless someone explicitly told her something, she probably didn't know about it. She hadn't googled any of the rest of the Philly Finds team. Why did it matter if they'd been the top agent in their last office, she'd once thought, if they wouldn't be here?

Sure, she didn't feel that way now, singularly focused as she was on proving herself through work because it was the one thing she felt in control of, but she'd been absolutely disinterested—and sometimes downright unwilling—to be aware of what was going on around her.

Callie didn't answer until they'd merged onto the exit to head to Center City. "Probably not? It's just... you of all people probably understand what it's like to have a shitty experience and not want to talk about it." Callie threw a hand over her mouth. "I'm sorry. I didn't mean for that to sound the way it probably did."

Nora laughed and waved her off. "You're fine. But yeah, Gray working at Brenneman Brothers hasn't come up."

"Well, I hope she knows that she has a team of people in her corner if she does decide to come." Callie shot her a quick glance and a genuine smile. "Same goes for you."

Chapter Twenty

Gray had been at the happy hour for about thirty minutes. It was already busy. At least fifty Realtors and small business owners milled about, easing into the casual but focused conversation that networking required. She'd planned to go early, before the drunken revelry began and the Realtors dropped the niceties in favor of less guarded language, at least with one another. Brenneman Brothers would undoubtedly have a decent contingent of people flowing in and out throughout the event, though there was no one yet that she recognized.

The Philadelphia Realtors' Association had rented out a bar downtown, and for the next few hours, it was going to be Gray's own personal version of hell.

Still, the networking contacts could be invaluable over the coming months and heading into spring.

She'd met up with Trent for a drink beforehand, and they'd stuck close to one another since arriving. He was a few years younger than she was, but he'd gotten into real estate at twenty-one, so he'd been an agent for longer.

Still, he struggled with the networking aspect, and when

he'd asked if she wanted to go together, she was happy to help him—even if it meant running into people she'd otherwise rather not see.

His invitation had helped her make a decision she'd been waffling on. It was easier to do things for other people than for herself, even if she sometimes resented them for it. The last week of living with her sister had proven that point in spades.

And maybe it had provided a helpful distraction from Nora.

What to do about Nora was the million-dollar question on her mind from dusk until dawn each day, when she would lie in bed and ruminate over how catastrophically fucked she was.

Nora Gallagher had been a problem before, and now... she was so much more than that.

Gray liked her. Gray wanted to see where this thing between them could go. But she was also terrified.

When she'd let her guard down and they'd kissed, it had been better than she'd even imagined. And she'd imagined it dozens of times already. What would happen if she kept letting the wall drop lower? A little trust here. A little vulnerability there.

Brick by brick, she'd start to depend on Nora. To want things for them. To have hopes and dreams about a hypothetical future. It was too much.

But still... that kiss wasn't enough.

She'd thought about it almost every free second. It had made talking to Nora so difficult since it had happened.

Trent's voice was a welcome distraction for about two seconds—until she processed his words. "Bro. Callie and Nora are here. We should go say hi."

He was like an excited puppy, which she'd been trying to channel into helping him meet local businesses since they'd arrived. She'd also been trying to strike him calling her 'bro' from his vocabulary, but that didn't seem likely to happen anytime soon.

"Bro," she emphasized back, elbowing him gently in the ribs. "You already know them. That doesn't count as the networking we discussed."

"Bro," he pleaded, like she was legitimately the arbiter of who he could talk to for the night. "It would be rude not to say hi."

She rolled her eyes but smiled in spite of her effort to hide being entertained. "That's Cameron Calloway of Calloway Brewing," she said, tilting her head toward a woman dressed more casually than the rest of the guests, standing in a small group of people.

Trent nodded excitedly. "I love that place."

"She's who we should be talking to."

She sort of loved how Trent pointed obviously when he said, "She's already busy."

Gray nodded. He was making a fair, albeit annoying, point. "Fine."

She walked, Trent in tow, toward Callie and Nora, who stood at the bar. It was Nora who noticed her first, her blue eyes settling on Gray as they moved through the room, bobbing and weaving past small groups in conversation.

"Hey, guys. What's shakin'?" God bless Trent for his complete obliviousness.

Nora lifted an eyebrow and smiled, covering her mouth with her hand like she was trying to hold back a laugh. "We just got here, so that seems like a better question for you two," she said, her focus drifting back to Gray.

All she wanted was to be close to Nora, but when she was close to her, it was difficult to think clearly. Another reason why keeping her distance had made sense.

Gray rocked forward instinctively but broke eye contact to scan the crowd. "Still early, but it seems like a decent turnout."

Nora flicked her gaze around the room, never settling on any group for longer than a few seconds, almost like she was looking for someone.

Callie, two drinks in hand, turned away from the bar and into their group. She handed Nora a glass of red wine and kept a cocktail for herself. "I hope this isn't all work because this is the first night I've been out on the town in ages."

"To Jake not burning the house down," Nora said as she and Callie clinked their glasses together.

Gray noted the comfort between them. There was a familiarity that she knew hadn't been there a few weeks ago.

"Mind if I slide in to grab another drink?" Trent asked, surveying the space between Callie and Nora.

The group did a little shuffle to make room for Trent to stand in front of the bar, which led Nora toward Gray so they were now standing next to each other.

Trent looked over his shoulder toward Callie. "What are you drinking? That looks good."

"Oh, it's the..." Not coming up with the name, she turned around and faced the bar with him, picking up a menu to show him the drink.

It was just the two of them now. Gray looked up at Nora and tried to suppress the butterflies in her stomach that seemed to be present whenever they stood within five feet of one another.

"Probably not the best time to have our overdue conversation." The least she could do was acknowledge the elephant in the room.

Nora flashed her a lopsided smile and tipped her head down, her breath ghosting across Gray's cheek. "I was

221

wondering if we were just going to pretend like it never happened."

"I don't want that. I've been..." Gray gave into the pull by another inch. "This is a lot for me to process right now."

She could feel more than see Nora nodding next to her, their heads so close together they were almost touching. It was electric, and if Gray tilted her face ever so slightly, she could taste the lips she'd so desperately missed for the last week.

"I get that," Nora said quietly, her voice low and sensual in a way that Gray felt through her entire body.

"And you're just so..." Again, she struggled to find the words, but after almost a week of silence on anything that actually mattered, she knew she owed it to Nora, even if this wasn't the place or time. At the very least, she needed to communicate more than she had been. "Unexpected," was what she finally settled on.

"I wasn't expecting this either." Nora tilted her head back and made eye contact, like she was searching for something. "But I don't want to pretend it isn't happening. I've had enough pretending and avoiding for a lifetime."

Gray smiled, despite how the butterflies had gone rogue in her stomach and were now trying to flutter their way up her throat and out to freedom. "Can we talk? Tonight. After the event I mean?"

And yeah, she'd do almost anything to keep seeing the wide smile stretched across Nora's face for as long as she possibly could. She was already feeling more relaxed after this brief conversation, even if it hadn't actually resolved anything except that it got them talking again.

A voice cut through the din of the conversation in the bar. "Nora? I was wondering when I'd see you at one of these things."

Nora tensed, but she didn't move away from Gray. Her

smile, which was usually one of Gray's favorite things about Nora these days, disappeared without a trace. Which meant that Gray hated this woman on sight.

Nora stood there like a cardboard cutout of a real person, flat and one-dimensional, as she stared at the woman who'd inserted herself into their conversation.

"Andrea."

Hearing that name made Gray stand up straighter, too, and take an instinctive step closer to Nora. Because when someone cried in your car about their dead dad and a shitty ex-partner who made them feel like they didn't matter, it was pretty easy to put them soundly in the 'oh, fuck no' column.

Gray studied Andrea while Andrea leveled her attention at Nora. About Gray's height, she had dark, well-gelled hair that, contrasted with her makeup, made her look fairly androgynous. She was attractive—objectively—but her eyes were cold.

Even when Nora had been withdrawn, her eyes had always been so expressive. Clear or stormy or sparkling or pensive, there was always so much going on below the surface, even when Nora wanted to hide it. Imagining Nora in a serious relationship with someone like Andrea was more than a little difficult for Gray's brain to compute.

"Are you here with your team?" Andrea gave Gray a look that could only be called judgmental before she scanned past them to where Callie and Trent were still chatting animatedly at the bar. "Quite a ragtag group you've assembled," she said when her stare settled back on Nora.

Who, to her credit, was leveling a look back at Andrea that Gray would never want to be on the receiving end of. "It's a big event, Andrea. I'm sure there's enough room here for both of us."

Possibly hearing the strain in Nora's tone, Trent and Callie turned around, their backs against the bar to survey the situation as it unfolded.

"You two looked pretty cozy when I walked up," Andrea said, flicking her gaze to Gray. She gave her a dismissive once-over, then smiled at Nora again. "Did I interrupt something?"

Andrea exuded confidence, but Gray wasn't impressed. She knew the type all too well, and it was only a small consolation that she hadn't seen him lurking around yet tonight.

At least, even if it killed her to credit Andrea with anything, she seemed overt in her narcissism. She didn't disguise it as altruism like Paul had.

"You could walk into an empty room, and you'd still be interrupting." Nora took a small step closer, her fingertips settling against Gray's back. "And who I talk to is absolutely none of your business."

"Oh, the baby found some bite." The hollow laugh Andrea let out made the hair on Gray's neck stand up, making it hard to appreciate how good the casual yet deliberate touch from Nora felt.

Andrea drained the rest of her drink and rolled the wineglass's stem between her fingertips. The whole thing gave Gray the ick a million times over.

"I wanted to chat with a few people here before it gets too busy," Gray said, turning to Nora and effectively boxing Andrea out of the conversation. It felt way better than it probably should have. "Did you want to join me?"

The look Nora gave her almost made the last five minutes of torture worth it. "Sounds perfect."

They walked away, Nora's hand still settled against the small of her back. Before they stopped at a group to mingle, Gray leaned over. "That was your ex?" she said with as much self-control as she could manage.

Nora smiled sheepishly, but with even a few feet of

breathing room, she didn't look nearly as out of sorts as Gray would have expected, given what seemed like a long overdue run-in after parting on bad circumstances. "Yep. That's Andrea. Though, in my defense, I think she's worse now than I remember."

"And I can't imagine you remembering her very fondly, so that's really saying something."

Stopping, Nora shifted her hand over to Gray's hip and squeezed it gently. "Are we still going to talk after this?"

Gray nodded, finding it a little hard to breathe—let alone speak—with Nora so close.

Nora smiled and scanned the room that had grown busier around them in the last half hour. "Okay, good. You ready?"

Her heart beating impossibly fast, Gray tried to steady herself. She knew that Nora was talking about mingling, but it was what came after that gave Gray the feeling that she was floating at the same time she was free falling.

They were on the precipice of something, and ready or not, it was happening.

Gray pulled up outside of Nora's house and eased into a spot out front. She put the car in park and clasped her fingers together to keep from fidgeting. "I didn't know you lived in Northern Liberties. We're practically neighbors."

"Do you want to come in?" Nora asked, unbuckling her seat belt.

At the very least, she owed Nora an honest conversation. "Sure."

She followed Nora up the steps to a row home that looked very similar to her own from the outside. An original build that had probably been rehabbed at some point, the brick exterior was almost invisible except for what she could see around the porch light that Nora had left on.

"So your ex..." Gray said as she trailed into the house behind Nora. "Was she always..."

"Condescending?" Nora supplied as she unbuttoned her jacket in the doorway.

"I was going to say 'the personification of a Disney villain,' but sure, that works too."

Nora laughed and flicked on the living room light, stopping whatever Gray was going to say next. Nora's house was decorated beautifully, with rich colors and bold prints covering the walls. The left wall running along the ground floor and its staircase was exposed brick, which contrasted beautifully with the deep emerald of her sofa.

"I love your house." She didn't try to hide the awe from her voice.

"Thank you. Andrea always hated my taste in decor."

Gray rolled her eyes. "I think we can agree that Andrea is a complete idiot on so many levels."

"Do you want to sit?" Nora gestured toward the sofa. Her other hand reached out to take Gray's coat. "I can hang this up for you."

Gray took the extra few seconds to stare unabashedly at the aesthetic of a house that she never would have pegged as *Nora* but just, somehow, felt right. There was still so much she didn't know about her.

Nora moved back toward the sofa. "Did you want a drink or anything?"

"I'm good."

"How are things going with Willa?" Nora leaned back and propped her elbow on the top of the sofa, resting her head against her hand.

She looked so... cozy... was the word that Gray's brain settled on.

Still, all the enticing comfort in the world couldn't distract her from whatever the hell was going on with her sister. Gray wasn't naturally good at sharing things about herself. Still, she wanted to be honest with Nora. She deserved at least that much after dealing with Gray's radio silence. "They're... going. She got another job quickly, so at least she wasn't lying about that."

"I'm glad to hear that," Nora said sincerely. Gray watched her swallow and let out a deep exhale. "But I haven't really known what to think since leaving your house that day. You haven't really seemed open to talking." Nora's nose scrunched up with the cutest little hint of annoyance and embarrassment when she said, "It kind of seems like you've been avoiding me."

The fact that Nora was the mature, communicative one in this conversation was not boding well for Gray. At all.

Gray had worn her hair up tonight, and she smoothed a few flyaways against her temple. "My parents moved to Tennessee eight years ago."

"Oh?" Nora asked, raising her telltale eyebrow.

She nodded. Suddenly, it felt important to get the words out. And she knew if she didn't say them now, she may not pluck up the courage again any time soon. Not being honest would ruin whatever was happening between them, and for as terrified as she was of moving forward, staying still, for the first time in a long time, seemed worse. "I was twenty-three, and Willa had just turned eighteen."

Leaning closer, Nora brushed her thumb against the inside of Gray's wrist. "Why the move?"

Gray liked how much they touched, how sometimes it seemed like that was what Nora used to communicate if words were failing her.

Tonight, Nora was using both. Gray already felt like a goner.

She chewed on her bottom lip to avoid admitting how many years she'd spent picking apart that exact question. Finally, she shrugged, refusing to give what had happened the power it once held over her. "I think they were just done."

She watched Nora's head tilt to the side, blue eyes narrowing. "Done with what?"

"Being parents?"

She wasn't over it. She didn't know if she'd ever be, and the way Nora's face softened made Gray want to burst into tears. No one knew how she felt about her parents leaving except for Becks, since she'd been around when it had happened.

She'd never talked about it with Willa, who'd only just finished high school. Her parents had told them they were moving, offhandedly one day when she'd stopped by the house that summer to drop off a graduation present for her sister.

"You think they left because they didn't want to be in you or your sister's life anymore?"

Gray shrugged and wiped at her tired eyes. She tried not to think about her parents often anymore, since she assumed they weren't really thinking about her. "I'm not really sure what else to think. They just told us they were leaving. Didn't ask Willa if she wanted to go along. Didn't imply that they wanted us to go. They weren't actively involved in our lives before that, so it's not like it was the shock of the century."

She didn't pull back when Nora's hand shifted down to clasp their fingers together. "I'm sorry. That's awful. And that's nothing you could have ever deserved to have happen to you." Nora frowned and squeezed Gray's hand. "Do you still talk to them?"

"No. I decided that if they didn't want me, I didn't want

them." And she definitely didn't need them. She'd decided that years ago, too, and built her life to ensure the truth in it.

Nora's focused stare caught hers, so much emotion floating behind those blue eyes that it made Gray a little dizzy. "Does Willa?"

She shrugged. "I don't know. We don't talk about it."

"I'm sure that was hard on both of you. I'm sure it's still hard, some days. I try not to, but I think a lot about my parents. Especially lately."

"What do you think about?" There were very few people in her life she discussed her parents with, and Becks's own home life was so painfully functional that it made Gray embarrassed to pull at the threads of her insecurity over how she felt about her childhood.

Maybe Gray hadn't 'dealt' with her parents' abandonment and general reticence in the traditional sense, but she'd tried to move past it. That had seemed like enough. For a while.

And now? Maybe she didn't quite feel ready, but she also wasn't ready to be left behind by Nora.

Nora rolled her lip between her teeth, then stilled. Maybe she was regretting opening this conversational topic. Finally, she let her bottom lip go. "My dad's acceptance was very conditional. I still don't understand why. Maybe just so he could exert control over things?" She felt Nora's fingers fidget between her own, but Gray stayed silent, hoping she'd continue. "And my mom just... let him do it. She never defended me. Or herself. When I came out at twenty-two, my dad had a complete meltdown."

Gray pulled their past conversation up to the surface, trying to remember the few times Nora had mentioned her parents. "You said your relationship with them was strained."

Gray had never felt the need to come out to her parents,

since she didn't think it mattered to them. Would rejection hurt worse than ambivalence?

Nora nodded. "He basically told me that he wasn't okay with it and that I shouldn't keep coming around if that's how I wanted to live my life." She let out a hollow laugh. "I honestly don't even think that he cared if I was gay. It was always one thing or another. If I got a B, it should have been an A. If I got an A, it should have been an A+."

"Did you stop talking to your mom, too, when you came out?"

"Sort of? We never had the best relationship. I was always resentful that I knew she didn't agree with my dad but wouldn't stand up to him. So we went through the next couple of years talking intermittently. I think their deaths hit me so hard because my mom and I were finally getting to a better place." Nora's focus shifted down to their interlocked fingers before she made eye contact again. "I've never told anyone that."

Gray squeezed her hand. "What happened to them? If you don't mind me asking."

"Car accident. They were coming back from a party. He was over the legal limit to drive. Just barely, and I have no idea if that impacted things, but I know either way he would have insisted on driving." Gray felt Nora's hand tighten within her own. "And my mom let him. That's what they did. He made shitty decisions, and she went along with them."

"Oh god, Nora, I'm so sorry." Gray wanted to wrap her up in her arms, but she stayed still, waiting for Nora to continue.

Nora's voice cracked. "I was so mad at both of them. And my mom and I had been talking more. I was really optimistic that maybe she was going to leave him. I wish I would have pushed harder, been there for her more."

"You can't know what happened that night, Nora. And you

can't expect that anything you did or didn't do contributed to what happened." She had to know that, right?

"All I know is that I realized I was the equivalent of my mother in my relationship with Andrea. And still, knowing that... knowing how things played out," she said, her voice strained, "I didn't leave her."

"It's not that easy to see when it's happening."

"You're so much stronger than you give yourself credit for, Gray. You don't hide from the world, even if it hurt you. If *people* hurt you."

"I like that you think that about me." Even if it wasn't true. Gray was far more broken than she let anyone see. She talked to everyone, but she trusted no one. She went into every experience assuming that people would disappoint her, which was why she tried to have low expectations. All she wanted, not unlike the Nora from a few months ago, was to build a life that was impervious to anyone else. Because other people were wrecking balls to the carefully crafted security she'd managed to build.

Nora's free hand moved up to Gray's chin, knuckles ghosting along the edge of her jaw. "I'm sorry that your parents didn't take the time to get to know you. The more I learn about you, the more I want to know."

Her breathing hitched as Nora's hand changed directions. The light touch sent little sparks of awareness across her face. She knew there were unshed tears shining behind her eyes. The safety and comfort Nora seemingly wanted to provide was so tempting. She wanted to fall into it, to pretend like everything was okay.

But they'd already gone too far. This wasn't a casual hookup. Gray had feelings, and when this inevitably imploded, she'd be left holding the bag—another mess to clean up that she'd rather not make.

They'd both said so much. Shared so much. All the little threads of connection had woven together during this conversation to link them together.

Gray felt like she was physically being pulled forward. She was terrified, yet she couldn't stop herself.

Which she realized when she noticed how close their faces had gotten, Nora's eyes searching her own.

Nora's hand cupped her cheek, their lips only a few inches away from one another.

"Sometimes I worry that I'll be like my parents." Gray said the words like a confession, breathing them into the space between them, hoping that, somehow, they would be safe with Nora. They didn't feel safe to keep to herself anymore.

A gentle thumb caressed her cheekbone in slow, lazy lines. "You aren't like your parents."

"You can't know that." It was one of those secrets that lived deep inside of her, that she didn't even pull out privately to turn over in her mind. She resented her sister. She was afraid to get close to other people. Was it, deep down, because along with other people hurting her, she knew that she had the capacity to hurt them too?

Nora shook her head, hand falling down to cup Gray's neck just below her jaw. "In Bermuda, you were there for me. You didn't need to be, and yet you stayed with me during the hurricane, just so I wouldn't have to be alone." Gray moved to refute her words again, but Nora cut her off. "I saw the look on your face. You looked genuinely scared that I was so upset, like you'd do anything to take that look away, even if it meant spending twelve hours confined to a small hotel room with someone who wasn't very nice to you."

Gray managed a smile. "You could be pretty difficult."

"I'm aware," Nora said wryly, her face splitting into a grin that made Gray's heart skip a beat. "And you did it anyway. You're a good person, Gray."

"How do you do it?" Gray asked, finding it hard to get the words out with Nora's fingers massaging softly at the base of her skull.

Nora didn't answer for long seconds, focused on the pattern her fingers traced against Gray's neck. "Do what?"

"You just... decided things were going to be different, and now they are." Gray had spent so much of her life trying to live in an emotional stasis that the idea of willingly moving was terrifying.

She missed the soft scratch of Nora's fingers when her hand stilled. "I think at first it was easy to tell myself that I was doing it for the promotion. That was a catalyst that forced me out of my comfort zone, but..."

Gray sighed softly. "But what?"

"As soon as I started to come back to life, it felt like I was finally seeing things clearly."

"What did you see?"

Nora drew her lip between her teeth before letting it go, a shy smile on her face when she admitted, "I thought I'd been buried, but that wasn't true. I'd been planted. I realized how much time I'd wasted. How many people I was affecting by basically being a black hole of negativity. And how, if I didn't get it together, I'd miss out on getting to know people... people like you."

The moment shifted, the air growing thicker. Nora's fingers started moving against her neck again, and her other hand, which had been holding Gray's, started to trace a light pattern up Gray's forearm.

Gray's chest ached with the idea of the person that Nora seemed to see when she looked at her. She wanted to be that person.

And maybe, in this moment, she could be.

Gathering up all her courage, she leaned forward and placed a gentle kiss on Nora's lips. Her mouth parted, and a sigh slipped back into Gray, so perfect that it felt like air bringing her back to life too.

For tonight, that could be enough.

Gray pulled Nora's lower lip into her mouth, sucking gently before she let it go with a soft *pop*, anticipation and desire thrumming through her body just thinking about her words before she finally said them out loud.

"Do you want to go upstairs?"

Chapter Twenty-One

The tenderness of their kiss downstairs morphed into something else by the time they landed in Nora's bed. Heat had permeated the air around them, heady and encompassing as Nora sucked in a ragged breath.

Gray's hands explored, running insistent patterns along Nora's rib cage, fingers digging into her skin. Nora's stomach swooped with each close pass by her already sensitive chest.

She'd been wound too tightly. From Gray. From the stress of life. From this... desire. It had been growing within her, pulling at all those little strings she'd tried so hard to keep in place.

All she wanted to do was let go.

When hungry eyes above her scanned Nora's face, Gray's lip drawn between her teeth as she took Nora in, the last shred of resistance fell away.

"Come here." Nora pulled Gray down to her, their bodies colliding together, slotting into place so excruciatingly perfect that Nora wondered how long she'd last.

"Can we take this off?" Gray asked between kisses

peppered along Nora's jaw, her neck, the exposed skin at her clavicle, fingers plucking and pulling at Nora's sweater.

The last few months of soft, tentative buildup had erupted in what was becoming raw, electrified desire, zapping back and forth between them without losing momentum.

Nora's sweater came off first, and was thrown somewhere across the room.

"Fair is fair," Nora breathed, fingers scratching underneath Gray's T-shirt before tugging at the hem.

Gray sat up on her knees above Nora, arm wrapping back past her opposite shoulder to pull her T-shirt over her head in one fell swoop.

Nora groaned, watching Gray above her, chest heaving as she looked down at Nora with flushed cheeks and a focused stare.

It had been a long time since Nora had been in this position with someone—even longer that she'd felt like it mattered. That she'd wanted it to matter.

And when Gray's hand moved down to toy with the button of Nora's jeans, burning with a want that was quickly becoming uncontainable, something in her snapped.

She pushed herself up on her forearms before unbuttoning her jeans and quickly sliding them down her legs. Gray followed suit, easing off of Nora's bed to stand and strip down.

Nora's vision went a little blurry as she took in the black underwear set that perfectly highlighted all of Gray's excruciatingly sexy curves.

She'd moved across the bed before processing the action and was now on her knees in front of Gray. "This too?" Nora asked, jagged breathing cutting through the quiet, hands reaching up to Gray's chest where her bra could unfasten.

"Yes," Gray sighed, her chest pushing against Nora's fingers as she undid the clasp.

Wrapping an arm around Gray, she pulled her closer, the skin-on-skin contact electric, desire pooling low in her stomach. She dipped her head and swirled a taut nipple in her mouth. A moan of satisfaction broke free from both of them.

She sucked more purposefully when she felt a hand wrap through her hair, urging her closer. Gray moaned again when she scraped lightly with her teeth. It was a sound that Nora would never forget.

Her skin burned, the desire to guide Gray's fingers between her legs growing more insistent by the second. It was becoming a pressing need, but it wasn't the most important one.

What she needed—really needed—was to show Gray all of her appreciation for the last few months. Because Gray, she was realizing, seemed to have some notion that she shouldn't be taken care of, that life was about people taking without giving anything in return.

Nora swirled her tongue one last time against Gray's nipple before charting a path upward. Across Gray's chest, where she nipped and then soothed the flesh she kissed. Onto her neck, as Gray let out a soft sigh and tilted her head so she'd have better access. Nora trailed a column of kisses and soft bites along warm skin, desire tugging in her center with each new point of contact.

"God, that feels good," Gray said just as Nora reached her jaw, sparing a few light kisses before she pulled Gray's lower lip between her own and sucked gently.

The kiss, unsurprisingly, grew heated. Nora wrapped her arms around Gray's back to pull her closer, their chests brushing, Nora's already hard nipples practically begging to be freed from her bra. She dipped her tongue into Gray's mouth, loving the way Gray chased the movements with her own, crushing their bodies closer together.

Gray's arms wrapped themselves around Nora, and she let

out a surprised exhale when her breasts broke free, her bra straps sliding off her shoulders. Gray moved just enough to pull it down Nora's arm and let it fall to the ground, already forgotten.

This... this felt like heaven. Nothing but skin for her to touch, Gray's arms enveloping her in softness and safety and desire so intense Nora wondered how her legs hadn't buckled.

Nora's whole body went tight when she felt Gray's hand ghost along her underwear, fingers tracing a slow pattern against her entrance.

And god, she wanted to let Gray do it. Open her up and make her scream and leave her nothing more than a satisfied, panting mess under Gray's lips and fingers.

Instead, she wrapped her hand around Gray's wrist and held her still. "I want to taste you," Nora said against Gray's lips before pulling the bottom one gently into her mouth. When she let it go, she leaned back, taking Gray in.

Pupils blown wide, Gray hadn't moved her hand, fingers still making their presence known with light strokes that made it hard for Nora to stay on her knees.

"Please," Nora said, not caring if she begged for Gray, if it got her what she wanted in this moment, if she got to know what Gray tasted like, what she sounded like when she came undone.

Gray intertwined their fingers and slid onto the bed before she pulled Nora down on top of her.

It was the only invitation Nora needed. She slotted her thigh between Gray's legs as she kissed her way up her neck. She rocked her hips down, smiling against Gray's soft skin, though it was short-lived after Gray moaned in Nora's ear, the sound rushing through her body, making her toes curl as heat slid through her.

She wanted to continue on her mission, but Gray's light

scratches up and down her back, holding her close, made it hard to think about anything except this moment, about how good it felt where their bodies connected.

With one last nip against Gray's neck, she began kissing a path down Gray's body, muscles tensing against her lips.

"Nora," Gray breathed when Nora reached her hips, biting lightly at the same time she ran a hand down Gray's thigh.

She wrapped her arm around Gray's thigh, Nora allowing her torso to sink against the comforter, wishing she could get some relief from the ache in her center.

"Can I take these off?" Nora asked, her fingers plucking at the fabric she already wanted gone before she skimmed a finger up the length of Gray's entrance. She'd already waited for this moment for so long that a few more seconds to make sure Gray was just as enthused as she was would be worth it.

Gray's hips lifted off the bed at the same time she moaned a strangled, "Yes."

And then Gray was completely naked, like a vision out of Nora's dreams, laid out across her bed. One leg was bent, toes pushing into the mattress. Her other leg fell outward from where her hips opened, creating the softest pillow where Nora rested her head and nuzzled her nose against Gray's thigh.

She moved slowly, deliberately, loving how acutely Gray's muscles tensed with each new kiss and nip and caress.

Anticipation raced through her with each slightly ragged exhale from Gray's parted lips, and if Nora hadn't been soaked before, she definitely was when hands came down against her shoulders, fingers tracing errant patterns across her scorched skin as they held her down.

When her tongue slid against Gray's entrance, Nora met the cant of Gray's hips with her mouth, one of her hands sliding around to bracket Gray in place against the bed. Loving how the weight settled against her shoulder and pushed her deeper into the mattress, Nora wrapped her mouth around Gray's clit, sucking gently before swirling her tongue back and forth. Jagged moans cut through the air whenever she hit the right spot.

Nora was trying to take her time, to savor this moment that had been too long in the making, to pull every ounce of sensation from Gray's body. She wanted to be able to make her feel even half as good as she'd been making Nora feel the past few months.

Then Gray spoke, low and throaty and like she was on the verge of falling apart against Nora's lips. "Please, Nora. Please," she said, fingertips pulling at Nora's shoulder, encouraging her up the bed.

With one last taste, Nora slid Gray's thigh off her shoulder and crawled up toward her. Gray's eyes were so dark, a little wild as they took in Nora's ascent, tracking her like she was stalking prey.

Want reverberated through Nora when her thigh pushed against Gray's clit, and she rocked down instinctively to get more friction.

Gray pulled her down into a messy, frenzied kiss that had them both gasping for air before Nora pulled away, breathing hard into the space between them. "Tell me what you want."

"More. I want to feel more of you," Gray said at the same time Nora realized Gray's hands were suddenly everywhere. Cupping her ass. Running down the line of her spine. Curving delicately across the swell of her hips.

It all happened quickly then. Nora's hand disappeared between their bodies, her fingers rubbing against Gray's clit. The same thigh that had wrapped around her shoulder came up to bracket her hips when Nora eased two fingers inside, enveloped in heat and wetness that made her groan.

"Yes," Gray panted as Nora found a rhythm, her forearm

straining, fingers propelled by her hips. Gray's thigh was keeping them connected in the most excruciating way, their sweat-slicked bodies moving together, finding a flow that made Nora feel like she was in a trance.

Nora couldn't look away as she worked her fingers in and out, Gray's face cycling through a dizzying array of emotions.

"Oh my god," was all Nora heard before Gray's body went taut, back bowing off the bed as her thighs clenched hard around Nora.

She slowed her movements inside of Gray but didn't stop, helping her ride out her orgasm, only stilling her hand and sliding her fingers out when Gray's breathing started to return to normal.

Gray's arms wrapped around her and pulled Nora down on top of her. Nora was happy to act as Gray's personal weighted blanket and nuzzled in closer, placing light kisses against Gray's neck.

"That was..." Gray's voice trailed off, but her hands were still rubbing along Nora's spine, like Nora was the one who needed to come down from what had just happened.

Nora scooted to the side to wrap her arms around Gray's torso. "Hopefully that sentence ends in a positive adjective."

Gray husked out a laugh and held Nora tighter. "You're great at whatever you put your mind to, this included."

There was no point in being embarrassed at the little self-satisfied sound that she let out, but it was forgotten when fingers trailed against her soaked underwear. "Gray," she said, her voice throaty and full of the desire still bubbling just below the surface.

She looked up to see Gray's brown eyes trained on her again. Focused, like she was memorizing Nora's face. It made her heart skip a beat, the weight of the moment quickly expanding, taking up all that space she'd been creating in her world.

Nora found herself underneath Gray seconds later, surprised by the fluid ease with which Gray had managed to slide on top, looking down at her with a devilish smile when she said, "But I think I'd rather just show my appreciation."

* * *

"I get really hungry after sex," Gray said, peering inside Nora's open refrigerator with a bashful smile.

They'd wandered downstairs hours later, Nora impressed her legs were still solid enough to make it down to the first floor. Her thighs ached in the best way, her limbs loose and languid as she leaned against the kitchen island.

Nora scratched against the band of her sleep shorts that she'd pulled on to come downstairs and did a mental inventory of what may be in her fridge. "Whatever you can find is all yours."

She watched as Gray pulled out a carton of eggs and a couple of vegetables, bumping her hip against the door to close it. Gray set the items on the counter next to the stove, and turned toward Nora, who was still having a difficult time believing this moment was real. Gray was wearing an oversize sweatshirt of Nora's from college, which hung down to the middle of her thighs. Feet bare, her messy bun was almost unrecognizable, her lips tilted into a lopsided smile.

It was domesticity personified, and it squeezed at Nora's heart.

"I really can leave if that's easier. I don't need to clutter up your house at"—she looked at the clock on the microwave— "two a.m."

"I like you here," Nora admitted. She was past holding her

feelings in, definitely past trying to pretend like she didn't have feelings at all or that she was completely in control of them.

Gray ducked her head, but Nora could see the light color fanning across her cheeks. "I feel like Willa right now."

Instead of answering immediately, Nora stepped up to where Gray stood, back pressed into the counter. She kissed her softly before running her hands down Gray's arms. Stopping when she reached her hips, she moved her hands to wrap around the curves she'd spent hours mapping, wishing she could feel the heat from her skin.

Dropping a hand lower, she flirted with the hem of the sweatshirt, ghosting her fingertips against Gray's thigh. She pushed upward, the shirt bunching as she moved, tantalizing skin displayed, inch by inch, in an agonizingly slow procession.

Nora couldn't get enough. Of Gray's body. Of how good it felt to be close to her. Of how she wanted to ask a million little questions and understand all that she could about her.

"I assume comparing yourself to your sister is a bad thing?" she finally asked.

Gray stilled beneath her fingertips. Nora thought that she was going to push away from the countertop, but then her shoulders sagged, and she lifted her hands to play with the necklace Nora wore around her neck. "She reminds me of my parents."

Nora frowned. "That must be hard. To be continually confronted by something that you're trying to move past."

Gray nodded, her fingertips still playing with the necklace, though now she was ghosting her knuckles across Nora's collarbone while she did it. "I just don't know what to do about her. I mean, I can't *do* anything, but I don't know what needs to happen for her to take life a little more seriously."

"It sounds like you're just very different people. Maybe Willa's taken on less responsibility in life because she's always had you to fall back on. You didn't have that luxury." The look that Gray gave her made Nora's heart skip at least a few beats, thudding erratically in her chest from the weight of the conversation.

"I appreciate you saying that," she said quietly into the inches of space between them, their faces so close she could feel Gray's breath ghosting across her cheek. Gray drew her bottom lip between her teeth, letting out a sigh. "You're so different than I thought you'd be."

Nora's brow lifted, curiosity ebbing through her. "Yeah? And how did you think I'd be?"

She liked the little blush that fanned across Gray's face again, and she especially liked that she was the one that caused it.

"I don't know... I didn't expect you to be so warm. So present."

"Thought I was just a jerk with a panic disorder?" she asked as she brought her arms up to loosely wrap them around Gray's shoulders.

Gray laughed then, her own arms encircling Nora's waist. "I knew that there was more to you than that. I just... wasn't expecting to discover that I'd like what I found so much."

Nora's heart swelled, satisfaction and exhilaration sliding through her with the compliment. Like maybe this could be the start of something real. "I like what I'm learning too. About myself and you."

When Gray's fingers slipped underneath Nora's T-shirt, nails scratching lightly against her warm skin, all she wanted to do was lean into the touch. Gray had become safety and warmth and so many other things that all wrapped up into something Nora was still afraid to put a label on, even as she acknowledged the truth of how they swirled in her veins and made it a little hard to focus on anything else.

Her world was blooming brighter than it had in a long time —maybe ever.

Certainly not with Andrea. And not with the other people, including her parents, whose love she'd chased, always feeling like she was coming up short.

Gray didn't make her feel that way. She'd let Nora grow and expand and change, and she'd never made her feel like less because of it.

But what Gray wanted was still a mystery, one that, for all of Nora's progress, she didn't know if she was brave enough to ask about.

Chapter Twenty-Two

In the two weeks since Gray had awoken in Nora's bed for the first time, the idea of 'falling' had shifted into the past tense. She'd fallen. Hard. At least she was big enough to admit it, even if only to herself.

And it wasn't just the sex, even though that left Gray a little breathless when it popped into her thoughts throughout the day.

But since she was thinking about it now, the sex was... yeah. It was unbelievably, toe-curlingly, heart-thumpingly, moan-inducingly good.

Sometimes it was hot and fast and left Gray panting against the mattress, trying to catch her breath. On the weekends when they had more time, it was slow and deliberate, an exploration of newness. All the questions Gray had about Nora—at least in bed—finally got answers.

Because Nora wasn't afraid to let go, to let Gray see her messy and unapologetically wanting, Gray's name on her lips like a prayer uttered into the room when she came apart under Gray's fingers or mouth. It was a Nora she never thought she'd see, stripped down—in all the right ways—and ready for whatever came next.

And for as much as Nora liked whatever Gray had to offer, she also liked giving—a lot. Gray really needed to start doing more cardio because Nora was insatiable some days, almost like she was making up for all the time she lost, extracting every ounce of sensation and feeling whenever they came together.

They were becoming something, the two of them together, and Gray felt like she was standing in front of a door. Her stomach flip-flopped whenever she wondered if she was ready for what was on the other side. A conversation about what was happening had been on the tip of her tongue for the last few days, but she couldn't make herself say the words. Couldn't articulate what she was feeling, didn't know how to open the door for all the things still unsaid.

She knew that Nora cared about her, that she wanted to spend time with her, but they hadn't made any proclamations beyond that.

Did Gray want anything beyond that? Or, more accurately, could she handle anything more? Because the last thing she wanted to do was hurt Nora, who'd already been braver than Gray could ever begin to imagine. Gray had watched her pick up the pieces of a shattered life over the last few months, committed to doing things differently this time, to bouncing back to a state of excitement instead of dread at whatever lay around the corner.

They'd lain in bed about a week ago, Nora running her fingers lazily up and down Gray's arms, a soothing pattern that made it hard for Gray to think when Nora had said, "How are you feeling? About everything?" Her voice had been quiet, her hands still moving. It was the perfect recipe for a foggy brain and a lack of ability to articulate.

"This is good," Gray had managed, her own voice sleep-soaked and sated. She'd refused to give in to the little prickle of fear at the base of her spine. One day, Nora was going to realize that Gray wasn't enough, and she'd leave her just like everyone else. But hopefully today wasn't that day. Instead, she'd burrowed against Nora's sternum and slipped her leg between Nora's thighs.

Nora had tilted her hips so they faced one another, wiggling her body even closer. Instead of saying anything else, she'd kissed Gray, soft and yielding and like she was doing it for no other reason than because she could. It was a kiss that made Gray feel like time didn't matter, like they were cocooned from the realities of the world as long as they stayed in this bed together.

The connection she felt to Nora had also shifted. What had felt like a magnetic field, pulling Gray in with constant awareness, now felt more like gravity. She didn't notice it as much, just accepted the reality of it like she was staying tethered to the side of the earth by something more.

Gray had had lovers over the last decade, but there was no one except Becks whom she'd qualify as having loved. Maybe that was what had allowed them to stay friends, that she did truly care about her beyond their romantic connection.

She trusted Becks, who'd been there when her parents had decided to leave, who'd helped Willa move her stuff into the dingy apartment in South Philly that Gray had at the time. But they'd practically been kids. There was no expectation to have it all figured out, no awareness at twenty-three about therapy and processing and 'doing the work' to become a version of yourself that you loved. It had been minimum-wage jobs, academic struggles, nights out that went far too late, quiet tears alone in her bedroom after Willa had fallen asleep on the pullout couch she'd slept on for nearly a year, until she'd gotten her own apartment with friends.

Gray's entire life had felt like she'd been clawing her way toward... something. Stability, first and foremost. It was the cornerstone that she'd built her life around, even if most days, she felt like she was being pulled by the tides.

With Nora, she didn't know what rules would apply. Sometimes Gray sat at her desk, sneaking little glances at Nora while she worked, and she wondered how she'd feel if this thing between them imploded. Would she be able to go into the office every day and see her? When she got in her car in the evenings, would she instinctively think about driving to Nora's neighborhood instead of her own?

Those thoughts scared her. They'd probably have kept her up at night if she hadn't been spending most nights at Nora's, too exhausted in the evenings to do little except burrow against naked skin and fall into a dreamless sleep.

But still, it was there, picking at her whenever the promise of now, of the moment that they were existing in, melted away and the possibility of a future became more real. When she was with Nora, it all made sense. The touching and laughing and existing together was as easy as breathing. There were no unloving parents. No irresponsible sister. No rumors from people who wanted to cut her down and stand on her back as they climbed to the top.

She told herself that the stability she'd created couldn't be taken by someone else. It was hers and hers alone, and it wasn't dependent upon a fragile ecosystem of messy feelings that left her vulnerable to the whims of another person's emotions.

"You doing okay, Gray?" Becks's voice cut through the din of the new restaurant in Rittenhouse Square, where they were having a round of catch-up drinks. When she looked at her friend's face, a little worry line was drawn down the middle of her brow.

They'd just grabbed two seats at a new bar known for its in-house flavor-infused vodkas. Instead of looking at the menu, Gray had been wandering through her very potent and intoxicating Nora-infused thoughts.

She smiled apologetically. "I am. Sorry. How have you been? How was..." She couldn't pull the name of whatever city Becks had been in from her memory. It was full up these days.

"Los Angeles," Becks supplied, her head tilting to the side. "I was working on an indie film that I think could garner some awards attention."

"That's amazing! How did it go?" It wasn't hard to muster enthusiasm for her friend's success.

"I would have been happy to provide timely updates if you'd answered any of my half dozen calls," Becks answered, though there was no bite to her words.

"I'm sorry. I've been..." *Driving myself mad? Spinning in circles? Falling in love?* That last one caused a lump in her throat. She shook her head and offered another contrite smile. "Busy. I've been busy."

"Shacking up with your new girlfriend?" She could always count on Becks to call it like she saw it.

Hearing someone else call Nora that was equal parts exciting and terrifying. "We haven't labeled anything."

"You do realize that we have location services turned on for one another, right?" A bright, mischievous smile bloomed wild across Becks's face, like she'd been waiting to drop that tidbit of information since they'd walked in the door.

Gray's mouth dropped open. "You have not been tracking me!"

The satisfied nod Becks gave her confirmed that, yes, her friend absolutely had. "I was worried."

"You were not." Her incredulity rolled off Becks with zero impact.

"It genuinely started as concern, I promise. But then you

went radio silent and maybe I got a little bit curious about what or who was occupying all of your time."

Gray put down her menu. "And what do you think you've sussed out?"

"Well, I'm so glad you asked. I think I missed my calling as a detective, first and foremost." She took a long sip of water from the glasses the bartender had dropped off upon their arrival, drawing the moment out.

"Spit it out."

"We're in a classy place, Gray. I will not spit my water out."

Gray rolled her eyes. "I'm going to murder you."

"Solving my own murder from beyond the grave would be my greatest accomplishment yet."

Gray was caught between hoping she could distract Becks from this line of questioning and wanting to verbalize all the thoughts that had been swirling around in her mind the past couple of weeks.

Becks, intuitive as ever, watched the emotion flicker across Gray's face before she dropped a soft hand to Gray's forearm. "Hey, is everything okay? I was just kidding. You should do whatever you want with whomever you want."

"Proper usage of the word 'whomever.' I'm impressed." Apparently, she still wasn't ready to lay her thoughts bare.

"A truth for a truth?" Becks challenged.

That got Gray's attention. "What secrets are you keeping from me, your best friend?"

Becks laughed. "That is obviously a gross projection of your own feelings."

Gray lifted her brow and scanned her friend's face. Becks looked like she always did—ineffable. But there was also a softness in her eyes, a lightness that wasn't usually there.

The bartender stopped by then to take their orders. Gray

picked out a lime-infused gimlet, and Becks, really going for it, decided on a pickle-infused martini.

"Brave," Gray said to her friend as they handed over their menus. "Now spill."

"Well..." Becks tilted her body inward and leaned a forearm on the bar. "I didn't know it when I took the job, but Tatum had a part in the film."

Gray swatted at her friend's shoulder. "Shut up. How did that go?"

She could see Becks blushing even in the dim lighting of the bar. "It was... unexpected but very enjoyable."

"Is that what it's going to be? Enjoyable when you two end up in the same city? Or is it more than that?"

Becks let out a groan and scuffed one of her boots against the metal of Gray's barstool. "I like her. A lot."

"Why don't you sound happy about this?" Gray challenged, though, really, she understood the sentiment perfectly.

"I mean... it's scary, right? I think you were the last person I really had true feelings for, and my brain wasn't even fully formed then. I didn't realize how serious it all could be, how much having or losing someone could impact me."

Gray let out a low whistle. "Damn, girl. You've got it so bad."

"I know!" Becks wailed uncharacteristically at the same time the bartender put down their drinks. He departed without comment. She lowered her voice when she added, "I'm absolutely terrified. But I just... I don't know that I want to fight it. That I can fight it."

"Why would you fight it?" If she'd said it once, she'd said it a million times: Becks deserved all the happiness in the world.

"Oh, come on. Act like we're not in similar situations."

Gray downed half her cocktail to buy time. But loose lips weren't going to help her cause right then either, so she made the responsible decision and set the glass down on the long oak bar. "Yes, I've been spending a lot of time at Nora's. That doesn't mean anything."

"Gray, look at me." Becks pressed her fingers into Gray's forearm to pull her attention. "It's okay to fall in love. All the cool kids are doing it."

Love. That was a big word. A word that had the power to change everything in good ways and bad. Nora was bouncing back to a person she used to be, but Gray had never been this person. She'd never idealized a hypothetical future with someone, had never craved to get back to someone as soon as she left and missed them while she was gone.

"Nora is just so..." Becks stayed silent, letting Gray work out whatever she was gearing up to say. Finally, whether because she found the words or because she'd decided she didn't have the energy to keep them in anymore, she pushed on. "She's terrifying to me. She decided one day that she wanted things to be different, and then they were. And she has this misguided notion that I'm not a bundle of insecurity that's wound so tightly I could burst into flames at any moment if I so much as brush my hands together."

"You deserve to be happy." Becks's stare softened. "Does she make you happy?"

Gray sat, really considering the question. She loved Nora's laugh, how it was unexpectedly rich and vibrant. The way she'd catch Nora sneaking glances at her in the office while she was doing the same, like they were in their own little world. How, in spite of feeling like she could never measure up, it was never because Nora was making her feel that way. The intensity of it slammed through her chest. "Yeah, she does."

"Sounds like you have a good thing going then?" Becks said with a measured voice, giving Gray more space to sit with her feelings.

"I'm afraid I'm going to fuck it up." She said the words quietly, almost inaudibly in the din of the late evening bar crowd.

Becks pursed her lips. "You have a good heart and shitty life role models. You're figuring things out as you go, but it doesn't mean that you don't deserve them. And it also means you may fuck up once in a while. Everyone does." She leveled a smile in Gray's direction. "If you want Nora, you should go for it. Maybe have an honest conversation with her about how you're feeling, but you shouldn't wall yourself off from the possibility of happiness."

"And are you and Tatum having *honest conversations?*" Gray asked, drawing her brow upward.

"How about we do as I say and not as I do?"

Gray held out her hand. "How about I talk to Nora if you agree to talk to Tatum?"

"In for a penny, in for a pound," Becks said, slotting their hands together to shake.

The handshake, which was maybe the most adult thing the two of them had done together, morphed into a thumb battle within seconds.

Gray was good with words, as long as they weren't about her own feelings. And she knew, given enough time, that she'd chicken out on her promise to Becks.

Which was how she found herself in an Uber at close to midnight. She'd texted Nora an hour ago, asking if she could come over after drinks. Her next message had been to Willa, making sure she'd be home at some point to take care of S'mores since she wasn't coming with her to Nora's tonight.

Gray – 11:48 p.m.

Here!

It was cold, even by mid-December's standards, and she pushed into the house quickly once she input the keypad code that Nora had shared with her a few days ago. She'd tried not to think much of it at the time, when she'd been first at the door, Nora's hands filled with groceries as she'd rattled off the numbers to Gray.

She hung her scarf and coat on the rack by the door and eased off her Chelsea boots. When she came over, which was most nights, they had a routine. They'd shrug off their layers of winter wear, then their shoes, and then without fail, Nora would wrap her arms around some part of Gray's body and pull her close. They'd made out next to the door more times than she could count at this point, like Nora was so hungry for her that she couldn't wait.

Gray felt the same, but the appreciation for the act had started to settle deep in her bones. She'd come to expect that it would happen, and now, alone in the entry, she ran her fingers across her lips, feeling like she was missing something important.

Quietly, she moved up the staircase, then made a left to head toward the front of the house where Nora's bedroom was situated. Like the rest of the house, Nora's bedroom was quintessentially Nora in a way that Gray hadn't expected. Bold, big prints that adorned the walls. Floor-to-ceiling curtains that magnified the height of the ceilings. A comforter that was so soft it made Gray want to weep with joy every time she slid her body underneath it.

There was a chair in the corner she'd noticed after a few visits, constantly strewn with clothing. "Indecisive much?" she'd asked Nora at the time, her eyes flicking to the various blouses that were piled across the back of it.

Nora had been kissing down the column of Gray's neck, her voice unfocused when she'd said, "Not about this."

The conversation had ended there, as Nora had pushed Gray down on the bed and pulled two orgasms from her in rapid succession that left her feeling like she was spinning just as fast as the Earth.

Tonight, Gray slipped off her clothing and eased under the covers in her underwear. They'd done this before, just slept together, after long days or when they both had especially early mornings. And still, the novelty hadn't worn off.

Nora scooted closer to her, voice raspy from sleep as she threw an arm around Gray's waist and pulled her into the middle of the bed. "I didn't think I'd get to see you tonight."

Gray smiled and willed her erratic heartbeat to slow down. "I don't think you've looked at me yet, so technically you haven't."

Opening her eyes slowly, soft blue came into Gray's focus, stealing the air from her lungs. Nora's wavy hair was going in all directions, and Gray eased a few wild strands behind her ear, loving how Nora's face chased the movement of her fingers to prolong the connection.

"Hi," Nora said softly, the weight of the word enveloping Gray as warmly as the comforter she'd already grown attached to.

Gray leaned forward and pressed a gentle kiss to Nora's lips. "Hi."

She could see Nora trying to shake the sleep from her mind. Her nose scrunched up adorably before she scratched it and let out a yawn. "Did you and Becks have fun?"

Gray nodded. "We did."

Nora's hand ghosted along Gray's hip before her fingers settled against the hollow. "Get into any trouble?"

"If you count thumb wrestling at the bar and knocking over a glass of water, then sure."

She wanted to wrap herself up in the sound of Nora's soft, husky laugh. The moment took on a hazy, ethereal glow before it snapped into acute focus when Nora said, "I missed you. I'm glad you came over."

Gray froze, all the unsaid words choking in her throat. An hour ago, she'd deluded herself into believing that she could vocalize her concerns. Could lay her cards on the table and admit to Nora her worries and anxieties and fears.

But when she did, it would be a bell she couldn't unring. Nora would know how broken Gray truly was, and she'd see her differently. It would be impossible not to if she admitted that her parents had been gone from her life long before they'd ever moved, and that Gray felt like she'd never learned to trust people as a result. If she voiced that she loved Willa more than she'd ever thought possible, but that her sister was a constant reminder of a life that always made her feel like less than, unworthy in the eyes of the people who were supposed to love her no matter what. If her parents didn't even love her, what chance was there for someone else to? She felt like she'd never be enough, and chasing love was only going to leave her a little more broken every time they'd tell her what she already knew: that she wasn't worth the trouble. That she was too damaged, had too much baggage to ever be the partner that anyone would choose out of all the people in the world to love.

But she didn't want this to be over. She already couldn't imagine a world where she didn't fall asleep with Nora's touch on her skin.

She leaned forward and placed a lingering kiss on Nora's slightly parted lips. A pang of want shot straight to her center, and desire curled low in her stomach. Maybe she couldn't consider what it was also doing to her heart, but she wanted—no, she needed to show Nora, even if she couldn't tell her.

Maybe she wasn't ready to vocalize the messy bits of herself that could change everything, but she could make sure that Nora knew how much Gray wanted her, that what was happening between them was possibly the most exhilarating yet comforting experience of Gray's life. She was in a state of suspended animation, both ideas existing simultaneously in a way that sometimes made it hard to think.

And, maybe, she could make Nora feel a little bit like that too.

She slid her leg between Nora's and eased up onto her elbow, half covering Nora's body with her own. A soft, surprised sigh slipped from Nora's lips that Gray captured in another kiss. She ran her tongue along Nora's bottom lip at the same time she pushed her hips down, anchoring Nora against the bed.

"I missed you too," she admitted with a soft whisper before her lips began a trail of kisses and bites along Nora's jaw. She slid her free hand down to Nora's thigh, fingertips skimming against muscles that were already tight. She loved Nora like this, already turned on and ready to come apart after just a few soft touches.

Nora's legs rolled outward, and Gray slotted in closer as their centers brushed together. Desire shot straight through her, toes curling against the bed as she searched for more friction.

"I didn't expect this to happen tonight, but I'm not complaining," Nora said, her voice laced with desire as her hands began to roam, quickly finding the clasp on Gray's bra and undoing it. With her chest free, Nora began plucking at Gray's already sensitive nipples, which only served to make Gray push her hips down harder.

"Fuck," Gray hissed into the darkness that enveloped them as one of Nora's hands scratched down her stomach.

Gray dipped her head, burying it against Nora's shoulder, biting gently at the tight skin. "You drive me crazy," she said, hoping these words, the ones she could manage to say, would be enough for now.

Dragging her stare to Nora's eyes, she found them already trained on her, pupils so blown they looked almost black through the sliver of light streaming through the open curtains. The erratic thump in her chest was back, stealing all the air in the room.

"I want these off," Gray said as she plucked at Nora's underwear, already changing positions to ease them down Nora's long legs.

She was back on top seconds later, urging Nora to sit up before easing Nora's shirt off and flinging it across the room.

Gray wanted... everything. To taste Nora. To touch her. To press their bodies as close together as humanly possible. She wanted to live inside this moment. It was a safe place where she could let her wants escape inside the confines of this room, unbridled and wild as they moved against one another.

Nora gasped when Gray's fingers teased against her entrance, and she moaned when Gray pushed a finger inside immediately after.

"You're already so wet." Gray slid another finger inside easily. "I can't get enough of you," she admitted, sliding her fingers out and back in before curling them. She didn't care if the truth in her words settled around them like a fog or floated away into the air. All she wanted was to keep pulling these sounds from Nora, to push her into the liminal space where Gray now lived, always floating and falling at the same time.

Another moan, a little more wanton, escaped Nora's parted

lips, her breathing already ragged. "Fuck, Gray. That feels so good."

They'd had great sex already. Amazing even. In the shower. On the sofa. Against the kitchen counter. But this was something else. Gray was giving herself over to the moment, letting her body say all the things her voice couldn't, pushing every ounce of emotion she'd been bottling up into her actions as she worked her fingers in and out of Nora, sweat beginning to pool at her lower back.

Gray thrust harder, her fingers enveloped in heat as Nora's walls clenched around her. "This is all I've wanted all day. I love making you come. Will you let me see you come, baby?" As Gray said the words, Nora's whole body went tight, fingers scratching hard enough to leave marks in Gray's shoulders, a moan drawing from her body to fill the room.

Gray's body was slick with sweat, her hand bumping against her own clit as she continued to drive into Nora, pushing her into a second orgasm at the same time Gray fell over a cliff she hadn't realized she'd been so close to. A whine broke free from her own lips that Nora quickly swallowed when she pulled Gray down to her. They were a beautiful, messy tangle of lips and legs, so wrapped up in one another it was hard to know where one of them ended and the other began.

"Gray," Nora breathed raggedly against her lips, hands anchoring her neck as her fingers scratched softly against Gray's scalp. "That was..."

Gray removed her hand from Nora slowly before she drew her wet fingers up to her mouth and sucked each one into her mouth. Nora's face was inches away, watching as Gray tasted her on her fingers.

"I didn't want to miss tasting you," Gray said unapologetically before she lowered her hand down, palm flat against the bed.

One of Nora's hands moved to Gray's back, ghosting patterns across her slick skin. "I'm having trouble forming words right now."

Gray pressed in to capture Nora's lips before she bumped their noses together, smiling against Nora's mouth. "I just wanted..." What did she want? She took a deep breath and burrowed her face against Nora's shoulder. "I just missed you."

The gentle patterns on her back continued. "If this is how you show me you miss me, you're welcome to come over anytime."

"Not worried you'll get sick of me?" Gray's heart stuttered with the words, wondering if the hint of truth in them was covered up by her slow, sex-sated tone.

Nora's fingers stilled, tapping errantly before the pattern started up again. She pressed a kiss against Gray's temple and drew her in close. "I don't think that's possible."

Chapter Twenty-Three

Nora sat at her desk, very little registering around her. The last few weeks of her life had been the happiest in memory. No, scratch that. They weren't even comparable to what had happened to her up until this point.

She felt like she was floating, moving through her days like she was a goddamn Disney princess. And if you'd have told her that a few months ago, she may have thrown a phone at your face.

For the first time in years, she didn't want to shy away from it. She wanted to reach out and hold on to whatever was happening, cradle it gently in her fingers and give it space to blossom without crushing it.

She and Gray hadn't made any declarations or proclamations, but that didn't change how she felt, like she had a constant, pleasant buzz soaking into her muscles. And seeing Gray in the office almost every day didn't help keep her growing feelings under control; her heart was always a half step away from fluttering whenever their gazes locked. Soft looks.

Stolen glances. Sticky notes on her desk, left at odd moments. There was one she was pretty sure Gray had managed to leave, unnoticed, while Nora had actually been sitting at her desk.

Like fingerprints, everyone's tongue print is different, it had said. She held it between her fingers now, written in Gray's loopy scrawl that she'd recognize anywhere these days. It transported her back to a week ago, when Gray's tongue had mapped what felt like every divot and hollow on Nora's body.

Her finger trembled against the small note, remembering what she'd given in return. Because something had shifted that night. She'd thought she was being vulnerable before, by even being open to what was happening, but as Gray had climbed into her bed, something inside of her had cracked wide open.

She didn't have to make space anymore—it was already there. It was wild and expansive and it was being filled by a fierce hope that they could do this. Like it would be the greatest adventure of her life if they did.

Without a future, her present had stayed rooted in the past, weighing her down like an anchor. She'd thought she needed to stay still, to keep the feelings in a state of suspension so they didn't drown her. She'd been so wrong. What she'd needed was to move forward, to make new memories, to prove to herself that the world was a place with so many people she had yet to know. And to accept that there were already good people in her life she hadn't taken a chance on yet.

Cynthia. Callie. Gray. Even Trent, with his always excited personality. She'd been churning for so long that she was stronger than she'd given herself credit for, more ready to enter into the next chapter of her life than she'd wanted to believe.

Because belief, especially in oneself, was terrifying. It had been easy to accept, at the time, that things happened *to* her.

And now? Now she was making things happen. She was

going after the life she actually wanted. A life that made her feel whole. A life worth living.

She ran her finger along the loopy letters one last time before placing the note in a drawer and standing up. Cynthia's office door was ajar, and she slipped inside and closed the door behind her like she'd done so many times before.

Cynthia looked up from her laptop, fingers pausing against the keyboard. "What's up?"

"I wanted to talk to you about something. Is this a good time?"

Leaning back in her chair, Cynthia let her glasses drop around her neck. She gestured to the chair across from her desk. "Sure. Have a seat."

"First and foremost, I want to thank you for believing in me all these years." Nora swallowed the lump in her throat.

She could see Cynthia's posture change, so that she was sitting up straighter. "You're one of the good ones, Nora. You just got a little lost along the way."

"And then took a couple of detours, threw the map out the window, and eventually set the car on fire."

Cynthia smiled, studying Nora's face. "Really pushing this metaphor to the brink."

"I didn't even realize how lost I was until I came back."

"Well, I'm happy you're here now. What is it you wanted to discuss?"

"I don't want the promotion." There, she'd ripped the Band-Aid off. Quick and clean, hoping the cut underneath wouldn't be deep. She'd be devastated if Cynthia was upset with her, but she had to stop living her life for other people. It was a small step in a line of many steps that she was finally excited to start taking.

Cynthia's eyes flitted across Nora's face, an inscrutable look passing over her mentor. "If you feel like that's what's best, I support you."

Nora's shoulders softened. It wasn't what Cynthia had said, but how she said it. Her voice was gentle, and Nora acknowledged the weight of those quiet words and how much she valued her relationship with Cynthia, now probably more than ever.

"I've given it a lot of thought." She wanted to explain her reasoning. Cynthia deserved at least that. "You even considering me changed my life in ways I hadn't expected, but as we get closer to making a decision, I'm realizing it's not what would make me happy."

A soft smile broke out across Cynthia's face. "And what would make you happy?"

Nora couldn't contain her own bright smile. "I want to be part of the team. I want to travel. I want to..."

"Fall in love?" Wow, okay. For as much credit as she gave Cynthia, it wasn't enough.

"Yes, that would be a nice addition to my future life plans."

"Well... just for the record, since agents work independently, there's no issue with two co-workers dating." Cynthia smirked and glanced through her windows at the office. "You know... hypothetically, if that was something you're interested in."

"I really like her." Nora probably couldn't have kept the words in if she'd tried.

"She lets you shine," Cynthia said, her voice earnest in a way that made tears prick behind Nora's eyes. Nora's heart felt so full, like everything was finally coming together.

"She's given me space to become the person I want to be."

"That's rare. I'm glad you're not afraid to hold on to it."

Nora beamed another smile before it dimmed slightly. "I do hope I'm not putting you in a difficult position, though. That's the last thing I want, but I needed to be honest about where I'm at."

Cynthia waved her off. "It's fine. You're an amazing agent, but I always assumed you wouldn't want to do this."

That stopped Nora short. "Wait, what? Then what was this all about?"

"You're competitive. I knew you wouldn't want to let the chance pass you by. I also knew that it would get you out of your comfort zone."

"You mean my black hole?" Nora responded without a hint of frustration in her voice. There were worse fairy godmothers than Cynthia Lennox, that was for damn sure. "So, then Gray..."

Cynthia laughed. "That was all you. Even I couldn't have orchestrated that."

Nora knew she was blushing. "For what it's worth, it just kind of happened."

"Some people are just drawn to one another," Cynthia said before her face soured. "Andrea picked you out of the masses like she was bestowing some gift upon you. She made you feel special, and then the second she had you wrapped around her finger, she took you for granted."

"You really don't like her," she said, though Nora agreed with everything Cynthia was saying.

"I'm sure there was a lot going on in your relationship that I was never privy to, but she acted like you were a young, pretty prop for her to trot out at her convenience." Cynthia smiled sadly. "I'm not pretending to be completely selfless. She reminded me so much of my first husband that it made me want to scream."

That got Nora's attention. She knew that Cynthia had been married once before. Twenty years older than Nora, she'd been with her current husband, Robert, for as long as they'd known one another. "You never told me that."

"I let the weight of my past go a long time ago, but it doesn't mean it didn't hurt to watch someone else going through a similar situation. Still, it wasn't my life to lead or to interfere with."

"Mostly," Nora said, lips tilting into a playful smirk.

"Mostly." Cynthia smiled back at her before she grew serious again. "One day, about six months after you started working with me, Andrea came by." She saw a hint of contrition on Cynthia's face.

"I didn't know that."

Cynthia sighed and pinched the bridge of her nose. "We maybe got into it a little bit. I told her she was banned from this office, and that if she ever set foot in here, I'd call the police."

"Wow." Nora let out a surprised puff of air, thinking back. It was hard to remember much from that time, when she was building her armor like it was the only thing that would keep her alive. "What did she want?"

"I assume you. You'd blocked her number by that point and moved into a new house. It wasn't hard to find out where you worked, and she had the bad luck of finding me instead."

A lightbulb clicked on. "That day. That day when you were so furious when I came back into the office. You wouldn't tell me what it was about."

"I've done a lot of growing over the years, but something about a narcissist trying to pull someone back into the fold really raised my hackles. I wondered if maybe I'd made the wrong decision. I thought about telling you, but all I wanted to do was protect you. I hope you realize that, and I hope you don't begrudge me for the decision I made then."

Cynthia had protected her. And not as an overbearing boss would needlessly shelter someone from a battle they should face alone, but as someone akin to a parent, trying to let their child heal in peace. It struck her with such staggering clarity that unshed tears brimmed behind her eyes, threatening to pour over. A lot of things in Nora's life hadn't worked out like she'd wanted or expected. A lot of people had let her down.

But Cynthia? She wasn't one of them. She'd stuck with Nora during her darkest moments and supported her when she'd known that Nora was weak and probably couldn't stand on her own yet. And she'd never held it against Nora. She'd never made that love and acceptance conditional.

"I really love you, Cynthia. I hope you know that," she said with a full voice.

"I love you too. And when I heard how efficiently you handled Andrea when you ran into her at the networking event, I felt like a proud mama bear."

Nora groaned. "God, nothing gets by you."

"There's a lot that goes into leading this team. Not that you'll ever know now," Cynthia teased, her eyes bright, the same fullness in Nora's reflected back at her.

A pang of guilt struck Nora. "So, what are you going to do? About the restructuring?"

Cynthia waved her hand and stood up before walking over to the window and staring out at the street. "I already have a contingency plan."

Nora turned in her chair to face where Cynthia now stood. "And what's that?"

"I was more than a little curious about how *both* of you would handle Bermuda. And if Gray can make you turn into a puppy dog without so much as blinking, imagine what she can do for the rest of the team."

There it was, in black and white, making perfect sense. Sure, Gray was the newest person on the team, but she had a doggedness that Nora hadn't seen in another agent before, a dedication that maybe she herself didn't even possess. Gray was great with both clients and teammates alike, and she was genuinely curious about the world. About the footprints she left on it. The ways in which people connected with one another and built bridges.

She was, frankly, the perfect choice.

* * *

"Am I being replaced?" Gray asked as her fingers played against Nora's collarbone. She stood behind Nora, watching her through the full-length mirror as her hands traced along already hot skin.

Nora let out a shuddered exhale. "You have evening showings tonight," she pushed out. She was proud she'd pulled that memory from the hazy recesses of her brain, given the way Gray's fingers were consuming her awareness.

Gray, with an unrelenting focus, continued to trace light patterns across Nora's chest before she dragged her hands down and anchored them around Nora's hips. She scratched at the exposed skin, and Nora's breathing went shallow.

Nora caught Gray's petulant face in the mirror, her chin just able to rest on Nora's shoulder from behind. She smiled and turned, pressing a soft kiss to Gray's temple. "You're cute when you're jealous, but it's only drinks with Callie, who I know we both adore."

"I had plans for you later," Gray whined, her fingers edging around Nora's stomach.

They were getting ready for work, a process that had started to take twice as long with their frequent morning detours. Nora couldn't say she minded. She liked this version of Gray: wanting and not afraid to show it.

Her breath hitched when Gray's finger plucked at the

button on her dark jeans, arousal shooting straight to her center. She'd managed to put on pants a few minutes ago, but Gray had caught her in front of the mirror before she'd settled on a blouse, and she didn't seem intent on letting Nora finish getting dressed any time soon.

Nora's eyes fluttered closed as Gray popped open the button. "You can come over tonight if you want."

"I don't think I can wait that long to feel you," Gray said, slipping her hand lower, beneath the band of Nora's underwear. Her soft breath ghosted along the shell of Nora's ear, eliciting a shiver.

Nora's hips jerked instinctively, trying to get closer to fingers that she knew could expertly push her over the edge. She let out a deep, steadying breath. "You're teasing me." Not that she minded. Not one bit. Gray could torture her for the rest of their lives if it felt this good.

Gray's other hand came up to cup Nora's chest through her bra, rolling her already tight nipple between her fingertips. "Am I really the one to blame when you stand in front of the mirror looking like this? God, you're so beautiful," Gray said softly as she placed a featherlight kiss against Nora's back.

Nora let the sweet words wash over her, but the softness of the moment was quickly replaced with an ache in her center when Gray slid her finger up Nora's slit. She knew she was ready. Just a few playful touches already had her wet, and she whimpered as Gray slid two fingers inside. "Fuck," she breathed out, everything going a little hazy at the edges. Gray fucked her like she meant it, like there was nowhere else in the world she'd rather be. Like there was no one except Nora and the singular focus that Gray possessed to pull every ounce of pleasure from her body.

Gray bit down on Nora's shoulder, watching them in the mirror. Nora's chest was flushed, splotches of red contrasting with the black of her bra, her head tipped back and cradled against Gray's neck.

"You're so sexy like this. I love watching you," Gray said as their stares met in the mirror. Nora's breathing hitched as Gray started rubbing her thumb against Nora's clit, still moving her fingers in and out in a torturously slow motion.

She ground her ass into Gray's hips, trying to feel more friction. Her body was electric, her center hot and tight, begging for release. And yet still, Gray pushed in and out gently, the wave continuing to build.

"Baby, please," Nora begged, wrapping one of her hands around Gray's hips to pull them flush with one another. Her other hand wrapped around Gray's forearm, trying to make her go faster.

Gray, it seemed, had other plans this morning. The only sound in the room was their staccato breaths until Gray said, "God, you feel so good. So fucking good."

Nora's whole body was on fire, like she'd burst into flames if Gray didn't push her over the edge soon, the line between pleasure and pain blurring excruciatingly.

"I want to watch you come." And then, without preamble, Gray began moving her fingers faster. The hand toying with Nora's nipple dropped down to wrap around her stomach, pulling her in closer, Nora finally getting the friction she so desperately sought. Gray worked her fingers quickly, thrusting in as deep as she could go, rubbing her thumb against Nora's clit every time she did it.

And when Gray bit down against Nora's shoulder, maybe hard enough to leave a mark, she came undone. Heat exploded through her body, whiteness behind her eyes, as Gray continued to fill her, to push and pull and make her come unglued at the seams. "Look at me," Gray said, eyes focused on Nora's in the mirror, hungry and intent in a way that made

Nora unable to look away. The pleasure was indescribable, watching Gray watching her, their stares locked as Gray brought Nora back down, her fingers slowing until finally she stopped moving them and eased out slowly.

Nora turned in Gray's arms, her breathing erratic, her limbs untrustworthy after what she'd just experienced. She wrapped one arm around Gray's torso and tangled her other hand against the back of Gray's neck, toying at the soft hair there. "That was not a bad way to start the day," she said before kissing Gray soundly, melding their lips together.

When they came up for air, Gray tipped their foreheads together, breathing into the few inches of space between them. "I loved everything about that."

Nora laughed, because what else was she going to do after Gray had just pulled that impossibly good orgasm from her body? "I think it's pretty clear I did too."

Gray's face softened, and Nora's heart exploded when Gray brushed their noses together before planting a light kiss on the tip of Nora's. "Good. That makes me happy."

"You make me happy," Nora said, still a little love-drunk and coming down from the haze of her orgasm.

"Yeah?" The word was tentative, Gray's shoulders edging upward.

Nora nodded. "I was wondering... the office holiday party is on Friday. I mean, I know we haven't discussed telling anyone about us, but I..." Her words stilled. She took a deep, steadying breath. She wanted this. Wanted Gray. She was sure of it. "I was wondering if you wanted to go... together. We don't have to make a big deal of it, but I don't want to hide this. I don't want to hide something that makes me so happy."

Something passed across Gray's honeyed eyes before they softened, her hands squeezing against Nora's hips. "Yeah. We can do that. I don't want to hide you either."

Nora hadn't thought her heart could feel fuller before, but she'd been wrong. She'd been getting better at recognizing her feelings lately, at putting names to the new ones and dredging up words for the old ones back from her memory. And she knew, without a doubt, that she was one hundred percent falling in love with Gray.

Chapter Twenty-Four

Most nights, Gray took S'mores with her to Nora's, straight from the office. Nora didn't seem to mind the ball of fluff in her home, and Gray had noticed when a new dog bed appeared after a few consecutive visits. Her heart had tightened at the gesture, which made it so clear that Nora was confident in making space for Gray in her life.

Tonight, she'd gone to her own home after work. The Philly Finds holiday party would start at seven p.m., and Cynthia had rented out a small room in one of the restaurants downtown, a steakhouse that was likely hosting a rotating variety of holiday parties throughout December. They'd start with a happy hour, followed by a team dinner. They were just a few days from Christmas, and for the first time in years, Gray found herself excited by the bright lights and garish decorations.

Gray eyed herself in the mirror, arms behind her neck as she clasped a simple necklace into place. She fiddled with the small charm at the end and made sure it was even. Tonight, she'd opted for a black chiffon cocktail dress that draped to mid-thigh. It had long, flowy, sheer sleeves, showed the perfect hint of cleavage, and had an open back for a little pop of something extra. She'd left her hair down and wavy, liking how it looked a little wild.

She wondered what Nora was going to wear. No doubt she'd look beautiful in anything she put on, but they hadn't been to a semiformal occasion together before. Just the idea of it made Gray's heart beat a little faster, as it often did these days.

It only took another fifteen minutes for her to put on some light makeup, just enough to make her eyes pop and her cheeks look rosy. Then she stared at herself in the mirror. She'd thought she had a strong sense of self. That she did what she wanted and said what she wanted. That she was guided through life by some indomitable moral compass that she'd etched out all on her own. As she eased her black heels onto her feet, she wondered if that was really the case. For the last few months, she'd been changing too. Maybe she hadn't gotten into all the details of her past, about how she felt and why she felt that way, but she was more open in the present.

She was letting Nora in, and for the first time, the idea didn't terrify her.

After ordering her car, she headed downstairs. Willa and S'mores were curled up on the sofa together, watching a trashy reality show. Gray had even softened her stance on Willa staying here over the last few weeks, though it was probably made easier by the fact that she spent very little time here these days.

"You'll be here with S'mores tonight?" Gray asked, shrugging on her jacket.

Willa looked away from the television, her fingers still playing gently through S'mores's fur. "Yeah."

Gray's phone buzzed. "Okay, my car's here."

Her sister's half-hearted wave was the last thing Gray saw as she closed the door behind her. Typical. But even Willa's ambivalence couldn't dim the brightness radiating from her. It settled around her like a blanket during the fifteen-minute ride downtown.

When she exited the car, her heart knocked around in her rib cage when she saw Nora standing outside under the awning to the restaurant.

"Why are you waiting out here?" Gray asked, opening the restaurant door and ushering Nora and her impossibly rosy cheeks inside.

Nora's lips were painted a vibrant shade of red, and they split into a smile that stole Gray's breath. "I wanted to see you."

They made their way over to the small coatroom situated off the entry to the restaurant. Gray had been here once before, for last year's holiday party, though it couldn't have felt more different. She'd only been at the company for a few months then. Nora had shown up for the happy hour before dinner, sticking close to Cynthia but leaving before dinner was served.

This felt like a date, something Gray realized that they hadn't done much of yet. With both of their schedules and S'mores, they'd fallen into a domestic routine, spending most of their time at Nora's house. Maybe they could change that soon. When Nora shrugged off her coat, Gray realized they needed to change that as soon as humanly possible.

"Wow." Gray couldn't keep her eyes off Nora, her maroon dress a perfect match to her lipstick. She wanted to kiss it off her, both the dress and the lipstick. Leaning forward, she placed a soft kiss on Nora's lips. "You look beautiful."

The flush on Nora's cheeks from the cold was still there, but it grew darker under Gray's praise. "So do you."

Gray's own skin grew flushed as Nora's eyes raked down her dress and then back up, like she was memorizing every inch. "You have got to stop looking at me like that or I won't get through this."

Nora smirked. "Just thinking about peeling you out of that dress later, not that I don't love how it looks on you."

Everything in Gray's body thrummed with awareness, her stomach swooping low. Instead of responding, she grabbed Nora's hand and pulled her out of the coatroom, passing Kelsey as they exited.

She noted how Kelsey stared at their interlocked fingers for a few beats longer than normal, but she didn't want the prickle of judgment, if that was what it was, to dampen her mood. "Hey, Kelsey. See you in there."

It wasn't a question, and she led Nora through the restaurant, dropping her hand when they reached the bar where Cynthia stood.

Nora leaned closer, breath ghosting over the shell of Gray's ear. "For what it's worth, she already knows about us."

Gray nodded and tried to quell the little spike of anxiety that flared up. It was a good thing that Cynthia knew about them, that she'd seemingly given her blessing for an office relationship. God, a relationship. Gray had avoided using that word, even to herself, for as long as she could, but that was the path that they were on. Romance and dates and feelings, delving deeper into knowing one another. It was, in the abstract, something she wanted. In practice, it made her feel a little lightheaded, and she braced her hand on the bar to steady herself.

"I was going to find Callie," Nora said at the same time Cynthia noticed them.

Gray gulped in a breath of air. She could do this. "Sure, I'll see you in there."

Nora squeezed her hand gently and wandered away toward the Ivy Room, where the party was located.

"Feeling a little more settled this year?" Cynthia asked, turning toward Gray and gesturing around the room.

Words. Gray knew what those were, but she was finding it a little hard to come up with any. She nodded and cleared her throat. She could do this. "I am. It's been quite the year."

Dressed in a fitted suit, Cynthia looked every bit the fearless leader that Gray had come to think of her as. She had nothing but respect for Cynthia. For how she managed her company. For how she led the team. She hoped in the coming years that she could absorb even half of the leadership qualities that Cynthia possessed.

Cynthia laughed. "That it has. We'll have a waiter coming by the room soon, but I wanted to grab some of the good stuff. What are you having?"

Maybe a little extra liquid courage wouldn't be a bad thing tonight. "I'll have an Old-Fashioned. What about you?"

"Manhattan," she said as she caught the bartender's eye. After she added Gray's order, she turned back to her. "We should catch up after the new year, sync up on how you're feeling about your first year with us."

Gray wrapped her fingers around the cold glass of water the bartender had set in front of her moments ago. She was Philly Finds' second top-performing agent, but still, a little prickle of apprehension rushed through her that all wasn't well. Instead of voicing it, she nodded. "Absolutely. Happy to discuss whatever you'd like."

"You're doing great work, Gray," Cynthia assured her, like she could sense the tension in Gray's shoulders. "I want to make sure I keep you on the team and ensure you're getting what you need from Philly Finds."

Okay, that didn't sound so bad. Still, even if it killed her, she wanted to acknowledge the elephant in the room. It wasn't Nora's job to fight her battles, to take on the opinions of the rest of the team while she slunk around in the background. And, according to Nora, Cynthia already knew they were dating.

"Along with another great year, my only goal is to avoid any conflicts of interest."

Cynthia's lips tilted upward into a knowing smile. "That shouldn't be a problem. I'll continue to operate as Nora's lead, regardless of what happens between the two of you."

That gave Gray pause. Nora hadn't mentioned anything to her about not moving forward with the promotion. "Oh..." she finally pushed out, not really knowing what to say.

"You're great with people, Gray. It would be a shame not to support you in growing that if it's something you want."

"Does Nora know?" Gray choked the words out, the implication of what Cynthia was telling her weighing her down like cement.

Cynthia nodded. "Absolutely. Nora made the decision not to move forward with the role. I assumed she'd told you." For the first time, Cynthia looked unsure, like maybe she'd stepped into something she shouldn't have. Unlike Gray, she was much better at a quick recovery. "But we don't have to hash anything out tonight. What you should take away from this conversation is that you're doing a fantastic job, and I wanted to make sure you knew it."

"Thank you for that," Gray said, trying to let the compliment wash over her in spite of the uncomfortable churning in her stomach. She knew that she would need to be extra careful with certain situations, but she hadn't expected them to pop up so soon. Nora moving into a team lead role had been the plan for months now, and Gray hadn't hypothesized a world in which that changed.

Why hadn't Nora told her?

Their drinks delivered, Cynthia glanced down at her watch. "We better get in there."

Gray tipped her glass in thanks and followed Cynthia into the Ivy Room. The rest of the team was already there, along with any partners or dates they'd chosen to bring. Grant, Tamara, and Julian were there with their spouses, while it looked like Trent and Sage had both brought dates.

It was an intimate gathering, but it could have been a hundred people and Gray still would have zeroed in on Nora the second she walked into the room.

She joined Nora, Trent, his date, Callie, Julian, and Julian's wife. "Hey," she said, working to put the confusing conversation with Cynthia in the back of her mind until the new year. Or at least until she could talk to Nora about it.

Nora's eyes, impossibly soft, found hers. They shared a moment, and the rest of the party floated into the background. Gray leveled a smile at Nora and willed herself to remember that the erratic thump of her heart was excitement, not nerves.

After introductions, where she learned that Trent's date was a friend named Sophie and was reminded that Julian's wife was named Alyssa, a waiter came around to take their drink orders. She'd started to settle again, moving past her conversation with Cynthia.

"We went pescatarian last year," Alyssa said when Gray tuned back into the conversation.

She and Nora shared another private look, Nora's eyes bright and playful. They'd discussed Julian's love for fish in depth one evening over a few glasses of wine while they'd snuggled on the sofa.

"Is that so," Nora said wryly, her wine glass held to her mouth to cover a mischievous smile.

"It was something I really wanted us to do," Alyssa continued, giving her husband a soft look. Maybe Gray had to give Julian a little more credit and at least assume his frequent microwaved fish wasn't some passive-aggressive attempt to nauseate his fellow colleagues. "He's been a great sport about it.

I'm hoping we can transition to being fully vegetarian in the next year."

Oh, happy days. There was an end in sight. Gray resisted clasping her hands together.

"That's great," Gray chimed in, holding in a laugh thinking about the conversation she and Nora were sure to have about this later. "Reducing your carbon footprint like that. I have some vegetarian recipes that I can share with Julian if you'd like."

Nora had moved closer to her, their shoulders brushing. Gray could feel the other woman's heat, could smell the gentle scent of her perfume. Refusing to overthink it, she placed her hand on Nora's back, letting it settle there.

She could see Nora's brow lift upward, a smile blooming across her face when she said, "I'm a big fan of ceviche. Shrimp salads. Even salmon because it keeps so well and can be eaten cold. So convenient," Nora finished, her body practically vibrating with amusement.

"I'd love any recipes you have," Alyssa said, positively beaming.

They carried on in conversation for the next hour, a waiter stopping by from time to time to take drink orders. It was nice, Gray realized, to spend time with the whole team outside of the office. Little groups would join into larger conversations before splitting off again, like a living organism that was constantly shifting.

When they sat down for dinner, she had a pleasant buzz, and she didn't miss how Nora's hand immediately found her own under the table.

By dessert, people had started to wander. Some headed out to the bar for a quicker refill. Others stood in small groups around the table, trying to digest the insane amounts of food they'd all just consumed.

Gray, Callie, and Nora had all sat next to one another, managing to stay in their chairs as the atmosphere became more gleeful and, honestly, drunken.

"I'm going to head to the bathroom," Gray said. She stood up, hoping the food canceled out the few extra glasses of wine she'd switched to after her cocktail. The room had a soft glow, and it felt instinctual to reach out and ghost her fingers across Nora's cheek when she asked, "Do either of you need anything while I'm up?"

Nora shook her head, as did Callie, who'd finally decided their affection was worth mentioning. "Big fan of this," she said, pointing between the two of them but leaving it at that.

Gray practically floated to the bathroom. It was a nice restaurant, and the ladies' room was no different. There was a sitting area beyond the door, and the stalls were all floor-to-ceiling, giving a luxurious sense of privacy. She headed inside one, her body in that perfect balance of buzzed and aware.

She'd only just sat down when she heard the door open, voices floating through the air.

"It all makes so much sense now." *Kelsey*, Gray noted as she pulled at the toilet paper roll, not giving the chatter much thought.

"What does?" The other voice sounded like Sage, who spoke much more quietly so that it was hard to tell.

"Gray."

Gray's ears perked up at the mention of her name, but she was a little too buzzed to appreciate the harsh staccato of Kelsey's voice, especially muffled through the door.

"What about her?" Definitely Sage.

She'd noticed that Sage and Kelsey had started hanging around in the office more together after the happy hour at Mulherin's Sons last month. It was nice to see Sage opening up a little more and giving Kelsey a new work friend; Gray could admit she'd been so distracted by her own complicated life since then that she hadn't talked to Kelsey very much.

"She's fucking Nora." That caught Gray's attention, her brain snapping into acute focus in a way that had felt impossible seconds ago. "I knew she wanted to be successful, but I never thought she'd actually try to sleep her way to the top."

"I think they look cute together." Sage paused before she added, "And it seems like they really like one another."

Kelsey scoffed. "Nora's so frigid that's hard for me to believe. And Gray was all cagey when I tried to talk to her about the Bermuda trip before it happened, and she wouldn't talk to me about it when she got back." It sounded like Kelsey smacked her hand against her head. Gray hoped it hurt. "God, they've probably been fucking forever. No wonder the boss's pet's new girlfriend got to go on the trip."

Gray heard Sage defend her. Say that she was a strong agent. That they didn't know the details. And that meant something, it really did, but the little shreds of positivity that she was clinging to fell away when Kelsey spoke again. "I've heard rumors about her, you know. This isn't a very big world. My friend at Brenneman Brothers said she left because she got caught sleeping with Jonathan Brenneman."

"Wait, what?" It was the curiosity in Sage's voice that made Gray suddenly want to cry, like the version of events Kelsey was putting forth had somehow become much more believable.

"Yeah," Kelsey said knowingly. "She was hooking up with my friend Paul, but all the while she was screwing Brenneman himself."

Everything felt wrong right now. Gray hearing this. Kelsey being willing to say it. Sage's ability to believe it. Her stomach roiled, and she wondered if she'd throw up all over her heels. For the past few months, she'd let herself think that this was different. That what she and Nora had was special, and even if it terrified her, at least it was real.

And maybe it was, but it didn't change what people would think about her. What they'd always thought about her. Sure, there had been a part of her that had considered the possible rumors, but she'd never expected them to be thrown around behind her back at a place like Philly Finds.

Sage's voice pulled her attention. "Well, that's kinda shitty if true."

She could practically see Kelsey in her mind's eye, nodding resolutely. "Looks like lightning can strike twice."

Gray waited for what felt like hours until they left the bathroom. She couldn't move. Couldn't think. Couldn't catch her breath as the weight of Kelsey's assumptions, of Sage's easy belief in this version of events continued to wash over her in sickening waves.

When she realized that she was close to hyperventilating, she called a car. She couldn't face Nora right now, couldn't face anyone. God knows how many other people Kelsey had peddled this narrative to, how many of what she'd thought were curious stares had actually been judgmental ones, picking apart whether what she and Nora had was real.

She was in the car, almost home, when she got a text from Nora.

Nora – 10:11 p.m.

Hey, where'd you go?

Gray debated ignoring the text. Everything inside her screamed to turn off her phone and pretend like this wasn't happening. But still, she couldn't do that to Nora.

Gray – 10:11 p.m.

> I wasn't feeling well. I didn't want to interrupt the rest of the party, so I grabbed a car home.

She saw the typing dots appear and disappear in rapid succession before another text came through.

Nora – 10:12 p.m.

> Are you okay? Can I do anything?

Gray – 10:12 p.m.

> I probably just had too much to drink. Just got home. Going to sleep it off, nothing to worry about! Have a good rest of the party!

Besides Becks, who was physically in and out of Gray's life, there was no one who regularly checked in on her. No one that cared if she had a hard night, who asked if she was okay.

The sentiment made her want to cry, a recurring theme in the last hour. From this moment on, everything was going to be different. Still, she was warring with herself over whether to push Nora away or actually let her help. In the immediate moment, she'd chosen self-preservation and retreated inward, but maybe they could talk tomorrow, when Gray would be on more emotionally solid footing and could explain to Nora what was going on.

She tried her best to push the swirling feelings down, but all that was doing was making her alternate between feeling like she was going to throw up and feeling like she would pass out.

Tomorrow. She repeated it over and over again in her brain like a mantra. She'd deal with it then.

* * *

Sometimes life had a way of filling the clouds so full that there was nothing for them to do but unleash their power. Maybe Kelsey was right that lightning really could strike twice.

Gray walked into an empty house to find S'mores sitting alone, downstairs on the sofa. She hopped off immediately and ran through the living room before whining at the back door to be let out.

After the world's fastest bathroom break in the freezing cold, S'mores bounded in happily and ran back toward the sofa.

Where the fuck was Willa?

Any other day, Gray would have gone to bed. Or gone to Nora's.

Instead, something inside of her bent at an angle so harsh she feared it would snap her in half. If she was going to—as Jonathan Brenneman had once so illustriously pointed out—get punished for the crime, she may as well commit it.

She dialed Willa's number. On the third ring, her sister surprisingly picked up, music and people audible in the background.

"Hey, everything okay?" Willa said, her voice hard to make out over the noise.

"Why aren't you home with S'mores? You said you'd be home."

A beat of silence. "I came to the bar around the corner to meet a friend for a few minutes."

Gray was sick of this. Sick of everything. Maybe it wasn't fair for Willa to be the only one on the receiving end of her ire, but there was a part of her that still felt like it was deserved. And that part was the one calling the shots right now. "S'mores had to go out, so it sounds like you've been gone for longer than a few minutes."

She could hear Willa exhale into the receiver. "I've only been gone an hour. I promise."

Gray pinched the bridge of her nose as the words leaked out, her own voice foreign sounding to her. "I want you out of the house tomorrow."

"Wait, what?" her sister protested. "I didn't do anything wrong."

"This has been going on long enough, Willa. I gave you a place to crash, and my patience is gone. I want my house back. I want my life back."

"I'm coming home right now." The noise halted as Willa's breathing picked up, like she was already on her way.

"You don't need to come back right now. I'm home with S'mores."

"We need to talk about this. Are you okay? Because you don't sound okay."

Gray was done with this conversation. "I'm going to bed, and I'm not going to change my mind. I need you out by tomorrow. Maybe you can stay with the friend you were out drinking with."

The cloud wasn't done with its torrential downpour yet. Willa unlocked the door seconds after Gray hung up the phone.

"Gray, what's wrong? Did something happen at the party?" Her sister was out of breath as she unzipped her jacket and moved across the room toward Gray.

And then Gray really did snap, words she knew she could never take back tumbling out of her mouth. "Willa, I'm sick of this. I'm sick of cleaning up your messes. I'm sick of not being able to count on you, even for the most basic of things."

"Because I left for an hour?" Willa asked, genuinely confused in a way that only her sister could manage. She looked so young then, her eyes wide and unblinking. "First you don't want me here, then you want me practically chained here if you're gone. What's going on?"

Gray pushed past the pang of sympathy she had felt toward her sister's confusion and held on to the righteous anger that was clawing its way quickly up her throat. "I thought that supporting you through your fuckups was the right thing to do. That it wasn't your fault that our parents were useless. But you know what? I was wrong. You're twenty-five, Willa. When are you going to grow up?"

"I don't—" Those were the only words Willa managed to get out before her eyes filled with tears.

Gray could feel herself losing control. Hell, she'd already lost it minutes ago, but she couldn't seem to rein it in. She couldn't go back to the person she'd been an hour ago, optimistic about her future and in control of her emotions. The dam had broken, and all of her anger and hurt and frustration was flooding through her, threatening to drown them both.

"I'm not some surrogate parent. I'm not here for you to float in and out whenever you have a whim."

Willa nodded, her trembling chin jutting out as the first tear spilled down her cheek. "I didn't realize I was such a burden, that you felt the same about me that Mom and Dad do."

"They've been gone for years at this point, Willa. You need to move past it. I have."

Willa shook her head, another tear dropping to the floor. "I saw them, you know, when I went on that trip with Keith."

Gray felt like her body was going to collapse in on itself. She was a black hole, a word Nora had once used to describe herself, and it felt so painfully accurate. Something hot and uncomfortable bubbled up in her chest, making it hard to breathe. "Why?"

"You think I don't know that you're always annoyed with me? Or that I'm shit at relationships? News flash, I'm not always an idiot. Though in this case, I was. Because I stupidly thought that maybe they cared, just in their own way. It had been a long time, and I wanted to see them, to see if maybe I'd been wrong all these years."

Gray wanted to reach out and hug her sister, but she couldn't. Her hands stayed balled into fists at her sides, her rage the only thing keeping her anchored to reality. Her voice was hoarse, anger and sadness and an overwhelming desire to curl up in a ball crushing her. A part of Willa had always refused to accept the people their parents were, and the sooner her sister dispensed with those ideas, the better off they'd all be.

Willa pushed on, like her own dam was breaking. "They still don't give a shit. I'm not sure they ever did. You're the only person that really understands what it was like," she said, "and you never want to talk about it."

"Talking about it won't change anything." The hurt. The rejection. The abandonment. There were no magic words that would soothe those feelings.

Willa stood up straighter. "It would to me. You act like you can just white-knuckle your way through life. Like what they did didn't fuck us up. I'm sorry I'm not as good at pretending as you are. I'm sorry I can't just pick up and move on like it doesn't fucking kill me to be thrown away like that. They're our parents, Gray. Our parents, and they could literally give two shits about us. Why would I ever believe that anyone else in this world would?"

Gray knew, with excruciating certainty, exactly how her sister felt. It had been something in the past that she'd well and truly accepted—that everyone would leave. Maybe she should put that to the test. "So what, you just treat me like shit because you can? Because you think I'll always be here for you?"

"I'm not trying to hurt you, Gray. I am so fucking thankful for everything you do for me, but you won't let me do anything for you. You don't want to talk. You don't want to let me in.

Half the time I don't know if you want me to just disappear and never come around again."

"Me neither," Gray spit out. Her regret was immediate, sharp and stabbing through her body, so forceful it was hard to breathe. When she saw the haunted look etched across her sister's face before it settled into a rigid mask, her heart twisted. Gray's vision blurred at the edges, tears pooling behind her eyes. She'd gone too far, the room silent except for her own gasping breaths and Willa's quiet sobs. She'd known. She'd known what the rejection would feel like to Willa. A slap in the face from the only person she still considered family.

And she'd done it anyway.

She didn't have time to think about what type of person that made her because everything happened quickly after that. Willa grabbing her jacket. The front door opening. Another broken sob that Willa tried to keep in check but failed.

She had to fix this. *Fix it, fix it, fix it*, she repeated in her mind.

Regret clawed at her, the words she needed to find scratching at her throat so hard it burned. "Willa, wait. Stay here tonight. I had a horrible night, and I'm in no position to talk about anything. We can figure this out tomorrow," she begged, her voice breaking under the weight of her words. But those words couldn't fix the ones that had come before, even if she desperately wished that they could.

For the first time in a long time, she saw a hardened edge to Willa's jaw, and it reminded her so much of her own. She was anguished that she'd been the one to cause it, to teach Willa a lesson that nobody should ever be forced to learn.

"Willa, please," she said as the front door slammed against her words.

And then Gray was well and truly alone, with no one but herself to blame.

Chapter Twenty-Five

It was late morning the day after the party, and Nora still hadn't heard from Gray. A million possibilities floated through her mind, and she didn't like a single one of them.

Finally, when she needed to see for herself that Gray was okay, she got dressed and drove the ten minutes to Gray's house. At least her car was parked out front, which was a good sign.

Whether Gray was hungover or had actually gotten sick, Nora wanted to help her. It was the singular thought that had propelled her into action, and she hadn't questioned it once. She knocked and took a slight step back, rubbing her hands together for warmth.

The door opened surprisingly quickly, Gray's face coming into view. "Wi—"

Nora's face split into a lopsided grin before she had the chance to take Gray in. Once she did, her brows drew together, trying to figure out what she was looking at. Gray's face was pale, and she was wearing a mismatched pair of sweats and a sweatshirt that were sizes too big. And she looked tired, so tired.

Like she had the weight of the world resting on her shoulders. "Are you okay?" Nora asked, scanning Gray's face for any sign of what was going on.

Gray swung the door open. "Never better."

She'd never seen Gray sick before. Maybe she just got a little cranky when she didn't feel well. Still, she was a far cry from the woman Nora had spent the evening with last night, an evening she'd been very much looking forward to continuing after.

Nora shrugged off her coat as Gray sat back down on the sofa. "I wanted to check on you."

Gray made a motion with her hand, dipping it down and shooting it off to the side. "Consider me checked."

Something was wrong, though Nora couldn't pinpoint exactly what. "Where's Willa?"

"I don't know." Gray refused to make eye contact. "We got in a fight last night and she left."

Nora moved over to the sofa and sat down next to Gray, who made no move to get closer. "After you came home?"

Gray nodded. "Yep."

"I'm sorry, Gray. I'm sure that sucked when you already didn't feel well."

"My fault." Gray shrugged, pulling her legs up to her chest and hugging them like she'd fall apart if she didn't. "Always my fault."

"You're sisters. I'm sure you both give as good as you get."

"It wasn't her fault," Gray said, her eyes narrow as she finally looked at Nora. She looked so detached, so different from the Gray that she'd come to know.

Nora scooted closer and reached out to put her hand on Gray's knee. "Gray, are you okay? What's going on?"

"Look, I can't do this right now." Gray looked down at her

hands and then back to Nora. "Honestly, I don't know if I can do this at all."

Nora experienced one of those moments when time slowed down, every second settling achingly in her bones as she tried to process Gray's words. But she wasn't going to let herself spiral until she knew what exactly they were talking about. "Do what?"

"This." Gray gestured between the two of them. "Us."

Okay, there was the flash of panic she'd been trying to keep at bay. What was happening right now? She was missing an extremely big piece of the puzzle, and now that she knew that Gray was okay—relatively—her next priority was to figure out what it was. "Gray... what happened last night?"

Gray ran her hands through her unkempt hair. "I'm not the person you think I am. You'll see that soon enough. Maybe you're seeing it right now."

"Why don't you let me decide how I feel about you?" Nora said softly. She tried to take Gray's hand, but Gray moved it away and pulled her sweatshirt down until it covered her fingertips. The action was received loud and clear.

"Nora. This isn't..." Gray stood up and started pacing along the length of the coffee table. When she stopped moving, she squared her shoulders toward Nora, her eyes hard. "People think I'm sleeping with you to get ahead."

The hair on Nora's arms stood up. Of all the ridiculous things people could say about her, about them. She hadn't considered this one, and she couldn't help the burst of hollow laughter that pushed out. "Who would be stupid enough to think that?" Well, she had a few ideas.

Gray waved her off. "That's not important. What is important is that I knew this was a bad idea from the start, and I did it anyway. I deluded myself into thinking that this could work, that life could be all sunshine and roses."

Nora managed a half-hearted smile even as tension rolled through her body. The minute they both gave in to this pressure that threatened to spill over into their words, things would devolve quickly. "I don't think anyone would describe us finding our way to one another as 'sunshine and roses.'"

"Why didn't you tell me you turned down the promotion?" Gray clocked her with a stare, her words accusatory.

"Oh..." Nora took a few seconds. Her relationship with Gray had moved so far beyond that, and she honestly hadn't thought about it much after talking to Cynthia. And she'd wanted to let it be a surprise when Cynthia talked to Gray. She hadn't considered how the narrative could be twisted into something it wasn't.

"Why would you do that?" Gray said, her voice rising. "And then Cynthia was talking to me about a promotion at the party. Do you know how that's going to look?"

Nora put her hands up in submission. She wanted to get them back to an even keel. "It was a genuine mistake. Honestly, I didn't know that you cared so much about what other people thought. If I knew for a second that you were worried about the optics, I'd have mentioned it sooner."

Gray ran her hands through her hair again, exasperation evident on her features. "Well, maybe if you left your last job because people thought you were fucking your way to the top, you'd understand."

That stopped Nora cold. She hadn't assumed that Gray had had an easy path at Brenneman Brothers, but she wasn't prepared for what Gray was laying out for her now. Her heart tightened at the thought of how difficult that must have been, especially given how hard she knew Gray worked. "Gray, I am so sorry that happened, but it has nothing to do with us." And truly, it cut at Nora more than a little bit that Gray didn't see that. She'd be strong, but she didn't know how much longer she could let Gray cut at their relationship with a hacksaw.

Gray started pacing again, bare feet sliding against the thick rug so intensely Nora thought she may get a carpet rash. "The devil works hard, but the rumor mill works harder. I was so stupid to think that I could just move past it. That it wouldn't..."

Gray was obviously in a bad place, and Nora didn't want to make it worse. It was all tied into a knot for Gray, even if both situations couldn't be more different from where Nora sat. One was a baseless rumor by someone who was undoubtedly an asshole. And the other was... well, it was the start of something that had begun because of work but was miles beyond it now. And until last night, she'd thought that Gray had felt the same way. "We know that isn't what's going on here. Cynthia knows. Anyone whose opinion matters already knows the truth."

"I can't even think about what comes next professionally, about how to deal with this at the office. Willa hates me, and I deserve it. And you..." Gray's voice was wobbly, like she was on the verge of tears. "It's all just too much."

Nora waited, wondering what came next. What about her? She wasn't the right person to support Gray? Did Gray not know how to accept anyone's love? "What about me?" she finally asked.

"I'm not who you want."

Nora's own frustration mounted. For the first time in a long time, she was sure, and to have Gray continually tell her that she wasn't what Nora wanted was starting to cut at her. "Please stop telling me what I want. I'm trying to support you, to understand what happened. I'm trying to work out solutions for how we can move forward. I'm doing what anyone who lo— anyone who cares about someone would do. I'm not trying to be an asshole here, but it feels like you're the one who's looking for an easy out, who doesn't want to try and make this work."

That was obviously the wrong thing to say; Gray's features went hard. "All I've ever done my whole life is try. Try to get over how fucked up I feel about my parents. Try to support Willa in all the ways that Gray had never had. Try to carve out some small fucking sliver of success in the world on my own. I'm so fucking tired. I can't do this too."

Nora bit the inside of her cheek, taking a few seconds to let the moment settle before it combusted. "Gray, I know that you're trying, but you're also pushing me away right now."

Finally, when Gray didn't respond, Nora stood and walked across the room toward her. The space between them felt like a chasm. All she wanted to do was understand why Gray was pulling away from her, even if the churning in her gut told her what she didn't want to voice out loud. Gray was scared. Terrified that Nora would be like all the other people in her life who let her down. But Nora was only human, too, and she couldn't pretend to be impervious to the careless words that Gray was hurling at her like cannonballs to get her to retreat.

"We can figure this out," Nora said when she got close enough to touch Gray, though she kept her hands to herself. "I just need you to want to work with me instead of against me. That's the only way this works."

"Why did you give up the promotion? For me? Isn't that exactly how you used to act for Andrea?" Apparently, Gray had decided defense was no longer going to work, so she'd adjusted her strategy fully into the offensive and was going for pain with a pointed jab.

It landed, squarely.

"That's not what it was and you know it. Or, at least, you should. I gave up the promotion because it's not what I wanted anymore. I've spent the last five years clinging to work to feel some semblance of control. I don't want that anymore. I don't *need* it," she stressed, imploring Gray to understand.

She watched as Gray crossed her arms and closed in on herself, her face gaunt. If seeing the anguished look on her face hurt Nora, hearing Gray's words hurt worse. "Maybe what I want is for this to end before anyone truly gets hurt. Maybe I don't think the risk is worth the reward. I'm not going to be able to let you in in the way you deserve. I don't even know what that would look like."

Nora understood what Gray was saying, more than she even wanted to admit to Gray. There was the possibility of real hurt, of heartbreak even, if this went south. They were something already, and they could be something with a depth that could drag them both under if they weren't careful. But, to Nora, it was worth it. It would always be worth it if she got to wake up with Gray in her arms, to hear about her day, to know that she caused even a single smile on her pretty lips.

She wanted the hard stuff too. For Gray to lean into her, to let Nora carry some of the crushing weight that Gray still held on to from her childhood. For Gray to confide in her and let her help, the same way that Gray had helped Nora.

So yeah, it was worth it, but she realized, with staggering clarity as she scanned Gray's closed-off features, that she couldn't spend her life trying to make Gray see that. Gray was wrong about why she'd given up the promotion, but she had made a valid point. If Nora shrank herself, if she worked herself into a version that Gray needed her to be right now for her own self-preservation, Nora couldn't forgive herself. She'd come too far to give up on the progress she'd made. And, granted, that progress was due in large part to Gray, who was also a huge source of her excitement about what came next, but she wouldn't wither this time. She wouldn't beg and plead and mould herself for the chance to be in Gray's life. Especially if

Gray was too afraid to let her be there, if she insisted on pushing her away.

Tears pricked behind her eyes, and she took a slow, steady breath to keep them from falling. She wasn't going to fall apart. Maybe she was deluding herself that this wasn't the end, or maybe she was still in so much shock at the turn today had taken that she wasn't able to process it yet. She felt like she was straddling numbness and acceptance, waffling back and forth between the two depending on the second.

Nora leaned forward, lips trembling as she ghosted a gentle kiss on Gray's cheek. "I know what it's like to be scared. To feel lost and alone in this world. You offered me a lifeline when I didn't deserve one. The only difference is that I wanted to take it." Her lips twisted into a sad smile, the magnitude of this moment finally catching up to her. "And for what it's worth, I don't think you're the lost cause you think you are, but I'm not the one who needs to believe that."

Gray swallowed audibly as Nora stepped back, but neither of them wavered. It killed Nora a little bit, but with one last look at Gray, she grabbed her jacket and headed out the door.

* * *

The Philly Finds office was closed between Christmas and New Year's, so at least there were no inopportune run-ins with Gray while the wounds were still fresh. Nora's feelings were like one big bruise, so tender to the touch that even thinking about Gray made her hurt.

Not seeing Gray hadn't done much to lessen the pain, but she didn't want to put that idea to the test. She'd have to soon, but today wasn't that day.

Instead of wallowing, she'd been trying her best to keep busy. She'd spent Christmas with Cynthia's family, which was a welcome reprieve from the sound of her own thoughts. Luckily, she'd managed to skirt any Gray-related conversations, wondering how they were going to move forward with the entire office watching their movements after the holiday party.

More than a few times, she'd wondered if she'd made a mistake. If she should have fought harder, stayed longer, to show Gray that she supported her. Was leaving the wrong thing to do when she knew how much Gray's ache from her parents leaving still burned?

She hadn't felt like there was much of a choice at the time. Gray was intent on pushing her away, and she could feel them edging closer to a point of no return. One of them would have said something that would have done more than just hurt their relationship. It would have fundamentally fractured their ability to exist as co-workers, to manage seeing each other every day in the office. Not that it felt all that tenable now.

But maybe with time it would.

Today, she and Callie had plans to grab lunch at Calloway Brewery. Again, she was reminded how much her life had changed. She could never hate Gray—not even close—even if her heart felt a little broken right now. It was because of Gray that she'd opened herself up again, that she'd come back to the land of the living and experienced all she'd been missing for the last five years. At least this time she'd known she'd tried. She'd put herself out there, open to the possibility of hurt at the hands of someone she trusted.

She'd also thought about her past relationships a lot over the last few days. She'd loved her parents, but she hadn't trusted them. Even her mom, as they'd worked their way to a better place, was still someone she'd come to expect disappointment from. And Andrea... well, Nora had accepted her, but she didn't think, in retrospect, that she'd ever truly trusted her either. There was a part of Nora that knew that Andrea was always looking out for number one, that they only worked because Nora worked so hard to make it that way.

Not that things with her and Gray had been easy, but they were... different. Fuller. Richer somehow. The laughter and the sex and the quiet moments. It had all been real, so genuine that it made Nora's heart ache with the thought of it. Unfortunately, they'd butted up against a wall that Gray wasn't ready to break down, that no amount of emotion from Nora's side could lessen.

Pulling into the brewery, she shook her bittersweet thoughts away and parked her SUV.

The taproom wasn't very busy as she headed inside. There was a bar running along the right wall, and the main room was open, with impressively high ceilings that made sound carry. In the back were the large, stainless-steel vats that always looked impossibly shiny.

She spotted Callie at the bar and headed over to join her. "You're a sight for sore eyes." And she meant it, leaning in to capture Callie in a sincere hug.

"Right back at ya. How was your Christmas?" Callie pushed a pint she'd ordered before Nora's arrival toward her, then took a quick sip of her own.

Nora took off her scarf before hanging her coat on the back of the bar chair. "No complaints. I had dinner at Cynthia's. How was yours?"

Callie let out a long, punctuated sigh. "We did the divorced-parent holiday shuffle. I shouldn't complain that my kids have so many people who love them, but between my house, Allen's house, and both of our parents' houses, it was a busy day."

Nora nodded. "I can't imagine. How are things going between you two?" Nora wasn't Allen's biggest fan, but she wanted to support Callie no matter what, and she knew navigating complicated family dynamics was tricky. Callie always put her kids first, even if Allen didn't deserve her willingness to make things work so well.

"You know, it was the strangest thing..."

"Well, now you've got me on baited breath."

Callie laughed. "Maybe I'm being crazy, but I got the sense that he wanted to reconcile. Or at least start a conversation about it."

Nora's eyebrow lifted so high she wouldn't have been surprised if it disappeared off her forehead completely. "Really? Haven't you guys been divorced for, like, a decade?"

Callie nodded. "Close to it. And yeah, I think so. He was just acting so strangely." She stopped, like she was reassessing her words. "I mean, not strange. He was acting like he used to when we first got married. And he kept talking about the kids' first few Christmases. How much he loved those days but realized he didn't fully appreciate them back then. How nice it was for the whole family to be together. He seemed so wistful, like he wished we could go back in time."

Nora frowned but hid it quickly. "And would that be... something you're open to?" She chose her words carefully, knowing what a sensitive topic this could be.

"Oh, hell no." Callie's boisterous laugh carried across the room. "I will strive for an amicable co-parenting relationship with him, but the ship for anything else has sailed. I think he's lonely, and he's conflating that with thinking he misses me."

"Well, to be fair, you are pretty great," Nora said, hoping Callie understood how sincere she was being.

Callie flashed her a smile that Nora was sure would get her all kinds of attention from people who weren't cheaters. "The irreconcilable problem that he fails to grasp, like so many other things in his life, is that you can't go back in time. All you can do is pick up the pieces and move forward. I'm glad he's finally realizing what he threw away, but it doesn't change the fact that it's gone."

Gone. The word hit her like an arrow in the chest. "I'm sure it's still hard for you," she said, her own words hitting a little too close to home.

It was then that Callie studied her closely. "Are you doing okay? You don't have that 'I'm in love and about to burst from the weight of it' look today."

Nora rolled her eyes, even as her heart thumped heavily against her rib cage. But she didn't want to shut herself off from feelings anymore, even if she didn't much care for her current ones. "Probably not going to see that look from me again any time soon."

"Oh, sweetie," Callie said, placing her hand on top of Nora's. "I'm sorry. Do you want to talk about it?"

Nora willed her voice to stay even in spite of how Callie's soft stare was begging her to shed the few tears that were always on standby. She'd cried twice since the breakup—or whatever it was technically called—had happened, but she was trying to make peace with the situation, to accept the reality of it as best she could. "I don't really know what to say. I don't want to air Gray's business since we all work together, but unfortunately we just weren't in the same place to move forward."

"I'm just... surprised. The way she looked at you at the holiday party was something special." Callie smiled softly when she added, "You looked at her the same way."

Nora nodded and blinked rapidly. Goddamn tears. "It was something special."

"Speaking of the holiday party..."

Nora tipped her head up, finding Callie's stare again. "What about it?"

"Well, I was trying to figure out the best way to broach this conversation, but..."

Nora rolled her shoulders. She was sick of hiding, and she had no problem having this conversation with anyone who wanted to have it. "If you heard a shitty rumor, don't worry. I did too."

"Oh, well, that makes this easier then." Callie visibly relaxed. "I'm glad I don't have to be the bearer of bad news, but I wanted you to know."

"What I don't know is who started it. I'd be eternally thankful if you could help me with that tidbit."

Callie's eyes went wide, like she'd just placed the last piece into a puzzle. "Wait, is this why you and Gray broke up?"

Nora shook her head but then stopped, opting for honesty. It was complicated, like most things in life. "It definitely didn't help the situation. And maybe it was a catalyst for a breakdown that was always coming. Whether Gray and I are together or not, I don't want anyone thinking that it's true. Anything that has happened or will happen for Gray at Philly Finds is because she earned it. End of conversation. Period."

"You're sort of terrifying when you're in someone's corner. Like, even more than when you're ignoring everyone."

Nora flashed a wicked grin. "I am going to take that as a compliment."

Callie laughed. "Damn right it was."

Nora tapped her fingers on the bar. "Now please tell me who started the rumor."

"Kelsey." She appreciated that Callie didn't miss a beat, that she didn't waver on being honest with Nora for even a second.

Nora's nostrils flared. Fucking Kelsey. She knew it. "What a pissant."

Callie nodded. "Apparently, and I am not gossiping, just

relaying the story for damage control... Kelsey told Sage, who was very upset to hear this news but had no reason not to trust Kelsey. So Sage confided in Trent, wondering if it was true because she knew that Trent and Gray were friends. Trent, obviously beside himself because he worships Gray and she is his quote, 'favorite bro,' unquote, came to me at the end of the night." She cut off Nora's question. "You'd already gone home."

Nora took a few seconds to absorb the grapevine of information. "Thank you for telling me, Callie."

"Why do I feel like a kid who just got called into the principal's office to narc?" Callie joked.

Nora shook her head. "This is someone's livelihood. What Kelsey did was beyond the pale. Especially after..." Whether she wanted to tell Callie, it wasn't her story to share. And she'd respect that.

Callie lowered her head. "I still have friends at Brenneman Brothers. Not many, but a few people I care about have stuck it out there. One of them, Priya, told me what happened to Gray when she worked there."

Nora lifted a brow. "Oh?"

Callie nodded. "Priya said that Gray was one of the good ones. Asked me to look out for her when she came to Philly Finds, especially after what she'd been through."

Nora's whole face softened, and she was suddenly overcome with emotion. "You're one of the good ones, too, Callie. Don't ever forget that."

Callie ducked the compliment. "There's a lot of power in people supporting one another. I think sometimes it's easy to forget that. A loud, angry voice can make a lot of noise in the general hum of daily life, but it's nothing compared to the quiet making itself known."

"I like that." After her years of self-imposed isolation, Nora realized the undeniable truth in Callie's words.

"So... do you really think you and Gray are over? It seems like you still care an awful lot about her."

Nora didn't want to carry around a torch that would eventually burn her up from the inside out. It wasn't like she'd stopped having feelings for Gray, but she was trying to move past them to acceptance. Still, she wanted all the best for Gray, who deserved nothing less than that. She smiled sadly, feeling a little more resolute in her words when she said, "I think we have to be, for both our sakes."

Chapter Twenty-Six

Work was the only thing keeping Gray sane, even if she hadn't been back to the office yet. It was the first week of the new year, and she'd spent the last two days tracking down every lead she'd ever had and working to re-engage them. Showings meant distractions. Problems meant someone else's life to focus on.

For a second, she wondered if this was how Nora used to feel before she quickly pushed the thought away. She had no right to think about Nora, not after how she'd behaved toward her.

She was currently standing in below-freezing weather in Old City, checking her schedule for the rest of the late afternoon. She could care less about the cold, but she welcomed the intrusion into her rambling thoughts.

Her phone vibrated in her hand, a text from Becks appearing on the screen.

Becks Anderson – 4:15 p.m.

How are you doing?

Becks had been back in town over the holidays, where Gray had unloaded the magnitude of the mistakes she'd made in swift succession like she'd been watching dominos topple in a line. They were quite the pair. Becks had updated Gray about her fledgling romance with Tatum being snuffed out at the first hint of seriousness, both about where things were going and whether Tatum was going to come out at any point. Gray had cried over her sister. About Nora. Her anger at what Kelsey had said about her.

It had felt good in the moment, cathartic even, but the ruins of the chaos she'd unleashed were still just as real.

Gray had to give herself credit. Not even she could have guessed how spectacularly she could fuck up her own life in just twenty-four hours. At least she was successful at whatever she put her mind to.

She hadn't seen Willa in over a week. Finally, two days after she had left the house, she'd responded to one of Gray's dozens of texts to let her know that she was safe. It was the first time Gray had felt like she could breathe.

All she wanted to do was tell Willa how right she had been. Because Gray didn't let Willa in. She assumed that the weight of the world was hers to carry alone. She nagged her sister and was frustrated by her behavior sometimes, but wasn't part of that what Gray had wanted? For Willa to feel so safe in this world in a way that Gray had never had so that her sister could experience it to its fullest? To make mistakes and stumble and know that it would all still be okay?

She'd created a safe spot for Willa to land, and then she'd held it against her. And when Willa had wanted to create that safety for Gray, she'd pushed her away. She'd decided instead that Willa was undependable, reckless, immature. That Willa was forcing Gray's hand. All the reasons that made it easier than accepting the truth that she didn't even know how to let her own sister in.

So yeah, she'd fucked up. Badly. And Willa was just at the top of the list.

She couldn't even think about Nora without breaking down into tears. God, why had she done that? Why had she pushed her away when all Nora had wanted to do was help? It had all felt like too much. She still felt like throwing up if she thought about the holiday party and the subsequent night and next day for longer than a few seconds.

She'd been embarrassed, maybe more than at any other point in her life, when she'd overheard Kelsey in the bathroom. Her usual instinct, to retreat inward, had morphed into an ugly explosion of frustration at the world around her. And now she was sitting in the rubble of a situation that she'd created.

Nora had reached out once—but not since—later in the day after their fight. Or breakup. Or Gray's nuclear shutdown. Whatever you wanted to call it.

I'm here if you need anything.

Six simple words that cracked Gray's heart open a little more every time she read them.

And still, she couldn't make herself respond.

She swallowed the lump in her throat and started walking back toward the train. Driving downtown was almost never worth it. It was ironic, she noted, that her job was to traverse the city to different neighborhoods, and she still had a terrible sense of direction.

That thought stopped her short as she stilled and looked around. Familiarity washed over her. This was her old neighborhood. Her old street. She'd lived many places throughout her life, but this one had always been her favorite. Not just because she'd lived there the longest. It was the last time she'd felt like a kid, and it had been the first time she'd felt protected by someone in the world.

Ms. Gibson.

Did she still live here?

Suddenly, Gray needed to know. She had to at least try, even if it was a long shot. It morphed into a singular focus that pushed Willa and Nora and all the ways in which she'd fucked up to a blissfully quiet part in the back of her mind.

Gray had never been big on signs, but if there was ever a time to feel like there was a giant neon arrow for her to follow, it was right now.

Her feet moved without her processing where she was going. When she stopped, she was staring up at a nondescript three-story apartment building. At least it was still here, which was something. She only had to loiter for about thirty seconds before a delivery person exited the building.

Sneaking inside, she called up the layout of a building she hadn't been inside in almost twenty years. It was easier than she expected. Muscle memory took over as she climbed two sets of stairs to the third floor. She passed her own apartment without slowing down.

Two doors down and on the opposite side of the hall, she stopped. The door looked like it had been given a fresh coat of paint recently, and a festive holiday wreath hung on it.

She held her breath as she knocked.

Laughter filtered from behind the door and into the hallway when a middle-aged woman with light brown hair and a broad smile opened it. "Hi," she beamed, cocking her head to the side. "How can I help you?"

"Hi." Gray suddenly felt silly. Childish even. She'd wandered back to the last place she'd really felt loved and cared for, and for what? A walk down memory lane that wouldn't change anything? This woman obviously wasn't Ms. Gibson, even a two-decades-older version of her. She refused to let the disappointment settle over her. "I was just looking for someone, but it doesn't seem like she lives here anymore. Sorry for interrupting your day."

Gray turned to walk away when the woman touched her arm. "I've lived here for fifteen years, but my wife's been here for twenty. She'll probably know."

Everything in Gray froze until, just like she'd done when she was little, she peeked into the doorway to see who was home. "Ms. Gibson?"

Like Gray was transported back in time, Ms. Gibson walked out of the kitchen, which was off to the side, and stepped into the hallway that ran through the apartment. She came closer, her eyes drawing upward as she tried to figure out whether she knew the random woman calling her name. It was strange how she looked so different yet completely the same. Her curly hair was graying, but it still had the same vibrance. Gray had loved pulling at her curls and watching them spiral back into place once upon a time.

"Hello?" And then her stare softened, recognition dawning across her features. She held her hand over her mouth and let out a long breath. "Gray."

And just like that, Gray fell into arms that were already open to welcome her back, even after all these years. She didn't know when she started crying. All she knew was that Ms. Gibson was crying, too, her hands running up and down Gray's back in a soothing pattern.

When they finally broke apart, Ms. Gibson ushered her inside, leading her by the hand through the hallway and finally sitting them both down on the sofa in the living room. It didn't smell like tobacco anymore, but she swore she caught a whiff of cinnamon in the air.

"I'm so glad you stopped by. This is my wife, Abby," Ms.—

or now Mrs., presumably—Gibson said before looking back at Gray like she might disappear. Gray understood the feeling perfectly. "I've thought about you often over the years. Wondered how you were doing."

Gray nodded, a lump forming in her throat even as she said hello to Abby, who was already headed back toward the kitchen to give them time to catch up. There were a lot of things she didn't know how to articulate, especially to this woman who had been her safe place to land for so many years. "I've thought about you too. I'm sorry I didn't stop by sooner."

Ms. Gibson waved her off. "You were just a kid when you moved away, sweetie. I didn't even know if you remembered me."

"I loved being here. It's one of the only good memories from my childhood," Gray admitted.

With a sad smile, Ms. Gibson grabbed her hand. "Then I'm glad that I could give that to you. You were also very important to me." She tapped her finger against Gray's chin, just like she'd done when Gray was little. "So it goes both ways."

Gray smiled, deeply affected by the simple gesture.

"So, how are you doing? How's Willa? Are you both still in the city?"

The lump was back, but she pushed it down. "We are. Our parents moved to Tennessee eight years ago, so it's been just us since then."

"I'm glad you two have one another. You were always a great big sister to her."

Gray wondered if she'd start crying for the second time in ten minutes. It wouldn't be the first time it had happened in the past week. The words rushed out of her before she could stop them. "I feel like I haven't been much good to anyone lately. I guess I came back here to try and"—she ran a hand through her

311

hair—"I don't know, figure out where it all went wrong? Or come back to when it last felt right?"

"Oh, honey." Ms. Gibson took her hand. "You were just a kid yourself, but don't ever doubt all the good you did for your sister. Whenever I gave you a snack, before Willa started coming over, you'd ask if you could take one for her as well. I always thought it was so sweet, even if it made me sad." She could tell by the look in Ms. Gibson's eyes that there were a lot of feelings simmering below the surface, about how her parents had chosen—or not chosen—to raise them.

Still, she was grateful for what she did have. That she'd met someone like Ms. Gibson all those years ago. "You were a saint. If not for you, we'd probably have been surviving off of the vending machine snacks I got from school."

"I'm just doing what anyone should have done. Oh my gosh..." She stood up. "You'll never guess what I still have. Give me a second." Moments later, she returned holding a laminated card in her hand. "Here. I feel like I should return this to its rightful owner all these years later."

It was Gray's KidSafe card, which they'd had done at school. It had a photo of Gray, probably around age seven, her hair wild and unkempt, her smile showcasing a missing front tooth. She looked at her tiny fingerprint on the card, running her finger over the arches, loops, and whorls.

She remembered the day it had been taken. Justin Morris, the brat that he was, had called her a string bean and said that she was weird because she read so much. So she'd done what any kid in her position would do and had cornered him behind the swings and dumped dirt on his head. It had seemed more than fair at the time. Back then, she hadn't understood how unfair the world was. That the too-small clothes her parents hadn't bothered to replace didn't account for her first growth spurt and made her look gangly. That even though she loved reading, it was how she escaped from her own life, from a world that didn't seem to care whether she was in it or not—until Ms. Gibson.

They'd gotten the cards back the same day, and had been instructed to take them home to their parents to keep in a safe place. She'd already known, even at seven. Instead, she'd run over to Ms. Gibson's apartment after school and proudly handed it to her.

"In case of emergencies," she'd said, all toothless smiles. "So you can find me."

A strange look had flashed across Ms. Gibson's features, Gray remembered, before her face had blossomed into a wide smile and she'd accepted the card from Gray's outstretched fingers. "I will always keep it safe, Gray. Always."

Gray's fingers toyed with the edge of the laminate that was peeling apart. "I can't believe you kept this all these years."

"I told you I would. I know a lot of adults in your life didn't keep their promises to you, and I didn't want to be one of them." Ms. Gibson's voice was soft, so comforting that Gray had to swallow down the lump in her throat.

Gray's eyes filled with tears. Goddammit, she was a mess. She was a mess who'd been wrong. Who *was* wrong. She'd thought that, for her entire life, she'd been alone. That wasn't true. The card she flipped between her fingers proved that, if she needed it spelled out for her in black and white. And Willa, whom she'd always looked at as a chain holding her down, had actually been her guiding light, giving Gray a reason to keep pushing forward. If not for herself, then she'd done it for her sister. Done well in school. Gone to college. Created a stable life. So that they'd both always have a place to call home, beyond the comfort and safety of having one another.

And then she'd made the grave mistake of throwing the

things she'd done for Willa back in her sister's face, like any of this had been her sister's fault.

She knew that she still had a lot to figure out. And maybe she'd keep fucking up along the way. No, she'd definitely still fuck it up along the way. But it wasn't going to be because she rejected help anymore, especially not now that she'd been confronted with all the good it had done her in the past.

She'd been lonely, but she'd never been alone. That was the true miscalculation she'd made in all of this.

Squeezing Ms. Gibson's hand, Gray basked in the warmth and familiarity, in the comfort of a connection they'd shared so long ago but that still made her feel a little braver, like everything was going to be okay. "Thank you."

It wasn't going to be easy, and it might not be pretty, but finally, she had reached a point where she didn't want to keep pushing people away.

* * *

Gray didn't expect texting her sister that she'd gone to see Ms. Gibson would be the thing that finally convinced Willa to engage with her. All she'd wanted was to talk to her, to hear Willa's voice again, but still, she felt unprepared later in the evening when her doorbell rang.

She rushed over to the door and swung it open wide, relief and embarrassment fighting for dominance in her chest. "Your key still works. It always will."

Willa stood at the threshold, dressed in a bomber jacket, black, high-waisted jeans, and a slouchy beanie, looking cool in a way Gray could never pull off.

But still, she was *Willa*. Her little sister. Gray had wiped her boogers. They used to stay up way too late, watching scary movies that little kids had no business watching. She'd held

Willa's hair back when she'd gotten too drunk at eighteen, the same week their parents had well and truly left.

Gray had spent so long worrying that no one would ever see her, that she'd failed to see the woman standing right in front of her. She didn't want to make that mistake again. "I'm glad you came."

Willa followed her into the house and walked over to the sofa, where S'mores lifted her sleepy head. She gave Willa's hands a few gentle licks before Willa scratched her between the ears. "I can pick up the rest of my stuff tomorrow."

Gray put her hands in her pockets and rocked back and forth. "Can we talk? Please?"

Willa sighed. "I'm not really sure what good that will do. You made it pretty clear already what you think of me. I don't know that I need a replay of that."

"That's exactly why I want to talk." Gray took a step toward her sister and gestured to the sofa. "Sit, please." She wasn't above pleading if that was what it took.

Gray breathed a sigh of relief when Willa sat down. She picked S'mores up and held the dog to her chest. "What's up?"

Not wasting time, Gray sat down next to her. "I'm sorry. For so many things." She kept pushing the words out. She wasn't worried she'd lose her courage, but she was more than a little concerned that she'd start crying. "I'm sorry you didn't feel like you couldn't tell me about visiting Mom and Dad, regardless of how the trip went."

"Gray." Her sister's voice was quiet, a million unspoken memories of emotional hurt at the hands of their parents floating between them.

Gray shook her head and cleared her throat. She owed her sister this. She owed her much more than this, but right here in this moment was a good place to start. "I am. And I'm sorry that all I wanted to do was give you a safe place to land and then I held it against you. That wasn't fair of me."

She watched as Willa took off her beanie and ran her hands through her hair, exactly like Gray sometimes did. "I'm sorry too. I know that I don't make things especially easy. I'm not driven or successful or able to handle things the way you are. I just..." Willa bit back a sob that made Gray's heart ache. Her sister looked tired, the dark circles under her eyes covered with makeup. Guilt sluiced through Gray. "I've really been struggling for the last few months. Ever since I came back from my trip. And I wanted to talk to you about it, I just didn't know how."

Gray grabbed Willa's hand and held it tight. "You are passionate and fun and curious about the world. You're not afraid to try new things. You're probably the kindest person I've ever met. I love you so much. I love exactly who you are, even if I haven't been doing a very good job at showing it." She swallowed hard. "I didn't realize until recently how much I've been closing myself off. I think I did a pretty good job of hiding it from everyone... except you." She looked up to meet Willa's shiny eyes. A tear fell down Gray's cheek.

It felt like a little piece of her heart healed when Willa squeezed her hand back. "I love you too. I've been thinking a lot this past week. I know that I've been treating you more like a parent than a sibling, and that wasn't always fair. But you just always seem like you have it together. And I felt like you didn't want my help, but I still needed yours. I felt so guilty every time I took it, but I didn't know what else to do."

Gray brushed her thumb over one of Willa's rings. "Do you want to tell me what's been going on? Because as sisters, I want us to be able to talk about anything, even if it's hard."

Willa let out a strangled sound and wiped her hand across

her face before burrowing it in S'mores's long coat again. "Well, I should be honest about S'mores, to start."

"What about S'mores?" Gray said, a protective edge in her voice.

And then, like Willa couldn't hold it in anymore, the words started to pour out. "She was Mom and Dad's. It was clear they weren't taking care of her. I couldn't stand for her to suffer, so I took her when we left." Gray's jaw dropped, but Willa was just getting started. "And then we came back, and it was so embarrassingly clear to me that Keith wasn't the right person for me. I tried to talk to him about the weird visit with Mom and Dad, and he just... couldn't grasp why I was struggling. I didn't want to end up in some dysfunctional relationship where we were both just floating by. Or settle for not being able to have difficult conversations," she said with a resigned shrug.

"That's... a lot, Willa. But good on you for figuring that out. You're way ahead of me on the relationship front. I've just decided that it's better to completely shut myself off rather than fighting for what could make me happy." The dog-napping aside, she couldn't keep the hint of pride from her voice. Because it was for a good cause, and Gray absolutely trusted that her sister had made the right decision. "And I'm glad you took S'mores. She's one of us."

Willa let out a sad sigh and spun one of her rings around her finger nervously. "Do you know that job that I had, the one in South Philly?"

"At the dive bar?" Gray thought back to the time Willa had shown up back at home in the middle of the day, stating that it 'wasn't going to work out.' She'd been so frustrated with her sister. For ruining her moment with Nora. For flaking out on another commitment she'd made.

Willa nodded. "That's the one. I'd started when I got back from the trip, and it was awful. Misogynistic and just truly

317

gross. I didn't want to tell you, but I quit because I couldn't handle it. Enough unwanted advances, and suddenly even a decent paycheck didn't seem worth it."

"Oh, Willa." Gray held her sister's hand tighter. God, she'd been so insistent to put Willa in a box that she'd made it impossible to see her as anything else. Hurt. Afraid. Alone. Trying her best to make it in an unfair world.

Willa shrugged, but the rattled breath she let out told another story than indifference. "The night of your holiday party, I really was planning to stay at home, but another former co-worker quit, too, because she'd gone through the same thing. She wanted to talk about it. It seemed like she could really use some support. I didn't think you'd want a stranger in your house, so I got her to come to Fishtown, but we met around the corner. I really was only gone an hour. And I wasn't out getting fucked up or partying, just trying to help a friend." Willa was looking at her like Gray's opinion held so much weight that Gray had to bite back a sob.

Her heart broke for her sister. For all the ways that Gray wanted to protect her, there were still so many in which she couldn't. She wanted to wrap her sister up in a hug and never let her go. She wanted to shield her from the world, from people who were so selfish or thoughtlessly cruel. But she hadn't given Willa the space to feel like she could be honest, to let Gray help with the hard stuff. All Gray saw was the mundane, annoying friction of living with a roommate who, honestly, she didn't really know all that well. Active communication was sorely lacking, and because they couldn't talk about the big stuff, they couldn't talk about the little stuff either. Gray's annoyances with her sister had festered, in part because she'd only allowed them to exist on a plane where superficial conversation and passive-aggressive barbs were being thrown back and forth.

"I'm glad you're telling me this now. I'm so sorry I didn't make you feel like you could tell me before."

Willa pursed her lips. "It's not all on you. Please don't think that. I know you have a lot going on too. Work. Taking care of S'mores. Nora." That last one cut deeply to hear, given how catastrophically Gray had fucked things up. "I intentionally didn't say anything because I was trying not to add more to your plate."

"I want us to be able to talk to one another." Just like Willa had done, Gray ran her free hand through her wild hair. She smiled at the similarity, at all the things that tied them together in this moment—good and bad. She took a deep breath. "I really fucked things up with Nora."

Willa frowned. "I'm sure you guys can figure things out if you communicate with her even half as well as you're doing with me right now. And for what it's worth, I don't think I've seen you this upset since we watched all those scary movies at home alone and you couldn't sleep for a week."

"I'm still afraid of the dark," Gray admitted. The admission tugged at something in her brain, but she couldn't quite figure out what. She'd had the same strange feeling when she'd been talking to Ms. Gibson this afternoon, like what she was remembering was something rooted in both the past and the present. She'd shrugged it off earlier, assuming it was the weight of the long overdue reunion.

Willa bumped their shoulders together, pulling her fully back to the present. "Luckily, we got to have sleepovers every night."

Gray's shoulders slumped, even as she smiled at her sister. She didn't want to be afraid anymore. Of being honest. Of putting her heart out there. Of worrying that the people she loved would eventually leave her. She'd been hiding in plain sight for too long. "I have some stuff going on at work." She wasn't trying to be evasive. She'd talk about it with Willa soon, but there was already enough happening between them and to them right now. "I pushed her away because of it. I don't... I have a really hard time letting people in."

"You don't say." Willa's wry smile eased the tension of the moment.

Gray rolled her eyes. "I know. I want to work on it, but I don't even know how to start. And Nora's just..." She knew she sounded so wistful, so completely enraptured by everything about Nora. By what they'd grown to mean to one another. By how far they'd come. By all the things they still had left to experience together. "She's special, and she's been through a lot too. I don't want to hurt her."

"Seemed like she was pretty into you. I'm sure that you making the decision to push her away is hurting her more than baring your messy soul and worrying that it will be too much is hurting you." That was annoyingly insightful. Gray huffed, and Willa let out a knowing laugh, holding up her hand. "What can I say? I have my moments too."

"You sure do." Gray lunged forward and wrapped Willa in a hug.

"You give the best hugs, sis. Have since we were little."

Gray's throat was suddenly thick, and she couldn't help as the tears started to stream down her face. "I want you to stay here for as long as you want. We may need to have better communication, but you always have a home here." She pulled back and met Willa's stare. "Always."

Willa beamed a genuine smile back at her. "I really appreciate that, sis, but I did line up a new apartment. It's with three other women, one of whom I'm already friends with. I think it'll be a good step for me, learning to live cooperatively and all that jazz instead of bouncing between living with boyfriends who are in it for a good time and not a long time."

"Are you sure?" It sounded like a good next step for Willa, even as Gray's heart clenched at the idea that she'd pushed Willa away.

Willa nodded, her smile mischievous. "I am. Don't worry. I'll still be over here all the time eating your food and using your laundry and playing with my nibling, S'mores."

Gray laughed and slapped her sister on the arm. "Brat."

If Willa said it was okay, she needed to trust her. And she needed to trust that she could share the vulnerable parts of herself with her sister, that it would create trust for Willa to do the same. With that knowledge, she felt lighter than she had in days, like the pieces were finally slotting into place.

Now, she just needed to figure out how to make up for ruining the best thing that had ever happened to her.

Chapter Twenty-Seven

Nora wondered when this would get easier. When the sadness —the potent loss of Gray—would start to calm. Even if she'd known that walking away was the right decision, Gray still monopolized most of her thoughts. Nora missed her. Gray's big, bright eyes that took everything in. The giddiness in her voice when she was especially energized about something. The way, in the stillness of the night, she held Nora like, if she let go, they both might disappear.

They'd had enough time for her to fall deeper than she had before, but not nearly enough when it all felt so unfairly snatched away. No amount of time felt like enough with the possibility of what they could have been.

Earlier today, she'd seen Gray for the first time in the new year, though Gray had been squirreled away in Cynthia's office. Nora had wanted to stay until their meeting was done, just so they could breathe the same air. Instead, she'd made herself leave so that she wouldn't be late to her afternoon showing.

Intent to distract herself tonight, she'd just eased her sock-clad feet underneath her and settled into a (hopefully) good book and a glass of wine when her doorbell rang.

She put her paperback down and padded across the hardwood floors. When she opened the door, a bundled-up Gray stood on her front steps.

Gray looked nervous, even as a soft smile graced her face when she said, "You're here."

Nora lifted an eyebrow, but her heart betrayed her by doing a weird skitter through her body at seeing Gray again. She was so close that Nora could reach out and touch her. "Where else would I be?"

Gray shook her head. "Sorry. What I mean is that you said in your text that you were here if I needed anything. I need something. I'm asking for it." A myriad of emotions flashed across her face, and Nora felt them as if they were happening in her own body. "Is that okay?" Gray asked, suddenly looking unsure.

She opened the door wider to let Gray inside. "Come in."

"Thank you." Gray followed her into the house. "Is it okay if I take off my coat?"

Nora nodded, still unclear about what was happening. Gray wasn't making a whole lot of sense, but then again, Nora hadn't been expecting her to just show up on her doorstep, so maybe she wasn't picking up the plot that quickly.

Gray hung her coat on the rack, like she'd done so many times before, and Nora's heart constricted. She missed the two of them coming back to her house together, all the mundane moments that made up a lifetime of memories at the end of the day.

"What is it that you need?" Nora asked quietly. She wasn't angry at Gray, but she did need to be careful with her own heart.

Only a few inches of space separated them when Gray

turned around. She was close enough for Nora to see the flecks of gold in Gray's brown irises. "I need to talk to you. Or..." Gray pulled her beanie off her head and ran her hand through her hair. "I need you to listen to me. Can you do that?"

Now, Nora really was beyond confused. She nodded anyway. "Sure."

Gray walked over and gestured toward the sofa. Nora nodded again, and Gray sat down. "Will you sit with me?"

When Nora sat down on the sofa, too, she made sure to keep enough space between them that they wouldn't unintentionally touch. Five minutes ago, Nora had been sitting in the same spot she was now occupying, but her own emotional state had shifted by miles.

"First, and very foremost, I want to apologize to you. For pushing you away. For implying that what we have is anything like your past relationship." Gray let out a long sigh. "For making decisions about what I thought you could handle or would be okay with. It wasn't right of me."

Well, at least they were in agreement about that. "I appreciate you saying that, Gray."

Gray nodded and ran her hands over the soft velvet of Nora's couch, like it was comforting her as she geared up to keep speaking. "I retreat when I'm scared. I spent months watching you grow and work to become a version of yourself you wanted to be. And not that you made it look painless, but you definitely did it with so much grace that it was easy to take the process for granted. I just..." Gray's hand stilled against the fabric. "I kept falling and falling for you, wondering how I was ever going to keep up. Mostly, I didn't let myself think about it. We were so good together. We were having so much fun together, and I felt so comfortable with you that I pushed it out of my mind whenever the little fear would bubble up."

"What were you afraid of exactly?" Because it wasn't like

Nora wasn't afraid too. Of Gray. Of what they could be. Of how she'd never felt like she'd bared so much of herself, her heart in someone else's hands to do with what they wanted. Maybe losing Gray wouldn't break her—she wouldn't let it— but it sure would hurt a hell of a lot.

The embarrassed smile that Gray leveled at her was both charming and intoxicating to be on the receiving end of. "I was afraid that you'd outgrow me. That one day you'd see that, for as much as I project having it together, I'm, quite frankly, a mess."

Nora shook her head. "Everyone's messy. I think you're being a little hard on yourself. I literally shut out the world for half a decade because I didn't want to deal with it. It's not a competition, but I do know that you're trying your best."

Nora's heart fluttered when Gray smiled at her again. When it dimmed, Nora resisted the urge to reach out and grab onto Gray's hand. "When you came over last week, it was the first time in a long time that I'd felt completely out of control. What Kelsey said. How it would impact things at work. What was going on with Willa. How I felt about you. It was all just..."

"Too much," Nora supplied. She remembered Gray's words from that day, etched into her memory.

"Yeah." Gray nodded, her voice full with regret. "I felt like I was being pulled apart at the seams and if I didn't curl up into a ball for protection, I would float away into nothingness."

It meant something that Gray understood why she'd done what she'd done. And it meant something, too, that she was admitting it now. But still... where did that leave them? Nora couldn't be with someone who couldn't let her in, couldn't let her help shoulder the weight of life as a team. It was something she'd always wanted, and she wasn't going to settle for less.

"I'm glad you're telling me this, Gray. Truly, all I want is what's best for you. But as for us, I don't..." Acutely, Nora realized that it was entirely possible to make the right decision and also regret it.

Gray stopped making eye contact, letting her stare drop down to the sofa before she shifted her focus back upward and met Nora's again. Not defiant but... determined? The thump in her chest rushed through her ears at the intensity of that look.

Still, it didn't solve anything. They'd done this before. After their first kiss. After last week. Gray retreated and then came back, and on and on the cycle would go until it would break Nora one day, and she'd wonder how long things had already been broken but she'd refused to accept it with the death-by-a-thousand-papercuts routine.

Nora cleared her throat. She didn't want Gray to assume what Nora could or couldn't handle, and she should do the same in return. "I can't be with someone who wants to run away from me or shut me out when things get hard. It's not healthy for me. I need to be with someone who can let me in. Do you really think, given where you are right now, that you can do that?"

Maybe it wasn't fair, what Nora was asking. Gray had given her space, had let her grow and change and become a version of herself that she was coming to love. And maybe Nora could, to some degree, do the same for Gray, but it would kill a part of her to do it. To never know what fully having Gray's trust would feel like. To know that there were pieces of herself that Gray kept closed off, even from Nora, because she didn't want the world to see them. Nora wasn't the same person from months ago, and she didn't want to go backward. She refused.

And, whether it was fair or not, it felt like Gray hadn't taken any true steps toward her yet.

Nora was already so hopelessly in love with the parts of Gray that she had been able to share, but she wanted them all. She knew that she was asking a lot, but she only had this one precious life. She couldn't spend it with someone who always kept one foot out the door.

Gray's eyes were shiny. "I've been thinking a lot about that. About whether I truly believe I could let you in or not."

Nora tamped down on the flutter in her heart that happened without her consent. Traitor. "And what conclusion did you come to?"

Gray didn't break eye contact. "I pushed you away because I was so afraid that if I let you in, you couldn't love the real me."

This conversation was either an end or a beginning, and Nora's whole body vibrated with the weight of that understanding. "And who is the real you?"

Gray shifted an inch closer. "You know how someone's been leaving notes on your desk for months?"

Nora couldn't help how her lips tipped into a grin. She still had about a dozen of the notes in her desk drawer, even if she hadn't been able to bring herself to look at them over the past week. "I do."

"You know the one about the movie *Psycho*, about the toilet flushing?"

Nora nodded. "I found it on a weekend. I laughed out loud alone in the office."

"I'm glad it made you laugh," Gray said before a sadness overtook her features. "When Willa and I were little, we were left alone a lot. So we did exactly what we shouldn't do, as kids often do, and watched scary movies. I know that tidbit of information because I became so afraid of the dark that I needed to find a way to make the movies less terrifying. To break them down into facts so that I'd be less afraid. Especially when Willa and I were home alone and I felt like I needed to protect her if anything actually happened."

Nora's heart constricted, but this time, she didn't wish the feeling away. "Oh, Gray."

"I think I was trying to show you a piece of myself—of my past—by telling you that," Gray said softly, "even though I didn't realize it at the time. It was only after having a conversation with an old friend and then talking to Willa that I realized how much of my life I put into those notes. Even if I was terrified that I wouldn't be enough, there was always a part of me that wanted you to see me. That wanted you to know how I became the person I am today."

"I'll never think less of you for what you and your sister went through. If anything, I'm so impressed with the person you've become." And god, she meant it with every fiber of her being. Gray was amazing. How she could doubt that was beyond Nora's comprehension.

"You know the one about how there is one vending machine in Japan for every forty people?"

Nora nodded. It was the first one where Gray had gotten more creative in hiding it.

"Growing up, our parents weren't home a lot. And you can probably guess that, as a ten-year-old, I wasn't very adept at cooking. The elementary school gym had a vending machine in the lobby. I'd always scrounge money together so that I could get snacks for Willa and myself. Just in case our parents were going to be out."

Nora had heard both too much and not nearly enough. She reached out instinctively and took Gray's hand. "You're a good sister, Gray. I know that you and Willa struggle sometimes, but I don't want you to ever doubt that."

Gray squeezed her hand back. "She and I are working through some things, but I think we're on a good path." When Gray ran a finger along Nora's knuckle, she tried not to give in to how good it felt, to how much she'd missed this.

"I'm glad." Nora's breathing stuttered as Gray's finger started tracing patterns.

"Bermuda was only the second time I've ever been out of the country. Becks and I drove to Canada once, almost a decade ago. The note about Sudan having more pyramids than any other country in the world?" Nora nodded. "I was obsessed with reading about places when I was little, dreaming about one day visiting them. It's how I knew all of that information about the island. I've always wanted to travel. I never got the chance growing up, and at some point, I think I just sort of accepted that that wouldn't be a part of my life. I've been trying so hard to keep myself together that I haven't been leading a life worth living. I've been letting things happen to me instead of making them happen. I've been so afraid to chase anything except stability."

Realizing what Bermuda, and that trip, had probably meant to Gray caused guilt to wash over Nora. "I'm so sorry if I made it less than amazing."

"But it *was* amazing," Gray said, her brown eyes finding Nora's and locking their stares. "Admittedly, I'd always been attracted to you, but that was the first time I felt like I ever got a glimpse of the real you. The person that you tried so hard to hide from everyone. And Bermuda was also gorgeous, don't get me wrong," Gray said with a wry grin, "but seeing you in a new way magnified the intensity of that experience infinitely."

It was so hard to think with Gray touching her. "So you've liked me since..."

Gray laughed. "I don't know if *like* is the word I'd use, but I was attracted to you and curious about you, which has clearly proven to be a pretty potent combination."

Gray flipped Nora's hand over and dragged her fingertips lightly against Nora's palm. God, she'd missed this. How well they fit together. How easily Gray seemed to know exactly how to touch her to make Nora putty in her hands. Gray flattened her palm, fingertips ghosting along Nora's wrist.

"I want this. I want us." Gray said it so simply that Nora wanted to believe it, that everything Nora so desperately wanted could be hers, if she'd just reach out and hold on to it.

This was the moment to lay herself bare. She wanted to be brave, the way Gray was being right now. "You scare me, Gray. I stayed with people far longer that I loved far less than you."

Gray nodded, her eyes still trained on Nora. "I've never felt about anyone else the way I feel about you. This whole time, I've been sharing pieces of myself with you, I just didn't realize it. I wanted to let you in, I just didn't know how. I don't want to miss the chance at getting to know every single thing there is to know about you because I'm too scared. Since Bermuda, you've been with me every step of the way, and I didn't know how to accept that." Gray looked at her solemnly. "I won't push you away again, and I'm willing to do whatever I need to show you that."

"I want to trust you, Gray—"

"And I'll try to earn that trust, however long it takes." Gray tilted her hip up and reached her hand into her back pocket. She pulled out an old, laminated card that she handed to Nora.

Nora looked down at a young Gray, her tiny fingerprint next to her photo. "What's this?"

"You're it for me," Gray said, the determination in her voice back. "Someone returned this card to me a few days ago. I'd given it to them when I was little, since they were the person I'd trusted most in this world back then. Now, it's yours. You're the person I trust. The person I want in my corner. It's probably mostly symbolic at this point since I look slightly different," she said with a soft laugh, "but the sentiment is the same."

Nora ran a finger over young Gray's picture, her heart fluttering so rapidly she worried it would beat right out of her chest. "You still have the same smile."

Gray laced their fingers together. "I love you, Nora. And

I'm done being afraid of how I feel about you. Spending my life pushing you away because I'm afraid you'll leave me isn't much of a life at all. I'm done being afraid of the best thing that's ever happened to me. And if you need more time, if I'm throwing a lot of big words around that scare you, it's okay. I'm not going anywhere. I just need to know that—"

Nora crushed their bodies together, pinning Gray below her on the sofa. She was done being afraid too. All she'd needed was to borrow a little bit of Gray's strength, of the trust she was putting in Nora to keep her heart safe. And if Gray could trust her, she could offer some of her own in return. Because she wanted this. Wanted them. Spending another second pretending she didn't felt impossible.

And that was what love was, when it really came down to it. Giving someone the pieces of yourself and trusting them to keep them close, to protect them for you when maybe you weren't strong enough to protect them yourself.

So in this moment, she'd give Gray the pieces that still felt a little raw and messy and sharp, trusting that she'd keep them safe. "I love you too. I've felt it for a while now, but I was so afraid to disrupt what we had going. I want more, though. I want mornings and nights and the boring stuff and the hard stuff." She dipped her head and placed a kiss on Gray's lips, relishing their softness. When she pulled back, those lips bloomed into a smile that was as much a language as any words would be.

With their bodies pressed close, Gray's whole body vibrating beneath her, the air heavy with all the words they'd said and had left to say, it struck Nora like a bolt of lightning. They'd never know what they could be, could never let this love grow and strengthen and evolve, unless they went all in on a life worth living—together.

Epilogue

Eight months later

"How are the new agents?"

Gray looked up from her laptop to see Nora, long legs crossed as she leaned back on Gray's desk, an adorable smile gracing her lips. And as far as the two orgasms she'd given Nora this morning were concerned, she was going to take at least a little bit of credit for that lingering smile.

Her heart still did that erratic stutter-step whenever Nora was close, and she allowed it to thump wildly against her rib cage, enjoying how alive it made her feel for a few seconds before responding. "Probably still shocked at what a functional workplace they've found themselves in, now that we run like a well-oiled machine and don't have any bad actors left," Gray teased.

Nora's smile became a smirk. "Does that mean I'm officially redeemed in the team's eyes?"

"I don't know. Why don't you ask them when they come over tonight for game night?"

It had become a twice-monthly occurrence, when colleagues and friends would crowd into Gray's house. Some people played games, but others simply hung out in the kitchen and stuffed themselves full of whatever food Willa had decided to make for the party that night.

Her sister had started culinary school six months ago, and Gray had never seen Willa take to something with more passion. And hey... she wasn't going to complain, especially when Willa came over to cook her and Nora dinner at least once a week.

Kelsey was long gone from Philly Finds, as she should be. Cynthia had backed Gray every step of the way, and within a week of Gray's conversation with her boss, after Cynthia had confirmed the situation, Kelsey's desk sat empty. Gray had heard that after Cynthia let her go, Kelsey had gotten a job at Brenneman Brothers, but that was short-lived. Within weeks, they'd been embroiled in a very public sexual harassment scandal, and the legal fees alone had all but bankrupted the once historic agency. It was the least they deserved, after the culture they'd perpetuated for far too many decades. Gray had been happy to speak with a few detectives as well as a legal team, though her information was only supplemental in supporting stories with more evidence regarding the toxic work environment.

In the last few months, the Philly Finds office had grown much busier. They'd tipped into a well-known status among real estate agencies in the city, and they had no trouble finding new agents who wanted to join the team. Along with the three newest agents, Gray had started working professionally with Sage, so she had a small team with whom she worked and that she supported in a more managerial capacity.

And, honestly, she loved it.

Her own deals still got her excited, but professional development had settled a desire in her to connect with other people, to make sure she was making a positive impact.

Gray pulled her focus away from Nora and glanced at the time on her phone. "I've got to get going. I have a showing in twenty minutes."

Nora made a petulant face, which made Gray laugh. How Nora had played at being cold and detached for years seemed ridiculous when Gray was confronted with her true personality. Nora Gallagher was a big softy, and she showed Gray every single day with her words and actions.

"I love you," Gray whispered before dipping her head and placing a quick kiss to Nora's lips. "I'll see you tonight?"

Nora, with a smile on her face again, nodded. "Only if Willa is going to make those pastry pinwheels she made last time."

"I feel like you're enjoying the pastry classes even more than Willa." It still shocked Gray how close Nora and her sister had become over the last few months. Sometimes, Gray would come home from work and find the two of them in the kitchen together, Willa explaining some new technique she was working on in class to Nora.

Willa still had her own apartment with friends, but Gray had a personal kitchen for Willa to practice in, which meant that she saw her sister frequently during the week. There had been a few close calls with Gray and Nora in indecent states of dress, so Willa had learned the hard way to text before she was coming over.

"She feeds me with food and embarrassing stories about you," Nora teased. "What's not to love?"

Gray ghosted her fingers across Nora's knuckles, her voice

dropping low when she said, "I can't tell if you're trying to make me jealous..."

Nora flipped her hand over so that she could interlace their fingers. "She feeds me, but you complete me. There's no contest."

Gray would never get tired of hearing things like that. And while Nora shared them freely, Gray was also learning not to be afraid of asking for what she needed, whether it was reassurance or comfort or anything in between.

"Good answer," she said, placing another quick kiss on Nora's lips. Gray groaned and disentangled their hands. "Okay, I really have to go. I love you."

Nora looked up at her from her desk, eyes soft and a gentle smile tugging at her lips. "Love you too."

***

Nora walked into Gray's house about twenty minutes before the other guests were set to arrive for game night. She dropped her work bag by the door and slipped out of her heels. In a few minutes, she'd go upstairs and change into something more comfortable, but excited chatter and delicious smells were already drawing her toward the kitchen.

She saw S'mores first, happily wandering around the kitchen looking for any bits of food that were lost to the ground.

Gray sat on the island, watching Willa buzz around the kitchen. Trent, decked out in an apron for his own good, stood near the stove, very seriously watching what looked like water start to boil.

Willa and Trent had met at one of the first game nights that Gray and Nora had hosted, and Nora had seen an immediate change in both of them. Trent may have been a little bit of a himbo, but he worshiped the ground that both sisters walked on and was possibly the most dependable, even-keeled person that Nora had ever met.

And yes, she'd joined his fantasy football league this year, which had solidified their own friendship over the last few months.

These were her people, and every day she was grateful at how the last year of her life had played out.

"Hi, babe," Gray said when she noticed Nora standing in the doorway, taking the group in.

Nora walked over to where Gray sat and looped her arms around her before pressing a soft kiss against her cheek. Then, she shifted her focus to Willa and Trent. "I hope you're ready for a Codenames rematch tonight."

"We'll get 'em this time," Trent said enthusiastically before he extended his hand to offer Nora a fist bump.

Nora accepted the gesture with a fist of her own and then looked at Gray seriously. "Sisters on the same team feels a little unfair. I swear to god it's like you two can read one another's minds."

Willa laughed and hip-checked Trent out of the way of the oven to open the door. She pulled out a tray of perfectly golden pinwheels that had Nora's mouth watering. When the pastries were safely on a cooling rack, Willa placed one on a small plate and handed it to Nora.

"Consider this your consolation prize," Willa teased.

"Brat," Nora retorted before biting into the pinwheel and humming with appreciation. Within seconds, there was no evidence the pastry had ever existed. "I'm going to change before the party unless anyone needs help."

Gray's dark eyes found hers, and her voice dropped low next to Nora's ear. "Do you need help?"

Nora angled her body away from Willa and Trent,

mirroring Gray's look back at her. "I don't think that's wise. We'll never make it down in time."

"I can be quick," Gray said, her voice a breath above a whisper when she added, "And I definitely know you can."

It took all of Nora's willpower not to kiss the smirk off her girlfriend's face.

Gray hopped off the counter and grabbed Nora's hand. "We're getting ready for the party," she said, already dragging Nora across the kitchen.

Nora was led upstairs, through a house that now felt just as familiar as her own. Pictures of Gray and her sister, or Nora and Gray, or the three of them, were now displayed proudly on the walls.

When they reached the bedroom, Gray shut the door and spun Nora around so her back was against it.

"I've missed you," Gray said, peppering kisses along Nora's jaw.

Nora pressed her fingers into Gray's hips and pulled her closer. "I saw you a few hours ago, baby," she finally responded, her breath catching when Gray bit lightly against her neck.

Gray nuzzled her face against Nora's already hot skin. Her girlfriend's words muffled as she continued to place kisses wherever she could reach. "And it was torture." Kiss. "God, you looked so good today." Kiss. "It should be illegal." Kiss.

Her pants were already falling down her legs when she realized that Gray had unfastened them. "You're really taking this whole 'helping me' thing to heart," Nora said before Gray eased her fingers inside Nora's underwear and she forgot how to speak.

Gray slid a finger inside Nora's wet heat and curled it. "Move in with me."

Nora's legs buckled when Gray eased a second finger in.

"Oh my god," Nora said, her head thumping back against the door. "You're not playing fair."

Gray curled her fingers again. "Nothing about the way I feel about you is fair," she said seriously. "I want us to live together. I want to wake up with you every morning and drag your gigantic, comfortable bed into this house. I want your artwork on the walls and your hands on my skin. You're the best thing that's ever happened to me. I love you so much I can barely stand it sometimes."

Her body flooded with heat, Nora could barely think. Her hips were working of their own accord, rising to meet each intensifying thrust of Gray's fingertips. She wanted this. God, she wanted all of it.

Gray pulled back and looked at her then, big eyes searching Nora's own lidded stare. "I don't want to wait one more second for what comes next."

And what came next was Nora. She was shocked by the force of her orgasm, and her head dropped against Gray's shoulder, fingers slowly moving inside of her as she came down in a way that Gray knew Nora loved.

"Baby," Nora gasped. She wrapped her hand around Gray's neck and pulled her in for a hungry kiss. When she pulled back, Gray's face was flushed, and all of her attention was still on Nora.

Gray was waiting for an answer, but her being brave enough to ask the question was all the assurance that Nora had needed.

Gray had spent the last year proving that she was ready for them, that she could let Nora in.

She eased her hand around to Gray's face and ran her thumb along Gray's bottom lip. "I love you. Absolutely I want us to live together." She replaced her finger with her lips, capturing Gray's soft exhale in a kiss that made Nora's stomach flutter. She still got butterflies when they kissed.

Nora smiled as she pulled back, her own look of absolute love mirrored back in Gray's eyes. All those months ago, Gray had given Nora space for her to grow, and now... she couldn't imagine filling it with anything else except their future together.

THE END

About the Author

Monica McCallan was an enthusiastic fan of romance novels long before she began writing them. She currently lives in Philadelphia, shares way too much about her life on Twitter, and is obsessed with her dog.

A Quick Note

Thank you for reading A Life Worth Living!

As an independently published author, reviews on Amazon or Goodreads are greatly appreciated.

If you'd like to stay up-to-date on what I'm working on, you can find me on Twitter @monicamccallan

Made in the USA
Middletown, DE
29 September 2023

39778470R00213